Praise for Mercedes Lac

"Series fans will enjoy the v
while enough information is p...
cover a world of high adventure and individual cou...
Highly recommended."   —*Library Journal*

"Lackey is back doing what she does best, and the result is affecting and compulsive reading."   —*Locus*

"If you enjoy watching a plan coming together, if you like watching people work hard and sweat much in order to bring off the work of decades, if you don't mind just a bit of villain monologuing and love a story of unlikely heroes, *Beyond* is a delight. Especially if you've never been to Valdemar or are, as I was, looking for an excuse to go back."
                                        —Reading Reality

"The perfect spot for new readers to jump in. I loved *Beyond* and I can't wait for the next book in the series to find out exactly how we get from where *Beyond* started to the Valdemar I love so much."   —The Arched Doorway

"*Beyond* is an example of Lackey at the height of her powers. It features engaging and lovable characters doing their best, pastoral slice of life scenes blending with a tense main plotline, and enough political intrigue to keep everyone on their toes."   —Traveling in Books

"If you, like me, grew up on Mercedes Lackey stories, the tale of the founding of Valdemar has been a long time coming. And this opening volume did not disappoint."
                                        —Under the Covers

DAW BOOKS BY MERCEDES LACKEY

*Coming soon from DAW Books

VALDEMAR

THE FOUNDING OF VALDEMAR
BOOK THREE

MERCEDES LACKEY

DAW BOOKS
New York

Cover illustration by Jody A. Lee

Cover design by Adam Auerbach

Edited by Betsy Wollheim

DAW Book Collectors No. 1953

DAW Books
An imprint of Astra Publishing House
dawbooks.com
DAW Books and its logo are registered trademarks of Astra Publishing House

Printed in the United States of America

Library of Congress Cataloging-in-Publication Data

Names: Lackey, Mercedes, author.
Title: Valdemar / Mercedes Lackey.
Description: First edition. | New York : DAW Books, 2023. |
Series: The Founding of Valdemar ; book 3
Identifiers: LCCN 2023046383 (print) | LCCN 2023046384 (ebook) |
ISBN 9780756417390 (hardcover) | ISBN 9780756417406 (ebook)
Subjects: LCSH: Valdemar (Imaginary place)—Fiction. |
LCGFT: Fantasy fiction. | Epic fiction. | Novels.
Classification: LCC PS3562.A246 V35 2023 (print) |
LCC PS3562.A246 (ebook) | DDC 813/.54—dc23/eng/20231011
LC record available at https://lccn.loc.gov/2023046383
LC ebook record available at https://lccn.loc.gov/2023046384

ISBN 9780756417413 (trade paperback)

First paperback edition: October 2024
10 9 8 7 6 5 4 3 2 1

Dedication:
To Matthew and Maree Pavletich
You know why

When hen one is accustomed to constant work, anything but *work feels strange. Is it unhealthy if one finds the work itself pleasurable? What does one's work take the place of?* Kordas's perpetually active mind followed the branching paths of thought. *If it does take the place of anything. Done well enough, a labor can be a pleasure. I've always found my work enjoyable, except, obviously, for the lethality, danger, horror, and pain. And to be fair,* those *weren't part of the work, just the results of the work.* Stray musings like this cropped up any time he had a minute of peace. It was very hard for him to keep his mind from racing these days, and this torrent of thoughts was a slow one for him. *Being a leader makes me feel alive. Averting crises, creating quick plans, and guiding the lost is its own kind of recreation. Even when it is uneventful. Blessedly uneventful. We have lost so much, but discovered what we're made of. In crisis we display our truest mettle, but it is in routine that we exhibit our patience and willpower. Well, I have the willpower part, at least. In my youth I was*

raised into a position I couldn't leave, one of constant work—
so, ultimately, I became the work. Leading the Valdemarans
isn't something I do. It's who I am.

So, as pleasant as the moment was, it *still* felt odd for him
not to be at desks and map tables, hearing testimonies, and
making notes (that would become orders) for the benefit of
generations to come. It hadn't been by accident that his weekly
routine was engineered to include today's "work." Of all the
days of the week that Baron Kordas Lord Valdemar performed
his scheduled duties, it was this one he looked forward to:
Midweek Day, when his morning tasks were few and he made
rounds of his peoples' projects from horseback.

Midweek Day! The closest I get to freedom!

Above him a blue sky, below him grass studded with tiny,
cheerful fuchsia, yellow, and blue flowers his gardener grumbled about and called "weeds." Around him, the grounds of
his manor bore no boastful ornate topiaries or ponderous state
statuary, but rather, hubs of material goods and their shelters,
sturdy crops, livestock, and the two-by-twos of masters and
apprentices at lessons.

Take this, the lawn in front of the manor, stretching out
until it reached the wall and the main gate. Back in the Duchy,
this would have been a manicured green swath. Here it was
not only studded with "weeds," but with sheep and chickens,
both watched over by a very young shepherd and two old and
wise herding dogs. And in back and to the sides, what would
have been flower gardens and more lawn were instead very
practical vegetable and herb gardens that fed and medicated
the entire population of the manor.

The new-looking wall that protected it all hosted scores of
people and their animals inside its perimeter and out, carrying on their affairs at the brisk walking pace the whole settlement had adopted. Kordas rubbed his palms together, prepared
to be in the place he best loved—a saddle. He closed his eyes for
a count of ten, savoring the moment. He might have acclaim,

power, a decent throne, and twin desks, but in his heart, a well-worn saddle with one of his Golds was what he longed for. On horseback, he was complete.

Love every good day you get. Enjoy the peace. Accept that, for the moment, things around you are not exploding.

Even the weather conspired to make him happy today: exactly the right temperature, just a bit of a breeze, and a nearly cloudless sky. An inky wave of little black songbirds flowed with that breeze, and alighted along a roofline by the hundreds, unhurriedly chirping their songbird conversations with each other like flautists practicing flutter-tongue. And if the scents here were not *always* those of flowers, well, that was the hazard of being an agrarian leader, the vast majority of whose wealth lay in the horses inside and outside this wall, and a good thousand head of livestock. He'd *definitely* smelled worse. He'd *escaped* worse.

Midweek Day—the Imperial military form of marking time was brutal in its simplicity. The Emperor's scribes had been burdened with writing out flowery, elaborate calendar dates to please their nobles, but the military worked quickly. Short commands, ranks visible, flags distinctive—and days? First Day, Second Day, Third Day, Midweek, Fourth Day, and so on. Kordas's policies left the months' names alone, but adopted the simple military shorthand for all Valdemarans to employ. They were busy people here—nobody had the spare time to write out "Sixteenth Day of Sunrise Celebration, in the Height of His Imperial Majesty's Spring Rise of Fertility, as recognized by His Majesty's Loyal and Mighty Appointed Governor of the Fecund Vastness of the Realm" on a document. Day, Week, Month, Year, and done—and the year, of course, began at one, the year they had all escaped.

He had read the cardinal dispatches—summaries of notable issues divided by the compass points around the Court— over a relaxed breakfast. His true Midweek Day always began here, at the stables. It was a wonder they even *had* stables, but that was because Kordas, by virtue of having the largest household in the Barony, had the most available manpower to build them. And the only reason they had that manpower to use to build stables was because something other than humans had built the enormous manor that he and most of his highborn nobles lived in. That something had been a mysterious Thing that lived half in the plane where magic was more abundant than in the Material Plane, and half in the soil of the former Hawkbrother Vale. The Hawkbrothers called it "a Mother," and not even *they* knew what its actual overall shape was. He would keep that a secret from his people, who would be unsettled by knowing that their city was built upon a vast creature that consumed whatever was fed to it.

He glanced back over his shoulder at the manor, which was not impressive by Imperial standards, but was far more than he thought they'd have been able to manage on their own. Four stories tall aboveground, with the same amenities of sanitation and water, heating and cooling, he had been accustomed to back home. And all grown straight out of the soil. He'd watched it grow, and marveled.

Now, it was true he *could* have had an Imperial manor. It would "just" take the efforts of a dozen mages working together for about six months. Powerful ones, at that. But he could not, in good conscience—even though he'd saved the mages under his protection from being dragooned into service to the Empire—have asked them to do that. Not when there were upward of fifteen thousand people who had followed him out of the Empire. They trusted and believed in his wisdom, enough to leave ancestral lands to go into the wilderness, and through dangers that had literally been unimaginable to them. They needed homes, clean water, sanitation, vermin control, food, and farms and—well, everything they had known in their lives until then that had been a matter of paying some money and receiving finished goods. Including shelter, and the mages could help with that instead of giving Kordas and the Court a fancier dwelling! In fact, the now-revered mages were hard at work every day, wielding their power to coax back some of the civilized improvements his people had left behind.

"Still can't believe that it's real. The Palace, I mean," said his eldest son, Restil, beside him.

"Manor, son," he corrected absently, as he always did. "I think the bastion walls are a lot more impressive when you think about it. They probably cover the same distance as the boundary of our old estate. That's the equivalent of a whole lot of manors."

"Do you miss it much?" Restil asked, passing a daypack to his father.

"The old manor and grounds? Oh, of course I miss it. It was a place of my youth, where *all* things were simpler than now. That's how memory is. The way you remember things is not always accurate to what it actually was, but you know the way it felt. I remember the feel of the banisters, as if I'd just come off the stairs. I'd skip the first step to show I was a young man of action. Some things just stick in your head. I remember the crazing of the lichen and moss on the walls as if I'd touched them yesterday, and how the turret steps had worn-down smooth divots in their middles from so many years of use. That's what's real to me." Restil watched Kordas's face while he spoke. "And the old manor will still be utilized, and looked after. That helps me feel better, even knowing I'll never see it again. Now we have this, a place that never *was* before we came. *This* manor is where we'll prosper now. Our old home is a fond memory, but now is now. A memory is no place to live. It doesn't hurt to visit, though." He smiled at his son.

Restil smiled back, briefly, then said, "It's weird. Thinking back, I feel like I miss places I've never actually been to."

Kordas replied, "It's all right, son. I know that feeling, too. I think it comes from some trait you value coming to mind, and you want to experience it like a memory. You feel like you were 'there.' Real or not." He gestured with his left hand. "And now, this is real. I think I love it even more than the home in my memories. If you are self-assured, anywhere you are is home." They both glanced at the bastion wall nearest them, following two birds chasing each other. The same entity below had built the wall—initially a single wall for protection, but within the first year it had become more than that.

No, this was not exactly the same wall that had sheltered them from the attack of that semi-sentient, deeply lethal walking forest. It was much broader now. A second wall had been built inside the first one by the Tayledras-whatever-it-was that lived under their feet. Roofed and floored, two stories tall, the space between the two walls had been turned into housing, and the roof had become the walkway holding the guards, with parapets and embrasures to protect the fighters up there. It was a kind of village, although now that people were finally getting their own homes erected, it was emptying out a bit. "It's lovely to have it, but it's not a proper house," was the general consensus, and it was true, it was a challenge to make a home out of a string of long, narrow rooms about twice as wide as a big farmhouse table was long. The rooms were subdivided into four-room partitions with a shared latrine and bathing room with a rainwater cistern above. Each room in the manor side of the wall had a single window facing toward the manor; each partition had a door exiting to the manor grounds. Part of it was barracks for the unmarried folk of his Guard, but the living quarters for people who were not in the household had been spaced out near the four gates that led to the land beyond, so people didn't have to travel too far to get to their work. But the space was intended to be more than that. Even with a growing population, between the tunnels the *hertasi* had left behind, and the interior of the wall, the entire Barony's human population could have shelter in the event of a serious attack or other emergency—although that shelter was going to be wall-to-wall bedrolls. *And long lines for the latrines.* Still. Even if something like the Red Forest turned up again, the people would be protected.

Restil looked back at his father and replied philosophically, "I suppose any place can be a home, if you need it to be."

Clever lad.

"Let's get on our way, shall we?" Kordas said, mounting and settling himself into the saddle. Restil did the same.

Within the wall, well, no one would *ever* think, "Here lives a mighty Baron." Not when two thirds of the acreage was given over to herds of cattle, sheep, and the all-important horses. The rest was food gardens, with scarcely a purposely planted flower in sight. Flower gardens would come in time. Food for his people had priority for now, despite the constant battle against native insects, blights, and wildlife.

All of this land had once been what the Hawkbrothers called their "Vale," which had had magical shields rather than physical walls. And Kordas very much missed the enchanting place it had been under their care. He had apologized to them during one of the negotiations, lamenting that the beauty the Tayledras left to the Valdemarans could only decline in their care—and he meant it. He had been reassured that for centuries, Vales were just abandoned to be reclaimed by the wild, since the Hawkbrothers thought of Vales as places to work, not lasting homes—even though they might work in one for generations. As long as there was benevolent custodianship and joy in whatever the Valdemarans did with this Vale, the Hawkbrothers would be content. But nearly all of the soaring buildings, decks, decorative vines, and gardens could not exist without constant magical protection and magical tending, and none of *that* could exist without the stupendously powerful node they called a Heartstone providing power that was only limited by the magician's strength and ability to manipulate it. With the Hawkbrothers gone, and their Heartstone shrunk to a more normal (if still powerful) node, the huge trees that hosted their homes, the lush growth that had required year-round warmth, the marvelous hot springs and pools, and the invisible protective Veil that allowed midsummer temperatures all year round were gone with them.

The last of the Hawkbrothers to leave had helped to bring down those forest giants, "giving them a calm death," as they put it, because these trees simply could not, structurally, have survived a winter. They had never experienced a winter freeze, and the Valdemarans were warned that if these Vale trees were not felled before frost, they would explode from the expansion pressure of their own sap. And so, systematically, down they came. He missed them—but they had supplied so much lumber that no one had needed to cut any for some time after that.

He shivered. That thought triggered a stressful memory of incoming sawblades on a sinking barge, because what man could just forget *that*?

He forced his thoughts back to happier places.

If it weren't for the hertasi's aid, stripping the leaves and bark while everyone else slept, two-thirds of the lumber would not even be ready for dry curing by now. And the leavings provided the fuel for the baking, using kilns made from former tunnels!

The trees that remained were hardy, and handled winter just fine. But it was sad to him that no one born after they'd come down would ever see those towering beauties whose tops seemed to brush the very clouds. It made the glimmers of sun through the leaves all the more poignant, as father and son rode in no particular hurry at all.

"Good day for this," Restil observed, happily. Like his father, he looked his best in a saddle, and Kordas smiled to see it.

Aura, his current Valdemar Gold mount, pranced a little and shook her mane, as if she had read his mind. He patted her neck and winked at Restil, who was mounted on his own Gold, Stanzia. At nineteen, Restil was still young enough to think that to be truly impressive on horseback he needed to be riding a stallion, and Stanzia responded to Aura's playfulness by sidling over to her with *that look* in his eye. Aura tolerated his behavior until he was within the exact distance it took her to snake out her head and snap her teeth *at*, but not *into*, his neck, her formidable incisors just grazing his hide.

With an affronted snort, Stanzia somehow leapt sideways, bucking a little, and surely rattled Restil's bones. A true son of his father, the young man was too good of a horseman to be unseated, or even unsettled, but he winced, so his father knew he'd *felt* it.

He looks like his mother at that age. The only thing he got from me was my hair. That meant a slight build, an angular face that was attractive without being conventional, stormy gray eyes, and his father's black, curly hair.

Hair so abundant and so enthusiastic about growing that it was sometimes a nuisance. Kordas had his own crammed under a hat. Restil had his tied back. Neither effort at control was entirely successful.

Restil's mount was probably going to be the last pure Valdemar Gold stud. No time for studbooks and careful crosses when most of the people of Valdemar needed the brute-force multiplier of a horse or mule, and the mares needed to be bred as often as was healthy for them, staying mindful of their upkeep.

Another thing we are losing. I'll miss the Golds. His family had been famous for them: horses bred for a glorious golden coat that looked like the namesake metal in the sunlight, but also for intelligence, good disposition, strength, stamina, and endurance. His family had made their fortune with horses, but their reputation with the Golds—an honest fortune, earned with hard work and care, not stolen from someone else as was all too often the case in the Empire.

Restil tightened the reins to correct his mount, and flicked Stanzia's neck with the ends, assertively stating an admonishing *"No."* The flick wasn't hard enough to "punish," certainly less painful than a fly bite, but enough to be a reminder.

Stanzia laid his ears back and dropped his head, trying and failing to pull some slack out of the reins so he could get the bit in his teeth and resist being controlled. Restil was familiar with these antics, and held firm. Stanzia brought his head back up, sulking.

"Studs," muttered Restil.

"Second thoughts?" his father asked mildly.

He shook his head. "No, Father. The exercise of controlling him without harming him is good for me, and the discipline is good for him."

Kordas nodded and turned his attention back to the great wall around the manor—which, like his son, his people *would* insist on calling "the Palace"—and the guards on it, who were snapping to attention as he and Restil passed. Kordas raised his left hand to give an open-palmed wave, essentially the laziest salute he had in stock. The place had been without disaster, tragedy, or monster assault long enough that these Midweek Day rides were routine. This was what he did, sun or rain, cold or broiling, although *not* in one of the freakish downpours this place seemed to have on an irregular basis, nor the equivalent blizzards that locked everyone inside whatever shelter they'd taken until it was over. He sometimes rode alone, often with Restil, sometimes with his youngest son Jon, but at the moment not with his middle child, Hakkon.

Or at least, he would not be riding with his youngest until the duration of Hakkon's punishment had run out.

The reason for said punishment probably was rooted in youthful energy, but there were a couple of accompanying signs of problematic thinking that everyone wanted to stop before it progressed any further. So the punishment was probably—well, it wasn't particularly harsh, but it was somewhat in excess of what the boy would have gotten if he hadn't opened his mouth and said what he had.

Hakkon had gotten into a great deal of mischief trying to "herd" someone else's sheep. Without permission. With a horse. The horse had been bewildered, the dogs were confused, the sheep had gotten aggressive because they had lambs with them, and the farmer had erupted out of the sheep pen he was building, roaring in rage like Pebble's mother, and just as incendiary. So that was three infractions: endangering the horse, endangering the sheep, and interfering with someone else's property.

The farmer had, quite properly, hauled Hakkon down out of his saddle and dragged him straight to the manor by his collar, the poor horse's reins in his other fist. The first person of authority he'd encountered, suitably enough, had been Kordas's older cousin, whom young Hakkon had been named for. All three had headed for the Council Chamber, and Kordas had been sent for. After hearing what the boy had been up to, and shutting down every single "But—" that Hakkon-the-younger had tried, the last straw had been the declaration, "But the sheep belong to one of my father's subjects, so they belong to—" Summoned from *his* work by a servant, Kordas had arrived at the (fortunately deserted) Council Chamber just in time to hear that outrageous statement and to see the result.

Hakkon-the-elder had taken both the boy's shoulders in his hands and shook him until his teeth rattled and he was dizzy. "If"—shake—"I"—shake—*"ever"*—shake—"hear that"—shake—"or anything *like* that"—shake—"out of your mouth"—shake—"again"—shake—"you'll find yourself serving as a pig boy for the rest of your unnatural life!" He let the boy go, and the young Hakkon reeled back, face white.

"And I'll bind you out to the Young Squire myself," Kordas had said from behind the boy, making his son jump. *"We* Valdemars serve the people, not the other way around, and don't you ever forget that. What they own is *theirs.* They pay us for our service in governing and safeguarding them with tax. A free bargain, freely made, because if they don't like it, they are free to take everything they own outside the bounds of the Barony, resettle in a place of their liking, and deal with their own defense." Now he leaned down and stared into young Hakkon's startled eyes from about a thumb away. "That's how it will be in Valdemar's lands. Suggesting otherwise is *Imperial* talk. We are *better* than the thugs we once suffered under."

Somehow young Hakkon blanched even whiter. The word "Imperial" had come to mean the worst of the worst, and he obviously felt that comparison deeply.

"Now, since you don't seem to have remembered any of that when it mattered, there will be a correction in your education," Kordas had said, standing up as straight and tall as he could and staring down from his full height at his errant son. Who, thankfully, was still shorter than his father. Unlike Restil, who towered over Kordas by nearly a head. It was very difficult to be an imposing father figure when you had to look up to meet your child's eyes. "Your new lessons will be concentrating on the latter days of the Empire, and your uncle Hakkon's and my experiences at the Court. And you will continue those lessons until you can recite them by heart. Then, in addition, in what has been your free time, you will be employed in a manner meant to teach you what an honest man does for an honest day's work, so that you'll appreciate what that farmer has to do to feed and clothe the rest of us."

He had tilted his head at his cousin, who quirked his mouth and said, "I can arrange that."

So young Hakkon was currently spending his noneducational time alternating between cleaning the stables and cleaning kennels. There was no time for rides with his father; the only parts of a horse that he would see for the next couple of fortnights would be the rump and tail, and what emerged from beneath the latter. No time for socializing and idling in games. No time for mischief. But plenty of time to mull over what he said to his uncle, and why it had made everyone so angry.

Hakkon had never shown that kind of arrogance and

dismissal of his "lessers" before, but Kordas was going to nip this first sign of it right in the bud. The reason for assigning him to manual labor was two-fold. One, he was going to get a good idea of just what manual labor meant, so he'd never take it for granted, and would be grateful that other people were doing it *for* him. And two, he was going to find out that those he had mentally consigned as "lesser" in intelligence as well as status were as interesting or more so than his peers. Kordas preferred intelligent servants to stupid ones; he rewarded thinking and innovation, right down to the sculleries in the kitchen. He himself had learned everything he knew about horses from the servants in the stables and breeding farm. Hakkon would learn more about horses and dogs than he'd ever dreamed existed by the time he was done with his punishment.

Aside from the guards and the gardeners, there weren't many people about who weren't working on planting and wrangling. Most of the population were outside the walls, tending their own fields and beasts, and trying to build their own homes. Sadly, once the Heartstone was gone, that mysterious building-creature in the ground had lost the energy to create complicated projects.

But at least it could still do something absolutely vital, and something that had worried Kordas dreadfully until they'd seen the Vale. It had been explained to him that what was below would continue to make that most desirable—at least in his eyes—of *all* civic projects.

Sewers.

It had already built a network of sewers under the Vale long before he and his people had arrived. It had tied the latrines in the wall and the ones in the manor into that network. And now, all anyone building a house needed to do was to leave a small, enchanted marker the size of the drain they wanted buried below the surface of the soil, where they wanted their own latrine to go, and at some point the thing would find it and make a new extension just for them. The extensions had rubbery valves every arm's-length as far down as anyone could tell, and effluents went one way only, without foul odors.

Let's hope that lasts. The closest Kordas could imagine to what the burgeoning city would smell like without the Mother below was a battlefield after a week of decomposition.

There would be no need to worry about sewage in the streets, or horrible cesspits, or any of the other dangers and health risks he had worried about. Imperial history was riddled with disastrous fights against disease, and the Valdemarans had faced over a dozen entirely new afflictions already. And if they lost the value of that excrement as compost, what they gained more than made up for it.

History books seldom mention what any event smelled like, and so people come to expect no smell at all. The fact is, cities stink, as a side effect of functioning. A wise leader thinks ahead about abating the intensity of repugnances to improve the morale and health of his charges. One of his grandfather's precepts.

The unstressed wave to the fighters on the wall was a signal that they could go back to standing guard. Or, if they were on simple watch duty instead of patrol, sitting on tall swivel stools instead of standing. Imperial military doctrine required standing on duty, but Kordas didn't think that was necessary here. They weren't on a war footing, and he figured it was better to have the momentary delay of standing up if action was needed than a guard complement with aching backs, ankles, and knees for years to come. As he'd reasoned it, that too had a reassuring effect: if you had plans for people's long-term health, it told the people that they had a future.

"I rode out to check on the tree nursery yesterday as you asked," Restil said into the silence. "Healers managed to find a cure for that rust disease, and walked it back. There's no sign of it on any of the saplings now."

"Well, that's an arrow dodged." The Hawkbrothers had been very, *very* adamant about one thing: *Do not disrespect the land. It is your host. Let it breathe. Nurture it.* Kordas had decreed leaving numerous trees around and between buildings, and planting a tree for every tree that was cut down. And not just any trees; no single type planted in rows like a sort of tree farm. It had to be mixed trees, just as in a natural forest. Fortunately, no one had argued with this. He'd half expected a battle with farmers who were impatient about wasting planting time on something that couldn't be eaten, but no.

The discovery of native nut and fruit trees helped with that. The Hawkbrothers had passed along lessons in understanding local animal behavior early on, to learn about the land's health by its subtle signs. Where raptors gathered meant vermin infestations; where lavender or mints grew, beetles and larvae would avoid; and so on. The brightest farmers diversified all they could.

Kordas deeply appreciated how reasonable people had been once things settled down to the point where life wasn't a distressing struggle every day, and people had enough leisure to start to complain about the things they missed from back home. And he couldn't blame them. There were things he missed every day, and he was relatively sheltered and very privileged, and was well aware of it. Sometimes he wondered how people coped with good humor, because the changes and adaptations they'd had to make included everyone, from the highest to the lowest, right down to the sculleries and pot-boys.

That sent his thoughts drifting off to the very interesting breakfast he'd had this morning: egg pie, but with seasoning that was only now becoming familiar. *Gods know everyone in the kitchen has had to learn a hundred new things since we got here, at least. Old herbs and spices unavailable, new ones to adapt to the recipes, new woods to learn for a quick and hot or slow and steady fire . . . and it's the same for every other trade. Adapting what Was to what Is.*

Which just brought his thoughts back to the erring Hakkon. "Where do you think Hakkon got his inflated notions of self-importance?" he asked his eldest, who could generally be counted on to know exactly what his siblings were up to.

Restil snorted. "That's an easy one. He's been spending time with some of the highborn younglings I don't care for, a lot of sycophants that fluffed up his ego. He got snarky with me the day before the stunt with the sheep, and I warned him if he didn't make a course correction, he'd run aground."

"I see you've been spending time yourself with the ship-builders from the Duchy of Olinian," Kordas replied.

Under the original plan, they would *never* have had builders of proper sea-going ships among them. Canal boats and the small vessels that plied lakes were the closest to real ships that the Duchy of Valdemar made; the Duchy had no more than repair docks since several other baronies and duchies nearby boasted experts in naval architecture, with excellent shipyards. But the emergency evacuation of the Capital by every means possible, including the entire Gate network, had meant that their private Gate, the one to what they had initially thought would be their new home, had experienced what mage Jonaton had blithely called "little glitches."

In other words, we got plenty of uninvited guests. I love Jonaton dearly, but sometimes he can be aggravating. A glitch is a fly in fresh paint, not being re-routed across the world!

A number of people who were *not* Kordas's subjects had flung themselves into Gates without a destination key, and ended up coming out to safety through Valdemar's secret Gate back on Crescent Lake. In most cases, they had come through by ones and twos, but the civilian shipbuilders outside the Capital had crammed themselves, their pets, their Dolls, and their families into light craft at once, and left through a supply Gate at the commercial shipyard. That Gate had interpreted this as being a "single party" like a shipment of several barges, and that was why Kordas now had a small population of shipbuilders from the coast—people who built sturdy boats with crafted wood, not fungal paste. They had liked the Empire even less than Kordas, and were happy to stay with the Valdemarans rather than taking the Crescent Lake Gate back to their home.

Of course, their shipyard home had a strong chance of being incinerated after they'd left. No one had done any scrying to see what was left of the Capital once Pebble's mother had finished with it. That was partly because not too many people actually cared, and there were enough eyewitnesses and accounts of the annihilation that it was well-understood that there was nothing left to look at. The final decision against scrying was mostly so that, if there were mages left in what remained of the Empire with the capability of detecting a remote scrying spell, they wouldn't be alerted to the escapees.

Having people who built boats with wood had turned out to be a very, very good thing, since Kordas's live fungus had not taken to its new home. It had turned itself into a gray powder and blew away in the first year. The Healers thought it might have been infected by a local disease, like a couple of their food crops had. Some of those crops had produced twisted or inedible yields, but weren't completely lost. Others were.

No purple beans, no softbeets, no catbells anymore. There's a chance they could be reintroduced if we sent agents to Imperial destinations, but . . . I'd rather do without old familiar flavors than risk discovery. Thank the gods the Tayledras had their own analogs to what edible flora we completely lost. Some of them are better, actually. We've lost a lot of people, sad to say, but it hasn't been to famine.

The river, on either side of the rapids, had basins teeming with edible life. The rapids seemed to be virtually unsurvivable to anything, which made them like a wall for species diversification. As a precaution, Kordas ordered the debris from the Red Forest thrown into the river upstream of the rapids, for fear it might give rise to a new Forest or poison the ground—and down to the twig, none was seen again after entering the rapids. Downstream, water from the rapids was as clear as air, no matter how deep the riverbed. There were drastically different versions of the same species north and south of the rapids. To the north, the horrific underwater spiders had become something essentially like deepwater crabs, and just as delicious. Sunfish the size of pie plates, eels that tasted like beefsteak, and catfish from the southern side—the Valdemarans would need dedicated fishing boats before long, when barge- and bridge-fishing weren't enough. Right now, the shipbuilders applied their woodworking skills to building houses, barns, and sheds, but their real love was ships. Anyone unwary asking for tales could find themselves drowning in stories about *real* ships and the beauty of them, with only the slightest provocation.

Restil shrugged. "I like boats. I like how they look, and how they move. I like how they feel under my feet. For all we know, someday we're going to discover a big enough body of water that actual ships are required. So I've been talking to the shipmen, writing everything down, and getting them to make drawings for me about how to make those big seagoing ships, so we can have records in the Archive when that day comes."

"Well, if that's what you're doing, you have leave to recruit a helper or two, and let it be known I've said that's your permanent assignment when you're not with me. And you might want to think about any other trade that we don't need *now*, but might need later, and get those recorded as well. We won't live forever. Mastery dies with the master, unless their knowledge is recorded." They approached one of the three smaller side gates in the wall now, which would lead them out into the half-built city they were calling Haven. A tunnel led through the wall, dark and unexpectedly chill, with stout iron portcullises at either end, heavy iron-bound doors, droppable spike chains, *and* murder holes in the ceiling.

Those had been added by human builders, not grown. Without the full Heartstone, only a node, it was better to rely on physical protections than magical. Spells could fail, but gravity was reliable.

The horses picked up their pace through the tunnel. They either didn't like the darkness and close walls, or were eager to get out of their usual pastures and into something less familiar. Horses got bored, too.

Right outside the gatehouse was what would eventually be the most imposing structure in the city besides the manor itself. They stopped long enough to observe the work. "I see Lord Hedron found something else in his hoard to entice another half-dozen carpenters to come work for him," Restil observed, after some silent tallying. "I wonder what it was?"

"Who knows?" Kordas replied, mentally comparing the building in front of him with the plans his Lord Chancellor had shown him. "When we all made those jokes about Lord Hedron and his crazy collecting—and how it was even crazier that he managed to bring it all with him—who would have guessed he'd be just about the only one of the highborn with goods that actual workers wanted! What was it the last time?"

"Needles and pins. There was almost a riot over them," Restil supplied.

His father nodded. The "really good" steel that they had brought with them was all that they would have for quite a while, until there was time to use the mine and the smelter—a gift from the Hawkbrothers—to make refined metal for things that were not strictly necessary. And until the steelworkers managed to hone their crafting techniques to create delicate, specialized objects like pins and needles, if you lost or broke something like that, you'd be doing your sewing with a clumsier bone needle, and pinning with thorns. So every lost pin and every broken needle was a notable upset in most people's households.

All the things we took for granted that we'd never thought of, even with the decades of planning that went into our escape. Things like, certainly, every village blacksmith was a fine metal craftsman, but they couldn't make precision items like needles and pins. The same theme arose all the time, like discovering that the clay here was like nothing the potters had ever seen before, and there were actually a few moons where some folks were eating off turned wooden platters, or on washed leaves, and drinking out of horns and wooden cups because their crockery had succumbed to wear, and the potters hadn't yet mastered how to reliably work and fire this new clay.

The question of currency arose after only a few months. The Council had agreed early to disdain Imperial coinage, so it was only worth its melt value regardless of denomination. Practicality ruled the day, and the value of currency was ultimately based upon what could be *made* with it. If a cup cost twenty copper, it was because making the cup required twenty copper pieces to be its raw materials. Craftsmanship fees came after. Paper notes wouldn't *make* anything, but royal clerks could keep tallies of values for later days. Copper was the most versatile metal they had, followed by brass and tin, and it was in short supply compared to the demand. Claiming a copper deposit was proposed, but that would have meant an armed expedition going into land that was only *just* cleansed—an expedition of fighters, plus some miners and metalworkers who were needed doing things here, not wandering around fighting off who-knew-what sort of perils. "Cleansed" only meant the rapidly mutating, actively murderous conditions of an area were eliminated, not that lethal monsters were *gone*.

The dilemma had been solved not by the highborn and Guildmasters on the Council, but by the people themselves. *They* had come to the Council in the form of one of the master smiths and one of the master potters with their idea. A trade, in which Kordas would pay the smiths and potters with foodstuffs or beasts from his herds to make exclusive goods for that trade, and would in return get back all the copper that came in. "Copper for crocks," they called it, although those who turned in copper cooking utensils got cast iron in return rather than more fragile pottery. With the copper under Baronial control, pricing standards were established, there was no waste, and there was no arguing. Kordas had been touched deeply when he realized how much they all trusted him to be absolutely fair.

Kordas realized his mind had been wandering when Restil flicked him with the end of a rein and said, "For the third time, Father, what route are we taking?"

"East to Inglenook Hall, then onward," Kordas replied. "We haven't seen the Young Squire in far too long."

They rode along the windowless side of the wall until they came to the road going eastward. A proper road, this was, and all thanks to Pebble, the young Earth Elemental, who would somehow lay down a resilient yet impervious surface anywhere you put a line of the sorts of things he liked to eat. Fortunately, two of those things were manure and iron tailings from the nearby iron mine. Sometimes Kordas felt terrible about taking advantage of the Elemental, but Pebble seemed to enjoy it-her-himself, and certainly Pebble could leave at any time and absolutely no one would be able to stop them.

There was something *like* a city spreading all around them, but one in which every single part was still under construction. Roads were there. Wells everywhere, and aqueducts bringing water from the river. Houses—not so much. Quite a lot of people were still living in their barges on the plots they had staked out as their homes, if they weren't living in the wall. Not the highborn—*they* were living in the manor. *And when they complain about the lack of space, I point out that there is plenty of room in the tunnels and in the wall.* But everyone from tradesmen on down to hired farm laborers was still making use of the barges. For the farm laborer, first came work for their master. Then shelter for their own chickens and other small personal stock and storage for their garden harvest, *then* a "proper cottage." For the trades and craft folk, the priority was on the workshop, then the place to hold and sell what was being made. And with an entire population competing for labor with a limited labor pool and limited supplies, most people were forced to build their own homes in their spare time.

So spread out before them was a strange sight indeed: plots of land along the roads with barges lined up jammed together, next to (in this part of the city) workshops from which came the sound of hammers on anvils, large and small.

At least we planned this much properly by centering the escape around the barges, Kordas thought with a sigh. There was absolutely nothing wrong with the barges as dwellings—there had been cottages on his estate that were smaller, and people seemed happy enough in them. And there was the wall. But living in the wall might mean a long walk to the workshop, since the highborn had staked out their plots nearest the manor. And it would mean a very long walk to a farm, far too long to make it worth a farm laborer's while.

Expansion could be aided by employing wagoneers to travel in a circuit, in light-duty, single-animal setups, giving rides to and from the hard-walk destinations. They could stop for anyone who would join them. It would also be a good source for monitoring rumors and domestic issues, since the passengers would talk. Also a good way to spread news, if the wagoneers carried briefings with them.

If only I'd thought of that years ago, I could have had passenger wagons made in the old country, and stacked on a barge.

"You have that look on your face again, Father," Restil said, interrupting his thoughts.

"What look is that?" he asked, fairly certain that years of

dicing with the Empire had given him a highly inscrutable face, and not one his son could easily read.

"The one that means you're feeling guilty because you couldn't somehow manage to transport an entire city here, ready-made, and pick the one spot that has metals and minerals all within easy reach," his son replied, startling him so much that Aura felt it and kicked up her heels. "Instead, you should be congratulating yourself on getting as much here as you did."

"How did you—" Kordas paused, and narrowed his eyes. "Has your mother—"

"Of course she has," Restil replied with amusement. "And you aren't as hard to read as you think."

"Then I'm slipping," he muttered, chagrined, as people paused in their work to bow to him. *Gah. I hate that. I wish they'd stop doing it.* There had been altogether too much bowing and scraping in his life in the Empire, and damned if he liked seeing other people doing it to him. They meant well . . . but it made him squirm inside.

"You don't need to hide things anymore," his son pointed out. "Not from your family, anyway." He nudged Stanzia with his heels, and the stallion moved off. "Come on. It's a bit of a ride to the Young Squire's, and I know we both want to get there in time to have a good chat."

Aura didn't like that Stanzia was getting ahead of her, and picked up her feet to move before he could urge her. Restil was right, of course. He didn't need to hide anything from his family.

And now it's come to this, getting good advice from my child. He found himself smiling. *Not a bad sign, actually.*

Now that Restil and his father were into the "half-finished town" part of Haven, the sights, sounds, and smells were reflective of the trades and building going on. Lots of fresh-cut wood. The forge fires were much too hot to smoke, but they did give off their own distinct aroma. Hammering assaulted them on all sides. Adolescents from the farms drove pony carts laden with foodstuffs for sale up and down the streets, and building or work got interrupted when someone needed to buy from them. From everything Restil had heard, those carts seldom returned to the farms with anything but traded goods in them. Right now the big currency was nails and those oh-so-desirable pins and needles.

Restil was highly amused by his father's discomfort with all the greetings as they trotted their horses down the beautifully finished streets between the decidedly unfinished house-shop-whatever plots. Instead of waving hands and calling something along the lines of "Mornin', Baron," which was mostly how people had greeted him on the barge convoy, it was a brief bow—sometimes abbreviated into a mere nod—and a "Well met, your Majesty." And every time the word "Majesty" came out of a mouth, Kordas winced.

He's going to have to get used to it. They want a King and they want the King to be him.

Oh, Restil knew very well why his father was not in the least interested in the title of "King," but the reaction was, well, rather silly, considering that he wasn't *declaring* himself a monarch, he was being elevated into the position by even the least of his people. In Restil's opinion, his father should just relax and go along with it all. If anyone had any objection to him in the role, they hadn't voiced it in Restil's hearing, nor in the hearing of all the little birds he had out in the populace that reported back to him of problems, unease, or unrest.

Well . . . not entirely true, but the people who would have objected already packed up and left. About a thousand people, all told; unlike those who had stayed behind at Crescent Lake, who were entirely farmers, most of these folk were the families and retainers of a handful of nobles, who didn't want a "new" life, they wanted the old life, but with *them* in charge. Kordas had let them go. In fact, he had allowed them to take almost everything they wanted to take with them. Which, in Restil's estimation, was the smartest thing he could have done. Restil's "little birds" had welcomed their departure. A few folks had even thrown an impromptu celebration.

Kordas had his own network of information, of course, but Restil and Beltran felt that a second, less formal network had a great many benefits and no real drawbacks, so Restil had made use of the highly varied friends he'd made to create what he called "gossip gatherers." There were mostly servants in this network, people he'd worked with as a page and more or less an equal, not a highborn; people he first knew before anyone found out he was Kordas's son. The ones he knew introduced him to others, and they, in turn, to more, so at this point, while he didn't have an ear in every household, he at least had one in every nascent neighborhood.

That network was why he was less concerned about Hakkon's misdeeds than the Baron was. Hakkon was basically a good egg that hadn't yet learned the three most important things about "friends." First, that not everyone who *called* themselves your friend actually *was*, second, that anyone could act nice but not all are sincere, so pleasantness was not enough basis for friendship, and thirdly, that until you sorted out who liked you for who you were, not for what you were or what you could do for them, it was a lot smarter to take your cues from the adults you respected than from any other source. Restil had learned those lessons because he'd spent a good part of his childhood with everyone assuming he was Uncle Hakkon's bastard child. And while Hakkon had been living under the same presumption, he hadn't been old enough for it to really affect him and how he viewed others.

Right now Restil was pretty satisfied with his circle of friends. The pages he used to serve alongside? Rock solid. Didn't matter if now they were squires (otherwise known as knights-in-training), the falconer's apprentice, or highborn heirs. A very few of the other highborn offspring his age, though? The ones who had never had to work at all, and even *still* had parents sheltering them from dirtying their hands? *Wouldn't trust their opinion on the color of the sky, much less anything important.* Maybe when they matured a bit—if they ever did.

Stanzia gave him a quick backward look, prelude to shenanigans. Rather than wait for the stallion to act out, Restil gave him a stern glare and said aloud, "Don't even think about it, Stanzia." Correction *before* the behavior was always more effective than after, and Golds were smart enough to understand when he used certain phrases and intonations.

And as he expected, Stanzia snorted, as if in surprise that Restil had figured out what he was about to try, then went back to sulking.

Not unlike Hakkon, really. This morning his little brother had been just as sulky, playing with his porridge until their mother reminded him it was going to be unpleasant to eat cold, and slouching out to his lessons with Beltran like a condemned man on the way to the gallows.

Just wait until he starts work in the stables.

Restil himself had done his stints in the stables, and would again, but not as punishment. It was because there had been several times when they were short of hands, and while *he* admittedly wasn't up to the kind of all-day manual labor that a seasoned stablehand was, at least he could muck out and groom his own little herd of horses—and, besides that, he could clean tack while sitting down to rest from the mucking-out. He rather liked working in the stable. Horses and horse-men were fine company. Horse shit wasn't all that bad, not like pig. Or human, that was the worst. *I think I like horses better than people, to be honest.*

They left the spiderweb of streets, then passed through a passage in what was going to be an actual city wall when the Mother Below got done growing it—"Mother Below" was what the Hawkbrothers called the thing that grew walls and sewers. He'd taken to the name; Kordas had not. Right now the wall was just about chin high on him when he was standing, so the passage was just a gap where the road went through. This wall was growing a lot slower than the wall around the Palace had; there was a lot more of this wall, for one thing, and for another, the magic that had been so abundant when the Heart-stone was active was slowly dropping back to the level they'd had back in the Duchy. Eventually, so the Hawkbrothers said, the magic would drop down to a point where the Mother would go dormant, and they'd be on their own so far as public works went, so it was best to ask the Mother to make things that benefited everyone, like walls and sewers. Not houses. Certainly not the highborn manors the nobles all wanted to get back into.

There had been some grumbling about that among the

highborn, and some pointed remarks about the Palace, but Father had provided quite a number of salient points in a full Court Assembly speech. First, that the Palace (he called it the Baronial manor, of course), was the size it was in order to shelter the largest number of people, and that quite a few of the highborns complaining were, in fact, currently taking advantage of that. He also made the argument that the manors they wanted built weren't going to do anyone a lot of good if the cellars filled with shit every time it rained because they'd wasted the Mother on building homes instead of a sewage removal system. Then he followed it up by reminding them all that having proper city walls meant that minor threats that a simple wall could deter would mean that the still-frequent alarms didn't send half the population or more to be crammed inside the Palace—err, manor—walls until the threat had been dealt with. Logic and clear heads prevailed. Especially when people with rank and wealth figured out that getting common laborers—or mages, as there were a couple of manors being put up in the Imperial fashion—to work for them meant that those people had to actually *like* them. Because those with labor to sell were far fewer than those who were putting in labor on their own homes and farms, and they could pick and choose whom to work for.

This was a new experience for many of the highborn and wealthy. They were quite used to ordering what they wanted, and dealing with any complaints or problems with silver.

It wasn't nearly the disaster some people made it out to be. It really wasn't even an inconvenience. The highborn might be cramped in the Palace, but they had the best place to live in the entire Barony. And they weren't starving either, anything but. The highborn *had* brought their personal flocks and herds and stores of seed and supplies, and they had their own personal farms out here past the city wall, staffed by the same servants who had tended their manor farms back home, so they weren't without resources. In fact, they were in a better position to offer something valuable like food or materials in return for the labor on their new manors than, say, a candlemaker or shopkeeper, so their manors were going up in a conventional fashion . . . but of course it was never going to be fast enough to suit them.

Nothing was happening fast enough to suit people, truth to tell. He had the feeling that people had had this vague idea that "once we're settled, we'll get buildings and all up in no time, and everything will be back to the lives we knew in a year."

No.

There was an astonishing number of things that the Valdemarans had been forced to do without once the initial supply ran out. Well, for one thing, they'd had to learn how to do joinery with pegs and dovetails and whatnot, not just on furniture, but *on the houses*, because there just were not enough nails! That ate into your time something fierce. For another, there were all the shortages. *I'm pretty sure not even Father thought about all the potential shortages.* There were some things they'd begun running out of in the first six months, and that was with Hawkbrother help!

Like Father keeps saying: trade. We need to establish trade. They had the Hawkbrothers, who were generous enough, but they were also very self-sufficient, and philosophically they made, grew, or otherwise created *just enough* and no more. There were many things they just had never seen the need for—like nails!—and they could not supply those gaps in what the Valdemarans needed and didn't have.

Huh. . . . There was an idea tickling the back of his mind, but it wasn't fully formed enough to come popping up yet.

Still, they'd also learned things from the Hawkbrothers— alternatives they could use to substitute for the things they were running out of, for a start. Thorns instead of pins. Pegs instead of nails. There was plenty of wool and linen for fabric, and even something the Hawkbrothers called "raimie" and a kind of hemp that made good, strong, soft canvas that was better than they'd ever had before.

"Make do" should be our motto, not "There is no one, true way."

The deliberate maze of the half-built city's streets gave him an oddly unsettled feeling of *this isn't quite right.* But once they were outside the Haven wall, the landscape began to look more like the countryside he remembered as a child, with farms dotting the landscape. Out here were the farms—the real farms, not the limited one inside the Palace wall. Because a lot of these farmers had their own work crews, most of them were full-scale homesteads now, with actual houses, not rows of barges. Rows of barges serving as laborers' cottages weren't quite so obvious out here. And because the farmers were far more used to self-sufficiency than the city dwellers and tradesfolk, their homesteads looked "normal" to his eyes. The barges had become cottages, storage sheds, pig sheds, chicken, duck, and goose coops. A lot of those had been walled in with wattle-and-daub walls, then covered with roofs of thatching, both for insulation and so that the barge decks and roofs could be used for dry storage, making them look more "normal." There were actual barns and stables, and fields had been measured out, assigned to farmers on the basis of what their old farms had looked like. And then had come the "best part," as far as the farmers were concerned: the means to delineate all those fields and farms so there were no arguments about borders and boundaries. And how the Hawkbrothers had chosen to help with that had endeared the Tayledras to the Valdemaran farmers for all time.

Every single farmer's field, whether it was growing something or grazing something, had been delineated by a stout briar hedge, reinforced at intervals by handsome "young" trees. All of these had been grown by one of the Tayledras "green mages" who grew the enormous trees of their Vales.

And while it had not been overnight, it had all been done within the first year, and for a very, very good reason.

The farmers needed to be outside the walls of the city of Haven creating food, *immediately,* and they could not do that if their herds and flocks were preyed on by wild animals, or their crops eaten by deer and wild boar.

And the Hawkbrothers had an answer for that: the hedges. It was a system they used themselves, in fact, though not to the extent that the Valdemarans had needed.

Restil had been fascinated when he'd gotten a chance to watch the growing hedges in action—you could, *literally,* watch the hedges grow. They weren't spindly and weak, either, but good, stout branches with wicked thorns to discourage creatures from trying to get through. Meanwhile the Hawkbrother would just be sitting there with their eyes closed, perhaps humming under their breath. Only when Restil started to grow into his own magic was he able to see the complicated Working that they were doing.

And, sadly, for the life of him, he could not do it himself.

He'd have loved to have been a Green Mage. The discipline was something that appealed to him on a fundamental level, whereas the combat magic he was actually good at did not. But at least he had earth-sense, like his father, and if he could not affect the land, he could at least tell where it was in distress and why.

The people other than farmers might not realize it, but if it had not been for the Hawkbrothers, there would have been hunger and even starvation. *We'd probably be down to half the people we arrived here with, if we'd had to settle by ourselves.* Between starvation, wilderness dangers, disease, and insects—so many insects!

Well, we probably couldn't have survived the attack of the Red Forest when it followed us. We wouldn't have been here *when the damned thing caught up with us, and without the*

Tayledras mages and the Mother Below's wall, we'd have become Forest food in short order.

So ten years after the Hawkbrothers had first brought the Valdemarans here, life outside the walls was much more like what the farmers of Valdemar had been used to—barring the fact that back home they hadn't often had to contend with bears, wolf packs, and the other hazards of wilderness or the magically altered versions of the same creatures. An insect plague had been solved, and quickly, by sending all the avians that weren't raptors out of the protection of the Veil to gorge on bugs. The raptors had come out too, but not to eat bugs—though Restil had more than once laughed himself silly over an earnest eagle waddling through a field ambushing the hellish, hand-sized, flying crickets that had turned up. The bondbirds had been there to guard the little birds from the wild birds of prey—which had taken the hint and abandoned the neighborhood until the insect plague was over.

Nominally, everyone except the thousand or so people who'd just packed up and gone downriver was directly under Kordas's rule. But pretty much "in charge" of everyone outside the walls was the Young Squire. The farmers revered Kordas for getting them all out from under the Empire's rapacious rule, and they obeyed his laws with far less questioning than the highborn, but it was to the Young Squire that they looked for their day-to-day leadership.

The Young Squire was son Old Squire Lesley, who had been the tacit leader of the farmers back home. But the Old Squire had settled in an extant village back at Crescent Lake with his prize, precious sow the Empress and a modestly sized herd of his very fine swine to keep him in comfort. Without the old man's leadership to fall back on, people had naturally gravitated to the eldest son (who was Kordas's age, so "young" was relative).

The Young Squire was well placed to be the agrarian leader. The highborn here were "absent landlords," leaving the handling of *their* farms to the Stewards who had come with them. None of the Stewards had any interest whatsoever in anything other than making sure their masters' farms prospered, so these large "manor farms," which might otherwise have swung a disproportionate amount of influence outside the city walls, in fact left "local governance" to others. Meanwhile, Young Squire Lesley had himself a "manor-sized" farm. He had gotten the greater number of his family's farmhands and servants when the split of the family had taken place, because his father had decided on semi-retirement, and didn't need that much help. Besides, thanks to his pigs, the Old Squire had more than enough people who wanted to hire on with him back at that village he settled into. Bacon was well known for its persuasive properties. Plenty of people wanted to hire on for the sake of the shoat every hired hand got as a Harvest bonus for working for the Squire. Aside from his personal servants, housekeeper, house servants, and cook, all he'd needed was a few folk to take care of the much smaller herd of swine that was all he'd kept with him.

So the Young Squire was the happy owner of the largest herd of swine in the Barony, as well as the Empress's finest daughter, whom he was calling the Queen. He had the most laborers, farmhands, and house servants in all of the settled farms. Which made him the biggest landowner.

Although, initially, he hadn't assumed the same position his father had held back in the Barony.

That didn't last long. After the first defection, the farmers had voted to establish a formal grange as opposed to the informal one they'd had back home, and needed a leader for it. By virtue of both the size of his holdings, and his education at his father's side, the Young Squire was the obvious choice. He merely waited gracefully for his friends and neighbors to press him to take it. And when they did, the Young Squire had seamlessly stepped into the position of leadership his father had held. A good choice; the other farmers trusted him more than someone highborn, and he'd absorbed or inherited a lot of his father's wisdom and solid good sense. And Restil knew that Kordas depended on Young Squire Lesley's acumen and canny knack for sorting through gossip and hearsay to get to things that actually mattered.

"I know horses. Young Lesley knows everything," Kordas had once said.

Restil didn't know about that, but Lesley knew everything that was worth knowing about the state of the Valdemaran farms and their occupants, and Kordas often said that none of this would be going as smoothly without him.

The hedges stood proud sentry on either side of the road, coming to chin high on a man on horseback; Restil and Kordas were just barely tall enough that they could see over the tops of the hedges into fields beyond. And in a welcome change from back home, every farmer had enclosed enough land to put his fields in full rotation: fallow in the ones most recently used for grains, grazing in the next oldest, legumes in the ones that would take grains the next year, and cereals in the current "bread crop" part of the rotation. It made for a pretty picture, but far more important was that this made for a sustainable use of the land. It was the same system the Tayledras used, so of course they approved as well.

The pleasantly bitter scent of hops drifted over the hedge to the right, and Restil smiled a little to himself. Now *there* was one commodity that everyone appreciated—beer! Taverns in town might be nothing more than stump pieces set up around a trestle table inside a peeled-log building with a pounded-dirt or crude puncheon floor, but there was a lot less grumbling about conditions than there might have been because of the steady supply of beer coming from the farms. A fellow was inclined to overlook a bit of hardship when he could count on a filling meal followed by a good pint at the end of his day.

All the houses out here had the same sort of architecture, and that, too, was due to the Young Squire's influence. He'd shown everyone how quickly a home made from squared-off logs could be put up, how spacious it was, how sturdy it was even without a frame, and how well it kept out the weather. But then he'd gone a step further, and organized all the farmers into what he called "friendship groups," which were committed to helping each other, particularly with building. So instead of one family and their hands working on a house, a barn, or a stable and taking a long time about it, the entire group would drop all but essential chores to descend on the property and have what they called a "rising" to get the thing built in a day. It made for something like a holiday, because there would be a communal dinner and perhaps a bit of entertainment when the structure was finished. If Kordas got wind of the rising, he'd have a meat animal sent from his farm over to it, so there would be a roast. It hadn't taken more than a year and a half to get most of the necessary buildings up out here on the farms, because of those friendship groups. And even the least social of people had swiftly seen the virtue in at least putting a good face on, because of the advantages the groups brought to everyone.

I would have thought that the folks up in the town would have noticed how well that system works, and adopted it. But maybe they're more suspicious of their neighbors than the farmers are.

He set aside his ruminations as they neared their first goal. A break in the hedges opened to the lane to Inglenook Hall, Squire Lesley's home. This was a simple dirt lane, not a Pebble-laid road, and although it, too, was lined with hedges, the Squire had also planted a great many more trees among the hedges than there were along the roadways, and now that the trees were almost ten years old, they formed a lovely green tunnel leading to Inglenook Hall. The Squire could have taken advantage of Pebble's services for this private lane, but he hadn't, which had only earned him more trust, Restil figured. The Hall lay right at the end of the lane, and was the only building around that was two stories tall.

Not that it was a "proper manor," by any means. It was still more than a bit crude, and showed a much less welcoming face than the Squire's old home had. Windows were small and unglazed, because there were, at the moment, very few sources of pure enough sand to make much glass. So, instead, the tiny windows were protected by cloth screens in summer and stout shutters in winter. Restil had been inside many times, and knew that this made for very dark rooms. Water came from a well, waste went into a conventional cesspit. Every inch of space was utilized, because Lesley preferred that his farmhands all be under the same protected, communal roof unless they really *insisted* on having their own space. In that case, they could live in the crude extension that held their barges, because cottages were not a priority at the moment. There were no corridors in the Hall; the building style was a very old-fashioned, even ancient style in which the rooms led into each other, with bedrooms farthest from the front and rear doors, and common rooms closest to them. Lesley had had the place painted with sap boiled until it became tar, so it was dark brown, with a thatched roof. It looked nothing like the laid-stone beauty back in Valdemar, with big windows and a lane of little cottages to the side, but as far as Restil could tell, the people living there were satisfied with their lives.

Normally they'd have ridden up to the house, found the housekeeper, asked her where her master was, and gone out to find him. But almost as soon as they turned into the lane, one of the Squire's youngest children, who must have been on the watch for them, came pounding up to them on an absurdly short-legged pony. "Papa needs you!" the child cried as soon as he was in earshot. "Follow me!"

With a jolt to the gut, Restil glanced at his father, who cast his eyes up to heaven. They both knew what this meant. It happened about twice a month at some point in the Barony, though not often at the Squire's farm. "Boar or bear?" Restil asked, as he reined in Stanzia, who wanted to go into a full gallop and probably would have bowled that poor little pony over in the process. "Could be a catamount, or a pard," Kordas replied. "That would be a nice change. But it's generally a boar."

Wolf packs could be discouraged merely by fences, and *thank the gods* there hadn't yet been any of those flying or running horrors they'd encountered on the river. But roughly half the wild things around here were natural—which farmers could take on—and half were magic-touched, which they generally could not.

"Whatever it is, it must have stormed the hedges *today*, or Lesley would have sent for you," Restil replied, keeping Stanzia to a lope so he didn't overtake the pony.

"Without a doubt. Almost makes me suspect the Hell Beasts around here have gotten hold of my social calendar." It was a feeble joke, but Restil laughed at it.

The child led them to the Squire's largest barn, the one nearest the house, where he kept the sows with piglets until the piglets were old enough to go into the fields. There they found Squire Lesley purposefully—but not grimly—arming his male hands with stout iron-tipped hayforks in lieu of boar spears, which were useless against the enormous creatures touched by magic.

"Pig again, is it?" Kordas called from the doorway, where he and Restil stopped their horses.

The Young Squire turned; Restil was pleased to see that he looked more annoyed than alarmed, his square jaw set with determination, and his sandy-brown hair raked to the side to get it out of his eyes. "Aye," the man replied, in a pleasant baritone. "Heard it last night, trying the hedges. Wants to et up piglet, I've no doubt."

Restil and Kordas both nodded; long acquaintance with the Lesleys made them a great deal more familiar with the ways of pigs than most highborn, and Restil knew that a boar would often kill and eat a sow's piglets to put her back into breeding condition so he could have her himself.

"He's on up in that thicket they allus like to hole up in," the Squire continued. "Looks like he's 'bout the size of one of your False Golds."

"Not horrible enough to need any more mages then," Kordas concluded. "Actually, a bit on the small size. Maybe that means the Pelagirs are running out of monsters to send us?"

"From your mouth t'the gods' ears," Lesley said piously. "I'd'a sent for a mage or two, but I knew 'twas Midweek Day, and you were due by, so I set Chip to be watchin' for you." He cast an eye over his young child. "Job well done, Chip. Now back in house; boar'd make less than a mouthful out of ye."

"Yes, Da!" the child chirped. But Restil was pleased to see that the mite didn't just run off and leave the pony; the beast got its tack taken off, a quick rubdown, and was put in its stall before the child scampered out. Meanwhile the hands all assembled in neat ranks behind their master; this had happened often enough in the last ten years that everyone knew their job and their strategy, and they were as well-drilled as any of Kordas's Guard. The last rank in the rear had the Squire's boarhounds, one to a man, and all on a tight leash.

It was a far cry from the first two years. People had gotten hurt and even killed by these magic-touched beasts before they worked out an effective strategy.

"So," Kordas asked. "The usual?"

Squire Lesley nodded. "Surround the thicket, use the dogs to scare it out of cover, and then as the gods decree."

Kordas laughed. "A good way to say 'no strategy survives contact with the enemy,' eh, my friend?"

The Squire barely cracked something like a smile, then turned to his men. "Go get in place, lads, and be quiet about it. We don't want the damned thing getting wind of you and rushing you afore we're all set to deal with him."

The men went out on the trot, their faces grim. Despite

having done just this kind of hunt on a regular basis, the danger was still very high. A normal-sized boar could easily kill and main several men during the course of a hunt. A boar the size of a horse could do a lot worse than that.

"Afoot or a-horse?" Restil asked his father.

Kordas knitted his brows. "You'd be safer on a trained mount, but Stanzia is green. Afoot for both of us. Remember the contingencies."

Restil nodded, and dismounted. He took Stanzia over to a clean farrowing pen in one corner of the barn and tied him up there, leaving him with a bucket of water and some straw to play with, slipping his bit, and removing his saddle. His father was doing the same in the opposite corner with Aura. Restil thought for a moment, then, deciding that it would do no worse to Stanzia than hurt his feelings, took leather straps out of a pocket on the saddle and hobbled his front feet. If the stallion decided to get up to mischief and chew himself loose or break the reins, he'd soon discover he wouldn't be moving fast or far.

The Squire led the way, followed by Kordas, Restil, and four of the biggest men Restil knew. These men had boar spears of a size that *might* prove useful against a pig that size. *Might.* If the thing charged, even if the head could pierce that tough hide, it still might run up on that spear and kill the man.

But they weren't there to attack the boar. They were there to help defend Restil and his father.

It wasn't far to the thicket—more like virgin forest, actually—right at the edge of the Squire's fallow fields. Well, "not far" by their current standards—his father's protestations to the contrary, the current Barony covered about twice as much territory as the old Duchy of Valdemar because everyone had crop rotation in place, so there were "extra" fields. The hike wasn't onerous, but it did involve going over the hedges around each field in the only way possible: stiles. A ladder up, a platform across the top, a ladder down. The stiles couldn't be used by anything but a fox—foxes climbed very well—or the bigger hunting cats like pards. Fortunately, pards didn't much like people. They liked briars even less, and not even the smell of delicious pig would tempt them into trying to negotiate a ladder meant for human hands and feet over the thorns.

But as soon as they came within earshot of the "thicket," Restil heard something he didn't like. Yes, there was the snuffling and grunting of a boar at rest . . . but there was a lot more snuffling and grunting than there should be for just a single boar.

Alarmed, he was about to say something, when the Squire rang the cowbell he was carrying as the signal to the men on the other side of this thicket to let the dogs loose.

A thunderous roar of barking erupted, followed by squealing bellows of anger and breaking branches, and something Restil knew he would be seeing in his nightmares for the next year came crashing out of the thicket into the cleared space between the forest and the hedge.

A boar the size of the largest workhorse he'd ever seen, two sows nearly the same size, and a mess of piglets the size of mastiffs.

A combination of terror and the strange exaltation that fighting always brought him ran through his nerves like a lightning bolt. He braced himself, and gathered his personal mage-energies. They would get only a single try at this.

"Over the hedge!" his father shrieked—though Restil knew Kordas didn't include him in that. He was a Valdemar; he would stand beside his father and fight until everyone else was safe.

He heard the men making for the stile, but all his attention was on the monstrous pigs. *"One! Two!"* his father shouted, which was his signal for what to do, and on *"Three!"* they both threw up their hands, barked two words, and looked away, closing their eyes to save their sight as light exploded all around them.

Restil immediately looked back up and saw the sows and boar reeling back in confusion, partly stunned. He didn't waste any time. He screamed another word of power and threw his hand forward as if he was throwing a spear. A lance of fire shot from his hand right into the nearest sow's eye. She threw up her head in a squealing scream, then dropped dead as the fire burned its way into her brain.

His father had done the same with the boar; the boar's skull was thicker, and it screamed and shook its head wildly. Restil made a casting, looping motion with his hands at the creature's front feet, magically binding them together before it could charge. It tried to anyway, tripped, and fell to the ground with the impact of a toppling tree. Then he and Kordas attacked the wounded eye together, and between the two of them, they penetrated the skull and the beast died with a final screech.

Restil looked for the third pig, but she had decided this was too much for her, and fled, with quite a number of the piglets—the ones that weren't stunned and blinded—pelting after her, as fast as they all could run.

He and his father sagged against each other while the Squire's men scrambled back over the hedge and made short work of the piglets. They might be the size of full-grown natural boars, but they had none of the aggression and didn't yet know how to defend themselves.

He had just gotten his breath back when the rest of the men and the mastiffs made their way back to them. "Send for the butchers, lads," the Squire said with grim satisfaction, and then everyone looked expectantly at Kordas.

His father smothered a sigh, and managed to mostly hide his pained expression. "Tonight," he said, with a false heartiness, "we eat pork!"

There was a cheer, and an answering cry of "Tonight we eat pork!" Kordas just shook his head a little. That line had become an ongoing *thing* across the entire settlement, and there was nothing Father could do to stop it.

"That must have taken the wind out of ye," the Squire observed, as the spearmen lashed piglet hooves together and slid the spears between them to carry them out, while the mastiffs and their handlers made the climb over the stile to get back to the Hall and summon the butchers for the boar and sow. "Reckon you ought to head back, and not press your luck today. I'll send a piglet or two up to the Palace."

"Manor," Kordas corrected, weakly.

"A brace of giant suckling pigs ought to feed up that mob of highborn you got living with you for one meal at least," the Squire continued, unperturbed. "Do 'em a world of good to be reminded of what dangers you're keeping 'em out of."

By the time they had walked and climbed back to Inglenook Hall, even his father was willing to admit that it would probably be a good idea to head back. Restil was *really* pleased to hear him say that; his stomach still felt wobbly after that unplanned use of magic, which he'd had to draw from his own inner supply because there hadn't been time to tap into a leyline. Stanzia had not, for a wonder, chewed through his reins or jerked them loose, although the amount of horse spit on the hobbles suggested he'd tried to chew through those.

His hands shook a little as he undid the hobbles and put the bit back in Stanzia's mouth. And it took two tries to get the saddle back on the stallion's back. Then he had to pause a moment before he could buckle the girth.

He glanced over at his father, who was leading Aura over to a feedbox to mount her. That seemed like a good idea to Restil, who did the same.

Stanzia was *finally* displaying the empathy that the Valdemar Golds were known for, sniffing at his face, nudging his shoulder in concern, and behaving like a perfect gentleman. Restil and his father rode out of the barn just as the first of the butchering crew appeared with crudely butchered chunks of pork. They all cheered at the sight of the two of them, and Kordas waved back.

"Father, the horses aren't tired—" Restil pointed out.

"True." Kordas put Aura into a canter, and Restil followed suit.

They were well within the city walls and halfway to the manor when Restil caught sight of a horse and rider galloping toward them. At first he was alarmed, until the rider saw them, yanked off his hat, and began waving it, a huge grin on his face. By this time it was obvious that it was Beltran, and Restil felt a lot of his exhaustion melting away.

They halted their horses and waited for Beltran to reach them. But instead of saying anything, Beltran reached into his belt pouch, pulled out something, and in the last couple of paces, showed it to them on his flat hand.

Restil felt his eyes widen, and his father uttered the happiest profanity Restil had ever heard.

"Copper! By the gods, copper! How? Where?" Kordas demanded.

"Right in the iron mine. *And* tin! They brought Ponu down to have a look at it, and he says it's rare but this sometimes happens, and we are incredibly lucky, and both veins are very rich and will hold us for some time." Beltran tilted the nugget into his master's hand. "Who knows, maybe the Cataclysm churned three different seams of metal together. But there's plenty, and that solves one of our big problems."

"All three together," Kordas murmured. "I wonder if the Hawkbrothers knew, and just didn't tell us? I'm getting scared, now—too much is going right."

"Well, today really was a lucky day," Restil replied. "We don't always get lucky days. I say, ride that feeling while it's galloping."

*T*onight we eat pork, indeed.

There must have been an abundance of those huge piglets, because by the time Kordas cleaned up, dealt with the afternoon's mixed business of reports from his Seneschal Jase Krane and urgent petitions directly to him, the aroma coming from the kitchen was enough to drive a person mad. The other giant boars they had dispatched since founding Haven had all been single males, and had been . . . gamey. Not that they were not appreciated, especially in the first three lean years, but the meat had that sour, musky taste adult wild game tended to have. Not inedible, especially not to people who were hungry for meat, but it had taken a lot of Tayledras hot peppers and something they called "strong sage" to make it enjoyable. And the smell while it had been cooking had been . . . distinct. It reminded people that they were hungry enough to eat about anything, really. It was a good thing that the butchered portions had still been so large that all the cooking had been done in pits outside.

This aroma, though—this was utterly delicious, and it seemed to Kordas that more than just two suckling pigs were being dealt with down in the kitchen area.

And in fact, when he finally joined the rest of his family and all the "Court"—otherwise known as all those highborn families living within his manor right now, plus their personal servants—there was a handsome, crisp-skinned, golden-brown piglet the size of a full-grown Valdemaran sow on each of the six tables in the Hall, surrounded by vegetables glazed in the juices. With that scent wafting all through the manor, *no one* was late for dinner tonight.

It was past sundown, so the Hall was lit by mage-light, with a few sage-scented candles on each table for atmosphere. The candles had been made and gifted by Lady Justine, who was not, by any means, the only one of the highborn to take to practical crafting in order to contribute to their mutual comfort. Lord Neuland and three of his eldest children were making some simple but stunning furniture, slowly replacing all the simple trestle tables and stools here in the Hall with pieces lovingly pegged, fitted, and polished that showed both mastery and enjoyment of the craft. And a good many of the highborn ladies had taken to the loom and to knitting.

Isla and the boys were already in their places at the head table on the dais that Lord Neuland had insisted on building, together with Hakkon, Delia, Alberdina, and a selection of the mages. He couldn't help but reflect, as he hurried to take his seat, that no one back in the Empire would have thought this gathering was of anything but a group of well-off craftsmen and prosperous farmers. Their clothing was much, much simpler than these same folks had been accustomed to wearing back before the escape, with very little in the way of ornamentation, and no jewelry except pieces that had sentimental value or significance to the wearer. The colors, mostly of the natural fibers, were attractive to his eyes, but subdued. Trim was limited to simple card-, stick-, or finger-woven patterns in the same subdued colors, or to stuff that had been cut off garments too faded or worn to wear by the original owner. Nothing was ever discarded, of course. If a garment could not be cut down any further, it would be unraveled for the colored threads for embroidery or woven trim. Same for the scraps from the re-tailoring. Truth to tell, he liked how it all looked, like a harmonious whole, even if his folks were not always harmonious in fact.

A quick glance over the tables, combined with the fact that by this time he knew these people as well as he knew his own family, told him that, for tonight at least, there were no active quarrels.

Then again, probably the smell of juicy, succulent suckling pig had buried all feuds for at least as long as it would take to eat and sleep it off. Meat was no longer a once-a-week treat. There was meat on the manor table at dinner most nights, if only in soup or stew, but no one had eaten suckling pig except when hunters found wild (normal-sized) sows with piglets, and those were so small that, shared out, the portions were quite meager.

For once, no one really noted his entrance, except with relief that now they could all finally eat. Not that he blamed them. His stomach let out a distinctly un-Baronial growl as he sat down, and there was a strong temptation to just reach out with his bare hands, grab a piece crowned with that glistening, amber skin, and tear it off to cram in his mouth.

He didn't, of course. This was a Court dinner. Manners above all. He sat down, nodded at the carver to begin, and all through the hall the other carvers put wickedly sharp knives to their charges and began the serving.

There would have been *seven* piglets, of course, not six. The cook would have kept one back for the kitchen staff, given such an abundance of meat. The kitchen staff and servers ate first; that was the way it always had been in the Valdemar household, and he'd been shocked to discover that *wasn't* the case elsewhere, that the Imperial staff only got what was left over after their masters had eaten—or worse, were fed "inferior" meals while every scrap of the master's meal was used in pies and the like the next day. How unfair was that? It would have been folly to say that out loud at the time, though; he'd been held as a hostage in the Imperial Palace, and any empathy shown for mere servants would have brought him ridicule at best, and signaled the then-Duchy out for suspicion at the worst.

That's how the Emperor liked things. Why treat anyone as a subordinate, when one could treat them as an inferior, too? Keep them ambitious enough to try harder, but never let them think promotion or reward was at hand.

As the carver handed around plates loaded with meat and roasted vegetables, Kordas could not help noticing that his errant son's attention was split. Partly on the food about to reach him, and partly on his father.

You'd better not be asking for a reprieve, young mischief. You won't be getting it.

"Well," he said, signaling the start of "polite conversation." "You can see what Restil and I were up to today. Do you want the details now, or later?"

"Where there are piglets there are sows, so I expect the battle was exciting, but given the result, brief," Isla said sensibly. "Let's have the details over dessert. It's going to be jam tart. Hakkon has something he wants to ask you before we hear about your hunt."

Kordas's plate reached him, and he put a forkful of pork in his mouth and made sure to extract every particle of pleasure from it before replying. "Well, Hakkon?"

The floodgates opened.

"One of the lurchers whelped and I helped and SerKellan the Houndmaster said I can have one if you say yes and I know I said horrible things but please please please please please may I have a puppy?"

Fortunately Kordas was, by now, well acquainted with torrent-speech from his middle offspring (who, when excited, nervous, or both, tended to blurt everything out at the highest speed possible to get it all out at once) and had no trouble deciphering the fact that one of the lurchers—or staghounds—had just had her puppies, Hakkon had gotten right in there with the messy business, and as a consequence, SerKellan, who certainly knew his business, had deemed Hakkon worthy of a pup.

This sort of pleading might have seemed immature for a lad of fifteen . . . and Kordas was immediately struck by it. It occurred to him then that Hakkon never *had* seemed to have the "feel" for horses that both his eldest and youngest did— and that, due to the complicated situation while they were growing up back in the Duchy, and then all of the work every one of them had been doing since then, none of them had ever had a pet dog. Sydney-You-Asshole the cat was . . . well, not like a dog. Cats do not "do" unconditional love.

It appeared that Hakkon had just been smitten.

Well, that will certainly teach him responsibility. A horse teaches a man self-control. A dog teaches him kindness. Come to think of it, *he* had only had a pet dog when he'd been home with his father as a child, before being hauled off to the Capital to serve as a hostage for his father's good behavior. Never since then. His whole world had been horses, and he hadn't felt the need for a dog—but part of the wonder of dogs is that whoever's dog was nearest is generally yours for a while, too. Dogs that are not bred to be guard dogs tend to be generous with their affection.

Not to mention that I think Isla would have had strong objections to sharing our bed with the kind of mastiff or lurcher I'd prefer as a pet. There was no way a pet dog stayed out of your bed. That was a given. *And that's as the gods like it.*

"You shan't have one as a pet until it's weaned and house-broken," he pointed out.

Hakkon nodded, still so excited he was slurring his sentences into a single word. "But SerKellan says I should come play with it every day."

"So you should. You need to let your pup know that you are going to be his pack leader when he grows up, and that he can trust you to care for him and love him. You can even begin training it a very little from the beginning, just as Delia trains her horses. And you'll have to know how to train it, because we won't allow it in our rooms until it is housebroken and knows not to chew on things that are not toys." *Good luck with that last, but it's not as if Isla and I are going to be too fussed about a little puppy-destruction.*

"Yessir," Hakkon said, his eyes going very round and bright as he realized his father was going to allow the treat.

"Do you know which one you want?" Kordas kept his face as expressionless as he could, because ultimately the real decision would be SerKellan's.

"Yessir! The runty one, Father! He's all gray with a white front! SerKellan said he's a good choice for a pet because he won't be so big as to get in the way indoors. I already love him, Father, and he loves me, I can tell!"

Thank the gods I had already made up my mind, or I wouldn't be able to resist those eyes. How did children, kittens, and puppies all manage to make it look as if half the space in their faces was taken up with eyes when they wanted something?

"Well, then, continue your duties, but as part of those duties tell SerKellan you are to spend time with your pup, and start making things for him. You'll want a harness to control him at first, and a good collar and leash. You'll need a big bowl for water and a smaller one for food. Since he'll be indoors, he'll need a bed." *Unless he sleeps in yours, pup, which I more than half expect to happen.* But those tasks would send Hakkon to the harnessmakers to learn leatherwork, to the potters to learn how to make a simple, rough vessel, and to his mother to learn handsewing. More good, worthwhile manual labor. It hadn't been a dog when he'd been a boy, it had been a pony; the same for Restil and Jon. Jon shared Sydney-You-Asshole with Jonaton. Astonishingly, Sydney-You-Asshole was still alive, although peppered in gray hairs; he hardly left Jonaton's rooms anymore except on good days when he made the trek to the royal suite and spent all of his waking time observing life from a high, sunny window in good weather, and in his special bed on the hearth in bad. Yet, on occasion, he still turned up in unexpected places, and he had trained the humans and other cats to glance around for him inside the manor.

The Great Hall was somewhat quieter than usual for the evening meal, probably because people were far more focused on their meal than on the extremely thin gossip of the Court. The most exciting thing that had happened of late was that Lord Astelon's eldest daughter had defiantly announced that she was pregnant, that the father was the manor blacksmith, and that they were going to marry whether her parents liked it or not. There had been something of a riot about that, with the parents threatening to send her into a religious order, the blacksmith equally (but more quietly) as defiant as his beloved, and strong demands that Kordas Do Something.

Leaving aside the fact that the few religious orders in the Barony were all too busy getting their houses established to have time to take in a pregnant girl, even if they wanted to (which they didn't), the girl herself wasn't actually a "girl" at all. She was fully adult—in her twenties—and had been used as a pawn in her father's negotiations ever since she was old enough to be considered marriageable.

Well, Kordas *had* done something. He'd issued a new law that anyone above the age of majority was allowed to wed whom they pleased, and granted the blacksmith an upgrade in his quarters—a set of four rooms in the wall, where he'd been living in a lean-to next to his forge. "You can disown her all you like," he'd told the stunned and irate parents. "That's within your rights. But she's not a child anymore, so *she* has all the rights of an adult. If she chooses to forgo the manor for the equivalent of a cottage, and life with servants for life without, that's her choice. But I'll remind you, love overcomes hardship like nothing else, and to young people in love, what it costs them is cheap." He'd paused then, and added, "On a personal level—you might want to think twice about disowning her. There's no going back on that, and it will be painful for you to see a mob of happy grandchildren you are not allowed to interact with." Speaking on a personal level was not unknown for Kordas, but the Court interpretation was that he uplifted Court esteem by speaking personally, as a near equals. This immediately had the knock-on effect that nearly every noble wanted a crisis to get wisdom about, to gain more of Kordas's attention, so they would gain the prestige. He'd left himself open for that. Well, the family hadn't disowned her after all . . . though she *had* moved into those rooms with her love.

There had been some interesting fallout from that, completely unexpected. A baker's dozen of new adults (that he knew of) had declared that they were breaking off with their families and petitioned Kordas for separate quarters. He'd granted the petitions, not bothering to ask for details. There were probably a lot *more* than the thirteen he knew of; those had all been among his Court, which meant they actually needed to petition to get a place to live. They got their rooms—individual rooms in the "living clusters," which they shared with other singles in the wall. And they wouldn't starve; they continued to have rights at the Court table. But if they wanted clothing for their backs and shoes for their feet and anything else that didn't come with those rights, they'd have to learn or use a skill they could trade to others. That wasn't his business either. Meanwhile, outside the manor wall, word had spread, and he presumed there were others who had also broken off and gone elsewhere. If there were irate parents coming up from the farms and the city to demand that he Do Something, he never heard about it, because he had given orders to Beltran that he flatly was not going to hear those petitions. The law had been decreed, and that was the end of that.

That was about as exciting as things got now, up here in the manor. Which was a vast relief, and much preferable to contagious diseases, insect plagues, blights, and the occasional Pelagirs monster. He bit his cheek, riding out the shower of bad memories and visualizations of what all had gone wrong since the last sight of the Empire. And of the awfulness that came with being human; they'd lost roughly a thousand souls since the escape to rivalries, revenge, drunkenness, crime, and foolhardiness. A quarter of that number were not involved with the crises at all; they were simply in the way at the time. Regrettably, he knew some people on both sides of the crimes, and it kept him mindful of how far badly someone could go under the right circumstances. In quiet moments, memories he would be better off forgetting forced him to feel vigilant about himself. If they could do such things, so could he—but with far more power behind it. Kordas closed his eyes for the duration of a long sigh, only marginally better at dealing with those instants of pain from plentiful practice. He hoped the day would come when he wasn't consigning criminals to life forever at hard labor—or re-evaluating himself, overly vigilant that he not become like them. Immense self-control was a duty to his people, even when it was prompted by trauma and the human cost of failure.

By the time he opened his eyes and shook off the morbid direction he was headed, someone had begun playing a single gittern somewhere in the place. Only half of a single song, as if to prove they could play it at all. Since the conversation from the others nearby *was* nothing but conversation rather than a courtly machination, he deemed it a good time—once he was full—to stand up to make an announcement.

He got everyone's attention; anxious faces relaxed when they saw his expression was a pleasant one. "Thanks to our miners!" he announced. "We now have copper and tin! The copper shortage is over. We'll also be able to make bronze as well as iron and steel, and I'll be transitioning in copper pennies, half-pennies, quarter-pennies, and bronze ten-copper pieces to make trading easier again!" He looked around at his Court. "Those of you who have silver and gold, the Council will be working out a worth scale, so you'll be able to use that, too."

There wasn't a cheer, but there were murmurs of relief and approval. If things had been difficult for the farmers, trading-wise, the highborn had had it worse. Most of them had needed to assign a member of their household to the full-time duty of trading, and that was not even to live in abundance.

"And even before we start minting coins, I am putting a priority on creating bronze needles and pins, and sewing scissors," he continued, and smiled when a female voice cried out, "Oh, thank the *gods!*" "Sempsters, seamstresses, if you are not familiar with the care and handling of bronze implements, and what you need to take care with, Restil will be gathering that information and will have it for you before the first ones are created for use."

He glanced over at Restil, who greeted him with a broad grin and a two-fingered salute. *Good, sounds like this is work he is ideal at handling.*

"There are, of course, many other things that bronze is better at than iron and steel, and Restil will also be in charge of notifying all the metalworkers so those who can make various useful items in bronze can start posting their expertise on their booth boards. Do you have anything to add, Restil?"

"I'm already working on a city map that has all the crafts-folk on it. I'll make sure to add the bronze and coppersmiths to that as well, and what items they can make. I intend to have large signboards constructed and placed in each crafting district that echo the information on the map for that particular district." Restil grinned again at his father's look of surprise. "Jon's been helping me, and so have some artisans. I expect we'll have the signage up as soon as we add the copper and bronze-smiths to our list."

"Oh, thank the *gods*," someone else said, in more of a groan than an exclamation. Kordas sympathized. Right now, finding out who made what was a matter of wandering around and asking directions. Well, not that *he* would know that; when he was looking for something, people tended to fall all over themselves helping him to find it, but that was what some of the people in his personal household were telling him.

Well, that gave people something to talk about besides each other, which was a blessing. The meal ended without any of the usual suspects sniping at each other or looking daggers across the room.

Kordas was irritated with people who made trouble over the pettiest of petty things at a time when—no matter what was going right *now*—this settlement was still in a very precarious position. What would have been famines were averted only by adopting local crops. Green beetles, churgles, and nimworms savagely undermined Valdemaran-brought crops, and the local large fauna brutalized the rest. Arrowclick swarms had killed almost as many people as wyrsa packs, and allergic reactions among the populace felled more than a few. They might have carved out a settlement, and the Hawkbrothers had certainly cleared out and cleansed the most dangerous areas, but as today's boar hunt had shown, that didn't mean life was as peaceful as it had been in the old Duchy of Valdemar, and "cleansed" didn't mean "safe" at all.

People too easily forget that we're the interlopers here, and nature in general wants to kill us without a care. The only social order is what we brought with us, and wolves don't petition.

The entire family left dinner as a group, while many of the members of the Court were still lingering over their jam tarts. Dessert generally was fruit, fresh or dried; baked goods happened only once or twice a fortnight. Delia, Alberdina, and the mages—Ceri, Sai, and Koto—also remained behind at the head table, all of them with their heads together over something. Whatever it was, Kordas reckoned to leave them to it.

The manor had been "grown" in the modern style, with corridors and rooms coming off them. Technically a waste of space, but if it came to sheltering the populace here, those corridors could certainly house a lot of people on bedrolls without sacrificing anyone's privacy. The Hawkbrothers had consulted him closely—indeed, had conducted what had almost been an interrogation!—when directing the "Mother Below" in its task, and he and his family had a suite that was actually superior to the one in his old manor. This one was all on the same floor, and had a schoolroom that Jon still used, several currently empty rooms, and *two* of the sanitary closets, which was a blessing with five people and three servants living there. Delia didn't share it; she had her own room now— she certainly didn't need anyone's supervision, much less his.

Delia had come a very long way from the lovestruck adolescent that he'd had to avoid. Although she wasn't a Healer, she and Alberdina had been managing most, if not all, of the Healers that had come along with the exodus. They'd gotten the Mother to grow them a separate building for the Healers, with quarters and "infirmaries" that could be isolated from each other. They'd begged, borrowed, cajoled, and sometimes outright confiscated everything they needed to fully stock and supply those infirmaries. They'd consulted with the

Hawkbrothers on the local medicinal herbs, written up how to use them, created multiple copies, and distributed those copies across the breadth of the Barony. They'd made copies of every healing reference book that had come with them, and made libraries in each of the infirmaries—libraries where the books were quite literally chained into the bookcases so they couldn't "grow legs and walk off," as Alberdina had put it.

That had not been all; indeed, putting all the Healers on an organized footing had only taken Delia and Alberdina a fraction of the last ten years, and despite the number of casualties and strange surroundings, Valdemaran medicine had actually advanced from the Healers' efforts. With Alberdina now in charge of what they were calling "the House of Healing," Delia had combed through the populace, found literate folks who were unable to do physical labor, and put them to work as copyists, starting with copying those books—and any other books that seemed especially useful. Certainly they were slower than trained scribes, but *any* copy of a book was better than *no* copy of a book, and her efforts had saved many books that were fading, falling apart, or had been water- or insect-damaged, and would certainly have been lost otherwise. It also put food on those people's tables, gave them useful work to do, and raised them in their neighbors' eyes from "useless" to "productive." After all, if this was something the Baron wanted, then it must be important to all of them. Paper, at least, was something they could make in relative abundance, since the Hawkbrothers had shown them water-tub slurry-screening and pressing. Polished metal plates, well glued and mounted on backboards, became surface plates for the presses.

And as if that was not enough, Delia had gone from storage barge to storage barge, looking for books, making sure they were still kept safe from vermin, asking for permission to take books for copying, and returning those books to their rightful owners when the first copy had been made. The romantic, book-loving girl had become a fierce protector and disseminator of knowledge, all on her own recognizance, and Kordas could not have been more proud of her. And this was in addition to all the ways in which her Fetching power had been useful, from births going wrong—both animal and human—to their defenses when attacked by outre creatures, and even putting out fires by dumping several barrels' worth of water on them at a time from afar. Everyone knew Delia. Everyone valued her.

Some members of his Council had wondered aloud if the book copying was really necessary. Kordas had pointed out that it was none of their business. "It's all being done without troubling any of you, taking a single grain out of a storehouse that isn't mine, or depriving anyone in any way," he'd said, in tones they had come to recognize as meaning, "It's none of your business if I choose to endorse it. Just let it be." Given Delia's record in helping to establish the House of Healing, most people elected to let it go at that. And if some people ridiculed his choices, well, they didn't do so in his hearing, or Delia's.

"Kordas, wait!" he heard her calling behind him, as if thinking of her had summoned her. She came pelting up to him, dressed, as Isla was, in a simple tunic and split skirt that allowed as much freedom of movement as any male had, and was, except for the most stubborn and hidebound of the ladies of his Court, now the standard of female everyday dress. They all stopped and waited for her to catch up.

"What were you and the others so intent on over at your end of the table?" he asked with a smile. "Did Ceri find you a husband?"

She rolled her eyes. Ceri was an insatiable matchmaker, and was always trying to find Delia a partner among the mage apprentices. "I can't imagine why he persists. If I wanted a husband, I am perfectly capable of finding one for myself. No, he was telling me that there's a problem with some of the younglings he and Alberdina are getting for apprentices."

"Sounds like something you need to talk with us about," he replied—not *terribly* concerned, but concerned enough, given how important those apprentices were to the welfare of the Barony.

"I was hoping you'd say that," she replied with satisfaction.

There was a guard on the door to the Baronial suite, a new posting, something that Kordas himself was not particularly comfortable with, but which his Councilors had insisted on. Even the Old Men had agreed with them. "All it takes is one outsider wanting to throw us into chaos, or one of our own who is particularly disgruntled," they had pointed out. "You can't defend yourself if you're asleep."

"Evening, Rainel," he said to the guard, who went stiffly to attention.

"Majesty," the guard acknowledged.

"Baron," he corrected, for the thousandth time, and managed not to sigh. "There's not a lot that's majestic about me this late in the day." Rainel struggled to keep his composure and replied, "As you say, Baron."

"Oh, Kordas, stop harassing the poor man," Isla remonstrated. "I want to hear what Delia and the Old Men have cooked up."

The guard opened the door for her, and she nodded graciously and sailed through, followed closely by the rest of them.

"I liked being able to open and close my own doors," Kordas complained, as soon as the door had been closed behind them. "I miss the Dolls, too."

"And I liked any number of things we don't have now, but I don't complain about them," Isla replied, waving the others to seats in the "receiving room," and taking one herself. "People need to see you as a leader, and a leader doesn't open his own doors, nor does he go unguarded when he sleeps. Now, what's all this about the apprentices?"

Delia flopped down ungracefully into the inviting embrace

of a heavily padded chair. "They can't *read*. At least half of them, the ones who were small children when we first arrived here. So the mages and the Healers have to waste valuable time teaching them how to read and write, when they could be using that time to teach them their proper work."

He slid into place beside Isla. "How did that happen?" he asked.

She shrugged. "The escape happened. Then there were more important things to do than teach your child how to read. Both for the littles *and* their parents. People were sending their offspring out in the fields to scare birds, or to places it was safe to gather wood, or some other useful task, and by the time evening comes around everyone is too tired to do things like teach and learn. So the older apprentices are teaching the younger ones reading, writing, and ciphering, which cuts into *their* learning time as well. It's not a disaster, but it's seriously irritating the actual mages and Healers."

He pinched the top of his nose between his thumb and forefinger. "Well, having half the population illiterate is not an option either. I'll put this in front of the Council. I don't think there will be a problem with finding time in the day for younglings for lessons; the problem will be figuring out who can take the time to teach them. Especially since you absconded with all the literate adults who have mobility issues, and put them to copying books." He held up a hand. "And I am *not* saying to stop that, and I am *not* saying it was a bad idea. It was an excellent idea, and I'm extremely grateful you not only came up with it, but you and Alberdina made it work."

Delia nodded, looking gratified.

"And I am not going to allow our tradition of literacy for all in Valdemar to die," he continued, perhaps a little more forcefully than he had intended. "That's one of the ways tyranny is able to take hold. And—" he stopped himself. "I'm not going to lecture. You already know Valdemar's history, better than some."

"Being able to read, freely, to read anything, is the first thing a tyrant suppresses. The enemy of a tyrant is rational, informed thinking, and the ignorant make the best slaves," said Delia, quoting from Kordas's great-great-grandfather.

"Exactly. Well, things are a bit easier now. We're not frighteningly close to starvation anymore. We rebound from shocks better. We'll figure something out."

"That's all I needed to hear," Delia said cheerfully, and bounced up from her chair. "I've got things to do before bedtime. Thank you, Kordas."

He snorted. "Don't thank me. I wasn't the one to find out the problem. We'll sort out something."

"We always do," said Delia, on her way out the door. "That's one thing we can count on."

There was silence for a moment after she left; Kordas illuminated the mage-lights with a thought, but kept them at a level he considered "cozy." He had expected his boys would all depart to their "rooms"—more like cubbies than rooms, but they were quite private, and even if the manor was packed full of people escaping danger, the rooms would *still* remain private. Restil and Hakkon did—but Jon did not.

In fact, Jon was very clearly thinking about something. Kordas waited. His youngest might only be barely fourteen, but he was a deep thinker, and when he spoke it was generally with good sense.

"What about us?" Jon asked at last. "Highborns, that is. Highborn children. A lot of us don't have much to do—especially the girls. Learning Court stuff from the past just isn't relevant anymore, and there's not the whole heaps of fine things to make fancywork with that there used to be. Many mamas don't want to see their daughters at common looms, and who needs fancy tapestries right now? Well, some of the sons, too. There's only so much weapons practice you can do in a day, and not everyone is good at it. I'd like to volunteer to teach, in fact." He grinned a little. "I still remember every bit of how our page-teacher taught *us*, and I am pretty sure I can do the job."

"Now, *that* is a fine point, and one I'll make to the Council. It will certainly count strongly in its favor that you volunteered first." He smiled broadly as Jon blushed a little. His youngest was a fine hand with a bow, but not as robust as Hakkon and Restil—although there was *no* doubt who their father was; they all looked like he had when he was their age. If this idea was partly a ploy for getting out of hand-to-hand practice, well, that was fine. If Jon had any ability with magic, it hadn't shown yet, but then again, Hakkon hadn't shown anything either, yet, and Restil had come into his powers rather later than most. So until and unless that happened, he wouldn't need time training in magic either.

And it was true that a great many of the highborn younglings were a lot more idle than he liked. He couldn't tell their parents what they were to do with them—*he* didn't have that right. But a great many of them were *not* going out on foraging expeditions, or spending actual productive time in the gardens, or helping with housework . . . and bored youngsters with little to do in a Court where all their traditional outlets simply didn't exist now (and probably wouldn't until they had children of their own) was a recipe for mischief.

"If you go do this teaching . . . it'll be fashionable to do it," he said aloud. "I won't even have to ask anyone; people with offspring at loose ends will be asking *me* to let them do it. There will be security concerns, of course, and all who teach will need to be *taught* how to teach, so that students retain what they learn. Yes, this is good thinking." *I need to discuss this with Isla tonight. By the time I bring this up to the Council in the morning, we'll have just the right spin on it.*

"My work here is done," Jon said, standing up and giving his father a mocking little bow.

"Never," Kordas declared. "But you can retreat to your cubby and whatever book you purloined from Jonaton now." And as Jon sauntered off, trailed by a black cat, it occurred to him that this might solve a problem of his own. *I wonder how Hakkon would take to teaching.* . . .

"... It's got merit, Kordas. That idea has merit," said Lord Alden Marin, a gentleman with a spouse so enthusiastic about bringing babies into the world that he had some fifteen children now, and—at least according to Alberdina—it was only with great reluctance that his wife had been persuaded that fifteen was enough. This attitude baffled Kordas, because he could not imagine a woman *wanting* to endure the stress of pregnancy that many times, but it was also none of his business. Lord Marin, on the other hand, sometimes seemed at wit's end with the shenanigans of his tribe.

The important business of the morning concluded, Kordas and Isla's carefully crafted proposal for general schools had just been presented, and the Privy Council seemed, on the whole, positive about it.

The Council Chamber was a spacious room more than large enough for the four trestle tables turned into a square, and their relatively comfortable chairs. It had fireplaces at each end—sadly, the days of mage-heated rooms were gone—and hanging over the fireplace nearest the table was a map of the Barony inked out on a giant tanned boar hide. It sometimes seemed to Kordas as if he had spent half his life here.

"Jon is quite eager to begin," Kordas said. "And, of course, there's no concern about having him set up a school here in the wall for the children of servants and guards; we could do that without bringing it up to the Council. But his point about the general population bidding fair to be half illiterate is a good one, and I thought it should be addressed before the situation becomes a real problem, with mages and Healers forced to tutor Gifted children in the basics, perhaps for years, before they can begin their real education." He paused. *"Years,"* he repeated. "Our mages and Healers are getting older by the day. That could mean *years* in which we have no effective Healers or mages."

By the looks of alarm, he was satisfied that he had effectively lit a fire under them.

"I wonder who else is idling away their time that could serve as teachers," wondered Lady Bastien aloud. "Alberdina and Delia swept up most of the literate commons that aren't up to strenuous work for their copying, of course, but surely— ah!" She snapped her fingers. "The priests and clerics, of course! *And* they have *places* for those schools all over Haven in the form of their temples, which are half empty most of the time!"

"But my lady, their prayers and meditations—" objected old Lord Damberlin.

"Can be done when the teaching is done," she retorted firmly. "As my own tutor was fond of saying, basic literacy and ciphering can be taught in two or three candlemarks a day. It's the application of those skills, in learning history, literature, medicine, advanced mathematics, and so on that requires extra time." She nodded, very pleased with herself. "Those advanced skills can be part of a Healer or mage's education, of course, but secondary to what will be their profession. As for the non-Gifted, if a child wants to pursue learning beyond the basics, I would think that a person of faith and devotion would be happy to supply that want. And if they don't, well, we can find someone who will, to the betterment of everyone in Valdemar. And thus, we demonstrate that teaching is a very honorable way to spend one's time, as well!"

"Don't expect a dissent from me, my lady." The representative of the religious communities of Haven, Father Delephon, immediately agreed, although moments of agreement between him and the ultra-practical Lady Bastien were usually few and far between. "I may have to thump some heads, but it's only been ten years since the duty of teaching the young literacy and ciphering was *part* of our duties to our flocks. At least in the Barony, it was."

"Delephon, not every religious devotee is suited to teaching," said Master Smith Longhammer, ruefully rubbing the back of his head. "I do remember Brother Haycock's impatience with great clarity, and his swift and completely unnecessary application of a spoon to the back of me head on multiple occasions for no apparent reason!"

"That's where the manor younglings come in," the Seneschal said smoothly, eliminating the need for Kordas to say anything himself. "The highborn almost all have children beyond their heirs, who, at the moment, are engaged in—what, exactly? Hunting, all very well, but we get most of our meat from domestic animals now. Their parents consider them too lofty to do manual labor and too valuable for the Guard, and that leaves them doing make-work. We'll surely have enough who are willing to spend time productively to make up for those who are ill-suited to the task. And there can be no better way to demonstrate devotion to one's god and the growth of maturity and responsibility than to undertake to teach younger children."

"Rewards, though," Lady Bastien mused, thinking practically, as always. "There must be some sort of reward for a youth in this besides the sheer novelty of being put in charge of something. Titles? I should think a Court title would be an inducement. We can make one up. Master of Scholars has a nice ring to it. Some sort of ornamental bit of frippery to wear at ceremonies. Laurel is the symbol of wisdom, is it not? And there are plenty of laurels in these parts. A gilded laurel wreath in the hair is both showy and inexpensive, and makes a pretty display."

Kordas just sat back in his chair, nodding from time to time, as his Privy Council took the half-formed idea, molded and shaped it, and by the time luncheon rolled around, had beaten it into a decree, transcribed it to paper, and sent it to the clerks for copying and distribution. *Where* the schools would be was sorted—as the lady had pointed out, there were plenty of temples, pretty much evenly distributed across the city, and even a few out among the farms. The wagons that brought produce into the city every morning could also bring children, and take them home again at noon, well in time for chores. The second batch of wagons that came in at noon doing the same could bring a different batch of children. Three hours of teaching each day was deemed sufficient for active youngsters who would have trouble sitting still for very long. There would, of course, be people who resented having an entire afternoon or morning of their children's work "stolen," but Kordas suspected they'd go along with it anyway, because not going along would make them look bad in the eyes of their neighbors.

And just when he thought everything had been hammered out, Squire Hawthorn, who represented the farmers farthest from Haven, suddenly woke up and objected, because the distance from his farms to Haven by slow produce cart was half a day. And that began the debating all over again.

"Didn't the Valdemar villages used to have what they called 'dame schools'?" the Seneschal finally interjected, looking weary of all of this. "The village would put up a building for someone aging—usually a childless elderly widow, or someone

whose home was now overly crowded with grandchildren—
and they would live in a room in the back while the children
were taught in the front of it. As I recall, it was an equitable
trade; an older single person no longer able to keep up with the
repairs on their cottage, or living with a hoard of noisy children, got a solid small living space in return for teaching."

"Some of us did," the Squire admitted.

"Well, do *that*," replied the Seneschal, who clearly wanted
his luncheon. "If it's too far for the children to come to Haven
or a temple, get those friendship groups together, look for volunteers willing—and capable!—to teach the basics, and take a
vote on who gets the job. Then, if there's no temple large enough
to hold classes, get the friendship group to build the school."

"Aye," Hawthorn said, slowly and reluctantly. "But who's to
pay for building?"

A glance to his exchequer and a brief nod from the same
gave Kordas all the information he needed. "I will," he said.
"Out of the Privy purse. I'll take care of the building supplies,
you take care of the labor and the teacher."

There was some more back and forth, because people always like to argue and find fault (especially his Council), and
finally a compromise was reached. Instead of a single small
and clearly insufficient room at the back of the school, the
teacher would get one of the empty living barges meant for a
small family, fitted up as a cottage, as so many of the farmers
had already done for their laborers. "Fitted up as a cottage"
meant walling it in and topping it with a thatched roof, so it
stayed reasonably cool in summer and didn't need a lot of
wood in the little stove in winter. That meant the school could
be left unheated when not occupied (another sore point; Hay-
worth said his farmers would rebel if they had to cut the wood
to heat "an enormous empty room" all winter), while the
teacher remained snug.

*Sometimes I think my Council just likes to argue for the
sake of arguing.*

This was why he always put the meeting in the morning, and did not offer pages to bring in a meal. The more growling stomachs he heard, the more likely it was that people would wrap things up.

Finally he was able to bring the meeting to a close; he couldn't help but notice that Hawthorn was quite eager to assist with this, even though he'd been the one to object. Probably because the food that was laid out in the Great Hall for luncheon was on a first-come, first-fed basis, and even now, even though it was the most basic "plowman's lunch" fare of bread, cheese, pickles, and raw vegetables and fruits, there was never so much as a crumb left when the kitchen workers came to clear it away. *It's not fancy, but we* could *be starving right now, and we're not.*

He was looking forward to getting his own share, when a page intercepted him and told him that Isla expected him in their suite.

That could only mean one thing: a visitor who didn't want to be paraded in front of the entire populace of the manor. There were any number of candidates, but the most likely was one of the Tayledras.

No telling what brings them. I hope it's not to say a permanent farewell. That farewell was inevitable, as the Hawkbrothers migrated further and further away from Valdemar in their quest to cleanse what they were calling "the Pelagir Hills" from the ravages of the long-ago Mage Wars, but he was not looking forward to it. They were a valued and valuable ally, over and above their generosity in bringing the Valdemarans here and giving them their old Vale. And many of them were his close personal friends.

He hurried to the Baronial suite to find Isla and Jon playing host to Silvermoon, who was apparently enjoying his very simple meal. "Kordas!" the latter greeted him; today the Hawkbrother was wearing a wrapped top and wide trousers of gray ramie, and his snow-white hair was confined in what looked like hundreds of tiny braids, each ending in a silver bead. "I would be pleased enough to visit here for some of Sai's famous bread, but I actually have other reasons."

"Can those reasons wait until we finish eating?" he asked. "My Council was especially long-winded today."

Silvermoon gestured at the small table between their seats, on which rested a tray of sliced bread, a particular mild, white cheese he very much liked, pickled beans, fresh flat-peas (a versatile Tayledras vegetable that virtually everyone loved), radishes, and baby carrots from the thinning of the gardens. *Diplomatic protocols be damned, I'm starving!* He filled a plate and set about emptying it inside of himself.

Silvermoon had brought along Jelavan, the hertasi who had made such a friend of Delia. Silvermoon was eating, Jelavan was not, but that was because Jelavan, like all hertasi, couldn't eat raw vegetables or cheese, so he had probably filled himself up on bread before Kordas got there. Then again, he might not be hungry at all; hertasi generally ate only two meals a day, breakfast and supper.

As he had many times before, Kordas felt very sorry for a creature who could not enjoy cheese. Then again, the Tayledras didn't actually have herds of milking beasts, so they didn't have access to cheese. *Maybe that's why they still visit us so often.* Certainly they had been eager enough to set up light trade in the foodstuff, a bit of magical help in return for a wheel or two.

As if echoing his thoughts, Jelavan spoke up, because Silvermoon's mouth was full. "I came along because I brought Sai some seeds to save until you have greenhouses," the little lizard said. "They're herbs and spices that won't survive a winter without protection. You enjoyed some of them before the Veil came down."

Kordas nodded appreciatively. "We did indeed enjoy those, and I for one miss them. Once we have glassmakers able to make new panes, we'll certainly have greenhouses, especially

here at the manor. That has always been the plan. There are a
lot of herbs used in Healing that take better to sheltered conditions, or work better when fresh."

He turned to Silvermoon, who had set his plate aside. "So
what brings you here? And why so quietly? There was no
fanfare, no page running to announce you, and no procession
to the manor! I thought you lived to be admired."

Although the visits by the Tayledras had grown fewer over
the years, every time they appeared in public, they were
greeted as heroes. No one forgot that they had brought the
Valdemarans here and given them a Vale that had protection,
a controlled climate, gardens, the iron mine and smelter, and
places for them to live. No one forgot all the help they had been
in succeeding years. Whether it was advice or direct help, if it
had not been for the Hawkbrothers, the population would be
half of what had arrived here by now, if not less—rather than
increasing, as people became comfortable with the idea of
having children here.

"Well," said Silvermoon. "While it's true I enjoy your company, I did come here for another reason."

"Do tell," Kordas said, leaning forward.

Silvermoon, for his part, leaned back in his chair, satisfied
that he had caught Kordas's attention. "We discovered *after*
we had set up our new Vale that there was a cluster of small
villages inside the area we intended to cleanse. These are tiny
villages, no more than a dozen families at most, so most people don't have secondary names, just 'son of' or 'daughter of.'
This isn't unheard of, but it did complicate matters a little.
Among other things, this time the inhabitants were in a zone
of chaotic magic; a couple of them, mage-Gifted, of course,
had learned to use it after a fashion. Others found themselves
used *by* the magic. So our work had to include that reality. The
ones who styled themselves 'mages' didn't much care for us
coming in and making things orderly, for instance. They'd
cemented power by being unpredictable—and no one wants to

oppose somebody that *anything* could happen around. That, we handled by persuasion." He left that for a moment longer than he had to, implying that something more than asking was involved. "Corralling the chaos we could handle for ourselves, obviously, as it's largely what we do. But we have a . . ." Here he rubbed his temple, as if his head hurt. ". . . a situation we don't have experience with, and meeting your people, shall we say . . . broadened our minds concerning solutions."

Kordas couldn't see where this was going, but that was Silvermoon's way; he never gave a straightforward fact when a roundabout story would do instead. *So his reason for being here has something to do with those people. Hang onto that fact, or I'll probably lose it in the story.* "Go on," he encouraged.

"There are two villages in this story, far enough apart they don't interact often, but close enough it's an easy walk of about half a day to get from one to the other. Both of them are in the path of what I would call 'mage-energy squalls.' In the first village, there was a widowed woman with a daughter, Lythe, who had become a handful once she reached the age of rebellion. Had a habit of sleeping most of the day, would run off as soon as she woke up to idle her time away with her friends, rather than helping her mother in any way, and would return late at night and wake her mother out of a sound sleep to demand the poor woman cook her a meal. This was a fairly recent development in Lythe's behavior, and it left her mother doing all the work for the two of them."

"Let me guess, she's about sixteen or seventeen, and too pretty for her own good," Isla put in sourly. "We've had that situation here, though it's more often among the highborn, and I am usually the one called on to deal with it officially if it comes to that."

"Quite correct, oh lovely Lady Terilee," Silvermoon nodded, using the name that the Tayledras had picked for her. "To be sure, she's more flighty, impulsive, and selfish, as adolescents often are, than malicious, and not at all mean-spirited. But that didn't help her mother, who was left to do the chores and work to support two people, with only one person actually working. Her mother decided to teach her a lesson by not making any meals for her if she was not there, leaving nothing that could be eaten immediately except raw vegetables, not cleaning up after her, not mending what was torn or broken, or doing any of the things the girl should have been doing herself. So she came home on the night in question, almost at dawn, and pouted and had a tantrum because there was nothing to eat and her favorite chemise was stained and had not been washed. Her mother told Lythe that she had warned her this was going to happen. Lythe snapped back with something along the lines of *you have to take care of me, I didn't ask to be born!* And her mother completely lost her temper. That is where things got complicated."

Kordas quickly tracked back and picked out bits from the story so far. Woman suffering from righteous rage, emotionally wrought up to the breaking point, and "mage-energy squalls" . . .

"Oh, no," he and Isla said at the same time.

Silvermoon nodded, pleased they had already guessed what had happened. "The poor woman doesn't remember her exact words, but it was something to the effect of, if Lythe was going to lie about all day and play all night, then she ought to never wake up by day, miss all the things she liked to do with her friends, and see how she liked it then. Presumably, this was in the middle of one of those mage-squalls."

"A mother whose temper has been tried past all reason is certainly going to have a lot of will behind her words," Isla said grimly. "Enough to turn her anger into a curse. I will admit that there has been a time or two when I have had to stop myself from saying things to the boys, because I *am* a mage, and I know the power of words with will and energy behind them."

"Exactly. And since both of them by that time were in a screaming fight, neither of them realized that anything had happened until the first sliver of the sun peeped over the horizon, and Lythe dropped to the floor, unconscious."

From the look on Isla's face, Kordas had the feeling that his wife felt the girl had gotten off with a great deal less of a "punishment" than she deserved, but he held his peace. Silvermoon had mentioned *two* villages, so it followed they had not even begun to hear the whole of the story.

"Well, now, this had a couple of repercussions, the most important to Lythe being that once everyone in the village realized she had brought a curse on herself, *no one wanted to associate with her,* not even her former friends. So there she was, insensible during the day, and all alone and bored at night, with even her friends shunning her. Suddenly it wasn't so much fun to stay up all night, and she and her mother came to us for help." Silvermoon massaged his temple again. "Now, ordinarily, we'd only get involved enough to see if we could break the 'spell,' and if not, tell her, 'Sorry, but you brought this on yourself,' and go back to the Vale. This isn't the worst fate in the world. She could even have turned this into an asset, by taking on the job of night watchperson for the entire village, which would have enabled her to contribute to the household. But then there was the second village and a second arrogant adolescent, and an entirely different, yet similar, 'curse.'"

Well, this just gets better. But I wonder what he thinks we can do about it?

"Rothas is just as handsome as Lythe is pretty, but more than that, he's got Bardic Gifts, extremely strong, though he uses them only crudely at the moment. But because of that, he's extremely popular with all the villages, called on all the time for entertainment, very much the subject of praise and flattery, and actually makes his bread with his talents. To be sure, he was good enough we even invited him to our Vale now and again; he plays several basic instruments, and he's a wonderful singer and a fabulous storyteller. And, of course, with Bardic Projective Empathy, he can and does lead you around by the nose during his entertainment. He was between villages, coming from one celebration where he was entertaining and going to another, a wedding, which was the better venue of the two and where he expected to be compensated generously, when he encountered an old woman he'd never seen before, taking up the whole of a narrow path with her donkey and cart. It was brambles on either side and he couldn't get by and he was going to be very late."

"Oh, no. . . ." said Isla.

"Oh, yes. Demanded she get out of the way, railed at her, and called her a number of offensive names. Made up a chant about how useless and ugly she was on the spot, if you please."

"And of course it turns out she's a hedge-wizard," said Isla.

"Of course she is. Or at least, she's someone who's perfectly capable of using magic. We haven't found her, by the way, which . . . makes me suspicious she might be more than just a hedge-wizard. And she probably already knew about Lythe, because she cursed Rothas with the opposite effect—just as the squall struck, giving her plenty of power, and also altering whatever she had intended to do in unexpected ways. 'Since you favor the night so much, I say the night shall be taken from you. From the time the last light has left the sky to the time the first light enters it, you shall . . .' and so on. And so he dropped down right there in his tracks like a stone, and didn't wake up until false dawn." Now Silvermoon rubbed his other temple. "As I said, we have not found her, and some among us suspect she's not a human at all, but rather a godling of trickery or something of the sort. It wouldn't surprise me." He sucked on his lower lip. "It's certainly exactly the kind of mischief such a being would do."

"I don't know if I'll ever get used to the way you say things like that so calmly. So you have two brats under similar curses that I assume none of you have been able to break. But no one's being hurt or inconvenienced except them, and they brought it all on themselves. Seems to be appropriate punishment to me. So why—" Isla wasn't as used to Silvermoon's long stories as Kordas was. Kordas knew that Silvermoon was just getting started.

"Because these two cursed youngsters somehow managed to stumble across each other at twilight. And—" Silvermoon made a little gesture suggestive of being struck over the head. "Lifebonded."

Isla looked at him, stunned. ". . . oh, no." Kordas simply facepalmed and sighed.

"Oh, *yes*. And remember that I said Rothas has Bardic Gifts? He's perfectly capable of including *everyone* within earshot in his misery. He doesn't even have to sing or speak; powerful Projective Empathy, and he doesn't yet understand how to control it. Or why. And so, because he really does not know how to properly use his Gifts, he does, indeed, make everyone as wildly inconsolable as he is. Within a day, he had people at his home village weeping uncontrollably at the least little provocation—until they figured out he was the source. Moving to Lythe's village made things worse. *Both* villages want no part of these two. And given their ages and immaturity, turning them loose is not a good idea. We took them in and did our best, but because—"

Here Kordas interrupted him, holding up his hand. "To be sure, you have curses cast by one woman who doesn't know what she is doing, and another who may or may not, and all of it tangled up with chaotic power—it would take time *and* genius to figure out if the curses can be broken."

Isla sniffed. "Oh, it's probably something like, 'You must do one utterly unselfish act,' which sounds like the one thing these two are completely incapable of."

"Harsh, but a fair assessment," Silvermoon agreed. "But . . .

unless there is something we are missing, something as simple as unselfishness won't break the curses. Although, in our lore, you would have to be completely unaware that doing an unselfish deed breaks the curse, because if you know that, and you do an 'unselfish deed,' it won't actually be unselfish. The intent modifies the result, and doubly so with chaos-formed magic, and we agreed we wouldn't like the results. So we haven't told them that."

"It's a touching story, but where do *we* come into this?" Kordas wanted to know.

"Well, I was hoping I could persuade you to take them in. You have some of the finest mages I know of in the Old Men and Jonaton. You handle magical energies in ways we do not, and that might make the difference." He paused for a drink, which Jelavan had in Silvermoon's palm before his fingers were even fully extended to reach. Jelavan consciously slowed his movements around Valdemarans—who turned out to startle hilariously easily, the Tayledras thought—yet it was still swift. Fascinatingly, the hertasi's handoff was in a smooth arc, with the cup pitched forward and back in motion before being fully righted. It struck him as something perfectly Tayledras: quick, quiet, artful, and mindful of the way the world worked. In this case, the effect of motion on liquid and how to counteract its inevitable sloshing. Things like this delighted Kordas. His mind was fully engaged, and it felt good.

Silvermoon's pause was long enough for a deep drink, as he took his time arranging what followed. "You have a much larger population than we do, and certainly much, much larger than their villages. Novelty, and an entirely new environment, might keep them distracted for a while. Be careful to ensure they are guided well, and kept happy. And occupied. You can find ways for them to make themselves useful, and since you are not related to either of them, you can make that a condition of feeding and housing them, without them whining about it. And you have a great many sensible adults who will be able to keep them out of further mischief." He sighed. "I am *very* weary of having to reinforce everyone's shields to prevent thrice-daily emotional breakdowns because these two aren't grown up enough to control themselves. *We* start in training mental discipline before the baby's even dry." Everyone had a chuckle over that. The challenges of guiding youth appeared to be universal.

Kordas glanced at Isla, who nodded slightly. "Given how much we owe you, of course we will," he said.

"Then let there be love," Silvermoon smiled. "Let there be love" was a Hawkbrothers phrase that amounted to "Who am I to know fate? Allow it to be what it will." "I am almost speechless with gratitude," Silvermoon proclaimed. "In case you were generous in this, we brought them with us. They're waiting at the Gate now," he continued, getting up without haste. "We'll just send them through when we leave. Or rather, we'll put Shadowdancer in a wheelbarrow, and Sunsinger can tote her across himself. But there is something else that brings me here, which is not as promising as the lovers' future. It seems you have a neighbor."

Ha, so the Hawkbrothers have already given them names of their own. Well, Lythe Shadowdancer and Rothas Sunsinger will certainly do to differentiate them from the Valdemarans. They weren't exactly one people yet, but he had presided over a number of Hawkbrother-Valdemaran marriages in recent years.

"If you mean we finally found that Lord Legenfall set himself up off to the east, and managed to ally himself with a local mage, we know," Kordas told him.

"That 'local mage' is not someone to be trifled with," Silvermoon said warningly. "We've had our eye on him for some time. Well, we think the mage is male. I'm not sure of what his limits are, because we've observed him doing some impressive things from a distance. We're not sure why he never challenged us, but he *could*. And your runaway lordling could persuade him to challenge you. So be on your guard."

"We're never off our guard." Kordas sighed, joining his friends. "Well, let's go meet your two troublemakers. Or at least, the one that's awake."

". . . and as a condition of feeding and housing you two, you'll have to make yourselves useful."

So far, Restil had held his peace as his father laid out *how things would be done* for the two strangers. Kordas was to be the stern leader in this little display; Restil was to be the sympathetic peer, once his father had left. It was a game they often played, and they played it to perfection. Since it appeared that Hakkon had learned *his* lesson, Restil and his father had decided to bring Hakkon in on the game as well, so Hakkon was silently watching, listening, and learning.

For his part, Restil was sympathetic. He'd had two episodes of what his mother called "a pash" in the last couple of years, instances where he really did believe he was truly in love, and it had been . . . well, he'd had nothing to compare the feelings to, so he'd been upside-down emotionally, confused, and at once desperately happy and desperately unhappy. But he'd been able to get over them when the objects of his affection— one of them a Tayledras scout named Redarrow—had not reciprocated, and (fortunately) were kind about letting his hopes down. It had been the worst emotional pain he had ever felt in his life. He'd been sure he would never get over it. He had, of course, but at the time . . .

And he could not imagine how badly it must hurt when something like these curses kept you from your *lifebonded* beloved for all but a few precious moments of the day. Life-bonds were serious business. The intimacy of love, it could be said, as if you had been blended with someone. People had quite literally died of broken hearts and souls when they lost their partners. *People think a lifebond is something to be desired. Those people have no idea what they are talking about.*

"I'm not going to ask you what you can do. I'm going to tell you what you *will* do," Kordas continued. "You, Lythe Shadowdancer—since you are awake and aware all night long, you will walk the top of the manor wall every night from full dark to false dawn. You will deliver their midnight meal to the guards, and you are to make sure they are awake as they stand watch. I'm aware this is not a challenging task, but it's a necessary one, and by taking it, you free up someone who has senior skills to you."

Lythe Shadowdancer had the good graces to look chastened. Of course, by this time, she had already been rejected by her own village and friends, and was very well aware of how much of a nuisance she and Rothas were to the Hawkbrothers. So she just bowed her head, clasped her hands in front of her, and said, softly, "Yes, sir."

She certainly was very good to look at, and Restil, now with ten years of experience with how "village beauties" tended to run young men—and not so young men!—ragged to cater to their whims, had a pretty good idea that her current treatment alone would have been quite the shock to her system. And being subject not only to this curse, but to the repercussions of her lifebond, had surely shaken her to the core. But there could not have been a more perfect example of a "beautiful heroine" for a wonder tale, with her enormous violet eyes, her ravenwing-black hair, her perfectly sculpted face, and her exceptional figure. *If this was the Empire . . . she'd be snatched up and carried off to the Emperor's Court to join his private circle of . . . well, there's no polite name for what she'd wind up as once the Palace had her. And then no polite name for the only thing left if the Emperor was done with her. I'm glad she's here, whatever happens.*

"As for you, Rothas Sunsinger, you are to be given over to my mage Koto until you learn full control of those Gifts of yours. In the meantime, because my people are mostly *not* mages and don't have their own shields, Koto will put *you* under a very tight personal shield to keep you from affecting everyone around you."

Restil *felt* the reaction to that immediately: resentment and anger, like a jarring melody atop the droning misery the life-bond was causing Rothas. And Koto stepped forward and slapped the back of Rothas's very blond and very handsome head.

"*HEY!*" the young man shouted angrily—but the feelings he was broadcasting stopped—or in the case of the misery, dimmed. "What—"

"So smacking you in the head works," Koto observed dispassionately. "Good. I'll use that if nothing else works."

"You can't do that to me!" Rothas seethed.

Koto smirked. With his round, bald head and face a map of smile wrinkles, he looked very jolly, and mostly was—but he was, according to Sai, a "take no prisoners" type when it came to magical discipline. "On the contrary, I can," he retorted. "The Baron, our leader, has put me in charge of you. If you don't like it—" he pointed to the door, "—you can leave and take your chances with the wilderness. The Hawkbrothers have washed their hands of you. Your own people, as you know, won't have you, because you're projecting misery wherever you go. No one else in the Barony will help you—not because we tell them not to, but because you're essentially an emotional cesspool, and nothing you can contribute is worth having to put up with being as sunk in misery as you'll make them. You and love have not yet reached an understanding of who is in charge, and love likes to take up lots of room. You won't be severed from each other, don't worry. I am not the enemy of love. I am, though, *implacably* annoyed by what it does to the ordered mind. You both are going to learn how to live in control of your own selves. Or not." Koto added, "We aren't monsters. We'll kit you up with everything you need to live in the wilderness except food—which we can't spare—but you'll be on your own." Koto narrowed his eyes and smiled just a pinch. "And we'll give you two knives."

Ouch. Koto's implying they'll kill each other if they end up in the wilderness. That's diabolical. I love that guy.

Lythe clutched Rothas's elbow, face full of fear. She didn't have to say anything; after a moment where he seethed with rebellion, he abruptly deflated, and the waves of opposition stopped without Koto needing to smack him again.

Koto nodded. "Good. That's a good start. I'll come for you at dawn." He saluted Kordas with two fingers, and left.

They were all standing in the "main" room of one of the four-room living spaces in the wall. Kordas had assigned them one that was as far from anyone else as possible. It had been sparsely furnished with a rough table and four stools, a fireplace, a kitchen counter, a sink, and a hand-operated water-pump that was fed from the shared cistern above, which in turn was fed by rainwater and "pipes" grown by the Mother to the water table below. The next room contained the staircase up, a drain, a jakes, a tub, a second pump, and a water reservoir built into the back of the first room's fireplace, which held water for baths that would be kept warm by the fireplace in the first room. Upstairs were two rooms with bedrolls on the floor. Restil rather doubted that the second of those rooms would be in use, but you never knew.

The couple's belongings—probably more than they had arrived with when they were taken to the Hawkbrother Vale, since the packs were almost as tall as they were—were at their feet.

"Rothas, you'll eat with my people at the manor," said Kordas. "Lythe, you will eat with the guards. I'll be sending one of them at full dark to instruct you in your duties. Wear something sturdy." He glanced outside the open door, where the light was fading. "I'll leave you to settle as best you can. Restil can answer any questions you have." He turned on his heel and left, Hakkon going with him.

When the door closed, Rothas—who really *was* too handsome for his own good, and probably had been the "king" of his little villages and not accustomed to being treated as he had been—let out a *whuff* of anger, and a brief wave of the emotion as well. "Is he always like that?" the Sunsinger demanded.

"He's in charge of the welfare of thirteen thousand of his people," Restil reminded the young fellow. "And you aren't his people, you're a couple of strangers he's taken off the Hawkbrothers' hands because we owe them so much."

Rothas had been about to say something, but stopped, his mouth dropping open. *"Thirteen thousand* people?" he replied, incredulously. "There aren't that many people in the whole world!"

Restil chuckled. "I assure you, there are a lot more than that. Where we came from, the Imperial Capital held something like *thirty* thousand people, all within a much smaller space than this Barony. And that was just one of a hundred or more cities of similar size, and fifty or sixty various-sized territories called *principalities, dukedoms, counties,* and *baronies.* The world is very much larger than you think."

Rothas's bright blue eyes went blank with shock. *"How?"* was all he managed to get out.

Restil didn't even bother to answer that.

"And if that is true, why is he bothering with *us*?" Lythe asked, her voice trembling and low.

"Because he owes the Hawkbrothers, and the Hawkbrothers are committed to cleaning up magical messes. They can't clean up yours, and they are hoping we can." It was Restil's turn to glance out the door. It would not be long before Rothas was insensible, and he should be in, or at least on, a bedroll by then. "There's bedding upstairs. You just take care of tonight and let tomorrow take care of itself for now. You are safe. I'll be here at false dawn to bring you both to breakfast, and answer more of your questions."

Rothas's shoulders sagged at the reminder of their current situation, and a wave of misery washed over Restil. "Thank you, Restil," he managed, and it actually sounded as if he meant it. "I'm sure this is no pleasure for you."

Restil laughed. "It's better than shoveling horse shit," he said. "And yes, I am the son of the man in charge of the welfare of thirteen thousand people, the Baron of this Barony, and I shovel horse shit. None of us are 'above' whatever job needs doing. It's the only reason we've survived ten years here, and I'll tell you all about *that* in the morning."

And with that, he left them to ponder their situation. He hoped their thoughts would be fruitful.

Koto and his new "apprentice" appeared for luncheon in the Great Hall the next day, and Restil had no difficulty seeing the new shield surrounding the young man, although it would not be visible except to mage-sight. Rothas looked very subdued, still with that undercurrent of misery, although at least he wasn't projecting it past the shield. *If that's what a lifebond does to you, I pray I never have one!* Restil thought to himself, as he helped himself to bread, cheese, and vegetables and joined them. Koto wore stern expression, quite out of keeping with the way he normally looked, but Restil could tell he was pleased with himself. *It looks like Koto is playing my father's game. He is the stern taskmaster, and I am to be the one to coax Rothas and Lythe into better behavior. We'll see which tactic works!* Restil had never actually *had* a rebellious phase; he wasn't sure why, but he was glad it hadn't happened. Maybe it was because when the world was throwing emergency after emergency at you, rebellion wasn't very attractive.

Life was so much easier when you got along with your parents!

"Rothas needs a rest from his studies with me," the mage announced as Restil sat down next to him. "Perfectly natural; he's never properly learned to use his abilities, and doing so is quite tiring! So since your father suggested you also serve as his mentor, Restil, I'll turn him over to you for the rest of the day. Anything you need to attend to that would prevent you from doing that, lad?"

Restil laughed. "I have learned the art of delegation from Father, although if my memory is correct, you Old Men and mother had to teach *him* that skill! Turns out that, other than boatbuilding and several kinds of very fancy weaving, there aren't a lot of crafts that we aren't already practicing, so we are in no danger of losing them. The weavers are happy to do their own documentation. So there is nothing preventing me from taking Rothas around, now and in the future."

Rothas's face was a mixture of relief and apprehension. "We're not shoveling horse shit, I hope?" he said, his tone implying that yes, he actually expected to share in that duty. Then again, he did come from a very small village, and it looked as if he, at least, had not tried to shirk his mundane chores.

"I've already mucked out my horses' stalls this morning, you're safe from that particular task," Restil replied. Koto took this conversation as a cue to go join the other Old Men at the high table. "But you're going to have to do something useful— or learn something. Father counts *learning* as important as *doing.* So I thought what we'd do is I'd find the luthier and you could start actual music lessons, then you can come along and give me a hand with another project."

"What's—a luthier?" Rothas asked.

"It's a fellow that makes musical instruments. Mind you, there's not a lot of call for those skills right now, so mostly what he does is alternate cabinetmaking with music lessons, both mostly for the highborn." It took him a moment to register that Rothas still looked baffled. "Haven't you ever had music lessons?"

"What do you need lessons for?" Rothas asked ingenuously. "I mean . . . birds don't take lessons—"

Evidently he wasn't in the Vale long enough to have heard any of the Hawkbrother bards. "Because the gods don't put the ability to play an instrument into *our* heads at birth," Restil replied.

"I can play the drums and the whistle. . . ."

"And there is oh, so much more than that," Restil replied firmly. "And it's a skill you are going to *need* when you learn to properly handle your Gifts. All that business of *Projective Empathy*? You'll ultimately channel that through music, once you can control what you share with others and what you keep behind your shields. Sometimes you'll need to do that without words."

Rothas's face fell. "I just want to sing. . . ." he said plaintively. "Why can't I just sing?"

A hundred retorts ran through Restil's mind, so he ate a carrot to delay his initial response of, "Do you know how many people would *kill* to have your Gifts?" There were a lot of possible things he could have said, but the one thing that stuck in his mind was the one he eventually said, after he swallowed the last bite.

"You haven't even tried any of this. Yes, I know Koto can be a difficult teacher, but he's also the best there is, and you are the equivalent of a little taking his first steps. What if all children decided that walking was too hard and crawled all their lives? Think of all the things they'd miss—running, dancing, even acrobatics!"

Rothas chewed glumly on a stalk of celery. *Celery. The vegetable of depression.* "I don't know. . . ."

"Besides, if you're honest, you'll admit that you don't 'just sing' the way a bird does, and you never have," Restil continued shrewdly. "What about all the practicing you've done? Making changes to a song so it suits you better? *Learning* new songs. And the only instruments you've ever explored are the drum and the whistle! There are dozens of instruments out there! Surely you heard at least a few while you were with the Hawkbrothers!"

Rothas's shoulders slumped. "I didn't . . . I mean, it didn't seem worth the bother. Everything was going so wrong."

Restil gestured with his carrot. "I figure when things feel wrong is when you need your music the most. This is how smart people get smarter. They learn when their feelings have had their say, and don't drag it out. I was taught that when you're in conflict inside, learning new things helps the world make more sense. Learning new things helps you discover wonders, while moping only increases your ability to feel bad."

In other words, he's never challenged himself because there was never a need to. He could coast on his natural abilities. That's the obvious. But now, there's a lot more going on that has him feeling ready to give up on everything. Rothas's lifebond meant that his enforced separation from Lythe was driving him deeply into depression and making him lose all interest in practically everything. It was probably even *physically* painful. But Restil had a notion that giving the fellow something equally powerful—working to master his Gifts and his craft—might counter some of that defeatism.

"We'll just go see the luthier," he said, making it very clear that "no" was not an option. "Then tell me if it doesn't seem to be worth the bother."

Now, it was possible that Rothas was putting on a good face for the Valdemarans in general and Restil in particular, and underneath he might be the arrogant, selfish boor that the short version of his story suggested—but Restil didn't think so. *Probably "young and stupid" sums it all up, and if being young and stupid was a crime, I'd be shoveling horse shit until I died to pay for it,* he thought with a touch of amusement.

He's probably no worse than Hakkon, for that matter—momentary thoughtlessness and rudeness, and a bit of unwarranted arrogance. Well, he's learned that the world is a lot bigger than he thought, and he is a very tiny minnow in a very big ocean. That alone has upended everything he thought he knew, and the fact that he's not screaming about how unfair this all is probably means there's a decent person in that morass of woe.

Rothas sighed. "All right. It's . . . all this has been *really hard*."

Restil nodded with sympathy. "Leaving aside what happened to you and Lythe, you've both been hauled into the Hawkbrothers' world, had their language and ours shoved into your head without a by-your-leave, and didn't even have time to get used to *their* way of life before they dumped you here, in the middle of more strangers than you could possibly have imagined. In your place, I'd probably be hiding in my bedroll, refusing to take the covers off my head."

That actually teased a little ghost of a smile out of the young man—which was enough to make female (and probably some male, Restil wasn't taking a census) heads nearby turn toward him, and dreamy smiles to appear on lips.

Poor things. Wait till they find out he's lifebonded. The weeping and wailing will be epic. On the one hand, this was amusing. On the other hand, it was very clear that Rothas was in a lot of emotional pain. Restil opted to come down on the side of sympathy.

"I know you don't much feel like eating, but eat," he urged, making himself an example. "You're not going to learn how to help yourself and Lythe if you wither away from starvation."

Once Rothas had choked down enough food that Restil was satisfied that he'd manage to last out the afternoon, he led the young man out of the Great Hall. And by this time it was obvious that a *lot* of people, and not just women, were covertly watching him. Some were openly staring. Restil couldn't blame them. Rothas was certainly worth looking at, worthy of a wonder tale, every single cliche about a golden-haired hero packed into a single person. *I am going to be besieged by the curious tonight after he goes insensible. They're all going to want to know every single detail, and they're going to be awfully disappointed when I say, "Well, you can ask him yourself when he's awake."* The more new people Rothas had to meet and talk to, the less he'd be thinking about himself and Lythe. With the Bardic Gift often came the absolute need for an audience, so Rothas would probably actually enjoy the enforced socialization.

Since the luthier mostly worked as a cabinetmaker and didn't need to be down in Haven itself, he worked out of four rooms he shared with a fellow cabinetmaker. In fact, they often collaborated on large pieces, with the younger man doing the rough work and the luthier doing the finishing. It was in one of the wall sections nearest the manor, so it wasn't far to walk. Restil cocked an eye at the sky and frowned. The clouds had a familiar look to them. "At least all the untamed magic around here doesn't affect the weather much."

"Aye, I noticed that too," Rothas confirmed. "Rain by tomorrow. Weather in that Hawkbrother city?—that was odd. Could be pounding down everywhere except *there*, and then it was just a gentle patter of however much they'd decided they wanted."

"This place used to be a Hawkbrother Vale," Restil told him as they approached Marin Joiner's open door; a tap-tap-tapping came from within, so at least they weren't going to be interrupting a music lesson. "But when they moved on, they took the protections with them. Winters can be hard, but I expect you know exactly how hard winter can be in this part of the world. I'll tell you more about us later, when you don't have to cope with twenty new things coming at you at once."

Restil tapped on the doorframe, purposely out of sync with the tapping of mallet on chisel, and Marin looked up from his work. A thin but obviously strong man, his gray-brown hair hung in a tail down his back. He could have been any age from forty onward, and wore a pair of lenses in wire frames perched on his nose, a carpenter's apron over the ubiquitous Valdemaran "working" outfit of natural linen trews and tunic, and leather wrist binders. The room smelled pleasantly of freshly cut, aged wood. "What can I do for you, young Prince?" he asked genially, causing Restil to laugh.

"For all our sakes, don't let my father hear you call me that!" he exclaimed.

Marin raised an eyebrow and shrugged. "Like it or not, will-he, nill-he, the crown is coming for Kordas Baron Valdemar since he will not pursue it himself. And that will make you a Prince. But again, what can I do for you?"

Restil explained the situation in as few words as possible, and doing his best to spare Rothas's feelings. But Rothas's attention had immediately been riveted by a variety of wooden musical instruments on racks on the walls: lutes, gitterns, small harps, fiddles—stringed instruments, mostly, although there were a couple of hand drums and some flutes and whistles, large and small. As if caught in (another!) spell, he drifted over to the nearest rack, looking but not touching. Respect for the beautifully crafted instruments practically oozed out of his pores. So did lust for them. He knew instinctively what they were for without even knowing the names of them.

When Restil stopped speaking, Rothas interjected a sentence of his own before Marin could reply.

"What . . . *is* this?" he breathed, hand hovering near a lute resting with its face against the wall, beautifully striped golden and pale gold belly shining in the light from the door.

Restil glanced at Marin, whose usually dour expression had just lit up with the biggest smile Restil had ever seen on his face. "That, my lad, is a lute. Go ahead, take her down off the wall." He turned to Restil and made a shooing motion. "And you can leave, Prince. Either find a place to plant your behind outside if you are bound and determined to listen, or come back in a mark or two." He rubbed his hands together. "Haven't had a pupil with the Gifts in—well, longer than I care to say. This is a great day!"

"You mean—" said Restil, pausing with the master just outside the entry.

"Yes, yes, of course I mean I'm taking him as a student, I'm not daft or senile!" He jerked his head at Rothas, who had taken the lute down and was cradling it instinctively in the "playing" position, tentatively plucking an open string and cocking his head to hear the faint tone. "Just look at him. The lute wants to play him. They were born for each other. This is something special. A life-defining awakening is about to happen, and I'd be a fool to just let it go by. It would be—disloyal to music for me not to guide him." Marin gazed across the room at Rothas and the lute, not even facing Restil as he spoke. "I don't have an audience at my lessons, so go find something productive to do."

"Yes, Master!" Restil replied hastily, and all but fled, even though he very much wanted to be there to listen in. But it had to be this way. It wasn't because of rank. It was that Marin had apparently taken on students like this before, and had his own wise ways of handling it that required privacy for the experience to work out best. Restil surmised that just being present would undermine the moment, at a time this delicate.

Well, "finding something productive to do" was never difficult these days, so he dropped by the Old Men's section of the wall, reported to Koto, and quickly found himself dragooned into helping set up an intricate bit of spellwork for repelling pests that would require several storage crystals. No one wanted to face *another* infestation of green beetles. When he pried himself away from that, he reckoned by the sun it was time to check on his charge.

He heard the faint notes of a lute as he neared the open door, and figured from the way that the notes sounded "sure" and practiced that Marin was demonstrating a tune to a pupil who had never seen a lute before. Granted, it was just a simple child's tune, but there wasn't any fumbling for the right notes, or hesitation. And nothing out of tune or out of place.

But to his amazement, it was not Marin who was playing. It was Rothas.

He felt his jaw sag. Rothas sat with his back to the door on a little bench, Marin sitting opposite him and smiling broadly. When Rothas finished the tune and looked up, Marin nodded.

"I've seen this once before, when I had a student with the Bardic Gifts," he said, matter-of-factly. "Understanding music means understanding systems. There are combinations of finger, string, pressure, and timing to call out each note, and by using the combinations inside a vast musical pool you can play and create songs. One of the misunderstood secrets of the Bardic Gift is that it thrives on perception of systems and details. You, young Rothas, you'll be able to pick up just about any instrument, see it demonstrated, and play a simple tune immediately, because you will intuit its system. Mastery will take about a year, which is a fraction of the time it would take an ordinary musician like me."

Every line of Rothas's back proclaimed that, for the moment at least, he had forgotten his lifebond, and more importantly, his depression. "How many instruments can I learn?" he asked, breathlessly.

"As many as you want." Marin shrugged. "Practically speaking, though, you're going to be limited to the ones I know how to make, because I am the only luthier we have. Which means if you are pining to master the shawm or the rebec, you are out of luck. I mostly make string instruments. Which I suppose is just as well, because you'll want instruments you can use to accompany your singing, and that means stringed instruments for the most part. We'll start with the lute, and that one is now yours."

Rothas gasped. *"Really?"*

Marin smiled broadly. "She's made from the heartwood of one of those giant Hawkbrother trees. An experiment really, but one that turned out unexpectedly well. The tone isn't like we are used to; it's brighter and louder, more overtones than undertones, like the child of a standard lute and a gittern. But I think it will grow on people. You'll be worthy of her fairly quickly, and meanwhile, even a flubbed note sounds well on her." Now he looked up at Restil. "Shoo," he said sternly. "We'll be busy until suppertime. You can come for him then."

Restil gave the master luthier a silent salute, and took himself back off to the mages. There was still work to be done on that anti-pest spell-web, but he already felt joy and a little bit of wonderment.

———————

The change in Rothas was remarkable. When Restil came to fetch him to supper, he was just lacing his new lute into a leather carrying case after carefully detuning her strings. He stood straighter, and although there was still a kind of hum of sadness to him that penetrated even through Koto's shield, he was no longer crushed beneath the weight of it.

He was so full of what he had learned that it bubbled out of him, and as they made their way across the vegetable gardens to the manor, Restil just let him gush. This was probably the best the young man had felt since the unknown magician cursed him, and he was a better companion for it.

He stood taller, too, as if some of the weight of his situation had fallen from his shoulders, and his expression was alive in a way it had not been until now. And he certainly attracted attention the moment he set foot in the Great Hall; all eyes turned toward him, and Restil could almost *hear* hearts breaking all around him. *Hopefully who he is and the fact that he's life-bonded has spread at the speed of gossip, and everyone knows.*

His father looked up to see what the cause of the sudden

silence was, and beckoned them over. Nothing loath, Restil led his still-babbling charge toward the head table.

Once Rothas realized where they were heading, he shut up abruptly, and followed Restil's lead. Since the seating in the Great Hall was all shared benches rather than individual seats or stools, they took places roughly across from the Baron and everyone on that bench scooted over a little.

As it happened, they sat right next to Koto, who scooped up a bit of spiced bean paste with a bit of flatbread, popped it in his mouth, and swallowed before speaking. "Good. I don't like to talk about people behind their backs. Kordas, I can work with this boy. I have my own personal shield on him now, which should keep him from affecting anyone else *except* the girl. There, I don't know. Lifebonds have a way of tying people together in ways that shields can do nothing about."

Kordas nodded, but still looked concerned. "I do have a question about this, since all I know are shields for magic. Do emotions merely hit the shield and dissipate? Or do they bounce around in there, like a mirror-magic shield does? The latter would not be good."

Koto snorted. "I know my business, Kordas Valdemar. Dissipate, of course. Otherwise he'd already be a stewed little pot of misery, weeping his eyes out right now, and getting worse by the moment."

The effects of his first, and by all measures, highly successful, music lesson had begun to wear off on the walk to the manor, and now some of that profound misery was creeping back into his expression, though Restil couldn't feel it . . . thank the gods.

"Marin Joiner has taken Rothas as a student as well," he reported. "And gave him an instrument, the lute he made from Tayledras home-tree heartwood."

His father smiled. "Sadly, that last means nothing to me, but I assume it's quite a good instrument. But now I'm very curious, Rothas Sunsinger. We've heard all *about* your music,

but we've never heard the music itself. Would you feel equal
to demonstrating your talent?"

Rothas looked taken a bit aback. "I . . . don't know how to
play this lute well enough to sing with it," he said awkwardly.

"That's all right. I can play." This was Beltran, who nodded
at his own gittern propped against the wall behind the head
table. "I can't sing, but I can play."

"But I don't know any of your music," Rothas objected,
though it was obvious that the invitation had awakened his
eagerness for an audience, something he probably had not had
since he'd met Lythe.

"I can follow you," Beltran assured him. Restil knew this
was absolutely true; Beltran had demonstrated that quite fre-
quently during the ten years they had all been here. It might
have seemed unreasonably frivolous to concentrate on something as trivial as *entertainment* while scrabbling to survive—
but Kordas (brilliantly, in his son's estimation) understood
that *entertainment* was even more necessary precisely *when*
you were scrabbling to survive. You needed it to remind you
why you were trying so hard in the first place.

Rothas got up from his seat—pausing to drink down a full
beaker of herb tea first—and Beltran got up as well. They put
their heads together while Beltran removed his gittern from its
case and tuned it, there was a little bit of humming and nodding, and then they both turned to face the hall.

Please don't let it be a love song, Restil prayed. Not only
would a love song just make Rothas sadder, it would also
likely redouble the number of people who were fancying him.

*There are going to be a lot of angry husbands and be-
trotheds in Rothas's life, I suspect.*

But Rothas, showing an amount of good sense that Restil
would not have given him credit for, broke out into the kind of
song that tavern-keepers loved—a good, long, funny story
song, bawdy without being vulgar, with a repeating chorus of
"You never shall have me treasure chest. A maiden I shall die."

As near as Restil could tell, it was about a hedge-wizard pursuing a shepherdess who was having none of his sauce.

What astonished him was that a song that must *surely* have been in Rothas's native language was now being sung in Valdemaran, and the rhymes, while not flawless, were certainly good enough for a tavern song.

Maybe he translated it while he was with the Hawkbrothers to distract himself.

His voice was everything Restil had expected and more. He had never heard a better singer, with a range that started with a solid tenor but actually moved down into bass notes. Clear, in perfect tune, and as mellow as honey. Loud enough to be heard all over the hall without straining. Within one verse, he had everyone clapping; in two, singing along with the chorus. And when he got to the end, he had everyone standing on their feet, cheering.

He was generous about the applause, too, not bowing until Beltran had taken his share of the approval. It took Kordas himself standing up to get everyone to quiet down.

"I remind you all, of a courtesy, that Rothas Sunsinger has not yet eaten. And that after that, he has a pressing engagement at sunset. So first, he will eat, and then, if there is time and he and Beltran are willing, he will sing *a couple* more songs. And his engagement takes precedence." Kordas sat back down, having established that Rothas was not going to be taken advantage of, and the other two went back to the table.

After that, Kordas waited for Rothas himself to choose to speak, or not. Restil wondered at that a little, but reasoned that his father was assuming that Silvermoon would not have held anything important back—

And possibly he's assuming that someone like Rothas, from a tiny village, hasn't really had what you'd call an interesting life aside from getting cursed and lifebonded. And he's probably right. Rothas certainly did seem to be a little awkward and shy once his performance was over. But he spoke politely and cordially when he was spoken to, though the glow that he had gotten when performing quickly faded. *At least all he looks is melancholy, rather than about to jump into the river at the least provocation.*

But he was certainly eager to perform again, because he rushed through his food (fortunately Beltran had already finished everything but the fruit they were having for dessert) and was able to sing three more songs before the sun touched the horizon. All three were a success, and indicative of his ability to correctly read his audience and respond with what they wanted. The first was a song about a hunter who encounters a talking deer and spares its life—Restil had the shrewd notion this song had its origin with an encounter with a young dyheli stag. The second was a spring planting song, with a typical chorus farmers could use to keep in rhythm while planting. The third was a comedic song about a traveling peddler who was outwitted by a clever housewife.

Not the sort of thing the highborn were used to hearing, but they seemed to enjoy the songs well enough. And the servants certainly enjoyed hearing something that *wasn't* about the highborn for a change.

At the end of the third song, Rothas held up his hand to stop the applause. "You really must save your accolades for Beltran, who just managed to play four pieces he'd never heard before. I *must* go, but make sure you show how much you appreciate him."

Well! Restil thought with approval, as Rothas galloped out of the Great Hall, lute in one hand, case in the other, heading, without a doubt, for the rooms he shared with Lythe, wanting to be there when she awakened, to prevent missing the tiniest moment of their brief time together. The applause followed him out the door, then continued for Beltran's sake.

He glanced at his father for direction, indicating with a tilt of his head the direction of Rothas's flight. His father shook his head slightly.

So give them their privacy, then go at full dark.

"Well?" Kordas said to the entire table when the applause had died down, and people went back to finishing their meals. "Initial impression? Positive, at least of the boy," said Uncle Hakkon. "Really, none of this would be an issue for us or the Tayledras to deal with if that stupid lifebond wasn't part of it."

"He's the best musician *I've* ever heard," said Sai. "If we can sort him out . . . and his Bardic Gifts are as strong as Silvermoon says . . . Kordas, you'll have a hell of a weapon in your hands. He'll be able to quiet a mob, or rouse them to murder."

"He's *going* to be strong enough to overcome even someone with shields and resistance, who knows what they're contending against," Koto said flatly. "Eventually. The potential is definitely there. So yes, a weapon, and a powerful one."

"I like him," Restil said simply. "I don't think that's his Gift at work either. I think he's genuinely an affable fellow. I don't know about the girl," he added. "I've barely seen anything of her."

"That's where I come in," said Delia, from the end of the table. "I'd judge her to be indulged to her detriment, but not *spoiled* as such. She'd learned her lesson long before she and the boy met. Now he's all she can think of, and she's deathly afraid she's going to lose him to one of us."

Koto snorted, but Isla shrugged. "It's a legitimate fear," she pointed out. "Look at how everyone here reacted to his performance! At the very least, because he is a Bard, she is *always* going to have to share him with his music and his audience, and she can't really compete with either."

"It's not a competition!" Koto protested.

"A girl isn't going to see it that way," Delia replied with authority.

"Then we need to find something *she* can do," put in Sai. "Besides look beautiful."

"I'm working on that," Delia replied. "She's a bit of an

enigma; Jelavan told me she really didn't open up to the Tayle-dras, either."

Kordas frowned. "I hope for her sake she doesn't just become Rothas's accessory. That won't be healthy for either of them."

"That's not in our power to decide," Isla reminded him. "*There is no one, true way* applies to individual relationships too."

"Maybe. Probably." Kordas smiled at his wife. "I guess I'm just prejudiced because you can do everything I can."

"And backwards, in skirts," she teased.

The whole table chuckled, but not loudly enough to draw the attention of the other diners.

Restil returned his attention to his neglected food, but what Sai had said, about Rothas being a potential weapon, stuck with him. *I need to become his friend, not just his mentor. He needs someone in his life who can tell him "no" in a way that he won't dismiss. Will Lythe do that? I don't know. But I do know it's too risky to depend on her being able to.*

"Good work out there, Beltran," Kordas said quietly, as he and the Herald walked through the vegetable gardens in the darkness, bringing with them Lythe's breakfast out of the remains of the supper.

"My pleasure, sir," Beltran said sincerely. "In my opinion, sir, we have a good handle on the boy, but we need to get a fuller picture of the girl. Also in my opinion, if there's trouble, that's the direction it will come from."

"Mm-hm," Kordas agreed. "A dark horse indeed, is that one. I'm glad Delia is taking charge of her. Delia's not one to be trifled with, and all that time spent with the Old Men, the Healers, and Alberdina has made her very shrewd."

"Shrewd enough to beat me at kingsmen," Beltran said ruefully.

"Shrewd enough to beat *me* at kingsmen," Kordas admitted with a laugh. "But more to the point, all that time spent with people who have seen every trick manipulative people play has taught Delia a lot about seeing manipulation in action and what to do about it."

"Hopefully there is nothing to see." Beltran sucked on his lower lip. "One thing, though . . . I think we need to put some sort of guard on Lythe while she sleeps. Rothas is going to be busy all day, and she'll be left alone, unable to wake, *in a bed*. Not all of us are angels . . . if you catch my meaning."

"Mm-hm. Good point. I wonder how she feels about dogs?" Kordas wondered aloud, thinking that a couple of mastiffs might solve that problem without tying up a human with work to do.

"What if she's a cat person?" Beltran retorted.

"We'll have to consult Sydney-You-Asshole," Kordas replied.

And he was only half joking.

Perhaps . . . less.

Kordas and Isla had just settled down together in the relative quiet of their chambers. *Not* in bed, although he rather wished they were—but it was still early enough that people might turn up with something Kordas needed to address. Too early for it to be possible for them to get away with *"Disturbing our rest is high treason! Begone, villain!"*—which was as much of a joke as "Tonight we eat pork!" but was still actually funny most of the time. But although the furniture was still extremely sparse, Kordas had had a bright notion when they'd moved from the Hawkbrother dwellings into the manor, and one of the first things he'd commissioned was a conversion from a leaking rowboat to a sort of settle. The boat had been sanded and waxed until it glowed, the seats taken out; then the whole boat had been brought into the room, permanently affixed to stands so it wouldn't move or tip over, and lined with a wool mattress, with a featherbed atop that mattress, and furnished with furs and some of the fanciest cushions, blankets, and coverlets they'd brought from home. Then a short set of steps had been attached to the side for climbing in. Set up in front of the fire, it made a grand spot for the two of them to cuddle up together of an evening. The idea proved to be very popular, so popular that eventually Kordas had had to call a halt to the commandeering of rowboats, lest they run out of boats they actually *needed* on the river. "Build your own," he'd decreed. "Remember, they don't actually have to be able to float!" He'd thought about decreeing that only leaking boats could be appropriated, but that opened the door to people purposefully sneaking down to the boathouses to put holes in the damned things.

The innovation, though, had led to people making all sorts of seating arrangements out of boat-like shapes, from chairs made of coracles to beds that hung from the ceiling and actually rocked. Apparently some people had enjoyed the rocking motion of the canal boats and missed it, but that was a bit too precarious for his liking. Hakkon was campaigning to have a bed of that sort. For now, Kordas was limiting him to a hammock swung over the safety of his bed. *If he goes a year without falling out, then he can have his boat-bed hung from the ceiling.*

It made a grand spot to share a book. For a birthday present a few years ago, Restil had given a try at woodworking, making a lampstand that was attached to the prow and curved over the top, so the glow from a lamp with a mage-light in it fell just perfectly on the page.

Kordas read faster than Isla did—a hazard of having to read so many official documents—so sharing a book with her was an exercise in patience, but Kordas was not about to complain. After all, time spent with a slow reader was a longer time in the person's company. Besides, she'd only admonish him not to rush, and point out that he was missing half the book. It was not a terribly inspiring book—actually, it was a treatise on mining—but any book was better than no book. This was one of the new copies that Delia and Alberdina had

had made, and given the discovery of copper *and* zinc in their iron mine, Kordas was rather keen to know more about mining and smelting now.

The windows were open, and gauze screens had been fastened into the frames to keep bugs out. Crickets and a few night-birds sang, frogs croaked down on the river and toads in the garden, and some night-blooming flower sent its perfume in on the breeze. The only thing that would have been better would have been a gentle rain. They didn't get a lot of these peaceful evenings, and Kordas was relishing the quiet, when someone tapped on the door.

Because of course they couldn't have a peaceful early-summer evening without someone interrupting it. That was what happened when you were a leader, after all.

Then again, that intruder could only be one of a handful of people that the guards outside all knew, because otherwise the guard would have interrogated the visitor and determined whether their business was urgent enough to disturb the Baron, then would have poked a head inside and asked if he wanted to see the person in question. All three of the boys were in their own rooms, puttering or reading, so it wasn't one of them.

But Delia had volunteered to walk the wall a bit with Lythe Shadowdancer, and she had probably had had enough time by now to have gotten something useful—or at least informative—out of the girl, so it was probably her. If so . . . good. He hoped whatever Delia had learned would throw a better light on the girl than he had now.

"Come!" he said, as Isla put a sprig of pressed rosemary in the book by way of a bookmark.

It was indeed Delia, and as she entered, closed the door behind her, and came into the lamplight, Kordas could tell she had news. "Join us in the stern," he invited, since he and Isla were in the prow, and nothing loath, she popped into the boat with them, folding her legs underneath her.

Kordas considered that the last ten years had made a defi-
nite improvement in her. She'd risen to every challenge, didn't
complain of their hardships any more than Isla did—and always with good reason and usually just to vent frustration.
And best of all, from his point of view, that infatuation she'd
had with him had withered and died a much-deserved death.
From being a conventionally pretty and a little bit aimless girl,
she'd turned into a handsome, strong woman with equally
strong opinions and plenty of ideas of her own—a great many
of them damned good ones. One of the best, in his opinion,
was that she'd begun over the past couple of years to develop
an interest in Beltran, Kordas's Herald, and the interest was
mutual. And much more appropriate than a pash for her own
brother-in-law.

Gone were the pretty gowns, stowed away in storage. Now
she wore the tunic and trews of hemp canvas everyone else
did, with a bit of horsehair finger-braiding she'd done herself
by way of trim. Valdemar Gold hair, of course, so it actually
looked like gold-thread trimming. She'd never been what he
would have called "soft," but she was definitely tougher now,
her cheekbones and chin more defined. Like Isla, she wore her
golden-brown hair in a practical braid wrapped around her head.

"Well!" she said, brown eyes sparkling with mischief. "I've
heard both sides of Lythe's story now, and I am rather glad to
report that Lythe Shadowdancer is not the wet mess we all
thought she was. Or at least, she's not the dreary little brat *I*
thought she was."

"That's a blessing," Isla said dryly. "Because the side of
the story we've heard so far doesn't paint a very flattering
picture."

"Well, let me tick things down for you." Delia wriggled a
little to settle herself in. "First of all, pre-curse, she wasn't
entirely running off at night to cavort with her friends. There
was some of that, yes, but her friends had plenty of jobs of
their own to do, and parents who'd yank them right out of bed

by the foot if they didn't rise with the rest of the family to get their work done, so while they were probably staying up later than they should have been, it wasn't ever past midnight. No, once everyone else had gone to bed, she stayed awake because she had begun to see spirits, and she didn't want to tell anyone about what she saw, not even her mother, after her mother dismissed what she was saying."

That made Kordas sit up and take notice. "Ghost spirits?" he asked.

"I talked about that with her. We don't think so. She says they don't look much like humans. We think they are some kind of elementals. Like *vrondi*. They might even be *vrondi*, since I have no idea what a *vrondi* looks like to someone who can see its native form. They didn't seem to be aware that she could see them, so she pretended she didn't so that she could watch them covertly. As I said, she tried to say something to her mother about this, but her mother just told her she was too old to be making up tales and having invisible friends. Although *why* her mother would have just shrugged that off when they're living in the *Pelagirs*, I have no idea."

Isla sighed. "Most probably because she didn't demonstrate this ability as a child—and now her mother assumed she was making things up so she could play all night."

Delia nodded. "Her friends didn't believe her either, although you'd think they'd all be prepared to believe just about anything."

"I suppose it was one of those cases of, 'No one has ever seen anything like you're talking about before now, so it can't be real.'" Isla pursed her lips. "Or . . . the universal tendency to see a lovely girl or woman and assume she has a head full of air."

"A little bit of both, perhaps. She was trying to figure out what she should do about this when she and her mother had that fight. That was partly what the fight was about, in fact. Her mother demanded that she 'stop seeing things,' as if it was all under her control. Oh, and something else that came out of that fight was that her mother wanted her to settle right down, right then, and 'catch' a husband prosperous enough to take care of all three of them, and this staying out all night was really putting a spoke in the wheels of *that* plan. There was a lot of 'I sacrificed everything to raise you, now it's your turn to take care of me.' Apparently people were starting to talk, and assuming she was meeting someone clandestinely when she was out and not with her friends."

"Hrm. I think that's probably the root of the fight," Isla replied, brows creased. "Danger to her reputation, because who knows what she was doing or who she was finagling about with—and, sad to say, her mother probably was counting on her to marry well from the time it was obvious that she was going to be beautiful." Kordas sighed at that. *Common problem.* Highborn or low, some people looked on their children as property to be disposed of as the parent chose—and in the case of a beautiful girl, counted on that girl to be the source of future prosperity, and became incensed when the girl didn't follow their wishes. Shouting and fights ensued . . . and often beatings and other punishments.

Delia nodded. "So that puts Lythe in a somewhat better light, and her mother . . . well, was not perfect, let's just say to be generous." Delia twisted a lock of hair that had come loose from the braid at the back of her head in one finger. "I don't think she's making any of that up, about seeing things. It doesn't seem like the sort of thing a person *would* make up. She didn't gain anything by it, and not even the boys who were courting her believed it. In fact, she said it put some of them off. As for her mother, well, she says that when she asked, 'But what about love?' her mother replied, 'Love is for rich people. And you can learn to love a rich man just as easily as a poor one.' Which sounds about right."

"That does put things in a very different light. Why didn't she tell all this to the Tayledras?" Kordas asked.

"Because they terrified her. And they were all—rightfully, given his Gifts—concentrating on Rothas, and trying to break his enchantment so at least he'd stop broadcasting misery. Rothas *does* believe her, by the way. Everything about the Tayledras terrified her—the bondbirds, the casual use of magic everywhere, the way they lived, the hertasi . . . I mean, I can completely understand that. When you live in a tiny village in the Pelagirs, almost everything having to do with magic is suspect, because most of it *is* bad." Delia shook her head. "And no one was particularly interested in trying to coax anything out of her, or keep her company, so once she and Rothas were in the Vale, she spent most of her waking hours in or near the sleeping space they'd been allotted, all alone, with Rothas next to her as insensible as a stone. The nocturnal Tayledras were all out with their owls, doing what the Hawkbrothers do, and the hertasi reacted to the fact that she was afraid of them by avoiding her so she wouldn't be afraid."

Kordas chuckled and replied, "Ho, they'll do that if you aren't ready for them. Incredibly quick, then utterly still."

"And wonderful. I miss them," Delia confided. "A lot. Anyway, as long as we can keep the shocks 'good' ones, Lythe can handle it, I think."

Isla softened visibly. "Now I feel rather bad for thinking what I did about her."

"Me too," Kordas admitted. "I didn't need to be that harsh, but—"

"But we all assumed that because she is beautiful, she is a spoiled child." Delia nodded. "Honestly, brother, we're so used to how beautiful highborn girls are spoiled, we just assume the same is true for every girl that's pretty. Plus all those songs about haughty village beauties who scorn poor shepherd boys."

Kordas hummed a bar of the popular drinking song "As You Wish," a tale about that very thing. He bit his tongue to keep from reciting all the tales of havoc that lovely girls in the

villages of the old Duchy of Valdemar had caused, and that he
or their local highborn authorities had been forced to remedy.
*In the real world, you never hear stories about the good, the
kind, the obedient, the respectful,* he reminded himself soberly. For most people, demeaning was easier than praising,
so scandals were appealing as excuses to show righteous indignation. *You only hear about the troublemakers.*

"At least she's confiding in you," he said. "Did she see any
of these spirits when she was with the Hawkbrothers?"

"No," Delia told him. "But if they are Elementals or some
sort of nature spirit, they might not have gone near the Vale.
They might have seen the Hawkbrothers at work, assumed
that they tamed and neutralized *everything* magical, and
avoided the place. She says they did seem to move and act
with intelligence and purpose, more intelligence than an animal, so that's not an impossible idea. I told her that I believed
her, that you would probably believe her, and that she should
keep a watch for this sort of thing while she walks the wall at
night. She's not afraid to walk the wall, by the way, and I got
the impression she was not sorry to have something to do
besides feel miserable and hide in her rooms. Oh! And she can
see in the dark. Probably as well as a cat, maybe as well as
an owl."

"An excellent reason to have her on the wall, then. I had a
feeling about her and that station. I'll just leave her to it unless
one of the Old Men wants to examine her. Or, wait—I'll see if
Wis wants to talk to her. He's not an expert on spirits, but he
is kind and gentle, and I think she's got enough stern authority figures in her life right now." That notion relieved Kordas.
The girl wasn't going to be a liability, the only people that were
going to see her during her waking hours were his guards,
and while she was quite likely to be the cause of a broken
heart or two among them, she was *not* going to be the live coal
she'd be among the highborn boys. *Good gods, that would be
a mess. There are some that would make a contest out of*

trying to seduce her, there would be a lot of angry parents that I "dared" to have a mere peasant girl that pretty anywhere near their precious heirs and spares, and . . . well, the possibilities just get worse from there. Ah, and about that—

"Does she like dogs?" he asked.

"Dogs, cats, birds, fish, frogs, pretty bugs, rabbits, deer—name an animal and she likes it. She says they talk to her, so she might also have Animal Mindspeech."

This just gets better and better, in the non-sarcastic sense. "Well, good. Then at false dawn when she comes down off the wall, I'm going to offer her Trusty and Alfonse-You-Asshole." Trusty was one of his pack of mastiffs, trained as protection dogs; he was just about five, which was approaching middle age for a mastiff, and it was time to give him some lighter duties. Watching over Lythe while she slept would be perfect. And Alfonse was one of Sydney's great-grandchildren, who liked to partner up with Trusty. Often for shenanigans. When Trusty was working to protect one of Kordas's herds, Alfonse went with him, and would venture into the wilder parts and get something bigger than he was to chase him—right into Trusty's jaws. This ended in a feast for both of them. Of course, this also meant that they were known to partner up to raid the kitchen—like his father and mother—hence the inheritance of the -You-Asshole "honorific."

"Oh, I can get that. That would be perfect," Delia agreed. "They're handfuls, but they're affectionate. Having tailed friends can help so much for anyone in distress. All right, then, I'm going to go take a half-turn around the wall with her, tell her about her new pets, and see if she has anything else to confide in me."

She rolled over the edge of the boat onto the floor, and went on her way. The door closed behind her with a soft *thunk*.

Kordas and Isla looked at each other, ignoring the book. "Now I feel badly," Isla confessed. "Quite badly, actually. I assumed the worst without ever laying eyes on the girl."

"And she doesn't know that. She doesn't need to know." Kordas kissed her ear. "And I've lost the thread of the book."

"Well, then." Isla smiled. "It's late enough that we aren't going to get any more visitors unless it's an emergency. Besides, you'll need to be up quite early in order to take her those animals, and I can think of some other pleasant things we can do before sleep. . . ."

This was the first time that Kordas had actually laid eyes on the girl since receiving the pair, and he was rather more than happy he'd thought of placing the cat and dog to guard her when he saw her.

In a word, now she was *dangerously* pretty. Especially at the moment, when between the fact that Rothas had just awakened and she had had her precious hour or so with her lifebonded, and that Kordas had brought her Trusty and Alfonse, she was actually *happy*.

So was Rothas, which made them just about the most handsome couple Kordas had ever seen in his life. Rothas was a sun-king, and she was a moon-queen, with her dark hair, pale skin, and huge, dark purple eyes. He'd never seen anyone with eyes that color before.

She had good animal manners, too; she waited until Kordas had brought the animals into their little living space and told her to call Trusty. There was no point in calling Alfonse; he was a cat and he'd come and go as he pleased. Then she got right down on the floor, eye level to the mastiff, and made a chirping sound.

Trusty was a big brindle, and he probably was double her weight. Those jaws could crush a limb. Kordas wouldn't have been surprised if she had been afraid of him, but she wasn't. He looked right at her, and so did Alfonse. Then, as Trusty started a slow tail-wag and Alfonse raised his tail like a flag-pole, both of them took the couple of steps needed to bring them to her, sat down within a hand of her, and all three of them engaged in some sort of silent communication that only rein-forced his suspicion that she had Animal Mindspeech. Half-way through this moment, Alfonse began to purr, and Trusty's tail thumped the stone floor vigorously. Then Trusty broke eye contact with the girl and looked at his master, Kordas.

"Yes, Trusty," Kordas said, as if the dog could understand him. "You belong to Lythe now. Guard."

Well, the dog certainly understood the command "guard," and his tail thumped even harder as his jaws gaped in a doggy grin. Alfonse leveled a withering look at Kordas that all but said in words, "And what am I, the red-headed stepchild?"

"You guard too, Al," he told the cat. The cat seemed happy with that.

Then Lythe and Rothas sat down on the cold stone, regard-less of their own comfort, and gave the two animals the atten-tion they certainly deserved. Kordas let them be for a while, then asked, "Delia said something about you talking to animals?"

Rothas bristled a little, as if he suspected Kordas of making fun of his beloved. But Lythe nodded, keeping her attention on the mastiff and not looking at Kordas. "She said you would believe me. Mother didn't. So, do you believe me?"

"How do they talk to you?" he temporized. He might not have the Gift himself, but he'd known people who did, and he had a fair idea of how it was supposed to work.

"Not in words," she said, confirming what he knew. "More like feelings mixed with pictures. Mother said I was making it up, even when I showed her how I could call wild birds to me out of the trees. I thought about calling wild rabbits," she added, "but Mother would have knocked them over the head and added them to the stewpot."

"Well, you have what is called Animal Mindspeech. It's a

kind of Mind-magic. It's perfectly natural," he added hastily. "Just rare. I'm glad; that will make it easy for Trusty to understand that he needs to guard you while you sleep." Trusty gave the eyebrow to Kordas when he heard his name. She nodded, and Rothas looked relieved enough to faint. "I don't think anyone is going to take a chance with a dog with jaws like that around," Rothas commented—a statement vague enough that it stated the obvious without stating it obviously, displaying the Bardic talent for wordcraft.

"Alfonse said he will, too," she told Kordas shyly. "But—he is a cat."

Kordas had to laugh at that. "Well, yes, he is. It's not smart to *expect* anything out of a cat. Just be grateful if he does things you like." He was very pleased to see that she didn't have some airy, unrealistic notion of how animals behaved, which was another good indication that she did, indeed, have Animal Mindspeech. "They already know where to go to be fed, back up at the manor, so don't worry about that. They are both good about relieving themselves far from indoors. Plus, Trusty and Al are very good at hunting rabbits together, and Al is murder incarnate when it comes to vermin, so they can supplement their own feeding when you're awake and helping patrol the wall." He smiled. "You'll have all the benefits of having a pet and none of the work!"

"We had cats," she replied, with a faint smile. "Because Mother said that cats are the only pets that can take care of themselves."

Alfonse's purr deepened with approval.

Feeling increasingly that his presence was stealing precious moments from the lifebound couple, Kordas saw himself out, relieved that yet another potential problem with these two had been headed off. As his son had hinted, the temptation to take advantage of a beautiful girl who was and would remain insensible while you had your way with her, and thus could never accuse you, had the potential to be too great for some

people to resist. And he couldn't spare a guard to watch her—
never mind that would be broadcasting that he didn't trust the
people within the wall.

Ruling is such a dance.

At least now the two were both productive. That would be
good for both of them. *And one less headache for me.*

One less headache was a good thing for Kordas, because he
had one waiting for him when he took his place at the Council
after a hasty breakfast.

The Council Chamber was a far cry from the one he'd had
back at the old manor in the Duchy. The old Chamber had beautiful colored-glass windows that could be opened on clement
days and closed on cold, made in abstract patterns of golds and
warm browns that did a lot to brighten up the room on a gray
day. They had woven wire screens to keep out insects on days
when the windows were open to catch a breeze. Its "stone"
walls—since it had been raised by magic, the walls were no
more stone than these walls grown by the Mother were—had
long ago been paneled in wood, then covered in tapestries to
deaden sound and create warmth in the winter. It had fireplaces at each end, and had been furnished with a curved and
polished horseshoe-shaped wooden table and supremely comfortable high-backed chairs, two sideboards for holding whatever was needed during the course of a meeting, including
drinks and food if it ran long, and additional chairs for guests
and those giving testimony or advice to the Council. The floor
and ceiling had also been covered in wood, with wooden
beams from which hung mage-lights. Over one fireplace hung
a banner with the Valdemar crest, over the other a map of the
Duchy, renewed every year to allow for changes, beautifully
made and colored on an enormous piece of framed, thin board.

But here, in Haven, the only thing this room had in common

with that one were the fireplaces and the map and banner. Over one fireplace hung the Duchy of Valdemar banner, brought with them from the Empire. Over the other was a map of *this* Barony, unframed and uncolored, but inked like the old one onto an enormous, extremely thin board made up of many end-cut flooring flats nailed and glued together, then finished with a smooth, hard clay surface. It showed scores of spots where outdated symbols and lines had been sanded down and corrections had been made. The windows held fitted frames with gauze in them to let in light and keep out insects, with lockable shutters to guard from storms and winter cold, like the rest of the windows in the manor. The way this manor had been grown, none of its edges were *perfectly* straight or level, and its "trim" invariably had organic shapes of varying depth in its surface. The floor was "stone," the ceiling was "stone," the walls were "stone," with no softening by tapestries or rugs. Such things had been too bulky to bring many with them, and of exceedingly low priority to make right now. *Maybe we should have wall hangings like the Vale had. Thick, woven panels of leaves, vines, and cloth with gravel inside. Without any kind of spellwork, they made* all *kinds of noise turn calm.* The harsh acoustics were sometimes distracting. The Council table consisted of three trestle tables with not-so-comfortable stools, although those were slowly being replaced with actual chairs with backs, with priority going to the oldest Council members first. There were similar trestle tables to serve as sideboards.

It was not a "comfortable" chamber, but to Kordas's mind that was all to the good. It meant that people were not inclined to linger and obfuscate. Not when their behinds were slowly going numb on hard, basic wooden stools that might or might not have uneven legs. At least the floor was even. It wasn't a *shabby* place of governance, but it was austere, which mirrored how he liked work done in the place. Functional first.

And Kordas was thinking of just that when he strode into

the Council Chamber, hoping that this was going to be a nice, short meeting once he reported on the progress with their two newest problems. *I need a day on horseback. One in which nothing happens. I don't think I ever quite appreciated boredom as much as I do now.*

"So, Kordas," began his Lord Chancellor, but stopped short when Kordas raised a palm.

"Rothas Sunsinger has had shields placed on him by the Old Men, and is no longer a hazard, although I caution anyone with Empathy to stay clear," Kordas interrupted, and was backed up by a nod from Sai, who was the mages' representative today. "He has Bardic Gifts and is currently undergoing training, and I am sure will be happy to perform when he is asked. Lythe Shadowdancer has been assigned to walk the wall in place of a senior officer to see to the guards' needs and ensure they are alert. She has Animal Mindspeech and apparently sees as well in the darkness as an owl or a cat, making her quite useful there. Since she does not have Bardic Gifts, and inconveniences nobody, I judge that this is sufficient to earn her keep. Sunsinger's Gifts are also sufficient to earn him a place." He did not mention the mastiff. Not that he didn't trust members of his Council, but he saw no reason to stir up a debate about whether or not the girl needed to be protected while insensible. Too often, Council members raised debates not because they cared about the outcome, but rather, because they wanted to be noticed.

The Lord Chancellor blinked. "Ah, that's all very good, Kordas, but that's not what I was about to say. I was about to say that . . . well, I, we, have more or less all agreed. I know you have been resistant to this, but it's gotten to the point where it *has* to be done."

Kordas stared at him blankly, and stayed standing. *What is he going on about?* There was no small number of things Kordas was resistant to. Aside from the senior mages, he had the clearest view of the big-picture matters of his people's future, and while many of the Council's proposals were reasonable, many more were short-sighted. He frowned and scratched the back of his head. "Go on, then."

"A King, Kordas. We need a King. Not a Baron. Not a Duke. We are out in the middle of gods-forsaken nowhere, a land of tiny villages far apart, who know nothing about Barons, Counts, Dukes, and all the rest. But they know what a King is." Despite receiving a scowl from Kordas, he continued. "To be plain, we feel *this* is the time. A King gives us legitimacy and respect. The natives here place outsiders in few categories—warlord, bandit, mad, murderous, monster, or suspicious. We've stayed something like "huge horde of suspicious people with a passive warlord," to them, and that isn't enough. With the Pelagirs so near, the locals are jumpy all the time, expecting the worst of anything new, and our people aren't happy about it. We already have that breakaway group on our northern border, the east is twitchy, and our claim on the south isn't getting any stronger. Even with the people we brought."

Kordas folded his arms where he stood, but stayed silent, letting his Court discipline override his more unpleasant thoughts. The Lord Chancellor continued what seemed to be a practiced argument.

"Not the most palatable example, but the Empire itself grew out of a mere Barony. The first of the Imperial line simply declared himself a King so he could outrank all the other landholders competing around him, quell their feuds and squabbles, and close-knit their forces. You can do the same, and you should, and we in this chamber are all, to a man and woman, in favor of it."

"I don't—" Kordas began with some heat, then stopped flat. "Wait, wait. Are you electing me King? That isn't how Kings work." Kordas then paused for a moment, recalling no small number of lessons about rich, powerful, and crafty people who supported and sustained royalty, and how they tended to get their way. "No, that *is* how Kings work, but I don't mean it that way. We're still getting established here. Manpower and resources aren't *that* plentiful. If I was made King, that would entail registering official bloodlines and searching out any relatives, drawing up charters and naming offices, and a hundred other things, like couriers, celebrations, designing livery, and heralds to go far and wide. Nobody has time for that. It's a lot of fuss for no good reason."

"It's the fuss the people want," Jonaton added, cradling the venerable Sydney-You-Asshole as he stood. "Kordas, there are children past ten years old here who have *never had* a King. Scads of the traditions we brought with us center upon service and duty to a monarch. It means something vital to us, and the people are in need of reassurance that they're going to last. Maybe you or your descendants make something different from a monarchy, but for now at least, all of us from plowman to priest know the structure of a monarchy, and will feel reassured by it. Your people need that confidence in their lives. A King, a valiant, brave, and smart King, is someone to believe in, and nobody is better for that than their savior."

"That just makes me feel like a religious figure. I don't like it." Of course Kordas had thought about this over the years. What he did now was more or less the same as what he'd do from a throne. But. *It feels too big, too soon. There is so much more work to be done. The outermost palisades aren't even done, because we used up half the forest stock making buildings to live in. Everybody's fed, but not sumptuously, and while music, plays, and stories keep morale up, we don't even have theaters yet. We barely have enough perimeter scouts and guard towers for Haven. And—*

"It also has to be said," Sai began, in a tone that foretold a solemn lesson to come as he stood. "We have all thought it, but I will say it out loud." All attention went to the elder mage, and he counted off fingers as he spoke. "Someone saves a Duchy's-worth of lives, makes treaties with The-Strange-Giant-Bird-People, fights monsters, establishes a thriving colony, and then he just calls himself a *Baron*? He could have been King, and he uses *Baron*? To some, that *might* sound like somebody who *maybe* doesn't think very much of himself," Sai finished. "What happens if some monster, deity, or warlord barges in and demands to see our King? What can we say? We have a Baron, will that do?"

Snorts ands giggles rippled out from around the chamber, and one of the guards involuntarily blurted out, "I told you not to!" with indignity and an intense, wary glance at Kordas. Fortunately for the guard's career, Kordas got the joke, and it broke a lot of the room's tension. The laughter startled Sydney-You-Asshole away from Jonaton's arms, and the cat cruised slowly across the tables toward Kordas.

Kordas himself laughed near to breathless, stammering, "And some—" before laughing hard again, wiping his face with his hands. Clearly, he was trying to wrestle this back to Very Serious Business, but with the absurdity of the moment, he wasn't winning. As he steadied himself, he reached down to give his old friend a pet, and Sydney rubbed against him and flopped onto his feet.

"And some Kings become Emperors, don't forget," Kordas retorted, ineffectively. He was not succeeding at looking dour with his face reddened from laughing, and Sai wouldn't have been fazed by it anyway. Being a powerful mage was good, and being old meant you didn't worry as much, so being a powerful old mage suited Sai just fine.

"*We know* you don't want to be like the Emperor," Sai put forth. "Any Emperor. You've made that abundantly clear. On my name, I declare that it won't happen. Your friends won't let you turn into that. *Baron* has run its course, and it would be cheap to call yourself an *Emperor* of one city, anyway, so go with King."

The Lord Chancellor took up with, "Kordas, we've studied this. Our people have been struggling and adapting for so long that they *need* to feel at home now. Established. We agree that they want to be a Kingdom, and they want a King, and that King has to be you because you got them here safely, and kept them safe for the last ten years. You as their King says that Valdemar lives."

Kordas glared at him. *That damned old traitor. How dare he use a line that good on me!*

But Sai, Jonaton, and the Lord Chancellor were by no means alone in this. Within moments, every single member of his Council was saying exactly the same thing. Loudly. Insistently. Repeatedly. And the more he objected, the more insistent they became. Sydney sat near Kordas on the tabletop. He laid his ears back, perturbed, and flicked his tail quickly while he surveyed the Council. The cat judged all.

Kordas weighed every argument he could think of as he sat down in the center seat, and began listing them. That it really would make no difference (and the Lord Martial cited chapter and verse concerning their past interactions to prove that it would—and so did the Seneschal). That titles were meaningless out here (and Ceri helpfully supplied all the local names for "King"). That his people didn't care what he was called (and Beltran cited all the times when people had called him "Highness" or "Majesty" instead of Baron in the past several months). It was clear as springwater that they were not taking "no" for an answer, and that he had no choice and might just as well relax and go along with this.

"Isla will hate it!" he cried, his last line of defense.

"Mother told us to run you over if we had to," said Restil, who had been sitting off to the side, in a shadow and unnoticed, all this time. "I won't repeat exactly what she said, because in a man's mouth it's—well, it's not something a good or polite man would say. But the simple fact is, she totally agrees, and says she'll take care of planning the coronation so you won't have to worry about taking time off from your other tasks."

Venerable Sydney walked directly in front of Kordas, atop all of the table's papers, scrolls, and folios, and sat down directly facing him. His eyes were cloudy and his muzzle grayed, and his motives were as unknowable as ever. The cat reached up a paw—the Death to a Thousand Mice—and touched Kordas's beard. Slowly and deliberately.

Kordas returned the cat's gaze with a swell of emotion, wordlessly finding solace with the death-defying old fellow. *Gray in my beard, too, old friend. We've earned every one.*

Kordas looked away to find the room was nearly silent in anticipation. At that, he put his head on the table, his hands over his head, and sighed before raising it back up to declare, "I give up," with resignation. "You want me to be a King, I'll be a King. Do with me as you will."

Ignoring every other soul, the ancient cat flopped atop Kordas's left hand and nudged at the right hand for pettings. Which Kordas obliged. Sydney-You-Asshole purred, audible only to the future King amidst the room's tumult.

"Oh," said Sai, barely audible through the noise, but with a smile in his voice. "Don't worry. We intend to."

7

As Kordas expected, the news of the coming coronation had spread across Haven quickly, and morale had shot up. What followed were weeks of reviews and allocations of resources that could be spared for the event, but that was not all. Wisely, Kordas was advised by Hakkon-the-elder that this event presented high value for espionage, sabotage, and crime. There was no bigger preoccupation for Valdemarans, and that meant it'd be easier to slip trickery by while they were distracted. His few dedicated domestic spies went to work ferreting out potential trouble and neutralizing it. Even within the Palace, infiltrators might risk exposure from poisoning attempts, trapsetting, or similar power moves ordered by their distant superiors. *The ones we know about, that is. But there are always summonings and conscripted devils to deal with, self-appointed foes, and the monsters of the Pelagirs. Maybe not all native to* this *world, either. I'm no future-teller, but I've heard rumors that some Valdemarans are, and I'll trust in that and expert fieldwork.*

Soon enough, they would all know what all the local entities had to say about it.

Stevin, one of his long-established valets, helped him into clothing that had been in storage for almost ten years. It was also the first time in ten years that he'd *needed* to be helped into clothing; like everyone else, he'd adopted fairly simple garb as soon as it could be made, while they were all still living under Tayledras auspices—and hertasi care. Tayledras clothing was supremely comfortable and durable, even clothing as simple as workwear, and they had shared their textile secrets with the settlers gladly once they were offered the Doll-derived canvas treatment in exchange. Kordas had forgotten that the embroidered, brocaded, beaded, embellished, and elaborately contrived stuff was a lot less comfortable than the clothing he'd been happily wearing for the last ten years, and a lot heavier. He concentrated on that to avoid thinking about anything else—mostly avoiding the mental refrain that he really did not *want* the title of "King," which in his mind had far more negative connotations than advantages. It made his stomach knot up. *This could be far worse,* Kordas reminded himself.

At least I don't have to worry about it being out of date and unfashionable—despite the Tayledras, we haven't really embraced fashion. Probably to Stevin's chagrin. For a decade, no one highborn had been wearing anything other than the sturdiest of their old clothing or the simpler, harder-wearing garb that he and his family had adopted. Or at least they did so once they realized how poorly suited their existing clothing was to living rather rough and working alongside their underlings. Even the highest-born had realized that no one had the *time* that it took to keep fine garments in repair and clean—not when every available set of hands was involved in keeping them all fed, housed, and protected. There was probably a whole barge's worth of formal and court outfits pulled out of long-term storage in hertasi tunnels in less than a month.

This could have been much worse. I could have brought my High Court clothing with me. Ugh. He didn't miss those. The "in the highest style" garments that the Dolls had had made for him when he'd been at the Capital seemed to have been deliberately designed to be stifling. The Dolls had done their best to make it feel less like he was being strapped into a series of corsets, but it had not *ever* been clothing that was intended to put the wearer at ease; the Emperor had apparently found it amusing to contort and squeeze those in the Palace. This old finery, which Kordas had worn at home for official functions, hadn't been as bad as that—but it wasn't as good as the loose-fitting trews, shirts, and leather or knitted tunics, which he looked forward to getting into again more with each minute that passed. The more worn in and loose, the better.

Thank the gods that this coronation was timed for the cool of the morning, or he and Isla would have been melting inside their finery.

Did I ever actually like these high collars? he asked himself, as he inserted a finger between his neck and the collar in a vain attempt to loosen it. The delicate handmade lace edging the collar and cuffs of his shirt brushed his fingers like the wings of annoying gnats.

Stevin, a stern look on his saturnine face, slapped his hand away. "Your Highness will please to not destroy his neckline," the valet scolded, with a toss of his black hair.

At least Stevin is showing an appropriate amount of . . . sass. I don't know what I'd do if he went all obsequious on me.

He sighed, and acquiesced. At least he had the room to sigh in his clothing. He hadn't exactly been out of shape when last he'd worn this exquisitely laundered linen shirt with its frilled collar, the closely fitted weskit, and the jacket with brocade lapels that was so perfectly tailored that it *needed* Stevin's help to get him into it, but he was definitely leaner and tougher than he'd been ten years ago. The combination of limited food and hard work had honed him down rather than beefing him up. And the breeches instead of trews—he'd forgotten how tight they were, and it was a good thing they were made of flexible and stretchy lambskin, because otherwise he would not have been able to move. All of this nonsense was in colors of blue and white, with touches of silver, just like the Valdemar crest. The coat and trews were blue, the weskit was a darker blue, the shirt a white that seemed unnatural these days.

"I look like an idiot," he muttered, not at all used to the image in the heavily polished steel mirror. Mostly because the only reason he ever looked in the mirror was to make sure he wasn't about to embarrass himself.

"You look magnificent," countered Stevin.

"I can't move," he complained.

"Odd, you used to say this was your most comfortable outfit," Stevin replied serenely, lifting the silver-gilt and blue-tooled leather baldric with its Valdemar badge over his head, and settling it into place with the badge properly centered at breastbone, before hanging the dress sword he had not carried in *years* on it. No spitter, thank the gods. *I don't want to see another spitter, ever.* Well, that wasn't quite true, but a spitter was the last thing he wanted to see on a day in which he was being made into something he—mostly—didn't want to be. *I might be tempted to use it on myself!* Well, that wasn't true, but . . . at this moment, he very much wished that there was someone *else* being made King.

I know what my annoyance is all about, too. I got accustomed to riding against danger, spell-slinging and being heroic, the hands-on leader. Gods help me, I liked it. But this—doing this means I can't be that anymore, can I? I feel like Court let me out on a long leash and now it is dragging me back.

Stevin fussed with his hair until it lay the way the valet wanted it to. There would be a crown, of course. *Can't have a coronation without a crown.* But the one thing he had put his foot down about was that he was not, absolutely *was not*, going to wear the Wolf Crown. "It's a magical artifact," he had reminded them all. "From the head of the worst person we've ever known. We have *no* idea of everything it can do. It would be irresponsible to parade it around in public, or stick it on my head. What if the spirits of all of the previous Emperors are somehow tied to it and take me over? No, that thing stays in storage until we have the time and the safe place for the Old Men to study it properly! Remember, the Hawkbrothers wouldn't touch that damned thing with a barge pole!"

Not that he actually thought that being possessed by ancient spirits would happen, but . . . when he'd worn the damned thing before, it had made him feel things he really did not want to feel ever again. The crown made him want to vomit every time he looked at it, and it even gave some of the Old Men twinges of unease when they so much as looked at it. So he'd immediately gotten them to lock it up in an unused portion of the hertasi tunnels, where it would hopefully be forgotten. And for this coronation, he'd had a new pair of far less ostentatious circlets made, one for him, one for Isla, out of white-gold Imperial eagles melted down. The jeweler he had entrusted this task to had practically wet himself with the excitement that *he* was going to be making the first royal crowns of the Kingdom of Valdemar.

They were handsome things, those crowns. Simple white-gold circles about as wide as a thumb, with engraved horses chasing each other around them. Relatively light—they were still *gold*, after all, which by its very nature was heavy—but they weren't going to give the wearer a headache if they had to keep one on all day.

The boys, who would not actually have a coronation themselves, all had similar, simpler circlets to go with their new titles of "Prince." They all seemed thankfully indifferent to the fact that they had crowns and titles, and more thrilled by the fact they were now Princes like the protagonists of books and stories. And their beloved father—a King, like the biggest of fabled heroes. He supposed the boys' thoughts aligned with his own attitude about the position—most of being royalty would be just the same as they'd already lived, only with better hats.

Most of all, the boys were excited because there was going to be a feast using recipes from more prosperous days in the Old Land—especially baked and fried sweets.

The boys have their priorities straight.

Kordas wasn't genuinely out of sorts about being dressed, especially now. One of the functions of his valet was to inspect the noble's clothing *before* it went on, and he'd prefer not to be jabbed by any poisoned needles today, thank you very much. "Give over, Stevin, you aren't going to make me any closer to perfection," he said, finally, trying not to sound cross. "I am what I am, and a title isn't going to change that."

"It is not *your* job to determine how good you should look today," Stevin replied sternly, and with a hint of acidity. "It is *my* job. I don't tell you how to run a Council meeting. Don't tell me how to dress you for a coronation."

I believe I have just been put in my place!

Stevin nailed it home by finishing, "I know from past praise that you have *complete* faith in my expertise."

Just in time to save him from further fussing, Isla glided into the room in full sail, in a matching court gown she had probably worn three times in her life. And she took his breath away. She was completely stunning, as slim as a girl, and twice as beautiful as she had been when he married her. Her dazzling white linen chemise sported a high standing collar made of stiffened lace that rose halfway up the back of her head. The blue brocade gown had a belt that matched his baldric, complete with a Valdemar crest badge as a buckle in the front. The chemise was puffed out along slits in the narrow brocade sleeves and ended in cuffs ornamented with more lace on the chemise and on the cuffed brocade over it, and her hair had been arranged into an elaborate coil of braids on the top of her head. "He looks magnificent, Stevin, and any further primping you do to him will not be visible to anyone but me and Father Jorj. Time to go."

She took Stevin's arm before he could object, and led him to the door, but Stevin paused long enough to say, "You look the part." Kordas threw him a light salute, and both of them shared the crook of a smile.

"I'll try not to embarrass you," Kordas replied as they departed.

That left Kordas alone with his emotions, staring at the mirror to sum himself up. A momentous occasion such as this would be irresistible for those who would do him harm by spell or sword, and he would not let himself be less than supremely prepared. Shields upon shields, and for more than defense—engaging his shields was a calming ritual for him. His breathing steadied to a practiced rhythm and he grounded himself. He visualized much of it, mentally viewing his work from the inside and also from a viewpoint outside his physical body. His disciplined mental defenses locked into place, layering above, below, and around what he pictured as "him." Kordas's memory was too good for the last fifteen years to be a blur, but hundreds of individual events flashed by to form a shining chain around his mind. Bright like silver, draped but not heavy, the silver chain shone and glinted as it multiplied its length and breadth. It surrounded him. It defined him. It was borne up by the smiles, the saves, and each struggle he had triumphed over. All of the advice he'd taken, the tests of character, and the love he'd been shown were alloyed into its links. He armored himself with that chain, fusing it into the shiniest of reflective silver, and sealed his defenses with it. Then, outside of that, he called the Hawkbrothers' "three radials" technique into being. With the sphere of his core self as their centerpoint, three circles of defense, each at right angles to each other, drew themselves as expanding fields of energy. They formed not only a strong initial defense, but also a sensor: when attacked, they would not only resist, but also give a reading on the potency of the attack and its direction of origin. He murmured a prayer of thanks, too, while turning to leave the chamber—one of deep appreciation for those who had believed in him, and stayed true in the hardest of times.

The walk down the hallway was silent, save for the click and shuffle of his bootheels. He felt as if he strode through his own history, and without pause he pushed the doors open to step out between the waiting guards and join the distinguished company he would walk the rest of the way with.

The coronation was to be held outdoors, in front of the—well, it wasn't the manor anymore, it was now officially the Palace. As they exited the main front doors, the crowd that packed every inch of space between the raised steps and the vast expanse of grass (normally used to graze sheep) between the Palace and the wall erupted into a deafening cheer that brought blood to his face in a blush. It was an unexpectedly colorful crowd—he hadn't been used to seeing massed people as anything but a brown, tan, gray, and cream patchwork for the longest time. Polished metal glinted, and colors that had been safely kept in storage for the last ten years flaunted their brightness in the sun, like a massive—and *noisy*—ornamental flower garden. Among them was Pebble, who slowly waved a massive arm, while the elemental's other arm and both shoulders bore a half-dozen revelers.

For once, Kordas was speechless. There was a flutter in his stomach and his heart pounded; he strode out in confidence, but was struck by the feelings that cheer brought on. He had never been more embarrassed or more gratified. And at the same time, the weight of his new responsibility settled on his shoulders like a too-heavy cloak.

Kordas felt the invisible defenses set up to defend the event with each step he took, a sensation that made him feel a bit like a rag squeezed through rollers. A glimpse with mage-sight showed arches and domes of force grown upon each other as far as he could see, arrayed in geometric patterns as high as a sparrow's flight—a sure sign that the Hawkbrothers' mages had been at work.

"No procession," he had decreed. And so, indeed, there was no procession for him and Isla. They simply exited the front door, and stopped beneath the portico. But as they came into view, the massed trumpeters of the ten heralds to the left (led by Beltran) began a brand-new fanfare and processional song anyway—written by Rothas Sunsinger, with help from his mentor. They weren't all *his* heralds; he'd borrowed them from some of his highborn. But today they all wore the blue and white Valdemar-crest tabards that had also been taken from storage. And to the right, a massed choir made up of anyone with a decent voice and a good memory sang the words.

That choir had been a stroke of genius on Isla's part. It was a microcosm of all of Valdemar, with people from every possible background and profession, and every age from adolescent to Old Man. He felt his eyes burn with tears of pride as he looked at them.

Voices together, a shared song. This is real. It's all come to this, and it is real.

And up a cleared path leading from the gate to the Palace came the various religious dignitaries led by Father Jorj, and including Silvermoon, who represented the Hawkbrothers' Star-Eyed Goddess Kal'enel. And the cat, Sydney-You-Asshole, who marched ahead of them as if he was their leader. Improbably old—especially considering his bold life of mischief— white hairs sprinkled his coat like stars in the night sky, but age had not diminished his sense of self-worth in the slightest. Which was, of course, that he, Sydney, was worth ten of any human god-botherers, and he, being *cat*, would go first.

All of them were clad more or less magnificently, except Father Jorj. Silvermoon was particularly resplendent in flowing green robes cut to resemble leaves and made of silk taken, it was said, from very cooperative spiders. His long silver hair had been turned into an artwork of braids, beads, crystals, and feathers from his bondbird, and he sparkled in the sunlight, putting some of the more soberly dressed clerics in the shade.

Rather than start any kind of a quarrel among the various representatives of the various religions of his people about who was to do the actual crowning, Kordas had, from the start, put his foot down again and dictated *that* part of the coronation, at least. "My family has always had the patronage of Lady Epona, the Goddess of Horses," he had said the *moment* the entire Council and all of the representatives had met for the initial discussion. "Isla and I will be crowned by Father Jorj."

They'd all been taken aback at first, but after a moment of reflection, everyone agreed immediately, and not just because Kordas had made his feelings clear. Of all of the religious figures in the—now *Kingdom* of Valdemar—Father Jorj was probably the most humble and the least inclined to put himself forward or engage in disputes, and was universally regarded as a peacemaker. And no one could deny the long patronage that the Temple of Epona had had from the Dukes of Valdemar. Virtually every possible religious function in the Duchy household had been conducted by the religious leaders of Epona.

Now . . . this was not just a ploy to keep dissension to a minimum. Kordas was deliberately setting an example by choosing Father Jorj to preside over the event—beginning his reign as he meant to go on, displaying that he was serving his people rather than being served by them. So the relatively young Jorj strode along in front of the rest, just behind Sydney, blond head high, and his outfit could not have been more different from that of his fellows if he had tried. It was all of light tan-colored leather except for a white linen shirt: sleeved, front-laced tunic, riding trousers, boots. The metalwork was all brass and resembled horse furniture. The leather of the tunic had been tooled with a border of horses. There was nothing in his hands to represent power or authority, and nothing on his belt but a ceremonial riding crop. Behind him came a boy and a girl in versions of Jorj's ceremonial clothes, bearing the two crowns on miniature horse blankets made of the mane and tail hair from Valdemar Golds.

The coronation song—which, to be fair, mostly consisted of variations on "May the Gods save and protect the King and Queen, and the Land, Beasts, and Peoples of Valdemar"—ended as the procession of priestly types reached the steps. It was Jorj alone who ascended the steps, followed by the children.

The crowd fell silent. A light breeze sprang up, bringing with it the scent of trampled grass. Kordas had to control himself to keep his hands from shaking; this felt an awful lot like terror to him, and he reached for Isla's hand only to find her reaching for his, and squeezing it comfortingly. *And I am just waiting for something to go horribly wrong. This is the moment in wonder tales where something goes horribly wrong.*

Jorj turned to face the crowd. Kordas had no idea what he was going to say, only that he knew Jorj was a good speaker, and a good speechmaker, and he trusted the man completely.

And Jorj did not disappoint.

"Ten years ago, we all faced a dire threat, and yet very few of us were aware of that fact," his voice boomed out in the silence. "The Emperor had cast his greedy eyes on our peaceful home, and had decided that the time had come to pillage it for his endless wars. For decades, the Dukes of Valdemar had protected us from the rapaciousness of the Emperor by keeping us prosperous, but not *too* prosperous, by making us dull and uninteresting to their Court, and by keeping the politics of the Empire as far from us as they could. But that was to be no more."

Jorj summed up the story with admirable brevity, and although Kordas had to suppress several winces when Jorj trumpeted out what was commonly known, rather than the actual truth, the fact was only he and Beltran knew the truth and that was how he wanted to keep it. So Jorj said nothing about how he had murdered the Emperor—only that he'd freed the child-Elemental they now called "Pebble," and the Emperor had perished, along with the Capital, when Pebble's mother came to Pebble's rescue.

Then Jorj gave an even briefer summary of the temporary home at Crescent Lake, why they'd had to leave, and how Kordas had kept them safe until the Hawkbrothers appeared to offer them their new home.

Only then did he wax somewhat rhapsodic, thanking the Tayledras for their protection and hospitality, enough that he actually brought a faint blush to Silvermoon's cheeks. Kordas had to repress a grin, and felt any incipient terror bleed off to see someone else as the focus of all attention. *Good! Let Silvermoon suffer a little too!* And so far, nothing had gone horribly wrong.

"Together with our allies, we have prevailed against misfortunes that came our way. We drove off the green beetles. We survived the arrowclicks. We managed to eradicate the nimworms. The magic-Changed creatures of the Pelagirs discovered they had become the hunted rather than the hunters, and the cry of 'Tonight we eat pork!' rang through the land." He paused for the chuckles his tension-breaker called forth. "This was not an easy land of milk and honey, but it was, and is, a good land, and after its judgment, this land eventually welcomed us."

He paused to let everyone mull that over.

"But as we expand, we will inevitably meet more strangers, and there will inevitably be conflicts, though our intent be peaceful. These strangers will need to see that though we are many, we are one, united beneath an inspiring leader with proven vision, cleverness, and strength."

Kordas could not help but notice that Jorj had not said one word about the thousand or so who had broken away to form their own little colonies—and, if the Hawkbrothers were correct, a fair number had joined forces with a mage rumored to be quite powerful. *Probably a good idea. Let's not bring dissent into the picture at this moment.*

Jorj cast a glance behind him, and there was a twinkle in his eye that made Kordas suddenly wary of what the man was about to say. "So we need a King. And *you*, all of the people of Valdemar, backed by the Court, have agreed. That King shall be Kordas. It is said in the Book of Epona that the best leader is the man who resists being crowned, and I am sure you all have noticed that he has resisted with all his might and wit."

A roar of laughter greeted this statement, and it was Kordas's turn to blush and drop his chin a little.

Jorj waited until the laughter had died down before continuing. "And I have been given the blessed duty of crowning him on this day. Kordas, please come before me. And do not bow nor kneel, for you yourself have decreed that there shall be neither of these things in Valdemar, except as a *courtesy*, and not to show subservience."

Kordas took a single step forward and bowed his head slightly in respect. Jorj took the crown from the girl's pillow, held it up so that it gleamed in the sunlight, and placed it firmly on Kordas's head.

"And so I crown you King Valdemar, the first of his name. May you reign over us and guide us with wisdom, courage, and compassion!"

As Kordas stepped back, Rothas led the choir in a burst of "Gods save and bless the King!" Kordas had deliberately chosen his family name as his coronation name. It seemed fitting, since the plot to bring all of the Duchy's people out of the greedy hands of the Emperor had begun and been undertaken by his father, and his father's father. *If things had gone differently, it might have been an adult Restil who stands here now, and not me.*

When the choir was done, Jorj's voice boomed out again, enhanced and projected by magic, of course. And that telecaster that had provided so much entertainment at Crescent Lake had been unpacked and set up, so that all the people on the other side of the wall and down in Haven could see and hear what was going on—probably better than those massed in front of him.

"A King needs a co-ruler, a companion, an advisor, and if dire need calls for it, someone to take up the burden of rule should he fall. Isla, please come before me now."

Isla stepped forward, and bowed her head in turn. Jorj reached for the boy's crown, held it aloft like the first, and placed it on her head. "And so I crown you Queen Terilee, the first of her name, and co-ruler of this land. May you reign over us with patience, empathy, and wisdom!"

Isla had decided to honor their Hawkbrother allies by taking as her coronation name the one that they had given her, the same name as the river that flowed through this proto-city they were calling Haven. Kordas approved; it was a good choice, and he most certainly did *not* want her to, even implicitly, be tagged as secondary to him, which she might have been if she'd been crowned as Queen Valdemar. *Begin as we mean to go on.* That meant in equality. Queen in her own right.

She stepped back, Jorj retreated into the pack of prelates, and Beltran stepped forward. "People of the Kingdom of Valdemar!" he shouted, his face full of joy. "Behold your leaders! King Valdemar and Queen Terilee!"

The cheers almost drowned out Rothas's choir. Kordas couldn't help it—two silent tears coursed down his face as he clutched Isla's hand and waved his free hand to the crowd. Tears of relief, as well as the emotion that welled up in him.

They were crowned. They were King and Queen. There had been no explosions, no appearance of assassins or Imperials set to ruin, no swarms, murders, or disintegrations, all of which were historically frowned upon in public events.

Apparently, nothing had gone wrong.

By noon, enough congratulations and handshaking had taken place that Kordas's hands felt bruised. Out on the lawn a kind of "moveable feast" was taking place; anyone who volunteered to cook had been given wood for a fire and something to cook on it, and what they did with those things was up to them. Kordas and Isla wanted this to be a celebration of Valdemar itself, not a celebration of them. There was a series of trestle tables with flavored and embellished breads to go with what was being cooked, meats supplied by Kordas's farms and hunting parties that had gone out every day for the last week—yes, there was no shortage of pork—and vegetables from those same farms. Down in the town, exactly the same thing was going on, but with the breads supplied by the bakers there, not the Palace kitchens, and meats and vegetables bought from the local farmers and hunters by Kordas himself. And there was free wine. That was the contribution of the mages and even some of the various religious dignitaries that happened to have some magic. Water into wine was not a terribly difficult transformation, and although the nonexistent fountains were not flowing with it, there were plenty of vessels to scrub out and hold it. Low alcohol, of course. It would be a very, very bad idea for most of the population to be drunk and insensible! Because, after all . . . in tales, there was always some sort of emergency in the middle of a celebration. Your belly would burst before you could drink enough of this stuff for it to intoxicate you. That was a precaution suggested by Sai.

The ones who were not completely free to do as they liked today were the guards on their regular shifts, and those who had elected to cook and distribute food. But everyone had been able to view the coronation itself, and Restil and Isla had done their best to ensure that even those who were working would get some time off to enjoy the rest of the celebrations.

Meanwhile, the highborn had all crowded into the Great Hall to sit down to their own feast—dishes more elaborate than the simple grilled stuff down in Haven and out on the lawn, but nothing to compare to the feasts of the days back home. Still! Several special dishes appeared, and there were baked and sweetened treats in abundance, some of them the gift of the Hawkbrothers, most of them produced to Sai's recipes. Kordas's appetite was small, but watching his lads stuff themselves with the unaccustomed goodies at least brought a smile to his face.

Ball games spontaneously sprang up, interrupted when the Hawkbrothers played the grand joke of their bondbirds intercepting and stealing every ball in midair. There was entertainment too, although for the most part, babble and gossip muted it, and no more than half of the eaters paid any attention to it.

But not when Rothas sang.

If Kordas had not known that Rothas Sunsinger had never even seen a lute until a fortnight ago, he never would have believed it. The way he played sounded to Kordas's ears like the work of a master. And the music pouring from his throat, golden and full, somehow managed to ease his heart, his doubts, and his tension, all at once.

His Gift. He's using his Gift. The soothing, uplifting feeling, the happiness, those weren't coming from Rothas. They were coming from within Kordas himself, evoked by the Gift, which seemed to have no difficulty working through the shields. Rothas was the center of rapt attention, the focus of every eye. And the boy knew how to perform, in the sense of playing the audience, too. Somewhere he'd gotten his hands on, or been given, a good pair of buckskin trews, a white linen shirt embellished with embroidery, and a pair of fine boots, all of which were nothing like the simple garb he had arrived in. His golden hair had been trimmed and styled—Kordas thought he detected Stevin's hand there—and his posture was erect and at ease, his expression cordial and welcoming. Without a doubt he was the finest performer Kordas had ever heard, and that included in the Emperor's Court. Then again, the Emperor didn't use Gifted Bards for entertainment purposes. The ones he had been able to coerce or reward into his service were reserved for his personal pleasure or as what the Old Men had called Rothas—as weapons. The ones he hadn't were either executed or imprisoned, if they could not escape elsewhere. No one had been allowed to practice any sort of magic without the Emperor's permission and knowledge, and that included Bardic Mind-magic. The Bardic gift always came with ethical questions.

There wasn't so much as a whisper as long as Rothas performed; in fact, most people put down their food and listened with complete attention. And it wasn't that the songs were all that good—except for two that Kordas was pretty sure were the lad's own compositions. He sang what you'd expect of a rural musician at a happy occasion: a couple of simple drinking songs, story songs with happy endings, joke songs that had the audience roaring with laughter despite the fact that they weren't exactly sophisticated, and his two original pieces, one about the pleasures of a simple man's life, and one, his only love song, that could not have been about anyone other than Lythe.

This did not prevent people from staring at him in adoration and longing. And probably everyone either wished it was about *them*, or wished they had a love like that. Even Kordas, who had recognized the Gift at work and was somewhat armored against it, was moved. He reached for Isla's hand, only to find once again that she was reaching for his.

Fortunately, before anyone had a chance to act on whatever impulses that song evoked, Rothas went straight into a comic song, followed by that staple of the traveling musician, a "farewell" song. Essentially, "We've had a lot of fun, and now the show is done, thank you and good night. I've had a lovely time, glad you enjoyed my rhyme, and all these songs of mine. So now I'll drink some wine!"

And the Gift was put into use there, too; Kordas would not have been able to ask Rothas for another ballad even if he'd wanted to. *Clever lad.* If he *hadn't* done that, he ran the risk of annoying or even angering people when he refused to perform anymore.

My highborn are learning to accept the word "no"—but a celebration like this one does remind them of the old days, when no one lower-born than they are was allowed to use that word around them.

Rothas was the final performer of the evening, and now the servants all bustled in, cleared what was left of the food, left the wine, and bustled out.

But the evening wasn't *quite* done yet.

The Hawkbrothers hadn't yet added their contribution.

Beltran stepped out in front of the high table and quelled the noise with a short burst from his trumpet. "If you will all proceed to the Coronation Field," he pronounced, in his most stentorious voice, "our friends and allies, the Tayledras of k'Vesla, have a surprise for all!"

The "surprise," as everyone involved in the coronation knew, was to be a display of illuminations in the sky above the Palace, lights and music that would be heard and seen clearly from all parts of Haven and the Palace. Kordas set the tone by standing up, offering his hand to Isla, and making his way out to the somewhat trampled grass, where servants had brought out stools, rugs, and cushions from the living quarters all over the Palace. The sun was just setting, and Rothas was, without a doubt, speeding to his quarters to share his precious candlemark or so with Lythe before he fell insensible.

And probably tell her what a triumph he was. Well, he should. I just hope she doesn't start to feel like she's standing in his shadow.

Hawkbrother illusions were not limited to the darkness,

and he knew that they had a full program planned, so he and Isla settled into their chairs and prepared to be amazed.

All the colorful little messenger birds had been relocated to the new Vale, but thousands of their illusory counterparts filled the sky in swirling patterns that reflected the last of the sunlight, accompanied by a chorus of birdsong. The oohs and ahs of appreciation hopefully gratified the mages, who were arrayed up on the wall in order to have the best perspective on what they were doing. As dusk fell, the birds transformed to silver moths, and the birdsong to the sound of tinkling wind chimes that somehow played meandering melodies. The darker it got, the more the moths glowed, and they began to merge into larger and larger moths. Finally there was just a single, enormous moth, hovering silently over the Palace, its light obscuring that of the moon. Where it went, the eyes followed.

And then the real show started.

Fountains and cascades of colored light rose in the air and fell from the wall. Bursts of colored lights appeared in the sky and lingered. A gigantic dyheli King Stag whirled, danced, and pranced across the sky. An enormous pair of firebirds made a courting flight, skimming directly over the royal party. A herd of silver horses danced an intricate dressage performance high in the air. Wonder after wonder etched in all the colors of the world flamed and faded, until at last, the show ended with curtains of color swirling around the sky to the sound of Tayledras harpsong, and a single silver horse galloping in and out of the sheets of color so that its silver turned pink, blue, purple, green, yellow.

The horse grew to enormous size, filling the sky, then faded along with the curtains of light. A streak of red to the east went from north to south, followed by another to the west. Another, closer this time by a mile, and then another even nearer, until finally, the red glowing ball shattered across the Hawkbrothers' largest shields, illuminating their entire structure to the visible eye for a moment in red embers. The ball careened in a spiraling fall to the east, appearing to drop into the woods across the river, where a slow explosion of red light then bloomed. And then the darkness fell, the night air filled with the sounds of chattering, and the servants came out with mage-lanterns to light everyone to bed.

Kordas and Isla remained where they were, savoring the quiet after what had been a long and strenuous day. Out past the wall, he could hear the celebration still going on, but here, finally, there was darkness and peace.

"I trust you enjoyed our contribution," said Silvermoon, from behind him.

Kordas had more or less expected this, knowing Silvermoon, so he didn't jump. "More than I can say. Was the end piece modeled on anything?"

"Actually yes. A pleasant phenomenon associated with not-so-pleasant warped nodes," said the Hawkbrother, settling cross-legged down on the trampled grass, regardless of his finery. "I'm told there are also lights in the sky like that in the far north in winter. I couldn't say; I haven't seen it myself. Well, Kordas, you and Terilee are King and Queen now. Was it so bad?"

"I wish anyone but me was under this crown," he said honestly. "But . . . no. It was not so bad. In fact . . . it was rather flattering. So now we've solved one set of problems, but an entirely new set will spring up in the morning, all because Valdemar now has a King and Queen to place the burden on."

Silvermoon laughed and shook his head. "You! You are not 'oh my glass is half full.' You are not 'oh, my glass is half empty.' You are 'Doom! There is a hole in the bottom of my glass and everything is draining away!'"

Isla added with a grin, "And I am 'Why was the glass that big to begin with? It's wasteful! Melt this down to make two smaller glasses!'"

Isla started laughing, and, although he flushed with chagrin, so did Kordas. "You both know me too well."

"Then take my advice and wait for the problems to come to you, for once." Silvermoon slapped his knee. "Meanwhile, let us enjoy a brief moment of peace, all the sweeter for knowing that it will be brief."

"Listen to the man," Isla chided.

"Yes, dears," he said, with just a touch of mockery, and sipped his wine.

Because, after all, they were right.

8

Kordas's first day as King began with a mystery.

Sai, who never paid any attention to anyone else's privacy unless it suited him, just barged into Kordas's suite while Kordas was still getting dressed. Without Stevin this time—Stevin had more important things to do this morning, such as gather up all the household finery that had been used yesterday, make sure it was in good order and clean, and put it back into storage in the hertasi tunnels where it would be safe from moths, vermin, and temperature changes. It would be a very, very long time until the King of Valdemar's Kingdom could produce those embroidered tabards, silks, and brocades, and for the foreseeable future any ornamentation on new garments was going to be stuff that had been cut off garments too worn or ruined to wear, or had been created and added by the wearer. The only gold was in the form of coinage, and no one here had the skill to make gold thread. He could count on the fingers of two hands the number of people who could embroider to Imperial Court standards, and they were all busy doing work that was more needed and less time-consuming. Even the highborn ladies were sewing and mending common garments for their families, because their maidservants were probably helping with the building, decorating, or furnishing of their new manors. So . . . best take great care with the beautiful things they had already.

Under most circumstances, this job would have been handled by the housekeeper, not Stevin, but the housekeeper was tied up making sure all the common linens had been gathered up and sent to the laundry, and that nothing had "walked off" during the celebration. So Stevin had volunteered, much to her gratitude.

And this was just for the relatively small household that Kordas had—the highborn who lived here were expected to tend to their own household goods themselves.

In fact, it would be a very long time before most people had the kind of household they had enjoyed in the Duchy. For one thing, many servants had peaceably defected to start their own farms, which would not have been possible for them in the Duchy. What land was for sale in the Duchy was at a price a servant could not afford—as opposed to being free for the labor of turning it into a farm. So a good many of his highborn had come to the shocking conclusion a year or so into their escape that they were going to have to do many things that a servant had once done for them. Few of his highborn had been as "hands on" with the work of their estate as he was.

First there had been anger, and the demand that he "do something" about it. Then had come attempts to bribe the servants back—some of which had worked, since household servants trained in household tasks were somewhat ill equipped to farm. Finally had come resignation—and calluses and sore feet and the ongoing lament of "If only we had hertasi!"

Indeed. If only!

He considered it a good lesson for them; it made them understand just what effort their servants made—and it wasn't as if they didn't still have quite a few hands left to serve, and far more leisure time than any of those servants got.

As for his own household, well, back in the Empire his personal household had been . . . adequate to his needs, but far smaller than most of his rank. For a household the size of a "real" King within the Empire—or the Emperor himself? The number of servants would be staggering. There were fifty servants now tending to Kordas and his family and the Palace, and that included vegetable and herb gardeners, the stablehands and livestock tenders, and the kitchen staff who served *everyone* living in the Palace. It was the same number he'd had as a Duke, and he probably should be employing more, but the simple fact was that there were not enough people willing to *be* servants now, and he was counting on the personal servants of the highborn living here to take up the slack by doing everything that was needed to keep their quarters in good condition, as well as tending to the needs of their masters. *I certainly hope that as they move out into their own manors, we won't end up shorthanded.*

It would be a very, very long time before he could boast a household the size of even an Imperial Prince, much less a King. There was no way there would be that many people willing to be servants in his lifetime. Maybe Restil's. Not before.

Nominally the household was Isla's purview, but . . . well, he did worry about everything. And the fact that Sai had just barged in on him while he was dressing triggered his easily triggered alarm.

"So what went wrong?" he demanded. "Something must have gone wrong. Are half the mages down from overwork? Did someone among the religious Foresee a disaster? Did all the leftovers spoil?"

Sai rolled his eyes. "Nothing went *wrong*," he said, with a touch of exasperation. "You could look at this as something going very, very right. But—well, last night, the illuminations? The dancing silver horses? And the red thing? *None of us did that.*"

For a moment Kordas was sure he had entirely misheard the Old Man, because he had certainly *seen* those silver horses, and so had everyone else, because the buzz of conversation had been full of them. "What do you mean—" he began.

"Exactly what I said! *None of us did that.* Not us, not the Hawkbrothers, not the priests and what-all. Not even Father Jorj, who in any event hasn't got a magical bone in his body, but he swears he did nothing to evoke his goddess. None of us." Sai waited expectantly for Kordas to put two and two together.

"So . . . either it was some mage or mages down in Haven that we don't know about—" he began.

Sai snorted. "*Un*likely."

"Or it was a mage or mages outside of Valdemar—" he continued.

"Equally unlikely, or so say the Hawkbrothers."

"Or . . . the hand of the divine, on its own, without evocation." Goosebumps prickled his arms, and a chill ran up his spine.

"So say the Tayledras," Sai nodded, his white braid bobbing. "If not, well, we need to go hunting for someone with mage Gifts who's been hiding among us."

"It's probably Epona," Kordas replied after a few moments. "Not that She has shown her hand *at all* that I know of for generations, but it seems the most likely."

"It does seem like the sort of thing She would do, except that the Tayledras think it's Kal'enel. The Star-Eyed. They think She is *probably* showing Her approval of you taking over the old Vale, what you've done with it so far, and what you plan to do.

The rest of us—" He shrugged eloquently. "We don't have any opinions. Only questions. Which, to be honest, would mostly be answered with, 'Well, gods can do what they like.'"

"Well, at least Epona isn't going to smite us. We're a long way from her home. That could have seriously annoyed her, I suppose." Granted, Epona wasn't known for her temper or impatience, but gods could do, or be, what they liked.

"Something to be said for that," Sai agreed. "And the red thing? We think it was meant to show that the Kingdom is defended, but who did it is a mystery, too. Now, we've all had a bit of a palaver, and Silvermoon just came out and *said* to say that if anyone asks, *he* did it. We don't think anyone will, but that's our story and we're sticking to it."

Kordas could certainly see the logic there. *Yes,* the Hawkbrothers were allies, and *yes*, they were almost universally considered to be benefactors, but there were always dissenters, and there was no point in giving them more to work with. "Silvermoon did fantastic work with those sky horses, especially considering the Hawkbrothers had never seen a horse until we arrived," he deadpanned.

"Yes," Sai agreed. "Yes, he did. Well, put your boots on and get going. Just because you were crowned yesterday, that doesn't give you leave to have a holiday! Isla's been up since long before breakfast!"

"Isla can do everything I can, backwards and in skirts," he reminded Sai. "You should have made her Queen alone, and retired me to a pasture."

"That can still be arranged," Sai retorted, with a deliberately sinister laugh, and left.

The first part of the Council meeting this morning was, as he had more or less expected, devoted to discussing the coronation. *Mostly* people rehashing the parts they had liked the best. Kordas really couldn't blame them; it was the first time in years that any of them had enjoyed being dressed finely and fed the way they had been accustomed to back in the Duchy, and there was a lot of wistful talk about how nostalgic it had made them feel, how homesick they were, and how his Councilors wished that could happen more often.

Not that they'll go back, any of them. By now some new strongman is Emperor, and he's likely to be as bad or worse than the old one. Or, more likely, the Empire has collapsed into localized chaos. One thing's for certain—no one will be in the old Imperial Palace unless they can swim in lava.

But of course, they all knew that a celebration like that couldn't happen very often, and more importantly, they all knew *why* it couldn't, because they had all been intimately involved with the preparations. They knew, one and all, how much scrimping and improvising and work had gone into making sure that there would be enough food for a real celebration everyone remembered *without* robbing from tomorrow's breakfasts, lunches, and dinners. How much even the highborn had sacrificed, with many of them actually doing servants' work as they had in the first two years, sacrificing their own leisure on coronation preparations.

"Well, I'm not sorry we put all that work in," said the Lord Chancellor, who himself had spent the day before helping to police the grounds for horse pats so no one in the field in front of the Palace would have an unpleasant surprise. "It was worth it, every bit." And he didn't add, *I just wish . . .,* probably because everyone, especially Kordas, *just wished* that some things could be the way they had been back in the place they had all once called home. "I must say, Kordas, that light display would have been almost enough all by itself. I did wonder, though, why the horses were silver instead of your Valdemar Golds."

Kordas had been expecting a question like that. "I suspect because they were modeled after the crest, rather than the Golds, and they were meant to represent where my family came from, rather than some mythical winged beast," he said, and added with regret, "After all, the Golds as a breed are not going to be around much longer. Better to look ahead than behind."

"And speaking of that," the Lord Martial broke in, taking advantage of the cue, "you do remember that I sent off a couple of clever youngsters to see what they could find out about the renegades and their ally? They got back yesterday morning and reported to me before the coronation itself." "Clever youngsters" was code-speak for junior spies.

Kordas stifled his immediate reaction—to ask if they'd been caught, or had to flee because they'd stood out, or anything of that nature. The Lord Martial was perfectly calm; there was nothing in his voice or demeanor that suggested anything had gone wrong with his operation.

Sai's voice rang in his mind. *You are not "the glass is half-empty." You are not "the glass is half-full." You are "The glass has a hole in the bottom and everything is draining away!"*

Well, someone *has to be an alarmist!* he thought with irritation.

"Did they learn much?" he asked instead. "At least, did they learn anything we didn't already know?"

The Lord Martial nodded. He was a heavyset, usually somber man, who could have been a member of Kordas's own family, given his black hair and dark complexion. There were thick silver streaks in his hair and beard that gave him an aura of age and dignity, and those he certainly had in plenty. He was in charge of the Guard—one of the first people Kordas had delegated a major task to, once he had the opportunity.

Lord Ventis Endimon was his name, though by this time, everyone referred to him by his title, and his wealth had come from the excellent weapons his family had produced for as long as the Valdemars had produced horses. He was no slouch at using them, either, and his hobby of replaying old and new battles with counters in his leisure time had certainly fitted him for his position.

"I ordered them to be careful; they used to be gamekeepers on my estate, so it wasn't likely anyone would recognize them, but two new faces would certainly stand out if they weren't extremely canny," Lord Endimon replied, taking a sip of leftover wine. "But it turned out that they didn't stand out at all. The mage's stronghold has about the same population as we do, and it covers about the same expanse of territory. So they stole some local clothing and slipped into the enclave where our defectors live, making out as if they were common laborers from the mage's people—which, of course, meant the defectors thought they didn't speak *our* tongue, and ignored them as they made road repairs or toted objects around. The defectors are very pleased with themselves. The mage is treating them well. They're living as well as they did back home—well, the highborn and formerly wealthy ones are. For their servants, it's pretty much the same as it was back in the Duchy, and there was quite a lot of quiet debate about whether it would have been better to stay with us, and at least have the chance at a farm of their own even though they'd be sweating themselves and their families to get it, or do what they'd done and follow their masters and end up in the same position they were before the exodus."

"How much discontent is there?" Kordas asked.

"None, from the privileged. About fifty percent of the working class wish they'd stayed. The mage didn't bother giving anyone the local tongue except the people he wants to talk to, so that leaves everyone else living inside a kind of 'foreigners enclave,' and they're stared at or ignored when they venture out of it. Mostly they're kept around, or so my informants think, as sources of information about Valdemar. They were given holdings equivalent to their original lands. But they're not encouraged to live on those lands. The mage keeps them in his main city. Well, I say 'he,' but we are still assuming the mage is male. We don't actually know for sure."

"The better to control them." Kordas nodded.

"Exactly. The biggest pieces of information they brought back is that the mage is building heavy fortifications in the far south of his country, and he's not at all pleased about us being here, even though we're not exactly sitting on his border."

"In the strategy game," Kordas said, thinking aloud, "building fortifications tended to mean that you didn't expect to attack the other player, you expected them to attack you."

"Now, Highness," the Lord Martial rebuked, *much* more at ease with using the title than Kordas was with hearing it, "you can't believe he was trained on the same game as you!"

"No, but . . ."

"It seems reasonable, but reason and fear don't have much to do with each other," Endimon pointed out. "But . . . yes, that would have been my reading of the situation too. And now that I've sent them in and they are familiar with the main city and those border enhancements, we come to the next portion of the plan. I've told them to report to the mages once they're fully rested so the mages can use the pebbles they brought back and the knowledge in their heads to see if they can set up some scrying."

"And then what?" asked Lady Amberdin.

"We keep an eye on them. No more, no less," Endimon replied. "That's all. He's got to be powerful, this mage. Styles himself 'the Archmagus Renariel,' and although my people didn't see anything of his work, he has to be powerful if he's built himself a city and a kingdom as big as ours."

"Well . . . he has the advantage that territory that far north is probably better cleansed than ours is," temporized the Seneschal.

"Maybe, maybe not. It's not worth a debate," said Endimon. "Best we keep an eye on him if we can, as close as possible. I'll be consulting with the Old Men about what can be done when this meeting is over. If I have my druthers," he added thoughtfully, "they'll be able to get the local tongue, and someone can plant it in my spies' heads and I can send them back. I don't know if that's possible, but I intend to ask."

The usual minutiae of the day was discussed and disposed of, the usual reports summed up and the originals passed to the Chronicler, and the meeting was finished in good time for Kordas and the rest to be among the first to select their noon meal from yesterday's leftovers. What wouldn't keep longer than a day had already been sent down into the city to be distributed—well, fairly randomly, first come, first served. At the moment there were no "poor" for the food to go to, but everyone knew that when the carts came down from the Palace, it was time to grab a basket and come get a share. Granted, *some* carts went straight to various temples to be distributed from there to the sick, injured, and elderly, but only because those three classes would not be able to move quickly enough to get their portions before it was all gone.

Kordas reflected that in the eyes of some, these would be halcyon days indeed. Imagine having no poor! Even in the Duchy, there had been poor. *I'll enjoy this while it lasts.*

Because people would always be greedy, the strong would always take from the weak, and there was only so much even a King could do about that. Only a fool would think otherwise. *All I can do is my best. And that goes for Restil; at least we've brought him up well.* But when the rot set in, as it inevitably would, would it penetrate as far as the now—royal family?

"Did you bite into something sour, or are you worrying again, Father?" Hakkon asked, a little anxiously, from his left.

"Worrying again. Worrying always, Isla would say," he responded. Hakkon was an adept pupil when he chose, and his uncle had deemed him both suitably educated and suitably chastised to be released back to his normal studies and duties. But he was spending time every day with his new puppy and the Houndmaster, as much time as Restil and Delia had spent with their first Valdemar Golds, so Kordas was pleased with the results of the corrective discipline.

"I know how to make you smile!" Hakkon declared. "Come see my puppy when we're done!"

For a moment Kordas was inclined to make an excuse, but then he thought better of it. He *did* have some time. Hakkon deserved some of his undivided attention—gods knew Restil got enough of it. And no one can be sad for long in the presence of a puppy, especially not a lurcher, who was the most comical thing on four legs when young. "Let's finish quickly, then," he agreed, and Hakkon's face lit up.

The dogs' kennels were as good as the stables. Solidly built by the Mother of her peculiar "stone," with fireplaces at either end, kept as spotlessly clean as it was possible to do with several bitches with full litters. The kennels served as the home to several breeds, each with its own particular purpose.

At the large end were the mastiffs, huge creatures mainly for the protection of the herds from wild beasts, although their mere presence was a significant deterrent to humans as well. The working dogs, except for Trusty and some of the dogs that the guards on the walls used, were all out at farms. Only the breeding bitches were kept here. At the small end were the rat terriers, who vied with the Palace cats to keep the place free of vermin. With poultry on the premises, Kordas had placed a Palace-wide ban on ferrets, no matter how many people asked to have them as pets. The Palace bred and kept their own lines of rat terriers, but puppies were available to anyone who needed one. In between the largest and smallest breeds were a half-dozen other breeds: boarhounds, lurchers, retrievers, beagles, greyhounds, and bloodhounds, all of which were used in hunting. The ones here were all the packs strictly belonging to Kordas and his family; the highborn and moneyed either kept their packs at their manors (if the manor was livable) or at their farms.

Lurchers—the breed that Hakkon's pup was—looked rather like hairy greyhounds; not quite as fast, but heavier, and less fragile, good for general hunting. Like greyhounds, although they loved to run, when they weren't running, they loved to sleep and be petted.

Then there were the herding dogs, but none of them were kept at the Palace. The shepherds of Valdemar were very proud of their dogs, and kept the breeding of their charges in their own hands.

The puppies that Hakkon led his father to were being weaned. Their relieved mother—who by now was very tired of being assaulted for her milk at every opportunity—was resting in a pen next to them. *She* could easily jump into and out of that pen if she chose, and if the pups were truly in distress, she would be with them in a heartbeat, but they couldn't see or get to her. They were all milling about and playing, or whining at the side of the pen, because they could smell their mother. All but one. Not the runt, nor the biggest, but somewhere in the middle, he was clearly looking for someone when they came into view, and as soon as he spotted Hakkon, he ran to the front of the pen—or rather, blundered, because he was not very graceful at this stage. Hakkon got down in the straw and made much of him, as Kordas entered the pen, determined to test this pup to see what he was made of.

And the first thing that the puppy did was pass the initial "test"—he looked up fearlessly at Kordas, and sniffed loudly in his direction, showing interest and curiosity, but no fear or aggression. "What's his name?" Kordas asked, getting down in the straw himself.

"Kirren," Hakkon said proudly. "I thought of it myself. It means 'watchful' in Tayledras."

Kordas made chirping sounds and called the pup by name, and the gray lurcher blundered over to him, tail wagging so hard he was constantly off balance.

Kordas rolled him over on his back to test for dominance acceptance and submissive behavior. He picked the pup up, legs dangling, to test for his reaction to being "restrained" and unable to do what he wanted. He tested the pup's sensitivity to light and sound—no wincing away, no fear, no barking. Then he suddenly whipped out a bright red handkerchief and thrust it in the pup's face. There was a startle response, as was natural, but there was no fear, and no attempt to run. "He's going to make a fine pet," Kordas said with satisfaction. "The thing I like best about lurchers is what I like best about greyhounds. When they're not running, they just want to be loved."

"That's what the Houndmaster said," Hakkon replied, getting his pup's attention again and bringing him back to lie down on command. "Kirren already knows come, sit, and lie down. He walks on a lead pretty well. He doesn't stay yet—"

"He's a puppy. His idea of 'stay' is 'I'll hold still for a moment.'" Kordas could not have been more pleased that Hakkon had already begun training his pup. "If he is that clever, he'll—"

Hakkon tilted his head when Kordas didn't finish the sentence. "He'll *what*, Father?"

"I've just had an idea. I want you to get your pup just after supper and join me—oh—let's say at the East Gate." To forestall any questions, he added, "Let's just say if this works, you can bring him into our quarters as soon as he's ready to leave his dam altogether."

———

"Kordas, what are you doing out here?" Delia asked, as he and Hakkon approached her and Lythe out of the darkness. Trusty, practically glued to Lythe's side, raised his head, recognized Kordas's scent, then recognized by their scents that Hakkon and Kirren were both "puppies," whuffed, and sat.

Lythe and Delia were not up on the wall yet; Kordas knew that Delia was spending some time with Lythe every night, starting from when Rothas went insensible, and ending when Lythe went up on the wall.

It appeared that they were on their way to one of the external staircases to the top of the wall, because—as Kordas had anticipated—they were following the path at the base of the wall, with the wall on their right and the vegetable gardens to the left. A rich smell of freshly turned loam told Kordas someone had been weeding or harvesting this patch recently.

Delia had a lantern, Lythe did not, but then, Lythe supposedly did not need one. And she proved it by first exclaiming, "Oh, what a nice puppy!" and only then belatedly acknowledging the presence of the humans. "Good evening, King, and who have you brought with you?"

Her voice was high and breathy, and she sounded younger than she actually was. Kordas wondered if that was natural, or an affectation.

"This is my son Hakkon, and the pup is his," Kordas explained, rather amused by Lythe's naive salutation of "King." "The pup's name is Kirren. Did you get a chance to watch the illuminations last night?"

"Yes, once Rothas . . . after dark," she replied. "Rothas brought me a feast, and we ate it together, so I didn't see much of the ones before that. Bits and pieces. The birds were lovely."

She meant to say, "once Rothas was insensible," I suspect.

"He told me about his performance, and what a success he was." Something about her tone alerted him, and confirmed in his mind that he needed to have an in-depth talk with her— well, less "talk" and more "interrogation," although he would try to keep it friendly. *No time like the present for that little talk. Or rather, no time like the present once we deal with what brought us here.*

"Can you talk to this puppy?" he asked. Lythe laughed, as if the question was absurd. And there was, he thought, a little touch of pleasure there—pleasure that someone believed in her abilities and didn't ridicule her.

"Of course I can. I've talked to most of the dogs on the night watch." She got down on her knees, and the puppy came to her without prompting. She took his head in her hands and looked into his eyes. "He really likes you, Prince. He thinks you are his pack leader."

"That's what the Houndmaster said," Hakkon told her with pride.

Kordas smiled. "Well, good. What I want from you, Lythe, is this, if you please. Once the pup is fully weaned, I want you to meet with Hakkon and the pup. I want you to make Kirren understand that when he needs to go, he's to take himself from wherever he is to the dog-walking trench and do the business there. Then I want you and Hakkon to show him the way from our quarters to the trench and back again. I'll instruct the guards at the door to let the dog come and go as he pleases."

He glanced at his son in the lamplight. Hakkon's widened eyes and the shape of his mouth told Kordas the boy had had no idea that someone could do this. "It's Animal Mindspeech, son," he said. "Lythe has it."

"I wish *I* had it," Hakkon said enviously. "That would be— above everything!"

"I can certainly do that, King," Lythe agreed. "Am I now to teach all your dogs to be housebroken?" It sounded like she was more than willing to take that on.

"Only if you want to. I'm mostly asking you to do this with Kirren as a favor to Hakkon's mother, who is not entirely pleased about the idea of cleaning up after a puppy." Kordas smiled. "Housebreaking takes time, and there are always accidents."

"There may still be accidents," she temporized. "But there will be fewer of them. Yes, I can do this." She got to her feet again, and Kirren returned to the feet of his master, looking well pleased with himself.

Kordas turned to Hakkon. "Take him back to the kennels now. Tell your mother I'll be along shortly."

"Thank you, Father!" Hakkon crowed, very obviously thrilled that he was going to be able to bring his pet into their rooms much sooner than he had thought. He and the pup trotted off into the darkness in the direction of the lights of the Palace.

"Do you have somewhere you need to be, Delia?" Kordas asked, turning to the young woman with the certainty that she'd take the hint.

Which she did. "Actually, I do. Alberdina and I have some things to go over. Here, take my lantern. I'll see you tomorrow night, Lythe," she added cheerfully, then it was her turn to vanish into the darkness. At least, from Kordas's point of view. Lythe could probably still see her.

"I'd like to talk with you a bit more, Lythe. Will you walk with me?" Kordas asked.

"Of course," she said, but her tone signaled reluctance.

Hmm. I sent her friend away, and now she's sulking, but she doesn't dare make it obvious or argue with me. That didn't bode overly well for the conversation he intended to have with her, but . . . well, that didn't matter. He was older, and much more used to manipulating people than she was. She'd tell him what he wanted to know whether she realized it or not.

He didn't need *vrondi* for this, though he had asked for their help in ferreting out the truth several times in the last ten years. She was utterly transparent; he'd know if she lied.

So they walked on the paths between the vegetable and herb beds, and he asked innocuous questions. What were her friends like back home? What was her village like? What had her life been like? How were things now for the two of them, her and Rothas?

Delia's version of her story was all very well, but Delia wanted to be her friend. Kordas's view of her was that she was lifebonded to someone who could become a weapon—and through that lifebond could, potentially, affect Rothas's mental and emotional stability. That was a bad position to be in.

He had been afraid that she would be reluctant to talk to

him. He kept his tone light, but curious, and leaned heavily on being an amiable figure of authority. Soon she was chattering away guilelessly.

"Oh, my friends. They were always complaining that their parents would be angry if they stayed out too late, but they never stood up for themselves like *I* did." Her tone was dismissive enough that he was fairly sure that these were less *friends* than *the only people my age in the village.* Her only peers. And she didn't think much of them, after coming away and discovering how much more the world held.

She also didn't think much of the fact that they didn't disobey their parents just to please her, so she must, as a younger girl than she was now, have gotten very used to the fact that they generally *would* do what she wanted if it pleased her.

"Geffird's Well was so *small.* I had no idea how small it was before we met the Tayledras. And almost everyone was already spoken for—for marriage, I mean. Most of my friends were already betrothed by their parents. The only boys near my age were Lerys and Timman, the only ones not betrothed to someone, but my mother wouldn't have stood for them anyway. Nobody's parents would have them for their daughters; they'd never inherit their farm, they'd always be working for their da or their big brother. I didn't like them as a husband anyway. Mother wanted me to—" She stopped and shook her head. "But she knew it was no use, because she'd have had to drag me to the priest tied to a hurdle."

Crickets sang in the silence between them. So far his reading was tending back to *definitely spoiled and a bit thoughtless.* Not bad, she wasn't a *bad* girl, but he sympathized with her mother.

On the other hand, I have to think that her mother is mainly responsible for her being the way she is now. Probably indulged her, because it's hard not to indulge a pretty child. And it was clear that her mother had had a much older man in mind for her daughter. Probably someone who had already buried one or more wives. It was also clear that Lythe saw no future for herself as anything *but* someone's wife, and she was trying to put that future off as long as she could. And in that, he sympathized with her, not her mother.

"Well, what did you want to do?" he asked, trying to sound sympathetic.

"I . . ." She shook her head. "I don't . . . I tried not to think about it," she admitted. But something about the way she said it made him think it was . . . less than the truth. She had thought about it, but probably hoped that one day a handsome stranger would come into her village and ask her to marry him and take her away to some place grand and interesting. *And plenty of girls dream of just that.* Delia certainly had. And she *almost* got her wish too, except for the tedious fact that her rescuer was married to her sister.

Which might explain why Delia has decided to be friends with Lythe.

Then they got to what he really wanted to know. What, exactly, was the relationship between her and the boy? *Life-bonded* didn't mean *love*. It usually did, but not always.

And it was entirely possible that if they hadn't been life-bonded when they met, they would have hated each other. Both, being extraordinarily good-looking, were accustomed to being the center of attention, not sharing the center of attention. Both were headstrong. Both were . . . an amiable sort of arrogant. He suspected Rothas of having been spoiled as much as Lythe.

"And are you all right here?" he asked, as Trusty trundled alongside them, occasionally stopping to sniff the air for a particularly interesting scent. "I know it's not as comfortable and nice as a Tayledras Vale, but it's probably closer to what you know."

"It's . . ." She sighed. "It's very nice here. Nicer than home!

But there aren't many people awake except the guards, and they aren't allowed to talk to me for too long, because I have to keep making the rounds on the wall. I haven't really seen *anything* of the Palace, and nothing of Haven. It's all so different from Geffird's Well! *And* from the Hawkbrother Vale." She sighed again. "And Rothas is only awake for a candlemark or so, and when he is, he wants to talk about what he's learned, what he's been doing, all the compliments he's been getting. He never takes me to meet people, or see anything. I mean, I know that we don't have very much time together, and no one else would be awake at dawn but people who have jobs to do, but . . ." Her voice trailed off, and she glanced at him with an expression of guilt, as if she was afraid that she was asking too much.

Ah, yes, there it is. Definitely jealousy of a sort. Her handsome stranger never takes her to meet all the important people here. Everyone she encounters otherwise except Delia is too busy with their own concerns to pay any attention to her. She's feeling very neglected and it's at least partly Rothas's fault.

"But don't you want to spend the little time you have with Rothas?" he said.

"Yes . . . no . . . I don't know!" she cried, her voice breaking. "It's—I have to be with him, but I don't even know anything about him!"

"Didn't anyone ever explain being lifebonded to you?" he asked with astonishment.

She stopped. "The Hawkpeople did, and . . . it's like being in love, but you can't help it, and you can't stop it, and it's for as long as you live," she replied in a tremulous voice. "It . . . it sounds like a wonder tale, unless it's happening to you."

That may be the first sensible thing I have heard out of her.

Trusty sensed her distress, and plastered himself against her leg, whining a little. It was at that point that Kordas made a decision.

"Come with me," he said firmly. "You're off wall duty for the night."

"All right," she agreed readily enough. "But where are we going?"

He smiled. "To meet my wife."

Kordas exhaled from strain as Jonaton foisted yet *another* "liberated" Imperial Library tome down onto the stack the new King already held in both arms. Jonaton apparently didn't take any note of his liege's discomfort—being a little *too* much like the cats he loved—and scooped up a set of scrolls and paper flats, following Kordas. A good dozen cats were dotted around the room, atop tables, tucked between books and bottles, and occasionally chasing down some highly suspect mote of dust.

"You've known me all your life," Jonaton continued, "so the things I do can't be a surprise to you anymore. If I *needed* something, you'd give it to me, and if I *needed* something another person had, you'd persuade them to give it to me. All I do by *stealing* it is simply save some time for myself, and save you some bother." Jonaton then pointed to a cat-laden planning table. "Over there."

Kordas frowned before putting the stack down heavily on

the table, scattering cats with the thump. "Well, I can assure you that everybody tasked with inventory duties loses their hair over you," the King replied. "I find notes in the margins saying 'Jonaton?' for about every twentieth discrepancy. A band of thieves could operate with less than you."

Jonaton, unfazed by the King's words, answered, "Open those to their bookmarks," like he was directing a hireling page. Kordas growled at the quirky mage to remind him there was a Serious Discussion going on here.

"I didn't come here to squire for you, Mage," Kordas replied, attempting to be at least slightly intimidating, which was utterly blunted by one of Jonaton's charming grins.

"Anytime you want me to stop my exploration, Kordas, just give me the royal decree," the mage replied. "Be sure to send Hakkon to enforce it. He'd love that."

Hakkon, of course, was in charge of the pages and squires of the Palace, and long-time partner with Jonaton. One of Hakkon's common grumbles was that he and Jonaton seldom got enough time together, and Kordas had to admit there was truth in that. The last few years had been "settled," but that didn't mean "idle," and both of the men were prone to overwork in service to the people.

"As the Old Men would say, 'I can arrange that.'" Kordas chuckled. "And I won't deny you're vital to us, Jonaton. As a dear friend to me, as an esteemed asset of the Crown, and as a bad example to all."

"It's settled, then. In this case, all the missing paper was for what I'm about to show you. I also took the last draft of the city map. Technically it was outdated. It said 'Manor House,' not 'Palace,'" Jonaton taunted Kordas, while collecting some marking and geometry instruments. Cats scattered when Jonaton kicked at a carpet to unroll it. Chalk arcs, spirals, lines, and abbreviations filled the darkened, stained pile of the rug, and Jonaton laid his instruments down on it from one knee. "Obviously, there were strange things happening at the coronation. I heard you were made a King or something, but my attention was on the sky."

Kordas was no stranger at all to Jonaton's ways of taking notes, and he read the new charting. It was a map, of sorts, and though the buildings of the city were barely approximated, the map was one of fields of tension and energy, not roads, around Haven. Jonaton pushed his hair back and then clapped twice. Yellow and green lines of dim light climbed upward from a handful of points on the carpet map, and they curved, united, multiplied into and around each other. New lines came up from the chalk in sheets of green, and Kordas surmised that this represented the Tayledras's protective shielding, which extended slightly across the Terilee River and its bridges. The fields bent in on each other in an architectural fashion, revealing buttresses and pointed domes to multiply their strength and disperse threats.

"The Hawkbrothers and my apprentices worked with me on these."

"Where *are* your apprentices? Why weren't they helping you with the books instead of me?" Kordas asked.

"I have them busy stealing things for me," Jonaton replied, and honestly, Kordas wasn't certain he was joking. "But to continue, this interlaced defensive structure was also readable by mage-sight as a direction finder, like the mental discipline we taught you."

Kordas nodded and Jonaton turned his palms in midair, bringing motion to the display of the energy structure. Stabs and flashes of light struck the midair shapes from the inside of the structure, much like raindrops falling upward might. "These are the shows and celebrations. The bigger wipes are the light shows and the big illusions. Here." He accelerated the display, and the area over and around the Palace popped and hissed like wet firewood, with dazzles of light to match, each traceable by lines of light to points on the "ground." "And this is fine—this is what we expected. For this next part you need some distance. Go over there by Sydney the Third."

Jonaton's jaw set firm as he clenched his teeth. "You and the Circle and I have dealt with some impressively high power in our years. You can read by the colors here which kind of energy is which—what affects the physical, emotion, mind, temperature, and so forth. This is not something I want to show the Council. I haven't even shown Silvermoon yet." Jonaton turned his palms again and the shimmering approximation of the silver horse came into view, over the defensive structure. Thousands of wisplike lines of white radiated out from it.

Kordas's jaw fell open slightly, and he all but whispered, "Its origin is—"

"Everywhere. Yes. You've seen that before, we all have. That's when something from outside our physical world comes "through" into ours. It didn't come from people."

"Divine?" Kordas ventured. "We thought it might have been a symbol sent by Epona to encourage us, but none of us actually know anything about its origin."

Jonaton pressed his palms together and then turned them, and the visualization restarted, but this time, the energy shown smeared into long paths, lingering in the air to form something like brushstrokes, which showed motion better than dots.

The white horse's path went across the river before fading above the forest there.

"This is for your eyes only, Kordas."

Kordas saw a red ball of light make its way across the far side of the room, maybe miles away in the visualization's scale. It winked out at the opposite side of the room. A few seconds later, another one came from the nearer side of the room to the King, and then it, too, dwindled away. Then a third one, and a fourth, and each time they grew closer to the Palace and the coronation gathering.

Jonaton gravely said, "Now what does that look like to you, from your war-college study?"

Kordas felt himself pale, and he visibly shuddered when it occurred to him. "Ranged warfare, on open water. Straddling the target—firing testing shots to either side of a target to adjust for range, until eventually the target is centered, and the heavier attack is unleashed."

Jonaton tapped the tip of his nose, and then a significantly larger red sphere of light cruised in from the wall and arced down to the Palace. It struck true, bursting over the layers of the defensive structure, and its displayed force whipped out, following the grooves and arcs of the shield layers. A core of red light reeled away like a stickball spinning out of control, to fall upon a spot across the river, where it struck and dispersed into white around its edges. A disc of white remained there—on what seemed to be the exact spot the white horse had drawn down.

"Everyone thought that the red thing was a great light show, and I admit, it *was*—but Kordas, it was unplanned. Un-invited. I don't think it was meant as any kind of gift we'd want, and it came in from the north."

———

Restil had only just come into the royal suite from an enter-taining card game—gambling for pins with his friends. These particular friends were a pair of highborn, Piet and Jarl, whom he had recruited for his archiving endeavors, Jarl's sister Elanir, and one of the senior horse trainers, Kanni Grimson, who cleaned them all out to great hilarity. Kanni was a fellow who had luck in as great an abundance as Rothas Sunsinger had musical talent. They all liked playing against him, though; he was a good (if rare) loser and gracious winner, and always happy to share his knowledge of cards. And while he enjoyed gambling (and winning), he enjoyed simply playing for points rather than for stakes, so they did that as often as playing for pins.

Restil stopped and put his hand on the door when he heard an unfamiliar voice inside. He glanced at one of the guards.

"The King brought that new girl back here to talk with the Queen," the guard—one Restil only knew as "Scar"—said. He sighed. "The real pretty one, I mean. The one that's got night watch on the wall." That sigh said volumes; Lythe Shadowdancer certainly left an impression wherever she went.

Huh. Well, if they want me to leave, they'll suggest I go to my room. He certainly wasn't going to let the presence of a stranger prevent him from being in his own home.

The King and Queen were seated at a table near the window in the sparsely furnished main room, with the girl opposite the King. All three were dressed in the usual sort of garments that everyone wore now, the simple canvas tunic, linen trews, and linen shirt—except in Isla's case she wore a skirt instead of trews. The main difference between the King, Queen, and highborn were the trimmings, sometimes elaborate ones, that had been cut from older garments and sewn on the tunic and shirt. Restil and his brothers didn't bother. All three were talking and sipping cool water. That made sense; she wasn't a close enough acquaintance to be seated in the converted (much more comfortable) boat-couch with them. *Which might be smart anyway. If they are trying to get information out of her, they want a more formal seating arrangement.*

She was *very* pretty, and she certainly didn't need the fancy gowns he remembered from the Duchy days to enhance her looks. She was beautiful, even. And she didn't have that vapid prettiness that girls with more hair than wit had. She was very pale, which only made sense since she never saw the sun, her eyes a strange purple or violet color, and her raven hair, though put up in braids wrapped around her head, looked as if it would fall past her waist in an ebon waterfall. Her features were, well, perfect. She was almost an idealized version of a beautiful girl.

He closed the door behind himself very softly, and paused

to gauge the situation. He could understand Scar's reaction to Lythe, but he didn't share it. The last ten years here in his father's company, where he could observe without being paid much attention to, and had Uncle Hakkon and his parents coaching him, had taught him a *lot* about people, and he'd learned to read them pretty well. What he saw now was an artless girl, used to being the center of a small, admiring circle, generally used to getting her own way, who was now completely out of her element. None of the little tricks and mannerisms that used to work for her back in her village worked here. Instead of being the one issuing requests, she found herself the one following orders, and now she was adrift. *Father was right to keep her away from the rest of the people here for now. She'd be eaten alive by some, scorned and made fun of by others, cause trouble among the lads and possibly even the married men, and break hearts without intending any harm.* He did not detect any sign of flirtatiousness when she talked to the King, and a naive but manipulative girl well aware of her beauty would surely have seen an opportunity there. So that suggested that while she was used to getting her own way, she wasn't deliberately doing so at the expense of others. *Been plenty of highborn girls here in the Palace that saw Mother, dismissed her as "old and no longer pretty," and tried to catch Father for themselves.* He'd seen it multiple times over the years—either the girls tried it on their own, or tried it urged on by their parents. The result was always the same: rejection and humiliation. But *never* public. Father was too smart, and too well aware of the delicate balance among his courtiers. He always gave the girl an easy "out," and only once had someone not taken it and embarrassed herself, but not in a way that would make the parents blame the King.

He knew that his parents knew he was there; the girl seemed oblivious, and was lost in her own confusion and distress. Finally the Queen, speaking too low for him to make out what she said, soothed her, and she sighed, closing her eyes, her head sagging.

"Restil!" Kordas called, once that had happened. "How was your card game?"

So they want me to join them. He sauntered over and took the remaining stool. The window beside them let in a fine breeze, and the ordinary sounds of the night. A few people speaking in the distance, now and then a dog barking, the rustling of leaves, insect noises. The scent was pleasant, but nothing like the Duchy had been. More herbaceous than flower-fragrant. *Practical gardens instead of ornamental. I bet Mother misses the flowers.*

"I lost, as usual," he said cheerfully. "And as usual, Kanni gave us half our pins back. He says he only needs enough to make good presents for women." He sat down, and nodded to Lythe. "Hello, Lythe Shadowdancer. I've been meaning to ask you, do you have a surname or is that something that doesn't happen in your home village?"

The unexpected question took her off guard, and lifted her for a moment out of what looked like despondency. "I—no, I was always just Lythe, or Lythe, Sussuna's daughter. I didn't know people even had second names until I met the Hawk people. We're somebody-or-other's son or daughter, unless there's two people with the same name. Then it's usually 'the elder' or something that describes them, like 'the tall' or 'the smith.'"

He nodded. "So what was home like?" He was very pleased to note that she wasn't showing any signs of making a play for him—which, again, would have been the natural action of a manipulative girl. When rejected by the father, try the son—*that* was a game that had been tried on him in the past, and he refused to play it.

Hmm. Need to have a talk with little brother Hakkon about that. He's old enough now that highborn girls and their parents could consider him a prize catch.

"Small," she replied. "A dozen families, a couple of single

men, and another widow besides my mother. There were four—no, five villages within walking distance, although the fifth one took half a day to get to, so I've never been there. Actually, I never went to the other villages without my mother. I guess I liked it there? But it isn't as if I had a choice in the matter. It was the only thing I knew."

"What does your mother do?" he asked.

"Weave. The Widow Tankel spins; Mother weaves, because she's the fastest weaver the village has. I'm . . . not very good at large weaving, but she didn't really care. She had me weaving straps and trim on a stick-loom instead."

Hmm. Her mother probably didn't care that she wasn't good at the family trade because she reckoned on bartering those good looks to someone who'd take them both into their household and support her in old age. Well, he certainly couldn't blame Lythe's mother for the sort of thing that was common as dirt even among the highborn. Actually, particularly among the highborn. You married to increase your family's prosperity, not for any emotional reasons. That was what was expected of you. That was changing, but not swiftly; it was hard for parents to stop thinking of their children as another kind of crop to harvest. It helped that so many customs had been upended during the mass migration.

"I don't really know how to do anything well, I guess," the girl continued, looking down at her hands, blushing a little with what he assumed was shame. *Huh. Self-aware enough to say that, and feel badly about it, at least now. Not a bad sign.*

"You have Animal Mindspeech," he pointed out. "That's not 'nothing.' Are you staying here with us, or planning to go back home?"

"Oh, we *have* to stay until this curse is broken!" she exclaimed artlessly. "No one at home wants cursed people around!" Then she dropped her head again. "I guess we're just really lucky that the Hawk people and all of you aren't afraid of curses."

He took a quick glance at his mother; she showed every sign of sympathy. *All right, then. She's a good judge of character. Better than Father is, sometimes.*

"What would you do if we manage to break the curse?" he asked, though he wondered if one or the other of his parents had already asked that question.

Evidently not. Her head came up, her eyes looking startled. "I—I don't know." Her face took on a look of panic, and Isla reached over and patted her hand comfortingly.

"If *you* want to stay here, we'll make sure that Rothas stays as well. I am sure we can persuade him," Isla said firmly. "After all, he's not likely to find larger audiences than he has here, and I very much doubt he'll find another teacher."

Restil's mind worked in odd ways—things would be tumbling into place in the background, completely unnoticed, and suddenly, something would jump into his head, fully formed. He'd learned to trust these sudden bursts of intuition, but not totally rely on them. Sometimes they were wrong, but that was mostly because he didn't have enough information.

Oh, dear gods. That poor girl. Hit in the head by a lifebond to someone she didn't even know, and still doesn't really know. She's worse off than if she'd been betrothed to some old man at home—at least she'd still be in her home village, and still have her friends. Rothas is a good enough fellow, but . . . I bet he can't stop talking about himself, because he's really *happy to be here and is learning things all the time. What a nightmare! The boy is as thick as two short planks when it comes to understanding girls.* Though he had to laugh at himself for thinking that. *Not that I understand them all that well, but I do better than he does.*

"I'd like to stay," she said slowly. "But don't you say that everyone has to be working and helping? I'm not sure walking the wall at night is all that helpful."

Kordas winked at her. "I'll tell you a secret. The only reason I assigned you to that job was to wait until I knew what you were good at. There are things you obviously can't do, because you are awake when everyone else is asleep, but you have Animal Mindspeech, and that is very useful already. You can start by helping in the stables and the kennels. With your help the horses and dogs will understand their jobs much better, much quicker, and will understand from a very young age that the things we are asking of them and exposing them to aren't at all frightening. We'll be able to *talk* to problem animals and sort out their problems quickly rather than guess and flail. Humans can tell a Healer what's wrong. Animals can't. Well, just ask Delia, she's the busiest person in this Kingdom when birthing season comes around, because she can reach inside a mother and turn the baby without ever hurting her or the baby. She can—" He stopped as Lythe blinked at him, perplexed. "Don't worry, we won't be asking you to do that. But there are so many things you can do to help us with animals— and you know, it's kind of a truism that everything that goes wrong with a valuable animal happens in the middle of the night."

Lythe put her finger to her mouth, thoughtfully. "That's true," she said. "Sen Shepherd says that all the time. He says that the minute he lays his head on a pillow, one of his sheep decides to drop her lamb early."

"And we haven't even properly explored your other Gift," Kordas continued.

She looked at him blankly, then flushed. "Oh! The things I can see? You mean, you believe me!"

"Of course I believe you. Which brings me to a question. Do you happen to see anything here, now?" He gave her an encouraging nod.

She paused. Then squinted. Then shook her head as if to clear it.

"I see . . . something that makes no sense," she said hesitantly. "There's a pair of blue eyes just over your shoulder. Just *eyes*. Nothing else. They're watching me."

He smiled slightly, and Restil knew why. "That would be a *vrondi*. They're air spirits. We have a bit of history with them."

Restil wondered why his father didn't tell the girl that *vrondi* were attracted to the truth—but then he realized that his father had been, well, very sly. He had probably *called* the *vrondi* here on purpose, to make sure Lythe did tell him the truth.

Don't blame him.

He hadn't invoked the Truth Spell from the *vrondi*, or Restil would have seen the girl glowing blue even if he hadn't bothered to use mage-sight. But Kordas's unique bond with the *vrondi*, with the ones he had called Rose and Ivy especially, probably meant they could still talk to him if they chose to.

"Do you see anything else?" Kordas asked. "I don't actually expect you to, but I haven't used my own powers to look."

She shook her head. "No, King, nothing but the blue eyes."

"Well, at least that means I don't have any spirits spying on me!" he joked. But then he turned to Restil. "You're roughly the closest thing Rothas has to a friend—a peer. Am I correct?"

Well, that threw him for a moment. He had to think about it. "I *have* been the one showing him around when he's not studying or practicing. Or performing, but he's been cautious about doing that without express permission. I think his mentor advised him not to."

Kordas nodded. "That's good," he said. And nothing more, but Restil got the hint. *Ah, great, I get to be the one to have the little talk with Rothas, and let him know he's neglecting his lifebonded and making her unhappy.* Now, that was probably mostly because Rothas was—to put it unkindly—something of a bonehead. He wasn't terribly observant, which hadn't mattered that much in the past, when he didn't actually *need* to gauge an audience's response, because his Gift would carry him through. He also wasn't used to needing to care about anyone's feelings but his own. He definitely wasn't unkind . . .

He's a great big blundering puppy, is what he is.

But Isla was back to the girl. "Suppose we were to be able to break that curse and you both were able to wake and sleep when you chose again. What would you want to do? Go home?"

Lythe shook her head. "Not home. My mother would just want me to marry . . . someone. Someone not Rothas. I'd never heard of lifebonds before this. No one in our villages has. She likely wouldn't believe it, just like she doesn't believe I can talk to animals and see things. Stay here, if you'd have me. I guess Rothas would want to stay here too, since he's getting all these lessons and everyone loves to listen to him."

But it was clear, at least to Restil, that she wanted more. He wondered what she had daydreamed about, before—

"I . . . you're going to laugh at me," she said plaintively.

"We won't laugh," Isla told her firmly.

"Before, I had this daydream that someone handsome and exciting would come to the village, and we'd fall in love, like in songs and wonder tales. He'd be completely devoted to me, and he'd take me away, and—well, I didn't get any farther than that, because I didn't really know what I wanted, I only knew it *wasn't* in our little village. And I really didn't think too awfully much about that dream, because really, what was the chance that someone like that would come along? I just *didn't* want to marry some old man with bad breath who'd paw me and lay on top of me and stuff me with children, and I'd spend all my time having babies and tending children, and running a household. I *didn't want* that! The whole idea made me feel like someone was about to suffocate me! I wanted my life to be . . . I don't know . . . special. Different. With fun in it. And being pawed by night and working like my mother did by day isn't any fun." She paused again. "Really, that was why I went out at night, to have fun while I still could, because the older I got, the sooner I'd be in a place where I had no choice, and everything would be dull and sad and ordinary."

She raised her eyes to Isla's, and there was pleading in them to be understood.

And of course they all understood. Isla nodded sympathetically. "And your mother didn't understand that at all, because so far as she was concerned, the height of your ambition should be to marry well and be in charge of your own household." Tactfully, Isla did *not* mention the part about Lythe's mother very probably wanting to be the one being cared for, for a change.

Lythe sighed with relief. "Exactly. And even though the curse was horrible, because no one wanted to be around me, at least no one wanted to marry me either. Why would they? They wouldn't want me doing all the chores at night when they were trying to sleep. And when there were children, I wouldn't be awake to take care of them. So at least I didn't have that hanging over my head. But then . . . I met Rothas. And it was wonderful, but it was also horrid. I didn't *know* him, and I still don't know him, not really! He seems nice. He's kind. He never forces me to do anything. He's handsome. But . . . this is like a nightmare version of my dream."

"I can see that," Isla agreed.

"*Why* did this happen?" Lythe cried.

Kordas sat back on his stool. "Well . . . no one knows. Was it the gods? Maybe. Something you were born with? Maybe. Another, unintentional effect of your curses? I can't say. All I know is that a lifebond can be stretched, it can be fought, but it can't be broken. I'm sorry, Lythe, but the simple fact is that no one else will ever be attractive to you, and no matter how far you are from him, it won't be far enough to rid you of wanting to be with him. And that would be true even if you came to hate him. We have . . . some very sad tales to that effect, including actual tragedies." He paused. "A lifebond can bring out the best in two people—but if it's ill-placed, it can bring heartbreak too. I'll just leave it at that. If you had never met, things would be very different."

"If we'd never met . . . at least I'd still have a life I understand," she said forlornly. "So would he, I guess."

"I wish I had a better answer," Kordas said, into a silence filled only with insect sounds and the snoring of Trusty at her feet.

If they'd never met—well, Rothas would have the better life of the two of them. He only needs to be in a safe sleeping spot before the end of twilight, and with his Gift, that wouldn't be hard to come by. Heh, easier than most wandering Bards. He'd still be in demand, still be able to carve out a living with his abilities. Huh. Since he'd be insensible at night, people would be more *willing to trust him around their susceptible wives and daughters! But Lythe, well, drifting around alone at night, talking to animals and spirits, may be romantic in a way, but it's a sad sort of life to have to live. And it would leave her vulnerable if someone in her village decided that he could do what he wanted while she slept and get away with it.*

He concluded that he was going to have to talk to the amiable blockhead. It would ease some of Lythe's unhappiness if she at least *liked* the silly goose.

Well, all this information at least told him—and, of course, his father and mother—that some of their fears could be put to rest. Lythe clearly had no idea of the power she could exercise over Rothas if she chose to. And he was pretty sure she wouldn't choose to do so anyway.

"Well, Rothas has his lessons and his performing to fill his days. So how can we fill your nights when you aren't working with the Palace animals?" Isla asked, practical as always. "What do you *want* to do? Is there something you want to learn? Helping the Healers? Learning to bake? There must be something!"

There was a long pause as Lythe's face took on an odd stillness, as if this was another totally unexpected question. "Is it too late for me to learn to read?" she blurted, and blushed. "I always wanted to—no one but Father Willum knows how at home—but my mother said it was a waste of time for anyone who wasn't god-called—"

Kordas nodded with approval, Isla smiled, and even Restil found himself nodding. "Actually, I can do something better and faster than teaching you how. I can put the knowledge straight into your mind, with magic. I'll stick to Imp—I mean, Valdemaran, though. We don't have any Tayledras books."

"You can always help Alberdina and Delia and the scribes who are copying books once you know how to read and write," Isla added. "With mage-lights, light to see to write clearly isn't a problem, and good copying is largely a matter of going slowly and taking great care. Our copies don't have to be fancy, just accurate."

Lythe perked up immediately, clasping her hands beneath her chin. "Would you really do that?" she asked, nearly breathless with excitement.

"Of course. One more copyist will be invaluable, and it will give you something to talk to Rothas about, so he isn't doing all the talking, and you all the listening." Isla smiled slyly.

"When?" Lythe asked eagerly. "When can I learn how to read and write? I don't care if it hurts, I can't wait!"

"Now," Kordas replied, and reached across the table to touch the middle of her forehead.

"Well," said Isla as the door closed behind a dazzled Lythe, who was cradling one of Restil's old books of wonder tales in her arms, with instructions to read it thoroughly first, then go to Delia and get the materials to copy it. "We've lost a wall watcher."

"It was make-work anyway," Kordas reminded her. "This is actually much better. I'll put her to making extra copies of schooling books in between entertaining ones, and that will help the literacy project immensely. And it will give her something else to think about besides her own emotions." He pinched the bridge of his nose, and got up from the table. "I think at least part of her problem is that she's been wallowing in those emotions far too much."

"What else did she have to think about?" Restil pointed out in her defense.

"Good point. I hope you didn't mind sacrificing your book—"

"She'll give it back once she's made a copy for herself, and I've memorized them all, anyway." Restil grinned. "I don't mind giving her that one even if she forgets to give it back. It's something Sai threw at me one day to make me stop pestering him. Now, if it had been one of the ones you and Mother gave me—not a chance I'd loan it out. Now I just need to figure out how to approach Rothas tomorrow."

"Ah, you caught my hint, did you?"

"*Hint?*" Restil choked. "It was practically a signed decree with all the royal seals on it!"

"You were not exactly subtle, dear," Isla said mildly.

"As long as Lythe didn't figure out what I was talking about, it doesn't matter." Kordas stretched. "I've had a long day. A long Council meeting, followed by a long Court session for hearing petitions, and then—well, I wasn't planning on this session with Lythe, but I'm glad we had it. At the very least, she has something to make her feel less miserable. If she feels less miserable, Rothas will feel less miserable. I'm not entirely sure I want them to be more than friends—outside of the lifebond, that is—at least for right now."

Well, that certainly seemed counterintuitive. "Why?" Restil asked. "What could possibly be wrong with them being in love?"

"Two people in love who barely get to spend any time together? The misery will be back, and this time I don't think we'd be able to distract them." Kordas nodded as Restil's eyes widened. "Yes, you see. Let's stick to getting them to like each other. And you see if you can keep Rothas from overwhelming her. I must say, I do find one thing quite . . . odd . . . about her."

"What's that?" Isla asked.

"Well, she was the little queen of her village, from all I can make out. Her mother indulged her, her friends all did whatever she asked—"

"But did they?" Isla countered. "They *didn't* stay up all hours of the night to indulge her. Her mother *didn't* believe her about her powers. By the way, what does 'seeing Elementals and spirit creatures' translate to in terms of a Gift?"

"That, I'll have to ask the Old Men about. I don't *think* she's mage-Gifted, but it might be something subtle. From what she said, she seems to be able to see things I can only see when I deliberately evoke mage-sight. It would be useful if she can see and talk to Elementals or spirits without needing to do that." He yawned. "But that will definitely be for tomorrow. In fact, I think it's already tomorrow, so I am going to go to bed."

Restil took that as the command it actually was, and went to his room.

He wrestled with what, exactly, he was going to say to Rothas. The fellow *seemed* to be oblivious to an awful lot that was going on around him . . . but that didn't mean he was insensitive.

It could just mean he has no practice in thinking about anyone but himself. He found himself yawning. *Tomorrow I'll see about getting* his *history. There may be something in it that will explain everything.*

Restil had decided to ease into things over lunch. Rothas was getting his lessons in the morning, and practicing in the afternoon—now practicing *three* instruments, since he was learning the fiddle as well. So Restil had helped himself to a basket, filled it with bread rolls, cheese, butter, and hard-boiled eggs, and taken it off to the workshop, figuring to catch Rothas as soon as he left the premises. And in fact, as he was coming through the gardens, he saw the unmistakable blond mane ambling away from him.

"Rothas!" he called, and the young Bard turned toward him and waved. He hurried to catch up. "You busy?" he asked, as soon as he got close enough.

"Not really," Rothas admitted. "I thought I'd check on Lythe and then get some food. I'm starving."

"You're always starving," Restil teased. "Lythe will be fine, she has Trusty and Alphonse with her. Let's go down by the river. Have you been there yet?"

Rothas shook his head, and followed along beside Restil. "No. Kind of afraid to. I can't swim! We just had streams and ponds."

Restil laughed. "You're in no danger of falling in by acci-dent. And I don't intend to push you in until after I teach you to swim."

Rothas rolled his eyes. "Oh," he replied sarcastically. *"Thank you."*

"So, when did you start trying to entertain people?" Restil asked as they approached the river and found a good spot on the bank, just under a willow tree. He dug out a little hollow between two roots and sat down; after watching him, Rothas did the same.

"As early as I can remember, which is just as well, since my pa went off hunting and never came back, and my ma died when I was about six," the young man said matter-of-factly. "I got passed around all the families in my village as they had food to spare, but nobody grudged it, on account of that. There was an inn the next village over—Lark Rise—and the inn-keeper offered to take me off their hands, permanent. Folks was a little sorry to see me go, but times was hard, I was get-ting bigger and eating more, and they reckoned they could always get me to come back now and again when times got better. When I wasn't singing in the inn, people paid me a bit to come do weddings and the like." He ate an egg, whole. "The only problem that curse ever really gave me was that I couldn't sing at the inn after sundown, which was hard in the winter, 'cause folks would come in and be disappointed I was already sleeping like a stone and couldn't be waked up." He frowned. "Well, that isn't quite true. When people got used to it, there was some as talked behind their hands about how my curse might spread to the whole village, and some that used to try to prove I was faking it. I got scars from where they'd stick me with a knife! Harcort Innkeeper tried to put a stop to it, but he didn't always catch 'em. He was getting a bit put out anyway, because he was feeding me full meals and boarding me too, and not getting what he called his 'full value' out of me. So I was going a bit further than I'd been doing, working, to bring in money so I could leave him eventually."

"You didn't care for him?" Restil asked, carefully peeling an egg of his own. The hens were laying well now, well enough that eggs could be spared for lunch.

Rothas shrugged. "Nobody much *cared* for me once Ma died. I was useful, so I got treated all right, but I wasn't blood kin to anyone, so they didn't put themselves out, either. And I had to be *real* careful about women and girls. Their menfolk were all right with me singing, but they didn't want me hanging around after. I weren't what you'd call *good marriage prospects*. And you know how girls act around me, you've seen it here."

Restil nodded. "Did you figure that out on your own?"

He laughed. "Me? I'm a blockhead. No, Harcort warned me when I was about twelve and not a cute little anymore. Gave me a big long lecture about it, then kept an eye on me on top of that, and smacked me when he thought I might be flirting. That's another reason I didn't much want to stick around."

"So you were out on a job—"

He nodded. "Like I said, went further than usual, took most of the day to get there, and I was looking for a barn or at least a haystack to pass out in. Finally found a woodcutter's hut. Was practicing before I passed out, and that's when Lythe turned up and—" He shook his head and sighed heavily. "Turned my world upside-down. And I had about a mark, a little more, just enough time to explain what was going to happen, and then I dropped off cold. When I woke up, I didn't know what to think, because she was still there, she'd been watching me all night, she even had food for the both of us. Then she explained *her* curse, and it was her turn—"

"Then what?" Restil asked. "How on earth did you find the Hawkbrothers? How on earth did you *travel* when one of you was asleep all the time?"

"They found us. Dunno how, but it was that very sunset. I'd never seen the like—well, *you* know how they dress! Thought I was in a song myself, first I meet this girl, and she's . . . it was like lightning hit me, then she has a curse too, and then this outlandish bunch of people show up jabbering nonsense, then *I* pass out, and the next thing I know, we're in the Vale and I can understand their gobbledegook. Which . . . wasn't so bad when I calmed down. Can't beat their food. They were plenty nice to us, explained all about how I was a Gifted Bard, said they were going to try and help, and if they couldn't, they'd pass us along to someone who had different magic. And meanwhile, I learned their songs, and told 'em all about all the villages I knew." He broke off bits of a roll and ate it slowly. "Wouldn't have minded staying, but it was . . . it was weird. And this lifebond thing. I dunno what to do about it. I mean, I want to be with her every single moment, and I don't hardly know anything about her. Anyway, they kept me pretty busy, figured out they couldn't help, asked me if I minded being passed on. I figured better not make 'em angry, so I said yes, and they said good, and here we are." He finished the roll and took another. "I like it better here. I mean, lessons and instruments and all. It's not as strange, even though the food isn't as fancy." His face lit up. "I never knew there was so much to know about music!" he enthused. "And I can *do things with it*, or I will once I learn how! I'm only supposed to try with my teacher, and I can see how that's the way it's got to be, but it's like getting presents every day!" Then his face fell a little. "I keep trying to cheer Lythe up, telling her all about it, but she doesn't seem to understand."

"Ah," Restil said, as everything fell in place for him. "Well. Let me tell you a little bit about women in general, and Lythe in particular . . . ."

After a very few moments, whatever Rothas had planned to do after lunch had been forgotten. As Restil had deduced . . . Rothas was about as innocent, well-meaning, and blundering as a puppy. *He* thought he was engaging with her. *He* was using his Gift on himself, because he'd been told that he was making everyone around him unhappy when he was unhappy, so the depression he felt because all they could have was a limited time together was partly mitigated, but of course, he wasn't using it on Lythe because he'd been told not to use it on other people. He also didn't understand that nonstop chatter about pleasures she couldn't take part in was not going to make her feel anything but left out. Restil patiently explained everything to him, or at least, did his best. Rothas hung on his every word, nodding vigorously in agreement the entire time.

"So you see," Restil concluded about mid-afternoon. "Besides all the other things, *both* of you are in the position where you know almost nothing about each other, with a lifebond that's—well, it's acting like parents betrothing you, and you got no say in it. It's confusing, it's irritating—hellfires, it's maddening. But you have a lot more to keep yourself busy than she does, so up until now, all she's had is time to brood."

Rothas heaved a huge, sad sigh. "I thought I was helping."

"Of course you did. Your intentions were kind. But now you know, so this evening, I suggest you try something different.

Ask her about *her*. And . . . I'll just go out on a limb and say it's all right if you use a little of your Gift to try and cheer her up. If anyone objects, you can tell them I gave you permission. All right?" Restil smiled reassuringly, and Rothas slowly nodded.

"I'll do that." He sucked on his lower lip. "I reckon I'll make up a song about her. Girls always like that."

"Yes. Yes, they do," Restil agreed, and stood up, taking the now-empty basket with him. "I look forward to hearing it."

Rothas chuckled. "So do I!"

10

"**W**ell, that's . . . odd," said Kordas, gazing at the anomaly in his horse pasture across the river with extreme puzzlement. Of course, there was nothing to be seen by those with no mage-Gift, but to him and Sai . . . this otherwise ordinary stand of trees was lit up like a festival.

"That's what we all think," Sai replied, arms folded over his chest. "All of us have been out here poking at it since young Lobo found it. I know it hasn't been there long. It's not connected to anything at all, much less anything inimical—and believe me, if it had been, you'd have thought Pebble's mother had returned when we got done scorching the earth. In fact, it seems inoperative and benign. As if someone was preparing the ground for a major Working, like a Portal, then changed their mind."

The "anomaly" was, essentially, something *like*, but not identical to, a summoning circle. Except there was nothing about it suggesting who or what had created it. More than that, there was nothing at all linking it *to* something to *be* summoned. Every summoning circle he had ever seen was heavily and specifically linked to exactly what you wanted to summon, usually by inscribing its various names and attributes.

Try not to scare yourself by thinking it's for something there are no names for.

He was not surprised no one had noticed that this place was now very different from the rest of the pasture, even though plenty of people came and went here, tending to the horses. Even the horses showed no reaction to it. To non-magicians, there was nothing at all different about this grove of lovely trees—well, except that about half of the trees were not a variety a Valdemaran could name right off the top of their head. These were Hawkbrother remnants, like other groves scattered about this field. Unlike the giants that supported ekeles, or the tender growth that could not take a hard winter, these were native to the area, and handled winter weather just fine. Some of these groves had once surrounded dwellings, some had merely been pockets of seclusion in the otherwise busy Vale, and some had been cultivated to conceal a hertasi tunnel entrance or something else "unsightly," like one of the many tunnel vents that allowed fresh air to flow underground.

No, there was nothing about this grove that looked out of the ordinary to the naked eye. It was only when you looked with mage-sight that you saw it was very different from the meadow around it. A perfectly formed circle surrounded it, but a blank one, as if someone had changed their mind in the middle of their working—or been interrupted—and just left it. He could tell from the movements of energy around it, however, that nothing he or his mages could detect ever *would* or *could* be purposed on it. It was not only blank, it was protected. Nothing would be "written" there. Nothing *could* be written there. It was a perfect, fully ordered, charged circle, but one that was as impossible to alter as fire-glazed pottery.

"What—why?" he asked Sai. The old mage shrugged. Jonaton interjected, from inside an array of brass and wood tripods and instruments that resembled a land surveyor's full kit, "I can tell you some interesting things about it, Kordas." Jonaton, with his sleeves rolled back, looked very free right now. He was in his element completely. He whistled and gestured for the rest of the onlookers to go to where the King was, and they ambled over. When it looked like they were within earshot, Jonaton spoke like a lecturer. "I don't know who it's from, but there's an energy grain to it. Squint hard with your mage-sight and get very close, and there are radiating surface imperfections all over this thing." With a bit of extra effort to make the illusion-work more understandable for those with impaired senses, Jonaton conjured a teaching diagram—a kind of simplified, very legible illusion used to show moving examples of places, items, or energies. It was many mages' favorite thing, both for its clarity and for its usefulness for proving someone—anyone—wrong. "In concentric rings, at widening intervals from the center. If there's one thing I know, it's explosions."

Kordas chuckled a little, as did a few of the Old Men. Back on the old manor fields, there were more than a few water holes not dug by the tools of laborers. Wis said loudly to Koto, "You hear? One thing! He knows one thing! The boy's been holding out on us!"

"These same dynamics are found in near-surface explosions," Jonaton continued, unperturbed. "And they imprint like this, too, except far more violently. In mage-sight, it is much clearer to see, once you know the range to look for." His illusory drawings, bright against a darkened background, faded in an ice-blue mountainscape of representative peaks and valleys, symbolizing shock waves, over the map of the immediate area. A sphere was expanded up to illustrate a falling fireball. "I've got a theory I'll get to later."

Ponu grumbled, "All I know is, there it is, and it can't be used by anything. I'm going back to bed."

Sai took up quickly, hearing his annoyed tone. "Maybe it's a gift of the gods? The Palace doesn't have a temple, and it ought to, or a meditation place, anyway. The timing's right for it to have been made during the celebrations after the coronation. I'd feel perfectly comfortable meditating here, myself." Sai scratched his head. "Sydney went in there, walked around, found a warm spot, and lay down in it, and cats have an instinct for things that are safe, magically speaking." He chortled. "And unsafe! Whenever Sydney flees Jonaton's rooms, we all know to prepare for something going wrong in there! Thank the gods it's usually just bad smells and scorched clothing!"

"I'll take that idea under advisement," Kordas replied. A temple wasn't a bad idea, actually. There'd been a chapel to Epona in the Ducal manor, but the Mother hadn't built a chapel into the Palace because Kordas hadn't thought to specify one. He had a moment of guilt over that.

"If you could make it sort of a—I don't know how to put this—neutral ground for everyone? You know, include the symbols for everything you can think of in the decorations, and lots of things like stars and moons and trees?" Sai continued. "Some of your courtiers are pretty religious, and they'd appreciate a place like that. It'd be useful for weddings and namings and funerals." Now he rubbed the top of his head. "But just going by my instincts, I can't feel that it 'wants' to be anything. It doesn't lean in any direction, good or ill. It's almost as if this place was created with neutrality in mind."

"That still begs the question, who or what created it?" Kordas replied, not entirely happy that something or someone had come right into his back garden, so to speak, and planted a magic construct there. Even if it was a god, which was looking more and more likely by the moment. First the silver horses in the illuminations, and the "Red Thing," and now this?

"If it's a god," Sai replied, "and said god didn't sign their handiwork, so to speak, it's because that god doesn't *want* you to know which one it is. Normally I'd be the very last person in this Kingdom to say this, but—let well enough alone."

Kordas gaped at him.

"No, I mean it. *Do* get Silvermoon or some other Hawk-brother out here to look it over, surely. But after that? Accept the gift horse." He shrugged. "I can think of a lot of things that could have caused this. A latent Change-Circle. Old Tayle-dras magic bubbling up to the surface. Something they built and forgot about, and maybe the Mother woke it up again—or it could be something *by* the Mother. Maybe something from some Elemental friend of Pebble. But given the timing and that it looks to me as if it's *deliberately* neutral, that makes me think it's a little gift from the gods, and you don't ask too many questions about what gods give you, if you know what I mean."

Kordas did, in fact, know exactly what Sai meant. *If you are very unlucky, the gods will answer your pleas.* The saying had two meanings: gods would help someone who cried for their help to survive misfortune, but if called upon without great need, the gods might give their attention in unantici-pated, even cruel, ways.

So, gingerly, he stepped over the border of the circle and into the grove. It looked as if this had been one of those groves that concealed a nice, secluded spot for—well, plenty of things. Maybe a little tea house. Maybe a place to meditate. Maybe a trysting place. Maybe a spot where two people would work out their differences without any interference. There was a path into it, and it was hollow, with a tiny meadow inside it, and yes, it was just big enough for a modestly sized temple or chapel.

Most likely a tea house was here. One of those things with a tent on a platform. There'd be no trace of it at this point except this pocket meadow.

He stood in the middle and cautiously allowed all his

shields and protections to drop, knowing that Sai was out there and could protect him if—

Except Sai wasn't out there. Sai himself had stepped into the little meadow, strolling as if he wasn't walking on ground so highly charged with magical energies that it glowed to mage-sight.

He stood next to Kordas and nodded. "Go ahead, keep on with what you were doing."

Kordas sighed. "All right." There was no point in remonstrating with Sai now. The old man was a force of nature like Jonaton, and did what he pleased. Kordas continued to drop his protections until he stood there, magically naked to the world.

And felt nothing but a deep sense of peace.

No. Wait. Not peace. Not exactly. More like . . . like one of those places where the Tayledras had performed what they called a "thorough cleansing." A sense of transformation permeated the space. As if something *bad* had been here, but had been turned into this, leaving nothing of its original behind. It wasn't an absence, it was . . . potential. Readied for what would become of it.

With his eyes closed, he continued to let the sense of the place soak into him, and described what he experienced to Sai. Then he opened his eyes again.

The old man's weathered, wrinkled face was thoughtful. "Now, that's interesting. I can think of something else now, though. Wait just a moment." He made a few gestures in the air, mage-energies leaving a trail of light behind his hands as they moved, then whistled.

And then he held his hands palm up, and filled the space with his own energies—but not bound to anything. The power was . . . well, it was like a bowl of magic, just waiting for something to come drink from it.

And drink from it, something did.

There was a tinkling of laughter in Kordas's mind. Before he could react to that, a coalescence of whirling blue leaflike motes blew in, twisted a few times around the elder's hands, pulled up, and settled before them as a misty, humanoid form, whose most salient feature was a pair of enormous blue eyes.

Kordas didn't even wonder which *vrondi* this was. He felt it. "Ivy!" he exclaimed with delight and surprise.

:Hello, Kordas, King and Liberator,: the *vrondi* greeted him. *:It is good to speak with you again.:*

He blushed and stammered a little. "Just Kordas to you, my friend. No need for titles and that nonsense between us."

:This makes me happy,: the *vrondi* said. *:But Sai would not have called me for simple pleasantries. Nor would he have given me this much power just to learn if you were being less than truthful about something to him. So?:*

He could not help but marvel at how much the *vrondi* had changed. Ivy no longer spoke of herself as a non-entity, as "this one." She had learned from them all, and he was glad to see it.

"So . . . obviously this . . . place . . . that we're in . . . it's—" He wasn't sure how to word what he wanted to know.

:Not natural, no. But transmuted. By greater power than you or I. A gift, I think, made from something else. Completely, so no trace is left. A gift that is made safe for the recipient to accept.: The *vrondi* sounded very sure of that, and given Ivy's experience with inimical magic, and her nature as an Air Elemental, he was inclined to trust her judgment. *:Such transmutation is unusual, but not unheard of, for the sake of those whom the Great Ones favor. Both Air and Earth owe you a debt, and that is no small accomplishment. So accept and be grateful and do not burden your heart with too many questions. Answers will come.:*

"Sai thinks we should put a kind of neutral chapel or temple here," he told Ivy. "Something that is open to any and all."

:I think that would be pleasing,: said the *vrondi*. There was a long pause, as if Ivy was trying to figure out a way to say something without saying it. *:I think that would show respect.:*

Sai nodded, as if to say, "Well, there it is," which was also what Kordas thought. "Seems definitive to me," Sai said. "Jonaton is packing up, so I think we're done here. If you want to stay here and catch up with our old friend, I have a budding Bard to attend to."

For a moment, Kordas was overwhelmed by all the things that needed doing. He had meetings, he had business with Restil. He had—

But—

But—

I'm the King. And surely the King can be allowed a few moments to catch up with an old friend. I wish this was Rose . . . but Ivy was as much of a friend to me as she was. I wonder where Rose is now? Maybe Ivy will know.

"I think that's a fine idea, Sai. Thank everyone for me," he said. "Let Beltran know where I am and what I'm doing."

Sai replied, "The longer you're King, the more valuable moments like this are. Try not to miss them. Be well, Ivy."

Kordas settled down into the grass as Sai strolled out. "So, Ivy, how is the free life suiting you?"

———————

For once, Kordas got absolutely no objection from any of his Council. They all thought that a "neutral" temple out in the field was a fine idea. No one objected to it being in a horse pasture. "After all," the Seneschal remarked sagely, "some people can get a little . . . *enthusiastic* when they worship. A little distance from the Palace is no bad thing."

Everyone nodded . . . because everyone had been awakened at least once at dawn by Lord Niel's family and retainers singing chants to Eeron, the Forge-Father. Loudly. And . . . not one of them could carry a tune in a basket. Apparently, the Forge-Father had a tin ear, no doubt from His holy hammering.

"I think," the Lord Exchequer said portentously, "that it would be both appropriate and pious for the Crown to cover all costs. And given that, it would also be appropriate for the Crown to dictate the design."

The two priests—of the rotating group that shared two Council spots—looked a little disappointed, but nodded their agreement. The Lord Exchequer smiled, knowing that this meant *he* would dictate the budget, and that the chapel in question would be as austere as he could make it.

And there's nothing keeping the various religions from donating their own decorations, either, Kordas realized. *I'll insist on keeping the altar area bare of anything that can't be easily moved . . . but that's not a diplomatic thing to say out loud, so that will go into the design. Note to self: make sure there is a good storage annex attached to keep everyone's panoply tidily packed away.*

The meeting concluded satisfactorily and early, and Restil moved through the crowd until he got to his father. "What brought this sudden burst of piety about?" he asked his father quietly, as they left the Chamber and headed to the Great Hall to eat. "It can't be your aversion to the sacred chants to the Forge Lord."

Kordas wasn't looking at Restil at first, occupied in thought. *Valdemar has changed with this crowning, and there's only ever going to be so much time to handle it all. So any time for yourself has to be stolen from that.*

"Let's get our lunch to take with us," Kordas said instead. "I'd rather show you. The Old Men already know about this; Sai was the one to show me. Jonaton took its measure, and I'd like your impressions without prejudice."

When he didn't say anything more, Restil cocked his head to one side. "Your silence speaks volumes," he said. "All right.

Rothas has lessons with Koto after lunch anyway. Koto thinks he might be on the track of a way to banish that curse, by the way, but it's going to be complicated."

"Everything always is," Kordas sighed.

Rather than collecting food themselves, Kordas availed himself of the privileges of rank and sent a page for it, waiting until the youngling appeared with his brimming basket before he led his son out into the sunlight.

"There's one thing to be said for the fact that everyone dresses alike right now." He laughed. "We can make our way to the pasture without anyone realizing it's the King and Crown Prince, and not some stablehand or groom off in the middle distance."

"I cannot tell you how many times I have taken advantage of that." Restil laughed. They did walk to avoid getting close to anyone, just to be sure. And it was a lovely—if hot and a bit humid—day. Well worth being out of doors.

Kordas kept the conversation to everything *else* that had gone on in the Council Chamber; there certainly was enough to talk about. Being a mere Baron had meant that he could instruct Restil on an informal basis, as his own father had instructed him. But the many obligations of being a King meant that *everyone* had to be aware that the Crown Prince was being suitably educated in everything going on in the Kingdom. That education had to be visible. So Restil was sitting in on every Council meeting and every decision, so that people would know that if something took the King from his duties, whether it be for a day or eternity, Restil was ready and primed to take over. So was Isla, for that matter.

Restil caught him up on the little the Koto had had to say about the potential curse-breaking. That brought them to the grove in question—and before Kordas could say anything, Restil stopped dead in his tracks, staring at the place.

"What—"

"My reaction entirely," Kordas agreed.

Restil readily followed his father into the grove by the thread of a path, and nodded to his father as the path opened out into the clearing. It was cooler here, shaded by all the trees, and it was obvious that the horses liked coming here in the heat of the day, because the grass and wildflowers were barely ankle height, as opposed to waist high, as they would have been had there not been regular grazing. Kordas sniffed experimentally, and his nose confirmed it: there was definitely a scent of cut grass in here. And, fortunately, not of manure. Lurking horse-apples in the grass should not be a problem.

Kordas put his back against a tree trunk, folded his arms, and waited while Restil prowled around the clearing, using his own mage powers to test it. Restil was long past needing any instruction from his father—he was at the point now where Kordas couldn't teach him anything, and his magical schooling was coming straight from the Old Men.

"This is perplexing," Restil admitted. "When did this happen?"

"Sai thinks sometime in the last moon. Maybe even during the coronation. Goodness knows we wouldn't have noticed it then." Kordas waited patiently for Restil to digest that, then continued. "Sai gave Ivy enough energy to manifest, and she agreed that it's *probably* the work of one or more deities, and that I shouldn't ask too many questions."

"Well, if it had been a *specific* deity, who *specifically* wanted a place of worship here to themselves, they'd have marked it in a way we wouldn't be able to mistake," Restil said, finally. "In studying all the lore from all the gods we know, both the ones that came with us and the Tayledras Star-Eyed, none of them are shy about making their wishes known when it comes to establishing places of worship, or branding places they want for their own." He raised an eyebrow at his father. "We're more apt to get talking burning bushes or visions three stories tall."

"So, evidently, whichever one did this is willing to share. That's a nice example for our people to follow."

Restil smiled. "Yes. Yes, it is. Do we want to make this public information?"

Kordas thought about that for a while. "Well, we took it to the Council, so I think that horse has fled the barn. But we don't have to announce where it is just yet."

Restil stopped in the middle of the clearing and gave it a new kind of measuring look. "I think I know who to go to to build this chapel. Ever seen a stave church?"

Kordas was a little taken aback. "A what? A slave church?"

"No, a *stave* church. It's a kind of construction, like a palisade that makes a whole building. Strong, airy, great acoustics. That little village of Nerdenlanders, the people the Tayledras wanted in charge of the heavy forests?" Restil prompted. "They built a stave church for their worship. We can lay down a stone foundation and build one here without disturbing any of these trees."

Since that was precisely the main thing Kordas was worried about, he resolved to ride out to the Nerdenlandcroft and have a look at this building. *I . . . actually haven't been out there, because they never give me any problems—and they've brought their questions and needs directly to Haven rather than expecting me to send someone to them.* He frowned to himself about that. *It should be the calm, polite ones that get attention, not the brats and histrionic ones.*

Well, and also because the Hawkbrothers had expressed themselves very satisfied as to how the Nerdenlanders were operating as custodians of the forest. If the Tayledras were pleased, who was he to argue?

"A stave church is the closest thing I've ever seen to a free-standing Hawkbrother building," Restil continued.

"That settles it. Can you add this to your plate?" his father replied. Restil laughed.

"Gladly. I can't imagine that they'll say *no*, though." Restil nodded at the path in, and Kordas led the way back out again.

"Sitting down to eat lunch in there just doesn't seem-—right," Kordas added, as they made their way out of the enormous pasture and across the river to the Palace grounds.

Restil just nodded, and suggested with a tip of his head that they take a seat in a rose arbor . . . covered with peas, not roses. It was still an arbor—one of several, in fact, made from bent branches, just as there was some very lovely furniture made from bent branches—and it was quite pretty. The pea flowers might not be as showy as roses, but they had their own grace, and the curling tendrils of the vines were lovely regardless. Once the initial need to get food crops in the ground had been satisfied, and the vegetables on the Palace grounds not only supported the Palace population but produced a surplus, the gardeners had begun to get creative. There were pleasant arbors containing wicker seats covered with peas, beans, hops, summer squashes—anything that produced a vine probably had at least one arbor, and the vegetables that provided the best combination of shade and produce would become permanent parts of the garden. Colored cabbages, red, green, and purple, some with frilly leaves, were planted in concentric beds the way flowers had been back in the Duchy. Patterned, slightly raised beds had been introduced for the perennials and herbs. Winter squashes were kings of small mounds that were further covered in herbs or edible flowers that repelled insects. Berry bushes and fruit trees got the ornamental treatment as well. From a distance it looked exactly like a well-planned formal garden. It was only until you got close that you realized everything here was edible or medicinal. Kordas was ridiculously fond of it all. After being surrounded by purely ornamental gardens most of his life, there was something hilarious about these pretty plants all being edible. And the alarmist in him, who wanted always, always, to have enough food stored and at hand to see them through any emergency, gloated and felt comforted at the sight of all this abundance.

"I am reliably informed that snacking on the peas is encouraged," Restil replied, taking a seat, setting the basket down on the ground between them and breaking off a young pea pod. He slit the pod expertly with his thumbnail, and inhaled the young peas from inside. Then he tore up the pod and added it to the mulch at the foot of the vine.

His father sat down and removed the cloth covering the top of the basket. "I suppose we'll have to hurry this," he said with evident regret.

"We will," Restil agreed. "But that doesn't mean we can't enjoy it, too. All we have to do is *not* talk about work while we hurry through our meal."

He smiled as his father's eyes lit up. "Have you seen how this year's False Gold foals are measuring up?"

Restil replied with the same enthusiasm. *It's not often I can give Father a gift. I'm going to enjoy this one as much as he is.*

Kordas stared at the candle burning on the otherwise empty hearth—mind not blank, but not exactly thinking either. The whole set of magical shenanigans after the coronation still had him convinced that he was missing something, somehow. But what was it?

And damn, I never did hear Jonaton state his theory.

As he had for years now, while his people established their home here, Kordas was just fine at directing everything on a baronial scale. Roads were laid, resources storehoused, and by their sixth year, even wine was made. The flying monsters, the Red Forest, the water spiders—they were more *existential* than he could plan defenses for. They already lived here—to them, the Valdemarans were invaders—so they had inherent advantage.

The Tayledras were brilliant, but also preoccupied—they were allies, but helping Valdemar was not their priority at all. More and more, the feeling that whatever the Valdemarans made would attract trouble only grew. Even founding Haven on a Vale site gave him pause, because making Valdemar prosperous also used his people's labor to create a tastier prize to simply *take*. Spitters and Poomers were in short supply, and while ballistae and perimeter traps were built to stop a horde, that was just it—there was no guarantee than an invader would be a "horde" at all. Like the beetles, or the blight—arrows and coldshot wouldn't defend against such things, and *those* threats hadn't even been sent to weaken Valdemar.

That I know of.

Even the Tayledras held a policy that it was better to be agile and educated, and to improvise what was needed, than to create a fortress prepared for anything. It didn't help Kordas's worry that his people didn't *have* enough resources to be ready for every possible thing, and aside from being able to put holes, craters, and cuts in things, they were riding too much on luck. He knew damned well, however, that if he thought too hard about the situation, whatever it was that was prodding the back of his mind would flee like a frightened trout. What he needed was to "not think" about it—just set his mind to rest and let things churn until the wary fact or idea or whatever it was finally showed itself. Fresh air could help.

Isla stirred a little in the seat beside him, closed her book, and set it aside. "I'm going to bed," she said. "But I know that look. I've seen a lot of it over our years. Don't worry about waking me."

He kissed her. "You are the best of wives. I think I'll go out for a walk."

"Take a watchdog," she replied, as she passed through the door to the bedroom.

He knew very well she meant a guard, but instead of beckoning one of the pair at the door to the royal quarters to follow him, he conjured up his own "watchdog," an enhanced version of a mage-light that would constantly seek things larger than a house cat approaching the mage, and spotlight them. It was an extravagance, but tonight he didn't want anything or anyone intruding. *Intruding on what? I don't know yet. I just know I don't want any interruptions.*

The Palace was much quieter than the old Ducal manor had ever been at this hour—much less the Imperial Palace, which had been buzzing whatever the hour. People were, unsurprisingly, in bed. Even the nobly born worked in Valdemar, and worked hard, and at this point, they were used to it—some even cheerful about it. But that meant that everyone was in bed early. Entertainment after dinner never lasted more than a mark. If anyone wanted more entertainment than that, they could amuse themselves in their quarters. So the corridors were empty, mage-lights were dim to save people's night vision, and only the occasional guard posted on night watch was there to see him pass.

His mind would be racing, if there were a race to win, but instead it ran in circles, like a restless horse on a longe-line running ruts in the earth. It felt like there was just too much to be done for him to think through and plan out, so he touched upon one subject after another, dipping into ridiculous amounts of detail. Every night since the coronation had been like this, increasingly so. There was a foreboding in his thoughts about the immediate future, that they simply weren't ready to withstand whatever came after Valdemar now that it was such a ripe plum. He could devise defenses and strategies for what he *knew*. But out there was the *unknown*, and the unknown had kicked the Valdemarans hard more than once when it finally showed itself.

Once outside, he did not regret for a single moment that he'd decided to walk. He could only describe the air as "soft"; it was skin temperature, with barely a hint of breeze, and perfumed by herbs and the faintly sweet aroma of blossoming vegetables and ripening fruit. A full moon shone down on the gardens with little in the way of clouds to obscure it—only very high, thin clouds, which created a halo around the moon and accented the light of the stars. This was the famed "silvery moonlight" praised in song, noted in romantic tales, and inevitable in adolescent poetry. There really was nothing else quite like it, he had to admit. It provided just enough light to taunt out adventurous thoughts and skewed estimates of abilities. It seemed to imbue all that it touched with strange powers worthy of wonder. Moonlight, however, conferred no invulnerability to accidents, and in inclement weather Kordas's bones often sounded off about his foolhardy youth spent learning hard lessons like that.

After all that's happened, I'd say I've had all the fun I can stand. I'll see Valdemar through to my last breath, but I wouldn't mind it if others had all the adventures for a while. I feel like I'll be restless if my future is just smiling, waving, and handling administrative issues, but I think I'd like to find out. I won't be around forever. Valdemar is—I hate to use the word "stable"—but the worst part seems to be over.

Some wise soul had laid out the paths between the planting beds with white border stones so there was no danger of blundering into the turnips, and that was all that saved Kordas from stomping through carefully tended crops. His blunder snapped him from ever-deepening immersion in his thoughts. His mind was preoccupied by matters higher than mere walking. He was in a good state of mind, equal in intelligence and emotion at the moment, and that—and maybe the moonlight—encouraged wild thoughts of the future.

Kordas had a seat upon a garden bench and gazed up at the full moon, speaking directly to it.

"Silvery moon, cast your rays from above. I'll catch them with thanks, and shine back my love." He was clearly susceptible to poetry at the moment. *Why not poetry, though?* "Poetry is the perfect language of specificity for emotions, which* *otherwise evade characterization." As my worldly-ways teacher said, "If a subject is complex enough to defy our existing methods of expression, then a new mathematics must be devised to describe it." I was lucky to know him—a kind soul in a wicked place. Wish he was along right now. "Poetry was made for this; it expresses relatable feelings in shrewdly considered, artfully crafted ways. Composing poetry requires a deep consideration of every element that something could be made up of. For a ruler, the practice of poetry enhances the ability to evaluate whatever presents itself, in a brisk manner, with the faculty of subtle analytic skills in constant practice. These skills are as follows—"*

Kordas blinked himself alert with some effort. Apparently, he hadn't moved a jot, not even breathing. He spoke aloud with a hint of a smile, "That kind of night, is it? The kind of night when anything feels possible, and we're just lucky to be there for it." He felt inexplicably embarrassed about letting his thoughts be so intense right now. "When you feel like both a catalyst of, and a witness for, whatever would unfold. Like when we were young—when Love was a fact, heroes got scars, and the power of Want was supreme."

Also, your mind will spin around in your skull for a while now, thank you. It felt as if he latched onto every fleeting concept in his mind, and then consistently dove *too* deep pursuing its nature. He needed to snap out of it before it exhausted him. *It's difficult to just stop oneself from thinking. Fear, danger, and horror can do it, but I'll go too far in thinking about those sorts of things if I start now. Spellcasting discipline can do it, though. Especially ritual spellwork, because there's an order to when and where to build with each gesture, calling, steadying, simmering, linking, partitioning—no, stop, you're going too deep again.*

A King, alone in a garden, considering his people's well-being under moonlight. This could not get any more storylike. It's as if I'm setting the scene, in a book or a play.

Which I might as well be.

And it was a pleasant setting for it, a garden, once wilderness, coaxed into fine yields by the hands of people who, twenty years ago, could never have predicted their fates going this way. *Well, maybe some could. There's always a tale about some folk or other who can tell the future, though I doubt I've ever met any. That seems like deities' purview to me. Imagine if gods could see the future, and know what would be needed by their followers—what would they do with that? Would they make that which was needed? Would they bother to? Do they work to prevent tragedy for their followers—things the followers would never learn about? Do we beg for help not knowing that the Powers we pray to already protect us, and maybe that's more than we deserve?*

Kordas stood slowly from the bench and started walking. These garden paths were laid out for efficiency rather than overt decoration, much like old Valdemar's manor gardens. With a very little stretch of the imagination, he might have thought himself home.

Not home now, he corrected himself. But he couldn't help that the word still conjured a manor he no longer lived in, gardens he no longer roamed, pastures that no longer fed his horses. It had been home for most of his life.

Although nobody was there with him physically, Kordas said aloud, for drama's sake, "And in dreams, I still find myself there."

I can't believe I actually thought that would sound good. My poetry's awful, and I know it. Hah! Nobody harmed, though.

"I should be more careful about my mind wandering, Jonaton would say. It's too little to be out alone!"

He didn't pick a path, but his ambling was in a direction just the same. He let that internal pull lead him—out of the gardens, and across the river, giving polite greetings as he passed the guards and other Palace denizens who worked the dark hours. Lythe Shadowdancer was surely awake and working at something at this hour. Preceded by his "watchdog," Kordas strolled through the night breeze, over the rushing river, and into the hilled, treed field where he and his mages had consulted with each other earlier that day. His horses blew at him with mild alarm until they recognized his scent, before relaxing back into a hip-shot doze. It occurred to him where he was headed, though it hadn't really been a conscious thought until he was two-thirds there. He eeled his way into that now-familiar grove, careful to avoid night-spun webs, and found himself in the center of a beautiful circle of moonlight. The place looked to outward eyes as enchanted as it was to mage-sight—and brighter.

That moonlight. Nothing else like it.

After a moment, Kordas stretched, and his manic, analytic thinking fell into a more orderly state. For half a minute, he emptied his mind as if preparing for a Great Working. Night-birds sang, and owls sounded off somewhere deep in the field, punctuated by a couple of Palace dogs howling to that magnificent moon. He walked widdershins around the clearing's perimeter, resuming his earlier talk aimed at no one. Speaking aloud helped his thinking, because of course it forced concepts into words. And he felt like he was freer to do so alone. Away from a desk, and expectant faces, he could be more honest with himself—and this may as well have been a hermit's mountaintop for all the solitude he felt. He spoke with what, for him, was simple honesty. He wasn't selling anything.

"I hadn't wanted to be a King. Well. Everyone wants to be a King at some point, but what I mean is, I didn't set out to be a King. I wanted my titles, because I was the best suited to be in charge, and I'd been educated at length in how to use them. I was careful with ambition, unless it aligned with looking after our people better. So, the end result was . . . now I'm a King. With worthy heirs."

But since he was stuck with the crown, he couldn't have

asked for better heirs than his three lads . . . *Restil was immensely helpful today. Like all days, really. He's a Valdemar to the core. Well, so are the other boys, aside from Hakkon's little wobble.* It felt like they were *nothing* like the increasingly vile tyrants that had worn the Wolf Crown. And he was only getting older, while they were getting smarter and stronger, so quickly.

And that was when a particular too-familiar twinge of misgiving hit him again, this time with force. And finally, *finally,* the unease, the actual fear that had been lurking emerged, and gave itself a name that he felt in his chest even before it formed a word.

Time.

He could not fight time. He was certain that, while he might not be the best King, he was at least a King who kept the welfare of his *people* ahead of his own. While he lived, there would be no tyrants on this throne. And Restil was of the same cut as he was.

Restil despises tyranny, and won't emulate any traits that the Emperor and his cronies practiced. He is considerate, responsible, and vigilant. So that's . . . one generation covered.

"But what about Restil's heirs, and his heirs' heirs? What about usurpers, and manipulators, and . . ."—he paused in his steps to look to the west, where the presence of the Pelagirs seemed to loom like a storm's ominous darkness—"things we can't even *conceive* of now?"

He resumed walking, rubbed at his beard, and laid things out for the night to hear. "We are just people, self-interested, distractible, and flawed. That nature isn't changeable, so Valdemar's future has to be considered from that basis. Any person, given any power, will drift from compassion. Purpose meanders, rot of the soul sets in—and being people, we all tire, and regret, and wear down. The brighter, compassionate things take hard work, but evil somehow *always* manages to make itself easy. Neglect is easy. Indifference. It's too easy to turn into a monster."

With those words, he stepped over the threshold to meet where he'd begun. The first circle around the clearing was complete.

Kordas's memory pressured him with the recollection of the monsters, human and otherwise, that he had witnessed himself—and been subject to. Slavering beasts and lethal traps were barely notable next to the complex, insidious, weakness-baiting horrors he'd personally undergone at the hands of other people. In the Empire, nobility wasn't noble. Expedience, self-aggrandizement, profiteering, domination, conspiracy, and influence had set the tempo for the wicked music he was supposed to dance to, composed by true human virtuosos of misery.

"And cruelty with a likable smile is still cruelty," he murmured.

Himself included—he knew he was a good man, but then again, wouldn't that always be the primary delusion of the truly lost? Numerous times, he'd chosen murder and injury over alternatives that—even though he *still* could not think of many—he felt *could* have been possible if he had only been clever enough. He'd put criminals to death personally, taken more game than he had to, and wasted opportunities for his people because the Plan might have been revealed to the Empire. And after the evacuation? He'd cut Valdemarans "free" over questionable loyalty, in overwhelmingly hostile territory—it might as well have been death by exposure, staked out for animals. He split his people up, when group stability became too tenuous for him. He freed his people from the Empire, but made them wholly dependent upon what he provided.

Maybe that is why this crown isn't such a comfortable fit. My people were forced into a position in which they were powerless against either the Empire or the unknown, and they made a monarch of the man who did it to them. I'm not who they think I am—or what they want me to be. What else can someone give when their best wasn't enough? I should have done more than this. Better than this.

Self-loathing for not having been smarter or quicker, and the aching need to feel heroic—those were a nasty combination he hated in himself. It seemed like before he could even spell his name, *that* feeling had beaten upon him—the feeling that he just wasn't clever enough, or smart enough, or good enough. It didn't even leave him when there was a new crown screwed onto his head. Logically, he should have taken the coronation as a message that, apparently, he was doing just fine. But here he was again, wracked by self-persecution.

Kordas walked a little more quickly. "That was the Imperial way. I couldn't help but feel inferior in the Empire, when the Empire ensured that was what we were taught. The Empire was structured to beat down truly feeling good about ourselves, so we'd be more productive. And manageable. Useful. Usable."

He was at a steady walking pace now. He hit his stride and took up a lecturing rhythm, throwing hand gestures like he was teaching. "It'll happen here, too. The Empire didn't start that way—it *became* that way, because of what people *are*. We aren't immune to being human just because we fled tyranny, and history shows that every age had smart people who did stupid things. Like me. I'm not the smartest man there's ever been, and I need to come up with an *edge*. A way for us to not fall into Empire. And I don't have it."

With that, he completed his second circle. Kordas ruffled his hair for a few seconds, trying to shed the body heat that made him sweat like a novice firecaster. His frustration pushed him into an unexpected shout of genuine anguish.

"Valdemar has earned *better* than me!"

Kordas took a few deep, quick breaths.

"I feel beaten. Some things are . . . just too complex for me to solve. I've talked this over with the Council, with Jonaton,

Beltran, Isla, even Silvermoon . . . I pored over history, and only came up with what *not* to do. Something good enough for Valdemar . . . I think it's beyond me."

He walked silently, unable to form speech for thirty heartbeats.

"I've agonized every day for years now, being wise with our resources and keeping morale up, but I concentrated upon *being*, only looking at the scope of seasons, not centuries. My resourcefulness has declined. I'm weary, and it feels like my wits aren't what they were. I couldn't figure out anything but orders, laws, and traditions. Treaties and deals, holidays and awards. Those could—those *can* make a passable enough monarchy, for a while. An adequate one, but I want Valdemar to be much more than adequate. For the stability of Valdemar, and a mere *touch* of happiness, it makes more *sense* to be static—to withdraw, fortify, limit expansion, enforce strict be-havior, and be a tiny city-state, isolationist and wary. Now we're a monarchy, but . . . a static one, in a land that *requires* adaptability. It isn't enough to just survive. We need to inno-vate. I want Valdemar to be extraordinary, and to *last*. But here we are, a juicy little prize surrounded by danger from all directions, and we're fragile."

Kordas stood upon his beginning point, completing the third circle.

"I swear I didn't come here to pray. It may be that I'm not a very pious man, but I've felt that any Power is already busy enough without me calling. I feel like it's better to solve issues *myself* instead of assuming a divine Power will think I'm so extra special that They will get *right to* whatever bothers me. But—maybe this *is* a prayer, after all. I don't know what to do now, except . . . tell You. You may not have even noticed us, but maybe a King declaring his heart counts for something special, like it does in stories. If my surrender would help Valdemar prosper, take me. I'll be a brief King, if You will befriend this tiny nation—I'll go with You right now. Truthfully, I'd prefer *not* to give my life, because my people would grieve for me—and they've been through too much already. I'll die for Valdemar, but I'd rather live for it."

Kordas felt physical and emotional exhaustion coming quickly for him, but he was intense, even fiery in his declarations. This was more than just the sum of his heart, it was all of his oration skill, flung toward the gods.

"This world is short-sighted, savage, merciless, unless we choose to act in mercy. I believe that a spirit of wisdom, rationality, and kindness can grow here, in this Kingdom's character, and propagate from Valdemar into the world. I believe that we are not *here* to wallow in mediocrity, we are here to *do* amazing things. That's all I really hope for—a wise way for *us* to do things, ourselves. This is not a plea for gods to do it *for* us. Just—to help Valdemar prosper by its nature, and do better after its mistakes. If I shouted my *greatest* prayer—to anyone, to everyone—*this* would be it."

Kordas pushed out one last demand, his voice growing louder.

"And—if we're not alive to change the world for the better, why are we even *here*?"

Kordas found himself shouting at the sky with the moon directly overhead, and he forced a more relaxed pose upon himself and clenched his breathing in to a deep pant in the deepening quiet. "Haaah. Ah. I didn't mean for that to come out so—strongly. It's how I feel. I'm not shouting at you, but my frustration with myself . . . makes my judgment slip."

A few moments after his explanation, he was aware of something strange happening around him. He felt himself poised between worlds, between potentials—an intuitive sense that his understanding of the world might change very soon. It felt a lot like dizziness.

Kordas caught an unfamiliar male voice echoing as if in a

concert hall, or far away. "I'm sure. He *could* do this without me, but he's a show I don't want to miss."

And then he heard—

Silence.

Leaves whispering in the breeze, birdsong, the sounds of the river and the noise of Haven were all gone. Silence enveloped the little clearing, a complete silence that made the hair on his neck rise. But he didn't stop speaking; if anything, he put more feeling into it.

Kordas wracked his brain, reciting a list of appropriately honorificked Names, Powers, and Deities. Kordas *had* a list to recite because of course he'd noted them so many times over the past years that they were imprinted on him. He felt a bit lost—this wasn't at all how he'd rehearsed his Greatest Prayer going—and frustrated, because he was certain his exhaustively edited notes sounded *much* better than what he'd actually said, and that he'd blown it by just gushing from his heart. He put some of himself into each entreaty; this was not reciting a list, this was respect given to Powers to give favor. After the sixteenth name, he paused.

He wasn't alone anymore. His watchdog light shone upon Jonaton, dressed in his nightclothes and boots, who elbow-waved to him from the path back toward the Palace. In his arms was a black cat twitching his tail in agitation—the venerable Sydney-You-Asshole, darting his eyes around the clearing as if tracking moths. There passed a moment of pure, distilled awkwardness.

"So . . . ah. Doing some moon-work, then?" Jonaton inquired.

Kordas could unclench with his dear friend, and talk about anything, but he couldn't quite cover his embarrassment at being witnessed. Sydney stared at him with kitten-like wide eyes. Kordas twigged to what Jonaton was doing, and the awkwardness passed. Barely. "Something like. Having a word with the Powers."

Jonaton slowly placed Sydney on the ground, whereupon the black cat sat down and started chewing the grass. "Nice night for it, then." He made conversational gestures indicating the moon, the circular path trampled in the clearing, and Kordas.

Kordas, in turn, nodded in an exaggerated way, to reply that he understood that Jonaton was spellcasting with those gestures, and that his consent was given. "Best night for it. Aye."

Kordas figured that while he had been caught up in pacing, Jonaton had probably scanned the area a dozen ways before even making himself visible, and had no doubt come at best speed when some alarm he'd conjured to watch the grove had been tripped. That meant that what he did now was probably threat assessment, innocuous to the outward eye as idle chat, but rigorous under the surface.

"Glad I dressed up for it, then," Jonaton replied agreeably, hiding further spellcasting behind a set of bored-conversation rubbing of hands and picking at insects. "You feeling good, out here, kinging around?"

Kordas exhaled gustily. "Just feel a bit raw, and that's fine. It's fine. I don't mind this at all." He fanned himself by flapping his open shirt. "I was losing it back there, and I'm unsteady right now, but this is the best I've got." He gestured at himself, head to toe. "This is what I had to work with. I need to get back to it." Kordas figured that ought to—vaguely—mollify Jonaton enough to stand down. The interruption had been opportune, truth be told, because he needed a breather amidst so much hard-summoned honesty and inner turmoil. Now was the time to end his litany. Kordas turned back to his prayer.

". . . Epona, and the Tayledras's Star-Eyed, wise Kal'enel. We are humble, and hopeful, that you find favor with us here." And as the silence deepened, the light in the clearing slowly increased, a strange, clear, thin light that seemed to illuminate every leaf and blade of grass—as if literally silvering the world. The feeling of Presence grew until it was nearly as unbearable as the air pressure of a sudden gale-change—and yet, at the same time, it was unthreatening.

With that light came not just the feeling of peace, but the *surety* of peace. A growing, gentle joy surrounded and enveloped him. His eyes closed, his troubles allayed for the moment, and tears welled upon his face. He hadn't *planned* to invoke the attention of deities this night, but here it was. This was *right*. This was *good*.

He felt singular and self-aware of his fleeting lifespan, conscious of being a tiny mortal object hoping to live through the unfathomable divine power he was surrounded by. He intuited that this wash of power that blended him into it, thorough to his smallest fiber, was a deity's equivalent of an interested glance. He had no measure of time for how long he was examined for his worth, from forethought to deepest instinct. He felt thankful that he couldn't feel himself being judged—he didn't think he could bear that, and would just dissolve completely. He was intent upon remembering every bodily sensation he was experiencing—if he was going to be examined, well, he'd give the courtesy of studying right back. A disturbance distracted him for a moment, but he mentally waved the distraction away. Unclear voices—one of them Jonaton's—were barely heard, murmuring. Apparently others gathered here, too.

Kordas felt no threat here; if anything he felt as if the entire area was protected.

Embraced.

Steps behind him jarred him again—and he opened his eyes to see that Restil and Beltran, each spotlit by the watchdog, stood midway between where Jonaton remained and Kordas's own chosen spot. The only other sound in the clearing was the rumble of Sydney's purrs.

I'm not doing *this. There is divine attention here, and it feels like I reached—Someone. This—feels like an Audience.*

With whom, though? With what—what Power could this be? And who am I to Them?

He faltered. The light dimmed for just a moment, but when he gazed around he caught approving, encouraging expressions from Beltran and Restil, instead of worry or dismay. That was enough to bolster his confidence.

They'd stop me if this was wrong.

He pulled himself up, and set his stance.

This is what I am made of, and I will pretend nothing. In the eyes of the divine, I present myself, with the truth of what I feel.

The light strengthened, and so did his resolve. It was time to—present his case? No, to beg a boon.

"I, Kordas, King of Valdemar, beseech Your goodwill and consideration, for the benefit of my people. We have come through terror and tragedy. Countless dangers await our every step, in every direction—above, around, and below. I fear we, as a people, will fall to predation, to our worst natures or to others'. We are mortal, and fallible, struggling amidst hardships we barely understand. We are weak in this new land, with but a single distant ally, the Tayledras. Threats will come that I fear we will not endure without divine help. The wonder that Valdemar *could* be will be lost, if we stay this vulnerable in our Kingdom's infancy." Kordas lowered his voice to a more personal expression of his feelings, beyond his diplomatic nature.

"I brought these refugees here as best I could, but *I* won't last. I know I will give my all to be a good man, and a good leader for them. I know my son will do the same. But what of his children's children's children? What if our line ends tomorrow? I do not want what happened to the Empire to befall them! Will you help Valdemar to be as magnificent as I believe it can be, and safeguard the lives and well-being of my people?"

He was not answered by words as such, but instead by an all-enveloping sense of *You have asked the right question.*

And then, out of the light, spun wonder.

It took his breath away. He felt as if he was trembling on the brink of something momentous, something that would change everything.

The light gave birth to sparkling motes of power that danced and flowed in three ever-changing forms so beautiful they made him gasp. He stared, mesmerized, as the lights coalesced into pillars, then between one breath and the next took full shape.

Three of the most gorgeous horses he had ever seen in his life stood in the middle of the clearing. Silver-white, silver-hooved, blue-eyed, they were incandescent with magical and spiritual power, and he found himself stepping forward, hand outstretched, longing to touch the arch of the middle one's neck, and aghast at his own presumption. Restil and Beltran each reached out to one of the beings of their own, who stepped forward to meet them, with the sound of perfectly tuned temple bells coincident with each equine step.

Kordas felt a lurch in his belly, and a non-sound akin to a massive door closing, far away. But that didn't stop him from continuing to move, as if in a dream, without mass or substance, until his hand lay gently on the center being's silken coat and muscles. He looked up into those sapphire-blue eyes. . . .

:Hello, Kordas. I am Ardatha.:

He heard the voice in his mind as though spoken by some giant in a great hall tuned for music. It had a tone like no other mind-voice he'd experienced before, with a sense of depth and reach to it. The stallion's lips certainly weren't moving, but it had to be his. He was distracted for the briefest of moments by the sound of a purr as loud as thunder, and the flicker of black against the shimmering foliage as Sydney unhurriedly walked off into the trees. The rich voice in Kordas's mind spoke with a nearly palpable, honest intensity.

:If you will have me, I Choose you to share my destiny with. For Valdemar.:

Kordas became aware that he was walking, and the white—well, it wasn't a horse—the *being* at his side had been talking to him for some time.

And he was nowhere he recognized.

Silver light surrounded them—"silver" came to mind because there wasn't any dust in the "air" to identify a light source by, only reflections from surfaces, and shadows were skewed as if light came from the two of *them*. They were on a path with no discernible ground around it, laid out in silvery sand, and outside of a circle of clear air around the two of them, there was nothing to be seen but silver mist.

He stopped. This was—so strange. Not at all dreamlike. He should have been in a panic, but instead, there was a deep sense of calm. And his mind had never felt so sharp. More than that, there was a deep sense of rightness here, and an ethereal joy that sparkled inside him like fireflies in the darkness.

Longtime habits of suspicion in the face of good appearances interrupted his reverie. *Hold up. This is far too perfect. Exactly what someone like me would dream of, presented with orchestrated, encompassing pleasantness, removed from any familiar location. I'm being set up.*

The being stopped at the same time he did. "Where are we?" he asked. *I should be in a panic. I'm not in a panic. Why am I not in a panic?*

Well, you dolt. You were *praying. Maybe you are not in a panic because this is your answer.*

:Ah, you woke up.: The creature—Ardatha?—nodded his head.

"I did—and where am I?" he repeated. The sense of *safety* and *calm* only deepened. *Surely this isn't some form of afterlife. . . .*

:My fellows borrowed this place from Kal'enel with her permission. It's where her Swordsworn train. This place will allow us to talk—and we have a great deal to talk about!—and yet your body will rest as peacefully as if you were in bed.:

He had no idea what Ardatha was talking about. Until a moment later, when he did. He knew who the goddess Kal'enel was, of course. But now he knew that the Swordsworn were Shin'a'in, and the Shin'a'in were once part of the same nation as the Tayledras and—

Well, it was as if several history books had just lodged in his head, and for a moment he reeled, disoriented. He'd used magic to give himself languages and other important information straight out of someone else's memory before this, but never so much, so quickly.

He steadied himself with one hand on Ardatha's shoulder. The creature didn't seem to mind. In fact, he seemed to welcome the touch. "What did you say you are?"

:We decided on the name "Companions." But the full what is why you and I are here. We're the answer to your plea to the gods. We have been centuries in the making. And I promise you that we are in no way the kind of answer you expected.:*

He looked the creature over; if this was an "answer from the gods," then the gods had created the most perfect horse he had ever set eyes on. Even his Valdemar Golds were a pale imitation of this beauty. Still. A . . . horse?

:We have a lot to talk about,: repeated Ardatha. *:Do you need some time?:*

That simple, commonplace question made him stop in his tracks and take stock of his surroundings. The mist seemed endless, the expanse of silver sand really didn't have anything interesting about it, and if this was, indeed, a place where a god brought people to train them—in fighting, presumably—it didn't need to be scenic.

Do I have any reason to disbelieve this creature? Well . . . no. *Everything* about this place screamed "you are safe here" to his senses, material, magical, and mental. And not in a way that would have raised alarm bells in him. Under the Emperor's tutelage (although he had faked being a lot less powerful, magically, than he actually was), he had learned scores of ways in which he could be magically tricked, and this place matched nothing he had ever trained for or heard of. Rather than lulling his senses, this place had them all wide awake and energized. Even his land-sense was telling him, "This is a safe and sacred space . . . although it's not 'land' as you know it."

:Would you prefer to stop for a while? Sit down if you need to,: Ardatha said, kindly.

"I need to. This is a lot to understand. If I even *can*," he said.

:Excellent.:

The sand rose up in six columns, which each split into six, and then each split again. They darted and wove into an elegant reclining couch shape. Gingerly he took a seat, and his "throne" rose so that he was eye to eye with Ardatha.

"This is nice. I need to figure out how to do this," he muttered. Ardatha snorted.

:Let me begin with the very basics of the . . . Way of things now. The Powers are more numerous than you know, and gods are made up of Powers. The gods do not directly interfere in mortal matters beyond a set level, though they easily could. This is a matter of a truce among all the gods, light and dark, good and evil. Exceptions, for emergencies, are negotiated. If it ever came to a god breaking that truce and striking down

mortals directly, there would be retaliation wholesale, and this world would not survive.:

He nodded. This wasn't exactly new to him, since it was written into *several* holy books he had read . . . but to hear it confirmed by an intensely supernatural creature gave him a chill, accompanied by a strange kind of joy, as if he had been entrusted with something very important.

:However, under certain circumstances—like, in your case, exactly the right, completely unselfish plea at the right time— Instruments are permitted. We are Instruments. We are not avatars—those are mortals who become the physical vessels for gods. We are mortal, like you. We have free will, like you. We are here to advise and help—but that help is mostly limited to what a similarly talented human could do in the same circumstances. We cannot see the future—that is not for us to do—but . . . we are good at guiding. Think of us as a sort of compass. We will always point true north.:

He found himself nodding, and stopped. A strong thought from his doubt and fear said, *This is not just pretty, this is seductive—all this is* engineered *to appeal to you. Seduction, challenge, majesty, mystery, promise? Hope? This is a set-up. This is too perfect for them to just intuit what would appeal to you—they must have already been in your mind, Kordas. They are* in your mind!

As is the way of fears, "they" had no firm definition; "they" was the sense of "others" as a foreboding force of judgment and power over him. These thoughts threatened him on a self-awareness level. Could he unravel from this? *How can I get a true confirmation of anything if they are manipulating my mind? The spectacle of this is fantastic, but a show is a show, and a show is a performer's best weapon. If they can play my senses this well—how could I—*

:How can you be certain I am telling the truth? Ask your friend Rose.:

And before Kordas could react to that extraordinary statement, the mist swirled and parted before—well, it looked like more mist. A little more solid, a kind of pale blue in color, and moving toward him in a slow vortex.

"Kordas!" said a very familiar voice, and one he had never expected to hear again. A pair of intensely blue eyes opened at the top of the vortex and blinked at him in a friendly manner. "Ardatha invited me here to reassure you that he is truthful. The Companions were not crafted to lie to you. I am not sure that they can."

"Rose—" he began, and then found himself choking up, with a lump in his throat and unexpected tears burning his cheeks. He covered his mouth with a curled hand.

"I know you miss us, and not just because of all the things we did for you," Rose said teasingly, her voice warm and loving. "But don't worry. We're not leaving your new Kingdom. And not only because we owe you our freedom. We *like* you. We *might* even love some of you," she added, sounding more mischievous. "What you are trying to do—this seems like a good home for truth. So we're staying!"

:Forgive me, my dear, but I have a lot to discuss with my Chosen, and there is a limit to the amount of time he can stay here.:

"Of course," Rose agreed, and a tendril of mist brushed the tears from Kordas's cheek. "You made me seriously consider corporeality for some time. Just to be closer. Pet Sydney's children for me."

And with that, she faded back into the ambient mist and was gone.

Kordas sniffed, and dried his eyes on his sleeve. *Huh. I'm material enough to cry. And have my eyes itch. This seems . . . very substantial.*

But if they control my perception, they could *have made me think that was Rose—and had her say to trust them.*

:Oh, Kordas. This is a show, a work of art, and true expression unbridled, as a moment of learning in a benevolent plot. I can tell what you feel, and I can't be flustered by your thoughts. I can forgive more than you might imagine, and I won't seek power through what you confide.:

"What exactly *are* you, Ardatha?" he asked—the first question to come into his head.

:Well . . . that's two questions, actually. The first of us are . . . I suppose you would call us pure spirits, who were never mortal. Whole creations, designed by a master of the craft. When there are enough of us here, in Valdemar, then we will begin mating and birthing, and those new Companions will be those who have once been mortal.: The Companion shrugged gracefully. *:The Highest Ones believe that ultimately it will be better having those who understand humanity from having* been *human as your Companions, than those of us who only look on, inexperienced with your aspirations.:*

"So . . . you're *new.* And that's not your natural form?"

:This is a very useful form. The unenlightened will see a horse and discount us. By design, we can travel faster and farther than a horse, and without exhaustion, giving you a mount that can cover great distances in little time. We are obviously not as fragile, unreliable, or as easy to frighten as a horse, and will take you wherever you ask us to, regardless of the danger.: Ardatha shook his head. *:We will fight beside you, carry you, and if need be, die beside you.:*

Kordas almost choked. *Oh, that's not ominous at all. But— let's test things a little.*

"Can I see your true form?" he asked, now prodded by his insatiable curiosity.

Ardatha's head came up with alarm. *:I don't think that is a good idea.:*

"Indulge me," he insisted. *Because when else am I ever going to get to see the true form of an Instrument of the gods?* He couldn't help himself. Maybe it was the feeling of complete physical safety here. Maybe it was just that he couldn't help but poke at things that perhaps he shouldn't. And maybe he should take the Greater Spirit's advice.

Too late.

:Very well,: said the Companion.

And a long, long minute later Kordas found himself convulsing on the ground, mind flooded with—too much. Just too much. It was like a deep intake of breath that simply never stopped—an inhale that persisted even when the body could bear no more. Kordas was *too* aware. And terrified, awestruck, and overwhelmed with wonder. Before him was an immense . . . *presence,* and a light too bright even to contemplate—and he wasn't seeing it through physical eyes. Inside the light were patterns, wheels of language and geometry, puzzles containing plazas and landscapes of unfolding details. They in turn divided into knots of magical energy, casting out and grasping fields and frequencies he couldn't interpret, and each of them opened into even more complexity. Clusters of concepts were linked by shining cords akin to lute strings, most of them extending into distances well beyond his confused perception. And yet they were all *here.* Embodied.

Kordas clutched at his sides and steadied himself. *This . . . was a bad idea,* was all he could manage to think.

Ardatha's "voice" said, *:You were very brave to try,:* but in a tone that meant, *I warned you. I did warn you. :There is a reason why we say "fear not," when we appear to mortals,:* Ardatha said, sounding just the tiniest bit irritated. *:We have a penchant for theatrics. We could perhaps appear as a harmless small animal, or ordinary object, but instead we appear as something dramatic, and then say "Fear not!" just after we've freshly terrified someone.:* Ardatha sounded amused, but followed up with a gentle, *:You did ask for it. And I did as you asked of me.:* Kordas felt sunburned, from his skin to his marrow. The light dimmed, and Kordas cautiously looked up. The Companion was back to his horse form.

"Point taken," he managed to gasp. He levered himself up off the sand and cautiously climbed back upright into the throne. "Now, this is a lot, but we have a purpose. Brief me on all these things we need to talk about."

:Excellent. Let's begin.:

Restil reeled a little and balanced himself with a palm on Darshay's shoulder. The transition from what the Companion called "the Moonpaths" to the real world was a bit like being suddenly very drunk, and then suddenly far too sober. But that wasn't what had him so disoriented that the world whirled around him. It was the sense that his head was stuffed full of a lifetime's worth of information, and right now it was all swirling around in there in no sort of order—like learning a hundred subjects by alternating one sentence at a time. But beneath it all was something else: powerful, deep emotions, and a sense of connection to Darshay that transcended anything he had ever read about or imagined. He clung to that as incoherent, random bits of thought and information tumbled him like a leaf on the wind.

:Steady, Chosen. Give it a moment.: Darshay's Mindvoice in his head—it gave him such a rush of joy that for a moment he could scarcely bear it. Until Darshay had Chosen him, he had never really realized how *lonely* he had been. Yes, he had

friends, almost all of whom had been his friends since childhood when they were all pages . . . but he was always the leader, always the one everyone else depended on for answers, and it had been like that from roughly the time they first settled here. As if first being a Valdemar, and then being himself, had made them decide he was their leader, his friends deferred to him. Rather like the way the rest of the Kingdom had decided his father should be King. And it seemed like betraying their faith to face them with anything other than confidence. That went doubly when he was acting as Crown Prince. Yes, this was exactly the same situation his father was in, with even more pressure, but his father had his mother. Restil hadn't had *anyone*.

Until now. Until now, when he had looked into those blue eyes and knew that he would never, ever be alone again.

That steadied him, even though his head was swimming.

Steadied him enough to notice that although it had been past midnight when he found himself drawn to the grove his father had brought him to earlier today, it was now dawn, and the dawn was glorious.

Delicate, transparent spears of pale gold streaked the pale blue sky, touching the bottoms of the few clouds with gilt. Still in shadow, across the river the Palace stood, blue-gray against the luminous blue of the sky. Not cold and oppressive, but a bulwark against danger, as it was meant to be. The gardens and lawns stretched out between here and the Palace, painted in the same blue shadows as the building, and interrupted only by the silver and splash of the river.

There wasn't so much as a hint of breeze, and flower-and-herb scent hung heavily in the air. Dew had formed on the tips of the grass stems, and the pearly droplets gleamed in the growing light. The horses didn't seem the least disturbed by this activity in the corner of their field. Most still drowsed, and instead of the steady munching sounds that Restil was used to out here, the air trembled with birdsong. It almost seemed as if he, his father, and Beltran were the only people awake in the entire world.

He felt alive in a way he had never been before; every leaf and grass-stem glowed faintly with the energies of magic and life. All his senses were preternaturally sharp, and his body felt as full of sensation as his mind was full of thoughts and information. He wanted to laugh. He wanted to cry. He wanted to leap on Darshay's bare back and ride like the wind to the end of the world and back again. And instead, he just stood there, paralyzed with joy and delight.

Movement caught his eye, the movement of people coming this way on the other side of the river, and with a start, he realized that people had emerged from the Palace and the wall, dressed as if they had just thrown on whatever was to hand, and they were moving toward the bridge to this field as if they were enchanted.

He jumped, startled, as a white form brushed gently past him, coming from the Grove behind him. Then another. And another.

Exquisite white horses, silver-hooved and sapphire-eyed, drifted across the flower-studded grass to meet the enraptured humans moving across the bridge toward them.

Wait—not all of them. Some of the Companions emerging from the Grove drifted off away, deeper into the meadow, to join the horses grazing there.

:They will Choose later. When their Heralds are ready to be Chosen.:

"So . . . we're to be called Heralds, now?" he managed.

:You first three are Kordas King Valdemar, Crown Prince Restil, and Herald Beltran. Only one person can be King. Only one can be Crown Prince. But anyone can be a Herald—and to be sure, at the moment there are no other Royal Heralds in the Kingdom except Beltran, so it will be easy to redefine the word.: Darshay tossed her head and looked exceedingly pleased with her own logic. *:Once we arrived and Ardatha*

Chose him, your father helped to define what a Herald would be, though he doesn't likely remember it now. He felt . . . very alone, like you, and was overwhelmed. When they emerged from their communion, we all understood what being a Herald would entail.:

He ventured to drape an arm over her shoulder. It felt right, and he sensed her pleasure in the contact. Slowly, his exultant joy subsided to something a lot easier to maintain. For a moment, he felt regret, but not for long. Being at the absolute peak of pleasure was . . . exhausting.

Together they watched the first meeting of Companion and—well, Herald—play out over and over in front of them. He was delighted to see that his mother was one of the first—and unsurprised a moment later to see Delia staring rapturously into the eyes of a particularly athletic-looking young stallion.

"Not my brothers Jon and Hakkon?" he ventured.

:For our purposes, now, we need responsible adults, who will be able to defend themselves at any time. Hakkon and Jon will be Chosen, unless by their own actions they render themselves unsuitable, but not now. You Heralds will be in danger . . . rather too often for us to risk a child. We will not Choose children until there is a pathway to training them and allowing them to become adults in safety, under wise care.:

For the rest, the people meeting their own Companions were a mix of high and low: at least one guard, a smattering of young nobles, a few Palace servants, one of Grim's best stablemen, a gardener, a huntsman, three apprentice mages. They were an apparently-random mix of complexions and genders, and Restil figured that was so there could be a voice for everyone, from their own perspective.

:Most of them have actual or latent mage-Gift,: said Darshay. *:We believe that for now, you will mostly need mages, since an expert mage is as effective as a full squad of trained guards. Being Chosen will bring that out now, and being paired with one of us will mean we can guide them as their*

own teachers cannot. The ones that don't have pure Magic have some form of Mind-Magic, and we'll bring that out, too, and teach them how to use their Gifts, although your mother and Delia need no teaching in mage-craft and Fetching. They are masters of their Gifts. All of you have Mindspeech now, at least with your Companion, and possibly more.:

"Well . . . if we didn't, my conversations would be very one-sided," he replied. She snorted, and bumped him with her shoulder.

:There are drawbacks to this form. For one thing, you Heralds are going to have to speak for us in the Council. I would suggest recruiting your religious leaders to help. By now I think you will find that they all know something momentous has happened, and to be frank, acknowledging that we are Instruments only helps bolster their own credibility. They'll be happy to help.:

This was clearly not a mere observation. "So that's my job to bring up at the Council meeting that will *surely* be over breakfast?" he hazarded. "And make sure our religious leaders verify we haven't all dropped into some terrible deception?"

:Exactly.:

Well, that certainly deflated his euphoria—though not entirely. There was still a part of him, deep inside, that was speechless with wonder.

"Will I have to bring a wooden cutout of you to the Council Chamber to represent you?"

Darshay laughed in his mind, and he took it as a good sign that he could joke amidst these momentous events.

:Will you make its mouth move when you speak for me?:

Restil laughed out loud. He hadn't expected that joke to work at all, much less that he'd get one back. At least there was one thing: his all-night sojourn in the wherever-it-was had left him feeling as if he'd had the soundest sleep of his life. He had never felt better, and more able to take on challenges, in his life. "I'm ready," he said. And then his stomach growled.

"As long as there's *breakfast* as well as a *meeting*," he amended.

Kordas listened with no small amount of awe as Beltran—*Beltran!*—gave a recitation of what had just happened in the Grove with the grace, poise, and articulation of a Bard. He held them all spellbound, including Kordas, Restil, and Isla, who had actually been there.

As for the not-small cluster of religious leaders, who had all turned up at this meeting as if they had all been alerted already, they were all nodding along with him, looking serious and portentous. So were all of the Old Men, who had somehow squeezed their skinny behinds into the Chamber. It was very crowded in here, and the Councilors mostly looked as if they were torn between feeling outnumbered and feeling thunderstruck at having an actual deific intervention happen in their own backyard. And, further, Beltran had implied that it could have been from any, or many, Powers and gods—no doubt to keep partisan conflicts from brewing early and ensure the clerics' best behavior.

Hmm. Ardatha said that the Powers and gods have treaties, and negotiate amongst Themselves. So, this may well be the work of many. I'll run with that as a baseline.

:I approve of that,: Ardatha responded in his thoughts.

Beltran finally concluded, and sat down, looking both uncharacteristically determined and a little astonished at his own temerity.

If this is what being Chosen did to him . . . I'm impressed.

:Now,: Ardatha prompted. *:Call for Restil to speak as soon as the Lord Martial says you need some sort of organization.:*

The Lord Martial cleared his throat in the silence. "Well," he said. "The gods have made their interest abundantly clear . . . but gods are notorious for being careless of details, or expecting petitioners to figure things out for themselves. Surely, we need some sort of organization—"

Kordas in turn cleared his own throat, interrupting him. "I believe the Crown Prince was about to address that," he said.

Restil stood up. He looked amazing—in fact, he looked as good as Beltran did, and as good as Kordas felt. Kordas had been . . . well, near desperation and exhausted right up until the point when Ardatha appeared. Now he felt better than he had since he'd left the Duchy for the Capital.

"The organization will be fairly simple for now; there are only eighteen of us at the moment, and that's manageable without a real hierarchy, just an agreed leader," Restil said smoothly. "Obviously the King is the ultimate authority. Beltran will be his second-in-command. Your King has developed an identity and structure, in concert with the Companions. Beltran's example of service and excellence is why we are going to call ourselves 'Heralds.' He's the only Royal Herald in the Kingdom, so now we will all be Royal Heralds, and he'll be the head of the Heraldic Circle. When there are more of us, we'll refine things, but this will do for now." He cleared his throat slightly.

"I mean no disrespect when I ask the heir this, but what will these Heralds *do*?" asked a Council regular.

We spoke about this earlier, but this is our chance to hear how Restil presents it. He's earned this.

Restil spoke to the entire Council Chamber as if he were at the head of a master's classroom—as the teacher, not a nervous student. "A Herald will be of positive moral and ethical character, of any origin or faith, and they will be educated in disciplines from riding and self-defense to the interpretation of law. Weaponry, protection, customs, and law will be of especial importance to a Herald, who will be an evaluator of situations and resolver of conflicts. Herald-and-Companion pairs will travel swiftly to all stations, farms, and communities in their rounds." That caused some approving rumbles from representatives of underserved and distant subjects.

"This will improve the granularity of our contact with our people, and with the Crown's approval, Heralds shall share their most recent knowledge with those people's representatives in Council. The Companions shall carry Heralds faster than race horses, without tiring. Obliged by their bond with their Chosen, the Heralds' oaths bind the Companions to the interests of Valdemar as well. Heralds will deliver new laws to the peoples' local leaders, act as intermediary judges, and correct injustices that threaten Valdemar. They will speak with authority for the Crown, as needed, subject to later revision, of course. Heralds may accept gifts, but are immune to bribery, by their oath and by their lack of need, and shall be supported by the Crown in all needs."

Some more rumbles were heard, as it dawned on Council members and clergy alike that knowledge would travel far faster than before, both outward and back, without embellishment. Kordas liked that part, because it would mean more precision in resource allocation, and in getting aid in a hurry to where it might be needed.

Restil opened his arms, getting the Chamber's attention anew.

"However! We, Valdemar's Heralds and Companions together, would like our esteemed guests to verify to their satisfaction that there are no dark deceptions going on here—"

Restil didn't even get a chance to finish his sentence. As one—and with indignation!—the religious leaders all proclaimed that dark forces were *not* in play here. He just sat down and let the whole scene play out, because he could not have coached them into a response better suited to convince even the most skeptical of the Council.

There you go, my boy! You read the moment!

The representatives interjected, commented, earnestly harangued, interrupted each other, and all with an intensity that surprised even him. It didn't hurt one bit that they all essentially agreed with each other, and all cited various signs and portents that had awakened every one of them around midnight, and left them sending messages to each other until they all concluded they needed to turn up at the Palace as soon as they'd be let in. In fact, this was the largest demonstration of amity and unity he had *ever* seen out of them.

When the last of them sat down, Wis, Koto, Ceri, and Sai—without prompting—stood up in turn and did essentially the same thing. The only difference between what they did and what the priests, preachers, pastors, and prelates had done was that they didn't speak over each other, and they kept their speeches a great deal shorter.

All the time he "worked the room," as his father called it, Restil was acutely aware of Darshay's presence, how she was hearing and seeing what he heard and saw. And far from being intrusive, it was unspeakably comforting. *I can't imagine even spouses and mates being this close,* was his sudden, intrusive thought—and with that, his first twinge of concern.

:Yes,: agreed Darshay. :*Unavoidable. The Herald-Companion bond is . . . something very primal, and short of one of you doing something unspeakable, it will not be broken. And this means that to some extent, even a mate you love and cherish is going to be left on the outside of that. Nothing is perfect, and that is the greatest flaw in what we have done. In principle, I find it . . . presumptuous is the kindest word. It feels too much to me as if we force a lifebond upon our Chosen. Even if all intentions involved are benevolent, it still feels intrusive to initiate something so life changing. I beg your forgiveness.*:

:Nothing is perfect,: Restil agreed. :This . . . is more than worth it.:

:*I hope that holds true for every Herald,*: Darshay replied soberly. Then her Mindvoice brightened. :*But look at your Councilors! They have conceded on all points!*:

It was true. Rather than the looks of concern and skepticism that had met Kordas's first announcement, now there were nods and expressions of intense concentration as they worked through the ramifications of it all.

"A uniform—and not the usual heraldic tabard," said the Seneschal, unexpectedly speaking his immediate thoughts aloud. "We need a uniform, as quickly as possible. That way people will not see a person on a white horse that *just happens* to look like the ones at the coronation illuminations, a person who may or may not speak with authority. And they won't see someone they used to know up on that white horse and start to ask questions about why he fancies himself so important. They'll see a single unit, something they recognize—it's a uniform with matching Companion—and something they don't— what the uniform conveys. That this isn't just some hodge-podge of random people who don't know what they're doing, elevated by who-knows-what whim of the King. No disrespect intended. This will be known as a *very skilled and specialized group* that has a job, knows how to do it, and will be guaranteed to be impartial doing it. Companions will be linked to Heralds visually that way—the uniform *must* be white! But I don't know about these things—uniforms— sewing—" Now he looked helplessly up and down the table. "Isn't white terribly difficult to keep white?"

Isla and Father Deskain spoke up at the same time; they grinned sheepishly at each other, and Isla gestured to the father to speak.

"Our robes are white, and we have several tricks, some of which are purely physical and one which uses just a *bit* of magic, which we'll be happy to share with the laundresses," he said, and deferred to Isla.

"We have stocks of that canvas that was used to make the Dolls. You couldn't stain that if you tried, and the canvas will certainly do for trews, outer tunics, and the outer layer of a cloak. Anything fancier can wait until we can *all* have the sort of dress we used to use."

"Oh, that will be very good," Lady Pellian said. "Make the uniforms identical except for the King and the Crown Prince, and even then, make the difference purely in extra ornamentation in blue and silver, the Valdemar colors. Make the uniforms otherwise all plain, utilitarian. So no one can accuse anyone of being 'jumped up' or taking advantage of the royal patronage. Look here, what do you say to using the stablemens' trews as the pattern for the bottoms—"

Isla got up and went to Lady Pellian's side; everyone else reshuffled their seats so the two of them, joined by Jonaton, put their heads together over the design that Lady Pellian sketched. Kordas noted with amusement that essentially all Isla had done was to move to her ladyship so it was obvious Pellian had royal approval, then let Pellian and Jonaton work out the least little details. He was very glad he was not expected to be part of that discussion. Strange terms like "gusset" and "armscye" and "flat-felled" were being tossed about, and he felt just as lost as he had when he first spoke with the shipbuilders.

:Don't look to me to help. I'm as baffled as you are.:

He almost laughed out loud to hear his Companion admit that.

Restil glanced at Beltran and his father to see both of them suppressing sniggers. Apparently their Companions felt the same.

Meanwhile the rest of the Council was deeply involved in working out what he considered to be meaningless trivia. Should the Heralds all be quartered together? It would have to be the Palace, obviously, but where? Should they be paid, as the guards were? Where were they supposed to eat?

:This doesn't matter!: he complained to Darshay. *:None of this matters!:*

:Well, not to you. You already have good quarters and you eat with the Court. But some of our fellow Heralds . . . don't.: He nearly kicked himself for being oblivious. Because of course only the highborn enjoyed that kind of privilege.

:Besides, right now, they are very shaken. I don't believe anyone in the Empire—even a priest—has ever encountered anything like us in fifty generations or more. It is easier for them to think about trivialities than about what we are, what we represent, and what else we might portend aside from the reason you asked for help.: Well, they were certainly neck-deep in trivialities. And right now he envied all the new Heralds, who had, for lack of anyone giving orders, had been sent to get their morning meal with the rest of the Court, and were now doing what *he* would very much like to do . . . rest and let some of that vast dump of information he'd gotten sort itself out in his head. The best way to rest would be to settle somewhere with Darshay for a few marks.

That was probably exactly what his father and mother were thinking right now, too.

:Why don't you go talk to the religious guests? They'll be the first ones who tell the people about us, after all. I expect they all plan to go right back to their temples and churches and all, and make this the center of whatever worship ceremony they have today. They'll probably continue to do so, off and on, for the next moon. So why don't you let them ask you questions we can answer?: He felt a little less useless and a lot less—well—bored. He was used to *doing* things. He wasn't used to sitting there and listening to people trying to avoid the warhorse in the room by chattering about uniform tunics and what part of the wall to put the new Heralds in.

So he stood up, picked up his chair, and moved it over to the gaggle of prelates. *Are they a "gaggle"?* What was the term for a group of holy people?

:Perhaps a pontification of priests?: Darshay suggested.

:I didn't think I could love you more,: he replied, as the learned gentlemen and ladies seemed to anticipate what he intended and made a space for him and his chair in the midst of them.

"Now," he said, settling in. "The King and the Queen can handle the Council. I expect you are all alive with curiosity. Ask me anything."

As they peppered him with questions, he saw out of the corner of his eye that Beltran was similarly surrounded by the mages.

:He's doing the same thing you are,: Darshay told him. *:Better him than you, because the Old Men are too used to seeing you as a magic apprentice and may not take what you say as seriously as if he says it.:*

The pontification of priests had regained some of their composure, and given the opportunity to cross-examine the Crown Prince themselves, with no competition from any other group, they managed to slow themselves down a little and not interrupt each other.

Restil really did not know any of them well enough to have put a name to them—to tell the truth he had been a bit hit and miss in his own religious pursuits, such as they were, and he'd mostly kept to the casual worship of Epona. As long "things" didn't interfere. Things such as monstrous beasts, Council meetings, helping manage the family horse herds, helping to save knowledge and skills from back in the Empire and make sure they didn't disappear, helping to organize the new schools and getting them the materials they needed to teach basic reading, writing and numbers, and running his own court of appeals. That last was what took up the most time: settling what he could, determining what needed to be brought before the King, and throwing out chronic complainers.

So he sat patiently and answered all the questions put to him, which ranged from the sublime—"Should we be giving the Companions some form of worship?" *(:No,:* said Darshay. *:Please not. We are as much servants as your prelates are.:)*— to the ridiculous—"Should we . . . put something down in case of 'accidents' if one of them wants to come to the Temple?" That had been the priest of Epona. *(:No,:* laughed Darshay. *:Tell him we're better behaved than some of his followers.:)* Another temple type asked, "But if they do, isn't it meant to be, and not an "accident?" Would it be blasphemous to just throw it out?"

:I am about to pee myself laughing, inside,: Darshay interjected.

"Should they bottle that as a relic?" Restil said out loud, keeping his face agonizingly straight. "She says no, the residue of earthly bodies is simply ordinary, and Companions are superior to horses in retention."

:I am so glad we came,: Darshay dryly commented. *:Please tell them that being respectful, even reverent, to us is fine, but we aren't to be worshipped. Neither should Heralds.:*

At least *they* were all secure in their faith, and absolutely certain that since their various deities were behind this manifestation, there could not possibly be anything sinister about it. The same was not necessarily true for the members of the Council, some of whom were looking anxious and pelting the King with tentatively phrased questions that essentially amounted to, *But what if these creatures turn against us? Will we be ground underhoof?*

Finally his father sighed and said, "Look, if something powerful enough to manifest dozens of Companions wanted to harm us, there are easier ways to do that. For instance— send a human agent to where Pebble is right now, insinuating that Pebble could be captured and held and forced to *only* pave lanes in *their* part of the Kingdom. And once Pebble's mother discovered her child had been subjected to restraint and captivity again . . ."

He shuddered, and went a little pale, but continued on.

"There would be nothing left of this entire Kingdom but ash and molten rock. *You* only saw her in action against the Red Forest. *I* watched her destroy the entire Capital City of the Empire, host to every major spellcaster and priest of the time. It's probably *still* a lava field. We have *nothing* that could stop her."

He paused, then concluded, "And if I need to remind you of what she can do, I'll be happy to establish a past-scrying viewing of just what I saw happen. Or, of course, you could talk to some of the people from the Capital who came through our Gate by accident—if you can get them to talk coherently about their experience. Most of them prefer not to think about the day they lost everything."

Silence in that part of the room as the Council contemplated that led Kordas to add, "I'd say that what Pebble's mother did took perhaps a tenth of the power of the Companions' manifestation. Now with them—if I may be so bold—Valdemar has a strong chance against those who would see it harmed." Then, abruptly, the talk turned to things like "How should Herald quarters be furnished"—as in, "Do we just give them a bed and a storage chest like the guards, or do we go further than that?"

His father let them natter on for a bit while he composed himself again, with an effort.

Ten years, and it still weighs on him, Restil thought, wishing there was something he could do.

:Leave that to Ardatha,: Darshay advised. *:He knows what to do.:*

I certainly hope so. If Ardatha can bring my father some peace of mind . . . it will be a true miracle.

Rumors as well as the actual truth spread around the Kingdom in the space of days. As was to be expected; after all, the majority of the "Kingdom" was no bigger than the old Dukedom had been, and rumor seemed to have the wings of a messenger bird. Almost all of the newly Chosen, especially the common folk, took it on themselves to ride out the next day, even though no one had the promised uniform yet, and other than the silver hooves and blue eyes there was nothing to outwardly differentiate the Companions from ordinary horses. The Companions themselves seemed to have some ideas about that, however. Restil certainly discovered that Darshay did when they began making the rounds of the farms and villages in and around the Young Squire's establishment. To the astonishment of the Squire and everyone who came flocking to see the strange new thing that the priests were all babbling about, Darshay was more than happy to demonstrate just how intelligent she was—first by parading through the farmyard, opening and closing doors and gates behind her, then by fetching whatever odd item she was asked to. This occasioned a lot of hilarity when the object was something she "shouldn't" recognize, in a place where a horse would never go. Like stealing the cook's favorite frying pan—Darshay let herself into the kitchen, snatched the pan from the wall with her teeth, and let herself back out again just long enough to display herself in the doorway with the pan in her teeth. Then, before the cook could erupt in a burst of fury, she replaced the pan, came back out, and closed the door behind herself. As the newly minted Heralds Mindspoke among themselves, either directly or via their Companions, Restil quickly realized that *all* of the Companions were doing things like that. And they *all* took the time to visit churches, temples, and sanctuaries to show their respect to the deities in question. Generally the religious leader in charge of a particular spot took the opportunity to preach a very short sermon on the beneficence of that particular god and a vague homily on how the Companions and Heralds were meant to serve the Kingdom. When they all returned to the Palace, at least the rumors spreading were now much closer to the truth.

There still was a lot of erroneous chatter, but at least now there was no hint that anyone considered the Companions sinister in any way. Mostly the chatter revolved around all the miraculous things that people assumed the Companions were supposed to do—blessing the crops, performing magic on their own, becoming invisible, speaking like a human. The rest—well, it was all about the "tricks" the Companions could do.

Beltran complained to Restil about this as they all began moving into the new "Heralds' quarters" in the wall. Restil had decided that he would join the others there as a sign of solidarity, but he did feel guilty that he possessed a lot of belongings to move in and servants to move them. He could loan out the servants, and did his best to find little extras like beds and bedding, curtains and chests, for the rest, but . . . well he was just grateful that they were all going to be wearing uniforms, to keep the differences in class and rank at a minimum. They were taking over a section that had been made into four-room "apartments" of a sort, the kind that shared bathing and sanitary facilities between every two. After his attempts at "scrounging," plus what the new Heralds themselves could find or make, the furnishings were sparse, but comfortable, and everyone had their own private room, which was something of a luxury to a number of them. They would take regular meals with the Court, but the fourth, common room in every one of these apartments, the one with the fireplace and hearth, did have a little stove on which a simple meal could be prepared at need, stoves taken from the barges and put into storage ten years ago, and fitted into the hearths once the Mother had finished growing the living spaces.

"There are still people giving me the side-eye," Beltran complained, as Restil helped him move his bed to another spot in the room less prone to getting the full morning sun. "Right now the Companions are . . . entertainment, I guess. A lot of people still don't see what actual use we are." He paused. "And a lot of the common folk are convinced that we'll be entirely at the service of the highborn and the Palace, not them. And I heard someone talking about 'trick riders and performing ponies.'"

"They'll learn," Restil sighed. A *thump* from downstairs told him that Delia was finally moving into the third bedroom, the one below Beltran's. This had been a scheme of Restil's; he knew that Beltran had had a wistful sort of crush on Delia for some time now, and although he was not about to play matchmaker, a closer proximity and shared duties just might turn her attention in that direction.

:If you are not playing matchmaker, you certainly could have fooled—:

—he staggered, and clutched the headboard to steady himself.

It wasn't Mindspeech. There were no thoughts, only a kind of punch to the gut. But he *felt* a flood of terror, and at the same time, his entire mind filled with a vision.

Dozens of children, screaming.

The vision expanded. The children, and one adult, were in a boat. The passenger ferry was on the river where there was no bridge, just above the rapids, outside the wall. It was a simple thing, a boat tethered fore and aft to a rope that crossed from one bank to the other, with a ferryman, a strong man who simply hauled the boat along the rope from one bank to the other. There were people on both banks screaming as well as the boat full of children.

The rope had snapped at the far bank. The current whipped the boat around, and the ferryman clung to the rope with all his strength, straining, while the children screamed around him. Restil sensed that his hands were slipping as the boat gyrated back and forth.

He and Beltran vaulted down the stairs and launched themselves out the door, Delia on their heels. Companions streamed toward the set of apartments, but Darshay and Kyrith were already waiting, and Delia's Companion was no more than a couple of lengths away. He and Beltran leapt onto the backs of their Companions and were away in a breath, Delia right behind them. He felt his stomach lurch as the vision played out in their heads. In moments, that boat was going to go into the rapids, and—

No saddle, no bridle, he knotted his hands into Darshay's mane and clung on like grim death. He was used to riding bareback—but not at this speed. Still. Gritting his teeth, he urged every bit of speed out of Darshay that she could give, as she raced for the tiny postern-gate beside the point where the river went under the wall. There was no other way. They couldn't just jump into the water; there was barely enough room for floodwaters to clear the bottom of the wall.

:I'm faster,: said Darshay. *:I'm fastest. We'll get there first.:*

They flashed through the gate and its tunnel through the wall so fast it was just a moment of darkness and then a burst into the light. He sensed the other Companions behind them, timing themselves so that there wasn't a crush at the gate, but all his attention was on the river ahead as his eyes strained for the boat. His heart raced in time with Darshay's hoofbeats, but his mind raced faster than she did. *The anchor spell. I can modify it to "throw" a kind of rope—*

:Passing that on.: The briefest pause. *:We have a plan.:*

That freed him. He knew his part and he focused on that, as he scanned the riverbank ahead for his target.

There! Faint screaming in the distance, growing louder as he neared. *This would be the afternoon lot of children going to their lessons at the Temple of Epona,* he realized in the back of his mind. And not just the children were screaming. By now, both sides of the bank held a crowd of helpless people—some of them the parents of the children in the boat—screaming in desperation. At the forefront of his mind, though—preparation for his spellcasting. This had to be fast, and sure.

Darshay skidded to a halt on the riverbank as soon as they

were within a stone's throw of the boat, near enough that he could see the terror and despair in the ferryman's eyes, see the blood on the rope where he was losing his grip.

With all his strength, he flung out a fat rope of his own magic, a creation of raw power, and seized the prow, bracing himself against the terrifying pull of the water. The boat shuddered, Darshay's hooves skidded and dug into the turf, and for a moment's terror of his own, he feared he was going to lose the boat, or be swallowed up by the river.

But that terror galvanized him as a reminder of the stakes, and he flung out two more "ropes," anchoring them to trees on the bank, with himself as the point in the middle of all three. Although feeling he was about to be ripped in half, he held, and sensed Darshay pouring power into him.

Delia and Valiance pounded up next to him, then passed him, only stopping at the point exactly opposite of the boat. Very small, screaming children began appearing beside her Companion as she Fetched them to safety.

In the next moment, the two apprentice mages, Fynn and Palonia, joined her, and he sensed rather than saw them creating the kind of magical bridge over the river that the escapees had used to cross from bank to bank during their journey. It took both of them *and* their Companions to pull off that kind of powerful working—apprentices did *not* even attempt this sort of thing!—but the rest of the Heralds arrived the moment it was stable, and they began a gingerly canter across it. The screaming stopped—

But not because the children weren't still terrified. They *were.* But one of the Heralds . . . was doing something to keep them quiet and cooperative. *Someone with Mindmagic.* Right now, Restil didn't care *what* that was, or who it was, as long as it kept the children from fighting their rescuers in their panic. *I'll find out later.*

The ferryman, brave heart that he was, had not jumped out and run to safety. When the rope he had been holding went slack, he began passing children too big for Delia to Fetch up over the side of the boat and into the arms of waiting Heralds, who loaded themselves with two and three children at a time.

Don't let them fall!

:We won't,: Darshay said with fierce determination. The mages widened the bridge just enough that a Companion laden with children could execute a spin-in-place and head for the bank, while another Herald and Companion took their place.

Restil felt himself starting to black out, but he grimly held, and held, and held.

Finally the last of the group half-pulled and half-assisted the ferryman up behind him. The moment the ferryman's feet left the boat, Restil let go.

He nearly blacked out; reeled on Darshay's back, utterly spent, as the boat whirled away and smashed on the rocks—and then vanished into the teeth of the rapids.

He slid bonelessly off Darshay's back onto the ground, and for a while just sat there, while Darshay nuzzled his hair, his vision graying around the edges.

Only then did he hear the cheers.

―――――――

By the time the frantic but hysterically grateful parents came to collect their offspring and the priests of Epona had gathered them all up to give them the shelter of the temple and tend to the ferryman's abused hands, Restil had recovered enough to think clearly again.

"What—did we just do?" asked one of the new Heralds, bewildered.

"What we're supposed to do," said Beltran with authority. "What we're meant to do. Serve the people. Act as one, at need."

They were *all* still at the riverbank, Heralds limp with the emotional and physical after-effects of what they had just accomplished, Companions bolstering them emotionally and in some cases physically. Fynn and Palonia lay flat on the ground, more exhausted even than Restil. Delia wasn't as exhausted—she'd had plenty of practice in using her Gift even after they'd all settled at their new home—but she probably wanted the stability of ground under her at this moment.

The fear of failure, the fear that he wouldn't be able to save them, drained away like water out of a pot with no bottom. He wasn't ready for elation, not yet, but there was profound relief and an upwelling of a chaotic mixture of other emotions, all of them tangled, but all positive.

He closed his eyes for a moment, and just allowed himself to feel Darshay's support, smell the fresh scent of the churning river, and even let the sound of the rapids become a pleasant background rather than a harbinger of disaster.

There was a growing crowd on both sides of the river, as word spread of what had just happened. The crowd buzzed with excitement, but had hushed when Beltran began to speak.

Seeing that, Beltran gathered himself further and began another one of those surprisingly eloquent speeches he'd been producing of late, pitching his voice high and loud enough to carry over the rushing water. Restil was more than content to leave him in control of explaining who had done what—and why, repeating with more emphasis each time that this was *exactly* the sort of thing that Heralds were supposed to be doing. He was too tired to do more than listen. It was an excellent speech, almost as good as one of his father's.

He did wonder, though, why Beltran was drawing it out as much as he was—until he felt recovered enough to stand, and with him, Delia, Fynn, and Palonia.

". . . and now we will return to our duties," Beltran finished smoothly. "Do not call this a miracle. Heralds and Companions, hand and hoof, making sure our people are *safe*. As it was meant to be."

Somehow the Heralds on the ground managed to pull

themselves back up onto their unsaddled Companions. *Unsaddled! No bridles! I am amazed none of us fell off! I am amazed we didn't drop any children!*

:We will never let you fall,: said Darshay.

With immense dignity, Beltran led the procession of Heralds back to the postern gate to the cheers of the two crowds.

Once they were inside the wall again, one of the former guards, now a Herald, let out a stream of oaths that those children definitely should not have been allowed to hear.

"How the *hell* did we—" he began, then stopped, probably because his Companion was explaining to him exactly how they had pulled that rescue off.

At just that moment, the King and Queen, trailed by the Council, arrived on *their* Companions. Kordas went straight to his son, and the Queen to Delia, and embraced them wordlessly. Because, of course, no words were needed. Not now.

We hadn't even practiced that. Everyone just knew how to position, and what to—unleash? There was a vigor while I was atop Darshay that made the spellwork stronger. It felt like the casting couldn't go wrong, and it was more effective than I expected. Restil didn't feel dizzy, but he was experiencing a sensation he hadn't felt before now. Heroism.

Is this what my father feels like as King? There are more stories about Kordas's heroics alone than most families have in their total familial history. And no wonder, if he felt like this *after every deed. This is—it feels like things went right, and not just by luck. There was precision, and no hesitation. None of us were tricked or forced to do the right things, and we* wanted *to do those risky things together.*

Darshay said nothing specific, but gave Restil the impression that while there was no lack of words to say, she felt that silent comfort was what he needed—she was infinitely considerate. Thoughtful—but understanding in context, and in the instant. He was sure *something* had gone on between the Companions at the speed of thought. Come to think of it,

Restil's own thoughts had felt quicker when he was responding and casting. Clearer. Purposeful, without the chaff that clung to regular thoughts. And they had all gotten there so quickly!

And it was—there was no doubt—truly heroic.

That is what we're made of, inside. We chose it.

We did it because it's why we're here.

:Yes. Thank you, Chosen.:

Next day, the Council, predictably, was furious. The Council Chamber was in a quiet uproar. People talking over each other, or talking *at* Kordas. He let them talk without saying a word. They needed to get it all out of their systems. He could understand their concern, but he was the King and Restil was *his* son, not theirs.

Kordas himself could not have been more proud of his son—of all the new Heralds!—but most of the Council members were appalled that the Crown Prince had put himself in potential danger. Kordas let them yammer on until they ran out of things to say, then stood up.

Silence descended on the room; at this point, his Council members had learned that Kordas seldom exercised his authority, but when he did, it was time to sit down, shut up, and get the hell out of the way.

"Restil's actions were entirely correct, and it would not have mattered if he was sitting on the throne, rather than being Crown Prince. I nearly bolted out of the Palace to respond, Isla beside me, but we were assured it was being handled. Did you think that the Companions were nothing more than pretty ornaments to bolster the morale of our people? Did you think he should have held back just because he is the Crown Prince, when he had *precisely* the skills that were needed? *Do you really think that I should have forbidden him?* Because if I had, there was *no one else* that could have gotten there in time to keep that boat from going into the rapids. There would have been dozens of *our* children drowned or smashed on the rocks. I could not have lived with that. I hope neither could you. But if you think you could have actually lived with those deaths on your conscience, rethink your position on the Council."

He paused and let that sink in, and if the silence had been heavy before, it was now laden with the burden of those words and all they implied.

Before anyone could stammer out an answer, Kordas continued. "I am the King. But I am also a Valdemar, and the Valdemars have *always* put their people first. Heralds are Valdemaran. How can I, as the King, ask my people to send their heirs into danger when I will not send my own?"

Well, there was no real answer to that question, and mouths around the Council table clamped shut on anything else they might have said.

"Now," he continued, softening his tone. "It is clear there is a need for a crossing at that point, or people would not have constructed that ferry. But it is also clear that a ferry is not the answer. Or at least, not that sort of crude ferry. This absolutely *is* a matter for the Council to solve, because the treasury must, in all fairness, cover the costs. Have you any suggestions?"

Koto—who was the mages' representative today—pulled at his lip. "Well," he said. "People will complain when we pull our mages off the work they are doing now, but we *can* raise supports out of the river, the kind we used to support the Gate pylons during our journey, and a bridge can be built atop them. It would be lovely if Pebble were here, but Pebble is building the north riverside route, and then is due back for the loop canal. We'll do it with *our* magic. Those giant tree trunks on the shore aren't decorative, they're a lesson about what will come downriver, so the stonework needs to be sturdy to begin with. That's not a casual casting. We'll need a lot of safety precautions during the building—nets in or over the river to catch whatever falls, for instance, and a dozen other things I haven't thought of yet—but a bridge is clearly safer than any second attempt at a ferry."

"Do it," Kordas ordered, before any of the Council—some of whom probably had projects the mages were working on—could object. "I don't want anyone to even consider putting another ferry there. And as the uprights are drawn up, I want chains, nets, whatever will work, anchored on them as a last chance before the rapids. In case *another* boat goes adrift. Whatever goes in the rapids, as best I can tell, never comes out. I think that may be the Mother's mouth."

"Let's hope she doesn't sneeze," Koto quipped. "I'll pass the request on to Sai, and his big mouth will tell the rest."

"If the mages can do the supports, the treasury can bear the cost of building the bridge itself." That was Isla, who had been consulting with the Seneschal and the new Lord Exchequer. "It might stretch things a little, since we have all these new Heralds to clothe and support, and sixteen sets of tack to be fitted, but we can juggle costs."

He and Isla had, of course, known exactly what was going on as the river crisis happened, but there was no way that either of them could have gotten out of the Palace and down to the river in time to do any good. Kordas would never allow anyone but Isla to know how terrified he had been, nor how hard it had been to let Restil take the lead in this crisis. Isla and Ardatha, that is.

Things are different now—I need to include Ardatha as a factor. I used to think privately.

Ardatha had started in that direction on his own, but the King's Companion hadn't gotten farther than the postern gate when the rescue was over. It had been a nerve-wracking period, but it had also been an enlightening experience to see for the first time how his Heralds and their Companions could move and work together, in an instant. And how Restil could form a plan in a few moments, then—and this was crucial—do his part and trust that the rest of the Heralds would do theirs just as competently.

It was uncanny how well they deployed, considering they must still have been in a daze over being Chosen, and they barely knew each other. Imagine how they looked to the bystanders!

And there had been another, entirely welcome development. Those crowds on the bank had spread the tale of the rescue through the town, and the story passed on the wings of gossip as fast as a storm wind. And now, *now,* no one had any doubt what Heralds were.

Heralds were heroes. Heralds risked themselves for *anyone,* not just the highborn and important. Since Restil had spearheaded the rescue, the word was that the highborn risked their lives to save the victims without a moment's hesitation—because they were Heralds!

Heralds served the people.

"Much more good has come of this than the rescue of our precious children alone," Kordas continued. "Now people know exactly what we are about. Now people will trust us. I would rather that none of this had happened, but in a single afternoon, we have cemented the Heralds' worth and our usefulness in everyone's mind. That is worth more than I can say. Think about this, for a moment, before you say anything else, and you will understand what great good has been done this day."

He let that statement sit there for a while, while the Councilors murmured among themselves.

:Ardatha, how is—everyone? Last I knew, the littles were all being calmed, then fed, then bedded down in the Temple of Epona until their parents could come get them.:

:The children are all safely back home as of this morning, escorted through the postern gate, across the grounds, and down into the city by Herald Tamver. The rest of the Heralds are back to putting their new quarters to rights. The ferryman is being feted as a hero, and rightly so, now that the Healers have tended to his hands. I do not believe he will ever need to pay for a drink for the rest of his life. And you have a procession of folk who are—now—arriving at the front gate bearing a great many gifts. I do not believe that outfitting the new Heralds and Companions will be an issue.: That last was said with a great deal of amusement.

He blinked. *:Wait. What?:* he replied.

Before Ardatha could reply, a page came to the door and tapped on the frame. "Your Highness, there is a group of people who urgently want to speak to you. There are a number of Guild leaders among them. They appear to have several work-wagons full of goods. They say they have come about the Heralds."

The Councilors stopped murmuring to each other, and looked first at each other, then at him. "Has Ardatha said anything?" the Seneschal asked.

"Yes, and I believe we need to speak to these people," Kordas said instantly. "And by 'we,' I am not being pretentious. I mean all of us, the entire Council."

Before they could reply he stood up and gestured to them to do the same. Koto had a twinkle in his eye, and Kordas suspected that he *might* have had something to do with this— but even if that was not true, there was something about this that had the old mage quite amused.

He took Isla's arm and led the way, following the page, who took them to the main gate in the wall. Of course on the way they picked up a gaggle of guards—it would have been irresponsible to have gone out there without them, after all. The best place to hide an assassin, as he knew from his studies in the Imperial schools, was in a crowd of supposedly friendly well-wishers.

The gate stood wide open, as it should, since any citizen of Haven and Valdemar should be able to walk up to it and petition for an audience with members of the Council or even the King. And there, waiting patiently, was a decidedly mixed crowd.

And behind them, a procession of laden carts carrying a motley assortment of goods. *Well . . . that's odd. :Ardatha, do you know why they are here?:*

:I try not to read minds without permission. It's rude, and in many cases, unethical. Enemies . . . certainly, but under normal circumstances, no. But I can tell you that there are no enemies at our gate at this time.:

The woman in the front of the procession, middle-aged, with her hair tucked up into an ocher scarf twisted around her head, brightened and then reddened as soon as she saw the King and Queen. Evidently she hadn't expected Kordas himself to come greet her group, and she was, for a moment, tongue-tied.

From the look of her, she was some sort of craftswoman, though *what* craft, he could not say. She had very strong hands, but no calluses that he could see. The fact that at the moment virtually everyone in Haven wore roughly the same kind of clothing—with variations on ornamentation and embroidery as time and skill permitted—made it a bit difficult to tell at a glance what someone's profession was. And the modest bands of tablet-work trim on her tunic and skirt didn't give him any clues.

"Greetings, my friends," Kordas said, as she tried to recover, and the rest of her party made bows, curtsies, or whatever their bodies would provide. "May I ask what has brought you here?" He pitched his voice so as to sound a bit apologetic.

"I'm very sorry, but if you have a grievance, you'll need to first take it to-—"

"Oh, King!" she exclaimed, interrupting him, still red. "Not a grievance! We are here about your hero Heralds!"

Bringing wagons loaded with what appears to be furniture? This is interesting.

He nodded to indicate she should continue.

"We heard about yesterday's rescue," she said, growing more confident. "We crafters had meetings about it last night, all over Haven. And askin' the guards, they allowed as how the Heralds was in need of some things we can rightly supply. I'm the leader of the Sempstress and Tailors' Guild, and we can whip up them uniforms you wanted—not overnight but right quick, something basic in two, three days at the most. Weavers Guild will supply the fabric if you don't have it on hand. Tanners got loads of cured white pigskin; splits for boots and uniform tunics and whole hides for saddles and tack. All them magic pigs you been killin' got a surplus built up. We tanned it, 'cause waste not want not, but some folks are chary of havin' leather from a magical beastie. Like they think the thing's going to haunt their dreams."

Kordas laughed. "If that were true, none of us would be resting easy after our pork feasts, now, would we?"

The woman flushed, and smiled, pointing around as she explained further. "True that! Well. Cobblers'll make the boots, we can make the tunics, shirts, trews—three changes each for summer, and we'll bring winter stuff later. Saddlemakers'll fit saddles and make bridles; that'll take longer, but the first ones will be done in about two weeks if the Companions can wear a standard design. Bein' as the Companions are all smart, the bridles will mainly be for show, with no bits or the like. We got a bunch of furniture the joinery 'prentices make to prove what they know. Every year what don't get bought gets broke up for firewood, and that's a damned shame. It's solid, just maybe not pretty. For right now, weavers brought up more stuff for curtains, sheets, an' towels, an' we got blankets too. Potters and metalworkers sent their goods so the Heralds got pots, plates, cups—well, I'm sure you're taking my meaning. We heard your Heralds are livin' sparse right now, so we're here to fit 'em up like new-married couples! Plus do up your uniforms and tack. There's plenty of hands to help, and the work'll go fast. Seems to us, they're gonna earn it all right quick if yesterday is anything to go by."

She waited, expectantly. Kordas was astonished. Actually, he was more than astonished. He had *thought* that establishing the Heralds was going to be an uphill battle, even with the help of the budding Kingdom's religious population, but yesterday's action seemed to have done everything he could have wanted and more. At least in Haven. *But word will spread out to the farms and villages very quickly once it's all over Haven. At least this time, it will be good news!*

The woman looked from him to the gate guards and back again. Finally one of the guards on the gate ventured to speak. "Shall we let them in, Sire?"

:Ardatha?:

:Definitely.:

"Then my guards will guide you to where the Heralds are setting up their quarters, and you have my endless gratitude," he said, picking out three guards with a look and a nod.

"We'll take measurements, and bring the new uniforms in—how many are there?" she asked.

"Sixteen, not counting Her Majesty and me."

She chuckled, more certain of herself now. "I misdoubt you an' the Queen be needin' uniforms from *us*," she said, and waved to the group. "No longer than half a sennight. Saddlers will come up in the next couple marks to measure the Companions, and the 'prentices are excited to meet the Heralds. Come on, lads and lasses. Let's get our heroes fitted up proper!"

The entire Council stared in astonishment as the parade went past at a brisk walk, some of the wagons laden with so much furniture it seemed likely the lot was going to fall over at any moment.

"Well. That should ease your monetary concerns, Lord Exchequer. Let's get back to the Council Chamber," Kordas ordered, once the procession had passed. "Among other things, I want to know how quickly we can get a bridge up, and why the ferry failed in the first place."

"Oh," snorted Koto. "I already know *that*. Bad construction. Amateur work. The children didn't want to walk that far, and someone who didn't know better rigged up that 'ferry'. Must have thought that a boat and a rope were all that was needed. Wrong kind of rope—too soft. Both ends were fraying and wearing through, but no one inspected it because it was new. We're just lucky both ends didn't snap at the same time."

Luck? Or more than luck?

:Sometimes it's just luck,: Ardatha said. *:Well, and there were probably some differences in how the ropes were anchored at either side.:*

:Should I direct them to find a way for the children to get to a school without a long walk—never mind. Restil will do it.: Restil had been proving himself more than competent before the arrival of the Companions, and that was freeing Kordas to take care of other things. *:Between Restil and Isla, I only have half the urgent tasks I had before!:* He chuckled to himself. Maybe being King wasn't going to be so bad after all.

———————

The Companions warned the Heralds that a virtual caravan of gifts in the form of household goods was coming, and Restil got everyone lined up in front of their quarters to receive the gift givers in proper style. When all the little speeches had been made, and the proper grateful responses given, the wagons were unloaded in front of their quarters, and everyone waited, so the Heralds could negotiate preferences with each other and everyone got a fair share. There was a surprising number of simple, functional pieces of furniture, all made to the same patterns: chairs, stools, wardrobes, chests, some beds (a good thing because not everyone had actual beds yet), pantries and tables. Quite a lot of it, which surprised him a bit, because he would have thought that people would leap to claim even apprentice work at this point. And most of it was mortise-and-tenon joinery, or peg joinery, so if something had to be taken apart to get it inside or up the stairs, it would be easy to put together again. The rest was all dovetail joints, of varying quality. It appeared to be sound work, though, which made sense; anything badly made would have been turned into kindling and the apprentice scolded. Still . . . it seemed odd no one had taken it at the low prices apprentice work commanded. But then again . . . a lot of disassembled furniture had come with them on their journey, and there were probably assumed defects in this apprentice work that would make people hesitate to *pay* for it.

Guild Mistress Merano confirmed exactly that, as Beltran and Delia made their selections and began hauling pieces into the apartment. "This's mostly last year's work, though we do save out things for longer periods that seem too good to discard. 'Tisn't perfect by any means, but it does the job; joiners put it for sale cheap, but not everything goes. Normally, we'd take it apart and use the wood for more 'prentice pieces at the end of the year or use it for firewood—not like we're short of wood here, but waste not, want not, and this is finished, seasoned wood, which isn't something to waste. We reckoned the 'prentices would be right chuffed to know you Heralds were using it. Oh! Remember them old wool mattresses the Queen had us make out of fleeces on the journey? Wool Guild brought the extras out of storage and we brought them too, figuring not all of you was able to take your bedding from where you were before." She waved vaguely down the line. "We heard a couple guards are Heralds now, and their commander wouldn't take it kindly if they ran off with stuff from the barracks."

"That's a blessing," said Delia, as she took a chair on each arm. "There *are* people making do with straw laid in an empty bedbox right now."

Merano beamed. The Heralds began unloading the cart with mattresses, towels, blankets, and fabric for curtains, and as soon as it had been *un*loaded, it got loaded again with the canvas the Dolls had been made of. Merano was most pleased with that, when she realized what it was. "I remember that!" she exclaimed. "Stout stuff, can't hardly stain it, and it'll last a good long time! Good for trews and summer tunics, and the outside layer of cloaks!"

The Heralds did not lack for eager hands to help them. Their neighbors in this part of the wall (mostly the families of guards), seeing what was going on, had come to lend a hand. Packed up in the linens were sets of pottery, more than enough for everyone, for cooking and eating if someone didn't want to traipse all the way to the Great Hall to get a meal. Metal pots, pans, and kettles too. A handful of Merano's people intercepted Heralds as they could catch them, taking their measurements with brisk efficiency and writing them down in notebooks. With so many Heralds and helpers, the unloading went surprisingly fast, and their benefactors could not stop beaming with pleasure every time one of the Heralds paused to thank them. And there were a lot of thanks. :*Quite the love-fest,*: Darshay teased. :*You all need to get used to this. You're going to get more kisses than blows from here on in, now that you've established your reputation.*:

When the measurements were all taken, and the goods all carried away, Restil took it on himself to invite the lot back to the Palace for biscuits and wine. Thanks to established vine-yards right there on the Palace grounds, remnants of the Hawkbrother plantings, one thing that the Palace had never lacked from the very beginning was decent wine. Nothing special, but eminently drinkable.

They all settled in the gardens among the vegetables. Restil went to the kitchens and found someone to help him carry out wine and savory biscuits, and alerted to what was afoot by her Companion, his mother had a page waiting there for him with the drawings and plans for the new Herald uniforms. When he got back with his loot, the Guildsfolk were admiring the plantings with some astonishment.

"Never thought vegetables could look pretty," Merano observed, accepting a cup of wine and taking a biscuit from a shared plate. "Think I'll do the like with me garden next year."

The rest agreed, and to tell the truth, it was exceedingly pleasant in the garden. Most vegetables were no longer in flower, but the herbs provided faint scent, and the breeze was just right, and felt damned good after all that work. Merano examined the papers Isla had sent, and agreed that these simple uniforms would not be difficult to make.

"Wouldn't have thought of these gussets myself," she admitted. "But they make sense, given how much jumpin' about you Heralds do. Wouldn't have thought the Queen knew that much about sewing!" It was clear from her approving expression that the Queen had just risen in her estimation, so Restil held his tongue about the other contributors to the designs.

Restil played host until a recollection of their own duties sent the Guildsfolk and their empty carts back down into the city, pleased, even delighted, that their offerings had been so gratefully received. Only then did Restil return to the Heralds' quarters and his own apartment to discover that Beltran and Delia had been hard at work in his absence.

He stood in the front door and marveled. He'd seen these installations when there was nothing but the Mother's stonework here, and while the potential was clearly there for making these apartments comfortable, initially they didn't look much different from a gaol cell. There was only so much that the Mother could build, but in these last years a lot had been done both in the Palace and out here. In the Palace, for instance, wooden floors were slowly being laid over the stone, and wood paneling over the walls. All of the openings in the walls had been fitted with windows made of small panes of thick glass in rotating frames that could be opened to let fresh air in. Curtain rods had been put up all over the Palace, and it appeared that someone had come out here recently to do the same, because there were double curtains on the window in the common room, and, he presumed, elsewhere in the apartment. The curtains were crude—they'd been made simply by draping fabric over the curtain rods, and there wasn't a hem in sight, but he reckoned the three of them could learn enough sewing to remedy that. There was a light unbleached muslin pair nearest the window, and a heavier canvas pair, better at blocking light, cold, and drafts, between the muslin and the room. The little common room didn't look so sparse now, with a wooden pantry currently displaying their crockery and pots, a table and three chairs, a couple of stools, and storage chests.

"We took care of your room if you want to go up and look," Beltran said, looking very proud of himself. "Delia is quite good at arranging things."

Delia dimpled at Beltran, obviously pleased at his compliment—
She never *dimples! Well, well, well. That's a good sign.*

"Oh, it's not that hard," she said modestly. "But go up and see if you like it."

Stout wooden pillars at the corners of each room supported the wooden second floor, with an opening cut to provide entry from below. A clever set of wooden stairs that folded up against the wall led up to the opening, which was more than big enough to allow even bulky furniture to pass through. That did make the room above the stairs a little smaller, but Beltran said he didn't mind and had taken that one—presumably he counted the Palace itself as being among his rooms, as could Restil. Being Heralds did not require them to forfeit their personal possessions, and he wasn't going to suggest *that* to anybody. The stairs led up to the back of the room; there was a wooden partition between the rooms, with a curtained door that led to Restil's room so they both had welcome privacy. He trotted up the stairs and through the partition to see what had been done.

Curtains at the window, as he had hoped. He hadn't needed a mattress; he'd purloined his own featherbed from his Palace room. The bed was neatly made up with the linens he had also requisitioned from the Palace, with more linens and blankets in a new blanket chest at the foot of the bed. A chair and small table stood at the window. An actual wardrobe for his clothing stood flat against the partition wall. He'd purloined quite a bit from his room at the Palace, so there were nice warm rugs on the floor, and now there were a couple of stools along with the cushions he'd fetched here, and a couple more chests and an armor stand, all of it arranged in such a comfortable and efficient way that he couldn't see a single thing to change.

"Delia!" he called, as he trotted down the stairs again. "It's perfect!"

He found Delia and Beltran sitting on either side of the table sharing a bottle of wine. He was quite satisfied to see that they seemed to be quite comfortable with each other.

"It's not quite perfect," Delia said, with a tiny frown, as he sat down to join them. "Those stone walls need some sort of fabric wall hanging or they are going to be quite cold in the winter. And we need more rugs."

"Furs?" Beltran suggested. "I've always wanted a fur rug . . ."

Restil laughed. "Furs, even furs from weirdling Pelagirs beasts, are extremely desirable. I don't think anyone is going to give us any." He sipped the wine. This was a nice respite from training with Darshay. "Still, if we Heralds get called out to help dispatch such a beast, I think if we ask nicely, we can probably get furs now and again." He sighed. "It's kind of nice to sit here and rest in *our own quarters*." Living in the Palace in the royal suite made him feel now and again as if he were still a child. Now, here he was, with his very own quarters. Not a child. Able to take care of himself without any supervision.

"I know!" Beltran agreed. "It makes it all feel solid and real! I keep waking up at night and thinking that being Chosen was some sort of fantastical dream. Maybe now that I'm here, that won't happen anymore."

They were all doing a lot of training with their Companions. Even his father and mother were training, slipping away from the Court just after dinner when the evening's entertainment had begun and working out in the horse meadow. And Darshay had nudged him into still more: morning training with one of the Old Men . . . augmenting his magic with hers. Sometimes she made even Sai speechless!

A tap at the door made all three of them look up, to see Rothas standing there with an expectant look on his face.

"May I come in?" he asked. "Have you got some time to spare?"

"A little," Restil admitted, "but not too much for me at least. I need to go talk to the shipbuilders about another bridge."

The budding Bard nodded. "That's what I wanted to talk to you all about. The rescue, I mean. Oh, and what it was like to have those white horses pick you. And—" He took a deep breath, and paused, because all those words had come out in a rush. "I want to write some songs! This is all material that is much too good not to make songs about!"

Restil stifled a groan, because he really did *not* want to be the subject of a song, but . . .

:It would be very good for us to have songs about us. Songs spread as fast as gossip, if not faster.:

:I know. I know.: He put a good face on it, and smiled.

"And Lythe is dreadfully curious. She's met Delia's horse, but not any of the others, and I want to tell her all about everything since she's not awake to see it for herself!" Rothas sounded just as enthusiastic about explaining to Lythe what had happened as he was about making songs, which was an excellent development. With a glance at Beltran and Delia, who each nodded, Restil gestured to one of the stools.

"Get a seat, and we'll tell you everything we can," he said. "I'll have to leave shortly, but I think Beltran and Delia can do as well as I could in that regard. Maybe better. Beltran is very articulate!"

Beltran blushed.

By the time he tore himself away, Rothas was hunkered down on a stool with a look of intense concentration on his face, coming up with a new question whenever one of them paused.

Restil's meeting with the ship-builders was entirely satisfactory. Like apparently *everyone* in Haven, they had heard the rescue story, *tsk*'d disapprovingly over the amateur construction of the ferry, and had strong opinions about the entire incident. But they were more than willing to build a good bridge.

"If you can get us supports to build on," said Jensom Hardhand, the fellow they all called their "captain." "That's not something we know anything about. We concentrate on keeping our work off the rocks."

"There's no one with that kind of skill at the moment," Restil admitted. "Stone-workers and brick-workers yes, but not anyone who can build supports in the middle of the river. So the mages are taking care of the supports, since we don't think we can get Pebble here any time soon. That's what we'll be working with." Restil promised. "The King wants to know, mainly, if you have enough experienced workers to put a small wooden bridge up in a reasonable length of time, something to allow for foot and light horse traffic, and what you think you need besides timber. We have ten years of being here to have a good idea of what the high-water mark will be, and I am told that putting the bridge on the level with the top of the banks will be fine."

The discussion didn't take long, and he went back to the Palace with a short list of materials and sketches for the bridge and the safety equipment they wanted. The bridge wasn't going to be elegant, but it would be enough for foot and light horse traffic—and it would be covered, with a kind of shed-like construction above it, opening to the banks at each end, to keep the weather off. A good point, since an icy bridge would be dangerous, and bridges froze before the ground did—and the sheer weight of snow buildup could crack a bridge to splinters.

What wasn't usual were the safety considerations the builders wanted. Nets both in the river and suspended from the side of the bridge to catch both falling materials and falling people. "You'll be needing to leave those nets in the river in place," Jensom cautioned. "They'll be the last way for people to save themselves before the rapids. And you'll need a crew of regulars that are good climbers and swimmers, with grapples and hooks, to clear the nets about once a week or so, or those nets will fill up full of debris and be more of a hazard than a help."

That sounds familiar, somehow. Restil was proud to inform them that those very subjects had come up in the Council discussions, and direct word from the King was to prevent harm befalling the building crew.

The ride back to the Palace was interesting. Being on Darshay made him highly visible, even if people didn't recognize him as the Crown Prince. But because people recognized him as a Herald first and foremost, he found himself grinning broadly at all the waves and even a few cheers—and he certainly appreciated the way folks cleared out of the way so Darshay could head for the Palace at a brisk canter. And that was when something occurred to him.

:Darshay, can one of the others be spared to go talk to the priests of Epona, and find out if whoever was teaching the

children can relocate to their side of the river on a temporary basis until the bridge is finished? And find a place to relocate the school to. If someone is going to have to travel for lessons, it's easier on a single adult than a gaggle of littles, and I don't want any of them to miss their schooling.:

:Absolutely,: came the immediate answer. *:Delia is going to talk to the priests. Beltran and Rothas are going to cross the river and find a suitable place for the children to take lessons. Beltran is taking Rothas because he can be . . . persuasive . . . as I am sure you know.:*

Indeed he did know. Rothas could exercise his Bardic powers now merely by humming under his breath. Restil knew that the Old Men had been pounding *morals and ethics* into his skull from the time they realized he *had* Gifts, and—

Well, this would be a test of whether or not he handled those Gifts appropriately. A touch of *please, we really need this, it's important for the children* would be ethical. *You'll give us what we want and thank us for the privilege* would not.

:Kyrith will be able to tell exactly what he is doing, and block it if need be,: Darshay assured him, which was exactly what he wanted to hear. *:And then, if he has been exceeding the boundaries, you may be sure that the Old Men will give him an earful when he gets back.:*

He thought about going to join them; after all, he was on the side of the river where they were going to look for a venue for the schoolroom. But then again—

If I start interfering when I've already set them to do something on their own . . . no, that's a bad idea. If they can't find a venue, they'll need to come up with another plan or ask for help, and that'll be a useful lesson in itself. Either way, it will be a good first task as a Herald.

:Second task,: Darshay reminded him, reading his mind. *:First was rescuing the children.:*

He took a moment to marvel at how comfortable he felt that she was reading his mind all the time. It didn't bother him at all, and if someone had described all this to him *before* he had been Chosen, he probably would have objected strenuously. But the level of trust he had in her was so deep it was instinct, and their connection went even deeper. *:Is this what it feels to be lifebonded?:* he asked.

:No,: she replied. *:Lifebonding is nothing like this. It transcends the intellect, and isn't logical. You can be lifebonded to someone you hate, in fact! It's just a good thing lifebonding is rare. This is emotional, instinctive trust, and we won't Choose someone who won't share that trust with us. Instinctively you understand that I will never do anything to harm you with what I know about you. And intellectually we are like twins who have always shared a bond of Mindspeech and Empathy.:*

Restil broached a question he hoped would have an understandable answer. *:How does a Companion know someone is—compatible with them enough to Choose them?:*

Darshay replied, *:I discussed this with the others some years ago.:*

:Years ago? You didn't just appear by a Power's wish?:

Darshay giggled. *:What someone here may perceive as a moment could be millennia in the making! The methods of our bodily creation were only a bit older than a single millennium, mixed with some from ancient deep-magic. Our centuries of refinement took more than wishing—it took failures and setbacks, and concerted effort by archmasters of physical secrets and subtlety. Once our souls were created, the mind of our bodies had to be refined in spectacular complexity, and, in all candor, we needed time to practice. We look good now, but—I shall not share with you memories of our creation. You might not eat for a week!:*

Restil nodded thoughtfully. Interesting that at least some of the Great Powers had foreseen a need for something like the Companions, that long ago.

:Our purpose is not to see the future, but that is the realm of others in the service of Powers, and they shared the knowledge.

Put simplest, Chosen, take comfort in understanding that those who watch over you knew that we would be needed long ago, and our creation by other Powers' hard work began then.:

Restil mulled that over a while.

:But back to your question. Think of it like music. A note can be perfect, but alone. It isn't until two strings pick up that note from each other that a rich, complex sound is built and sustained. People have countless traits in their being, and for someone with the right senses every person is an orchestra. Their traits add up to their own unique music, if you will. When a Companion finds that their tone mixes well with another person's tone, even at long distances physically, interest is taken in them and, with what even I call an amazing sensation, we simply know. *We must be very close for the music to follow. Our tones blend, and potentials unfold. Two strings speak in sympathy.:* There was a moment of silence as if she was thinking deeply. *:And, of course, there are traits we look for as well, which are part of that music. Empathy is an important one. A willingness to help others despite one's own expense. A broad mind. Intellect. The ability to listen first and speak second. There are others, but these might be the most important ones.:*

She paused. *:Ardatha tells me that we need to get back to the Palace and your father and yet another Council meeting to report on the bridge situation.:*

:I can get very used to this business of being able to communicate immediately with each other,: he said, with a smile. *:All right, let's get some speed on and let Delia and Beltran handle their duties.:*

Darshay obliged, moving into a slow gallop. Fortunately people were not so used to Heralds that a Companion pounding past at speed raised any alarm.

Well, that would probably come later.

But as he approached the main gate he saw a little knot of

people in front of it. There were three people in clothing of an unfamiliar cut and dull colors of dark green, ocher and dark brick, and a selection of guards who did not seem inclined to let them pass. *Huh. Wonder what's going on?*

Darshay didn't slacken her pace until they got to the gate, and Restil called out to the guards as they pulled up beside the group. "What's the problem?"

They all recognized him, and the fellow with the patch that marked him as a watch commander sketched a salute. "These folks insist on seein' th' King, Prince Restil. They say they got his seal, but . . . I dunno, such things can be forged—"

Restil hopped down off Darshay's back. "May I see the seal please? I can tell if it's forged or not."

The fellow in dark green looked very relieved, and handed him a bit of ribbon with a wax-seal impression on it. Restil invoked mage-sight, and sure enough, his father's initials, a K imposed over a V, appeared in faint glowing lines over the top of the seal. "It's genuine," he said. "The King is in a Council meeting. Is this urgent? If so, I'll escort you there."

All three of the people, two men and a woman, looked exhausted, and so relieved that their eyes got a little moist. "Oh, thank you, Prince Restil!" the woman exclaimed. "We—"

"You look ready to drop," he interrupted. "It's obviously urgent, so save yourself for the King and the Council." He turned to one of the guards. "If I unsaddle Darshay, can you please take the saddle back to the stables? Hand it to one of the grooms and ask them to put it away."

:I'll let Ardatha know you're coming. He'll tell Kordas.: Once again, Restil was profoundly grateful for the Companions' ability to Mindspeak with each other.

The guard didn't really have a choice—Restil *was* the Prince after all—but he didn't seem put out. "You do that, Tahler," the watch commander said, and once Darshay was unsaddled, she trotted away, the guard following in her wake.

"Let's go," Restil said to the three. He set off at a pace he hoped wasn't too fast for people who were clearly on their last legs.

"But Prince—" the fellow in green began.

"The King knows we're coming," Restil promised. They either believed him or were too tired to argue.

Fortunately the gardens had been laid out mathematically, so there was a clean, straight path to the door nearest the Council Chamber.

The door to the Chamber was flung open for them by one of the door guards, revealing that the King was waiting for them on the other side with a look of concern on his face.

"Your Majesty!" cried the fellow in green as Kordas appeared in the door. "We have—"

Kordas cut him short, and a page hustled them inside, all but shoving them down into chairs and putting cups of cider and chunks of bread stuffed with sausage into their hands. "It can wait while you eat and get a little strength back, Laramir," the King said. "Whatever is happening across the border is not going to affect us in the next quarter mark."

He emphasized his words with a look that brooked no argument.

Meekly, Laramir stuffed his face, took a long drink of his cider, and looked to the King for approval to speak.

"All right," Kordas said, as Restil took his usual seat at the Council table, setting down his bridge plans and lists. "What brought you hot-footing it back from our dissenters' refuge?"

"We know now why they have been kept isolated from the rest of the Adept's citizens," Laramir replied. "The Adept has made them into an army."

:The Adept? Who are they talking about?:

:Ardatha says that the suspected threat northward has been confirmed as an Adept-level spellcaster, who behaved aberrantly and then—left the Tayledras, absorbed the least-loyal Valdemarans and has—put them to use,: Darshay summed up delicately. *:Most of what we thought we knew about the "Archmage"—who is actually an Adept—is wrong. There has been a disinformation campaign for more than ten years.:*

"Is making," the woman corrected Laramir. "They're not an army yet. But they've conscripted everyone between the ages of thirteen and sixty, they've put Lord Legenfall in charge, and he's conducting Imperial-style training."

The Councilors looked appalled, and well they might. Restil knew enough about Lord Legenfall to know that this was a role he would relish. If he had still been in Valdemar, he would have been apoplectic that *he* had not been made King, rather than Kordas.

And Restil knew that, unfortunately, Lord Legenfall knew quite a bit about Imperial military strategy. He'd been a hostage too, and had gone through the same schooling as Kordas.

"There's some good news," the second man ventured. "The Adept seems to have lost interest in Valdemar for now, for some reason we don't know. Her attention is very much focused elsewhere, and that's what the army is for."

Kordas blinked at that. "I wonder why?" Then he shook his head. "We can't count on that state to last. But that does give us breathing room to decide how to fortify the border against a conventional attack and magical attacks. You were right to come straight here."

"We just barely got out in time," Laramir replied, his speech starting to slur a little with fatigue. "Lord Legenfall got permission to conscript from outside the former Valdemaran community, as long as those he conscripts are non-essential. People like us, who subsisted on minor labor jobs."

Kordas signaled to a page with a lifted finger. "Young Merlis here will escort you to—" He glanced over at Isla.

"I suspect all that you care about right now is a flat place with blankets," Isla replied.

"Yes, Majesty," Laramir said wearily. "It doesn't even have to be flat."

"We can do better than that," she said. "Merlis, take them to the squire's sickroom. There's no one there right now, it's close, and it has six cots and a full washroom in it. Round up some clean clothing for them and leave it on one of the empty cots. Then get food and drink for them." She turned back to Kordas's three spies. "Eat something more than a bit of sausage and bread. Get rest, and once you are rested, we'll hear all the details at the next Council meeting. Restil—"

"I'll get them filled in on what happened while they were gone; Heralds, Companions, all that," Restil said, anticipating what she was going to ask.

It was a sign of how very weary the three were that after a moment of confusion, they simply accepted that there was something they were missing and that they would deal with it later. Obediently, they put their empty cups down on the sideboard and followed the page out, and the door closed behind them.

"Well," Restil said. "After all that, my bridge news doesn't seem that important."

"Nevertheless," his father decreed, "Let us be the judge of that."

Kordas knew very well that the warhorse in the room would have to be discussed very soon—but an attack or attempted invasion was not going to be in the works for some time, and the need for the bridge was *now.* The covered bridge did not hold anyone's interest for long; the design was quickly approved, a royal commission for the building was written out, requisition permits were written out, the price was agreed on as fair and authorized, and the entire packet went off by page to the shipbuilders in half a mark.

"All right," he said, once that had been dealt with. "So . . . how long does it take to train a lot of civilians into an Imperial-style army?" The question was directed at the Lord Martial, who was in charge of the Guard.

"Normally I would say not more than a year, but—" He hesitated.

"But?" Kordas prompted, as the others stirred restlessly.

"But your spies just revealed that the leader of this city-state is not just a powerful mage, but an *Adept.* That changes everything. Your mages can put information into a person's head, but only one at a time. Is it possible that an Adept can create an army out of nothing by dumping weapons training and military discipline into this group of people all at once?"

Kordas ground his teeth a little, because he knew the answer to this question. It was how the Empire was able to fight on many fronts at once. "Yes," he said with resignation. "But they won't be in military fighting condition, physically or mentally. Even an Adept can't give someone that with magic. They would know how to wield a pike or a crossbow, but have no practice. They could use a shield, but not feel instinctively when to raise it."

The Lord Martial nodded thoughtfully. "Four moons. Two moons to form up the basics of a garrison. That would do it. At the end of twice that, especially if the Adept can keep them at training from waking to sleeping, she'll have a competent army that will follow orders. Only follow orders, not adapt or improvise—but enough to slaughter a hamlet or holding."

Kordas grimaced. Not the best answer. But not the worst. "Lord Legenfall is an adequate leader. Not brilliant. Not creative. And not a quick thinker. He also wasn't in the Imperial school as long as I was." He thought for a moment. "What does the land in that direction look like on the other side of the border?"

The Lord Martial consulted his fat notebook, and folded out a hand-drawn map from the many he kept at hand. "Largely unsettled. No point in extending the border though, since no Valdemarans have settled close to it in that direction, and the few people who are out there are either cautiously waiting a few decades to see what kind of people we really are or are just mistrustful; in either case, they don't seem inclined to take advantage of our protection." Then he grimaced. "Not that we'd be all that good at protecting them. The other reason not to extend the border is because we'd be stretched too thin."

"So we can booby-trap the border without putting any of

our people at risk?" Kordas grinned. "Excellent. I was trained in insurgency tactics. Legenfall wasn't."

"Neither was I," the Lord Martial said mournfully.

"I'll give you the benefit of my expertise. You can decide how to implement it. Loath as I am to give the mages yet more work . . . we should use both magical and physical traps and alarms." He looked over at the two of the Old Men who were representing the mages. "You mages need to think like Adepts, and try to come up with something an Adept would not be expecting. Then we can move a contingent of the Guard away from places where they are not particularly needed, and reinforce the border with conventional troops at that point. We should aim for a strategy of attrition." He smiled grimly. "One thing those people will *not* be, and that is used to the idea of getting hurt or dying. When that starts, expect a high level of desertion, especially if the Adept is not there in person to enforce her will."

"She won't be," Ponu said sardonically. "Mages gone to the bad never risk themselves when they can put arrow targets in the field."

The next couple of marks involved the two of them as well as Ponu and Dole (who were representing the mages) putting their heads together over how to best fortify that border with traps, because there was a lot of border to consider, and that assumed an enemy wouldn't somehow just Gate into Haven. They needed to avoid the sort of traps that an Adept might detect or be ready for, but Ponu and Dole both had plenty of ideas. Before the first mark had passed, Kordas had ordered the "Hawk Flag" flown, with a second flag of a pair of bendlets in gray on a red field below it, raised on the Palace's signal poles. Assuming the Hawkbrothers surveilled their neighbors regularly, he and Silvermoon had agreed that a hawk silhouette on a red field would catch a bondbird's eye, and show that the Valdemarans were in need of contact, and the flag below it would show the urgency by the number of stripes.

Eventually everyone's stomachs began to growl, the Lord Martial decided that he had enough to work with for the moment, and Kordas called for food and drink while they adjourned for a brief time.

Kordas left the Council Chamber intending to track down Sai—but the sound of muffled crying caught him off guard. It was coming in through a window that overlooked the gardens; concerned that *anyone* in the Palace was distressed, he found a door and went in search of whoever it was.

He found Jonaton hunched over on a garden bench, sobbing messily into one of his sleeves.

The mage looked up at him at the sound of his footfalls, and blurted, before Kordas could ask, "It's Sydney. He's been gone two sennights. By now—whatever his fate—"

Kordas felt a lump in his throat; of all the cats in the Palace these days, Sydney was the one who *never* went "missing"—very unlike his younger days. He always turned up punctually for meals, and registered his displeasure when his punctuality wasn't met. He always turned up to sleep on Jonaton, whenever Jonaton wasn't moving, and sometimes when he was. But in the last year he'd been getting slower and slower, doing more napping than mischief, and his muzzle had gone completely gray.

"He's—he's past twenty," Jonaton continued, wiping his eyes with his sleeve. "I never thought about it, though. He felt like a constant. I just—I guess I just assumed he'd be—"

The last came out in an anguished wail. *"I thought I'd have more time with him!"*

And he broke into sobs again.

Kordas knew better than to ask if Jonaton had used magic to search for him. He probably had since the day after the Companions appeared, and chalked up the lack of results to interference from the event. "The last time I saw him was when the Companions arrived," Kordas said around the lump in his throat and the sensation of burning in his eyes. "He was with you. You set him down, then he walked into the woods . . ."

He couldn't say anything more. Jonaton nodded wordlessly. "He never wanted me to see any weakness, and he hated it when I had to help him. I think he did what cats do. When it's their time, they go off to—to be at peace." Jonaton took a deep breath. "I went back to the Grove and called for him, day after day, bringing food. When I couldn't find a body, I held on to hope that he was off adventuring."

Maybe he is, Kordas thought. After he'd witnessed how interconnected the Companions, Powers, and even the vrondi were—and the Moonpaths—it was easy to visualize Sydney just vanishing from Valdemar, to—*to be an asshole in the spirit realms.*

"I think he waited. He must have wanted to make sure everything was going to be—all right. I can't explain it, I just feel that he—he wanted to *see it through.* That we'd be all right, and the Companions' appearance must have—told him it was all right now. He could take his end of watch at last." Jonaton scrubbed at his eyes. "I have to let him go," he said, broken-heartedly. "I have to let him go now."

Kordas went to his old friend, sat down beside him, and hugged him while Jonaton wept into his shoulder. To tell the truth, he shed some tears too. Sydney might have been Jonaton's cat, but the old bastard had a penchant for watching over Restil, Hakkon and Jon too. Particularly Jon. Jon had gone through a period of nightmares—not a surprise, given what all the boys had seen—and Sydney had slept on his bed every night during that period, patting him gently to wake him up when a nightmare started, even before he could make a sound to alert his parents. The cat hadn't stopped sleeping with Kordas's son until the nightmares had subsided.

Finally Jonaton gained fragile control over himself. "We should go back to the meeting," he said.

"Do you think you're up to that?" Kordas asked—knowing,

as well he did, that losing a beloved pet was just as hard as losing a member of your family. Maybe harder, because everything with a pet was wordless. You never really knew if they understood what you meant all the times that you told them you loved them. *Their* love was openly (if sometimes oddly) displayed. And they left you far too soon. The old dog that had been his childhood guardian. His first pony. His first horse. It hurt, and it never got easier. And when that pet was as special as Sydney had been . . .

Well, there was no consolation.

"I kind of have to be," Jonaton said, looking up with a watery grimace. "You know."

Kordas did, indeed, know. All too well. The burden of being the most powerful mage in Valdemar was just as great as that of being the King, without the benefits of rulership.

He stood up, and Jonaton accepted his assistance in rising. Together they went back to the Council Chamber, Jonaton guided by Kordas' reassuring hand on his shoulder, and by the time they got there, he was under control again, with nothing but his red eyes to show his distress.

But that was enough for the Council to notice, and look at both of them quizzically.

Damn it. I'm King. I can have a harmless indulgence.

"Some of you know all about the black cat, Sydney-You-Asshole," he said. Those who did, nodded. Ponu and Dole both looked alarmed, as if they intuited what Kordas was about to say. "He was actually the first creature to prove that Jonaton's Gates to this new world worked. As fiercely loyal as a cat could be, and never shy to add his opinion or open a door himself. He was present at—" and Kordas had to pause before summing up, "—a *staggering* number of the events that got us here. His antics gave a great many of us needful laughter during dark days. And by the tyranny of age . . . it appears he has left on that journey we all must take, into the country from which no one returns."

Jonaton's lower lip quivered, and his eyes brightened, but he managed to hold himself together. Sounds of sadness and mild cursing came from around the chamber.

Kordas drew upon the composure and dignity that making speeches gave him. "We care deeply for the creatures that depend upon us, expecting nothing, really, and getting so very much from them. Loving them takes courage, because love requires daring. Daring to risk the pain of loss—and accepting that they will only ever be temporary in our lives. Mourning them when they are gone speaks of our bond with them, and our willingness to give loss its due—by feeling it fully, then recovering wisely. Our animals make us better people. We do not abuse our strength, and we do not deny our empathy. That is essential to our character as Valdemarans, and that is why, I think, the Companions came to us in the first place."

:Yes. Yes, it is,: Ardatha confirmed in his mind, which provided Kordas a needed bump of fortitude.

"Now . . . I seldom indulge myself," Kordas continued. "But Sydney needs to be remembered, and not just through his numerous descendants. I *want* this. This will harm no one, and I hope you will humor me. So. Let it be, from this day forward, that the seal of Haven will include a small black cat in Sydney's honor, to pay respect to the—best asshole we were lucky enough to know."

The room fell silent, except for Jonaton and Ponu's choked sobs, and a couple of chuckles. But Kordas saw a lot of the Councilors looking at each other, and although he could not read their thoughts, he had a good idea what they were thinking. *Are we being pranked?* And *Is this a joke?* And *If it's not a joke, how long do we stay silent?* And *I don't know this tactic. Maybe he's testing our compassion.*

"Agreed!" Dole spoke up. That was impetus enough. One by one, the rest of the Councilors chimed in with support, even if it was puzzled or faintly annoyed support.

I haven't once asked them for anything for myself, until

now. I guess they all figure that if this is as self-indulgent as I'm going to get, they can live with that.

"I'll see to it immediately, Sire," said the Seneschal.

And with that, Kordas smiled a little. "Humor is healing, and indispensable for enduring dark times. Perhaps it would be a fine thing for Rothas to also write some about the confoundingly charming cat who left such an imprint on our hearts."

:Beltran is talking to Rothas now. I'll let Kyrith know that you want this, and Beltran has plenty of stories,: said Ardatha, gently. *:You know, we saw him too, when we entered your world. We recognized him at once as an audacious spirit. He will be missed.:*

"And may the stories and songs of Sydney-You-Asshole make us laugh as long as we are a nation. He saw to it that we remained humble," he concluded. He waited a few beats into the silence. "Now . . . let us turn our attention to the concerns of the Kingdom's safety that must be addressed, and matters of preparedness," Kordas said firmly.

And maybe this will pull Jonaton back from the pit. It's too easy to dwell upon a loss, and prolong grieving by feeling like one hasn't felt bad enough, long enough. Better to engage in accomplishing ventures in their spirit, rather than stagnating in misery. Sydney was a scrapper, so. Nothing focuses Jonaton quite like the promise of justifiable mayhem upon an enemy.

"We'll begin with a map overview and a catch-up briefing on our most recent knowledge. I judge us to be at an informing-in-generalities stage, so this isn't a full secure session. We'll discuss simple and effective defensive operations after that, then ways we can modify our known magic into—discouragement of aggression," Kordas said in his comfortable command voice. He gave Jonaton a respectful nod as their eyes met. They both assumed that would mean explosions.

To his credit, Jonaton wiped his eyes on his sleeve again, and went to work with the rest.

Restil and the rest of the Heralds had been invited to join the Court for meals, and did so unless something took them away at the appointed time—and so far the only time that had happened had been when a couple of the non-riders were so sore after practice that they just wanted to lie in their beds covered in liniment. Considering the things that the Palace cooks had learned to make with what was available here, eating with the Court was far and away preferable to soft-boiling an egg and dipping toast in it in your room.

And besides that, plenty of the new Heralds were unaccustomed to the kind of foodstuffs professional cooks could make out of almost nothing. The quality of that food was enough to make even those covered in liniment drag themselves to the table.

Ever since they had arrived here in Valdemar, the habits of the Court had changed in regard to mealtimes. Breakfast and dinner—what the farmers called luncheon—were the most substantial meals of the day; this echoed farm mealtimes. Supper was bread, soup, fruit, and cheese—something light, that wouldn't interfere with sleeping. And unlike Court meals back in the Empire, supper was eaten early in the evening, before the sun went down.

That meant that mouths and hands were not occupied for long, and it was possible for Rothas to supply some early entertainment before he went to spend their shared twilight hour with Lythe.

Kordas was pleased that he had turned up tonight. Jonaton still looked utterly devastated by Sydney's loss, only picking at his food, and Rothas's Gift would be sure to take him out of his grief, if only for a little while.

Kordas knew that Rothas had been working on a song about the appearance of the Companions and the Choosing of those first three Heralds for some time. So when Rothas sounded a chord on his lute, the King settled back, anticipating both pleasure and a certain amount of embarrassment.

But he did not expect what came next.

It was a comic song about Sydney. Specifically a lot of short vignettes in rhyme about the kind of chaos the cat had left in his wake back in the Duchy, all told from the cat's point of view. Which meant, of course, that Sydney felt perfectly justified in doing whatever he did, and it was hilarious.

"Those books I knocked down on the floor—I think I'll just knock down some more. Oh, you will thank me in the end— you need some exercise, my friend!"

Before two verses were sung even Jonaton was laughing. And by the time Rothas sang the last verse, about Syd leaping across that first Gate Jonaton had built and coming back at high speed—

"Found some wildlife, thought I'd share. And so I brought along a bear! What's wrong with you? You seem distressed. You know I only fetch the best!"

—people had tears in their eyes, they were laughing so hard.

Kordas was astonished as well as convulsed with laughter. He had no idea that Rothas was so good at comedic songs! Of course some of this hilarity was probably due to the Bardic Gift—which often gave rise to the saying, "You had to be there"—but this was genuinely a funny song on its own.

:And especially when drinking,: Ardatha observed. :It should be extremely popular in taverns.:

The Bard got not only tumultuous applause when he was finished but a demand to hear it again. And again. By the time people reluctantly let him move on to other music, most of them had it memorized and were singing along, banging on the table in time to the lively tune.

Even Jonaton.

Rothas only had time for two more songs before he needed

to leave (something everyone understood at this point, even if it was disappointing for most of them), and he kept to songs he had learned here, that everyone was familiar with, so there was more audience singing.

Kordas had the notion that by tomorrow, everyone living in the Palace would know the new song—and by tomorrow night, it would have spread down into Haven.

I think Sydney would be pleased.

Well, of course he would have been. Rothas was well on the way to making him immortal.

By the time the actual seal of Haven got painted and put up on the official buildings, everyone in the city would know who the little black cat was.

Kordas could almost hear Sydney in his head. *As it should be.*

Unfortunately, as he learned when he and Isla returned to their suite, young Jon had found out about the loss during supper and had slipped away, and they heard him sobbing desperately in his room the moment they opened the door. Kordas was taken aback; he would have thought that at fourteen, and certainly after experiencing the loss of so much else, Jon's reaction would have been like Restil and Hakkon's—sad, with quiet grief. After all, Sydney had been Jonaton's pet, not theirs. But as they saw when they went to him, Jon was utterly bereft and inconsolable. His brothers were utterly at a loss; Hakkon even offered his dog to cuddle, but nothing helped. They looked helplessly at their parents as Kordas and Isla entered Jon's room. Jon flung himself at his father. Kordas looked over the weeping lad in his arms at his wife, and all she could do was shake her head helplessly.

He was at his wit's end within a mark; the poor youngling had cried himself into inarticulate exhaustion. He could not even tell them why he was so bereft, and his grief showed no signs of ebbing. When a knock came at the door, Kordas was very much inclined to answer it, shout at whoever was out there to go away, and slam it again—but when he opened it, intending to do just that, the person standing there was Lythe.

At her feet was an enormous female black cat, the spitting image of Sydney. In her arms was a basket of three black kittens.

This was so unexpected, and he was so taken aback, that he just stood there with his mouth open. She cocked her head, obviously hearing Jon's crying, and pushed him aside gently.

"Excuse me, King," she said politely. "But I have come for someone other than you."

She and the queen cat marched right into the suite and straight to Jon's bedroom. Kordas followed, bemused. Without any prompting that *he* could see, the queen jumped up on Jon's bed rubbing against him and purring loudly.

Jon actually stopped crying for a moment, blinking at the newcomer, who took that as an invitation to shove her way between Jon and his mother, and plop herself in his lap. The cat looked up at Lythe and meowed silently. Lythe gently tilted the basket of three kittens, who tumbled happily into Jon's lap with their mother.

"This is Sable," Lythe said, sitting down on the bed where Kordas had been. "She's Sydney's great-granddaughter. As soon as she found out how sad you were, she told me I had to bring her to you. Of course, she didn't want to leave the kittens behind."

"Really?" Jon gulped, looking for the moment very much younger than his fourteen years, and utterly vulnerable.

Jon was always the most sensitive of the boys. I just didn't realize how sensitive he was. But there must be more to this than just that.

"Really. I have Animal Mindspeech, you know. That's how Hakkon's dog was able to join you all here, already housebroken." Lythe stroked Jon's hair once, then petted the queen in his lap. "Sable doesn't want you to be so sad. She knows how much you loved her great-grandfather, and she tells me—"

Right on cue, Sable meowed.

"—she tells me that it's *all right to be sad.* But she wants you to feel better. She says Sydney would want you to feel better. That was why he helped you with your nightmares, and why he got between you and those bullies. That's why he always came to you when you were lonely. So she came in his place to help you feel better. Do you want to know what the kittens' names are?" She didn't wait for an answer. "This one is a girl, and her name is Kallie. This one is a boy, and his name is Fisher. And this one is another boy, and his name is Edrik. Do you like them?"

"Yes," Jon managed. He took a deep, shuddering breath. "Thank you, Sable," he said, carefully.

Sable meowed, and bumped her head against his hand as the kittens began to nurse.

"I know you're quite the young man now, but even Jonaton and your father, and Dole, and Sai and his brother Ceri were crying about Sydney tonight," she said matter-of-factly. "Three wise old men were just as upset about this as you, and Jonaton needed a sleeping potion. So don't be ashamed to cry. The saddest thing in the world is when someone we love goes where we can't follow, right? And that's the worst part. You know you will be missing them for as long as you live."

Jon sighed, and wiped his eyes with his hand.

"But there will be other things to love. And Sable would like to love you, if you'll have her." Now she looked at Isla, who nodded—not the least because Hakkon's lurcher had put his head on Jon's knee, looking up at his face soulfully, and Sable stopped licking Jon's hand long enough to lick the dog's nose.

"Sable and her kittens are welcome to live here," Isla told all of them. "If that's what you want, Jon."

"I—I do, Mother." His voice was steadier now—and Sable meowed with what sounded like approval.

"Then it's settled." Lythe stood up, and put the basket

beside the bed. "You take care of each other." She caught Isla's eyes. "Sable will care for the kittens' messes, and knows to go outside when she needs to. She is a good mouser and ratter, but she will need meat and fish scraps to help her make milk; she'll get those herself in the kitchen, since the cooks already know her. If you give her scraps up here, make sure they are raw, or haven't any bones in them. She'll drink from the same water bowl as the dog."

Isla nodded that she understood. "When the kittens start to wander, I'll arrange for a sand box."

"And I'll make sure they know they need to use it."

Kordas saw her to the door and followed her outside, closing it behind them. "Lythe, that was extraordinarily kind and clever of you."

She shrugged, looking embarrassed. "You've already done so much for us. When Delia's horse—I mean, Companion—told me about Jon, I felt like I had to do something. I felt like I *could* do something to genuinely help, not just watch. I talked to Sable because she looks exactly like Sydney; and yes, she actually said most of those things. I don't know how she knew them, but she did."

"Wait, you can talk to Companions?" he interrupted.

"More like they can talk to me. Sometimes a bit too much. They're terrible gossips." She smiled, and shrugged. "They thought my idea of bringing the lad a cat was a good one. Sable was looking for a human to own, and it's very difficult to stay grief-stricken around kittens who are playing. And of course, I made it right with the dog as soon as I was within Mindspeaking distance of him. He took on, with great resolve I might add, the responsibility of safeguarding all of them when they are vulnerable. I hope you don't mind that I just *did* it without asking you first."

"I can't find it in me to be even the least little bit annoyed with you," he assured her. "I had no idea Jon would take it so hard." *And I didn't know about* any *of those other things she mentioned!* Guilt enveloped him. *I am a terrible father.*

"Sydney was extraordinary," she replied, her eyes looking wistful. "So clever I sometimes wondered if he was more than just a cat. Sable seems almost as clever. And she is a great deal less destructive." She sighed, and smiled at him. "Well, if I have repaid your kindness even in a small way, I'm satisfied. Good night."

"Good night, Lythe," he replied. "And thank you."

He re-entered the suite and went straight back to Jon's room. He sat down and offered a kitten a finger to play with. *I need to approach this carefully, and not set him off again. But I need to know what the hell has been going on with the son I didn't think I needed to worry about.*

"Jon, was all that true, about Sydney befriending you so much?" he asked carefully.

Jon sniffed, but at least didn't start crying again. "Yes, Father," he said, concentrating on Sable.

"The bullies?" he prompted.

"After we were here for about a year. Six boys. I didn't know them very well; they were all older than me. I wasn't even doing anything, I was just watching the fish in the river, and they just came up, started pushing me around, calling me names, and threatened to shove me over the bank. Sydney came out of nowhere and the first thing *I* knew, he'd jumped on the biggest one's back and was clawing his shoulders and biting his ears." Jon actually smiled a tiny, tiny bit. "He started screaming and flailing at Syd, but Syd just jumped off his back, then—he was like a whirlwind of claws and teeth, tearing up their ankles. They all backed off, and Syd got between me and them and started howling at them. It was such a weird sound! By that time we'd gotten the attention of some of the gardeners, who ran to us to see what was going on, and they ran away." He took a deep breath. "I never saw them again. I guess they must have been from one of the families that left Valdemar for the north."

Kordas felt awkward, but tried to cover it by patting Jon's shoulder. "Why didn't you tell us about this?" he asked.

"Because that was in the middle of when the *wyrsa* packs were attacking the farmers." By this time, of course, thanks to the Hawkbrothers, they had learned what those snake-dogs were. *Wyrsa.* Unnatural creations that dated to the Cataclysm and before. "You had so much to worry about, and I wasn't really hurt, and anyway, they disappeared right after that. I didn't want to give you more to worry about."

"And here I thought Restil was the responsible one," he said ruefully. "I wish you had told me."

"But there was no reason to make you worry, and maybe end up starting trouble with one of the highborn families. Or Restil would call them out, there'd be a fight, and more trouble than that, and it would be Restil that got the blame for the fighting. And besides, I knew Syd would fight for me." Two more tears crept down his raw cheeks. "And once, I got lost in the hertasi tunnels, and Sydney came and found me when I started to panic."

In his lap, Sable reached up with one paw, claws carefully sheathed, and patted at a tear.

"Why didn't you tell us how lonely you were?" Isla asked softly.

"Because there wasn't anything you could do about it," Jon said softly. "I just don't have much in common with a lot of people here. I don't like games or pranking, or just running about doing nothing but running about. I'm not good at anything but board games. I like to read, but they don't. I like just sitting and looking at things and watching people, they don't. But Sydney always seemed to know when I was lonely and feeling sad about it, and he always turned up and kept me company. It's not as if you could issue an order to make other people like me."

Kordas felt absolutely stricken. Why hadn't he *noticed* all of this?

:Probably because Jon kept it to himself, and all you saw was the good son who was never into mischief and never gave you any trouble,: Ardatha observed. *:And he was right. You were very busy, and just grateful that he wasn't constantly getting into mischief like Hakkon.:*

:But being busy isn't the same as neglect—is it?: Kordas pressed Ardatha.

Ardatha, for his turn, didn't answer immediately.

:You came close.: Ardatha felt guilty about saying it, but Kordas could tell that his Companion was meticulous about truth, and gave the most candid of opinions. *:No one has hours for everything, which is understandable. The difference is, you never forgot about him. You saw to it that he was looked after and educated, and time with you became special occasions to him. I would not call him damaged by your relationship with him, and there is much room for enriching what you have with each other.:*

:I can't believe they teach talking horses diplomacy.:

"I just don't have anything I'm good at," Jon said, dispiritedly. "I'm not smart, like Restil. I'm not good at fighting, like Hakkon. And I'm not brave. When bad things happen, I just want to hide, I don't want to face them."

"You *do* have things you are good at," Isla corrected. "You understand everything you read. Your handwriting is impeccable. What would you say to organizing the royal library and cataloging the books? It's a terrible mess in there, and we haven't anyone to spare to put it to rights."

"It *is* a mess," Jon acknowledged. "It always takes me a long time to find anything." He looked up at both of them. "But—"

"It's important," Kordas said firmly. "When we waste time looking for a book we need, we're not just wasting our own time, we're wasting time that could be used to fix things here in Valdemar. And you're perfect for the job. You are as well educated as the younger bookstaffers already." And then he had another idea, and snapped his fingers. Sable twitched an ear and the hound swiveled both of his. "You like to write and tell stories. I can think of another job you'd be perfect for, that no one—except probably Beltran—has even considered yet."

Jon looked at him expectantly.

"Chronicling the Heralds," Kordas told him. "We need *records.* The Heralds of the future will need them, because we are new and bound to make mistakes, but without records, we'll repeat those mistakes. Start with getting everyone's personal story, and you can start with me and your mother and brother, since you know us well. Then every time one of us does something, make an accurate report of it. Make reports on our training, and if there are mistakes in training especially, make note of that so we can do better, later." As light came back into Jon's woeful eyes, he patted the lad on the shoulder again. "There's no one better suited to doing that than you. And given how much you've kept your troubles to yourself, it's clear you are discreet, which is something that job really needs. The more you show that you won't gossip for the sake of being popular, the more the Heralds will trust you, too."

:Oh, we all trust him. I'll make sure all the Companions make it very clear that Jon is worthy of telling secrets to.: He paused. *:Some secrets. We'll discuss what ought not be said.:*

"Ardatha just told me that all the Companions already trust you," he continued, smoothly.

"He did?" Jon's eyes widened. "Oh, how I wish I could talk to them!"

:That's not out of the question,: Ardatha responded. *:Given that—well, I told you. When he's fully grown, he's going to be Chosen. But . . . :*

:But?: Kordas prompted.

:I believe he has latent Mindspeech. Perhaps we can

arrange for it to become active. There are plenty of Companions who have not yet Chosen who would very much like talking with him. There is much he can tell us; he is very observant. We know quite a lot about you and your world, but we haven't lived it like you have.:

"Ardatha just said that he thinks they'll try to find a way to talk to you," Kordas told him. He smiled. "I believe you might just have found a circle of friends. But that will be for tomorrow. Tomorrow, you can start in the library, and when you need a break, go out to the pasture and see if the Companions can figure out a way to talk to you. Then start on the chronicles. You'll have plenty to do tomorrow, and any time you want to rest, just come back here and Sable and the kits will keep you company. You look very tired, and I think you need to sleep. Cats purring are very soothing. Close your eyes, and you'll find out."

Sable purred.

"I am kind of tired." Jon knuckled his eyes. "I think you're right."

After reassuring themselves that he was going to be all right for now, Kordas and the Queen left him curled around queen-cat Sable and the kittens, making a kind of living bed for them. His eyelids were fluttering closed as Kordas gestured the mage-light in his room to fade out, and they left him with the door open a crack so the cat could come and go as she needed.

"Why didn't we *see* what was going on with our *own son*?" Kordas said with anguish, as soon as they were in their own room.

Isla shrugged helplessly. "I didn't see it either. I just saw that he was quiet, and I was grateful. I'm as much to blame as you are."

"Thank the gods for that asshole of a cat," Kordas said, sitting down heavily on the side of the bed. "At least he had *one* friend. Sydney was a better father than I am."

Isla sat down next to him and put her arm around him. "He was certainly a prolific one. There's no excuse for me either. What's past is done. I think we've gone a long way toward making up for that, though. We've given him something he can succeed at. Given him a sense of purpose." She paused, and tilted her head to the side, obviously listening to her Companion. "Dendalin says the same thing. And that if they can cultivate his Mindspeech, then the unpartnered Companions all are interested in becoming his friends."

He didn't ask if that was enough, because he knew that it would be. How could it not?

"We've made a start," Isla said firmly. "We can't 'make it up to him.' But we can make it better. And we will."

:Yes,: said Ardatha. :We all will, if I am any judge of Companions. Not to be overly dramatic—our numbers are few, and none of us are from this Kingdom. It may seem unlikely, but— we need friends too.:

Restil and Hakkon had overheard all of that, of course, and Hakkon grabbed Restil's arm and dragged his brother into his room. "Why didn't he tell *us*?" Hakkon demanded. He scowled, looking fierce. "I'd have punched those bullies' faces in! I'd have made sure my friends let him come along, when we were doing things!"

"And that's exactly why," Restil replied, feeling as guilty as Hakkon was angry. "If you'd beaten up those bullies—and I have no doubt you could have taken on all six of them—they'd have gone running to their parents, saying you started it. With no witness other than Jon, it would be your word against theirs, and their parents would have made a lot of trouble for Father. Father wasn't King then, remember. Those boys probably all belonged to the families that scarpered off, else they wouldn't have been bold enough to bully him. If you'd beaten their sons, they might have challenged him as unfit. Older people use the young to take blame, and act out their wishes. They are experts in how to work the levers and cranks of the young, because they are who installed them."

"They'd never have gotten away with that!" Hakkon objected, angrily.

"They certainly could have," Restil replied. *Time for Hakkon to get a taste of how the world works. He still thinks it's "fair."* "People are mean, Hakkon. They'll use trickery and deceit to take power from others, and keep it for their own. The parents wouldn't have to *prove* that challenge, only make people doubt that Father was impartial. Once that doubt was sowed in people's minds, it would *always* be there, and they'd second-guess every decision he made. Take the wyrsa attacks. People would start questioning whether he was responding equally to them. Did he favor protecting some people, like the Young Squire, over others? The doubt would grow. More people might have started to think about leaving. And all because you beat up some bullies that were tormenting Jon. And Jon knew that." He rubbed his head ruefully. "He's smarter than I am."

Hakkon pondered that for a while. "So why didn't they go after Sydney and Jonaton?" he asked.

Restil snorted. "I can think of a lot of reasons. They didn't want to admit they were afraid of a cat, first of all. But they had no way of knowing it was *Sydney.* There are a *lot* of black cats at the Palace and in Haven. A lot of them are pretty feral. And for all we know, they did tell their parents, and their parents either were afraid of annoying Jonaton because he's a very powerful mage and he could make their lives miserable in ways that couldn't be traced back to him—especially with all the Old Men covering for him—or they did go to Jonaton, and he said 'And how do you know it was *my* cat?' and they had no way of proving it."

Hakkon rubbed his temple, as if his head hurt. "I'm glad I'm not the Crown Prince," he confessed. "I'd be awful at it."

Restil punched his shoulder. "You don't have to be good at being anything but Hakkon, and you're the best there is at that. But if I were you—"

"Aye?"

"I'd see if the Lord Martial would take me on as a kind of apprentice. Other than Father, he was at the Imperial school the longest. There's a lot he can teach you, and I bet he could use an assistant at this point." *There,* Restil thought. *That should suit him down to the ground, and keep him from trying to drag Jon off with his gang of friends. Jon would hate that, and they'd get bored with Jon within a mark. Jon is smart enough to make sure of it, in fact.*

Hakkon's eyes lit up. "Aye, if he would, that would be great! The weaponsmaster keeps telling me to bugger off because he has other people to train besides me. I don't think he wants me in a mixed class because, well, a royal among inexperienced people with weapons could go pretty badly."

They talked about that for a while until Hakkon yawned. "All right, if I'm going to catch the Lord Martial at breakfast, I need to make sure I'm there when the first food comes out."

"And I have to traipse across the grounds to get to my quarters," Restil reminded him. "At least I don't have to remind you not to stay up reading in bed."

"Ha! No chance of that!" Hakkon laughed, as Restil left his room.

You'd think he'd be envious that I got magic, and he didn't. Or jealous that I was born first and became Crown Prince, Restil thought, as he left the building and headed across the darkened gardens, following the white stones on either side of the path.

:*He doesn't seem to envy anyone or anything,*: Darshay observed. :*Remarkable.*:

:*He's a good lad,*: Restil replied. :*Sometimes he's as thick as two short planks, but not because he's stupid. He's just not terribly observant when it comes to people trying to be deceptive. Actually, he's just not terribly observant when it comes to people, period.:*

He opened the door to his quarters to find Delia and Beltran waiting up for him. "Our Companions told us about Jon," Delia said, without any warming up to the subject. "Is he going to be all right?"

"I don't know. I think so? He's just been a lot more secretive than any of us guessed. Father's taking it hard. He thinks this is his fault. Mother, too." Restil sat down at the little table with them, and accepted a mug of cider. "Lythe seems to have hit on a winning strategy, by bringing Sable to him. Sable seems . . . well, if half of what Lythe said about her is real, she seems as smart as Sydney, without the chaotic streak."

Beltran nodded. "I hope the Companions can talk to Jon. Honestly, I think he'd be more comfortable with them than with people."

Restil snorted. "Honestly, a lot of the time *I* am more comfortable with them than with people."

"I like the idea that they want to take burdens from you, to make up for the peril they'll put you in," Delia acknowledged.

They sat in silence for a while. Then Restil decided to broach the other thing weighing on his mind.

"Well, we just might be facing imminent invasion," he pointed out. "I know you all know what happened at the Council meeting. So. What do you think we Heralds can do?"

Beltran perked up at that. "That is an excellent question. Let's work that problem."

Restil caught his father and mother just before the King laid a hand on the latch to the Council Chamber. "Did Ardatha tell you what Beltran, Delia and I thought of last night?"

Isla nodded. Kordas smiled. "Indeed he did. I have to say that even if they did nothing else, having the Companions able to Mindspeak with us is immensely useful. Menalus is discussing the idea with Celamir now, but I already know the answer is going to be 'yes.' They're just figuring out the best way to implement the idea. I'm going to bring it up with the Council immediately, but everything is in place but the details."

"And did he tell you what Hakkon and I decided?" Restil persisted.

"Oh, is *that* why Hakkon was up so early?" Kordas chuckled, and Isla made a face that said *Well, I never thought I'd see Hakkon up by dawn.* "I thought perhaps the Hawkbrothers had come in the night and left a changeling in Hakkon's place. He and the Lord Martial were gone from the Great Hall by the time Isla and I went down. Jon was still sleeping; I arranged for breakfast to be brought up and left on the table for him. Last night was . . ." Kordas shook his head. "Painful for all of us, on many levels."

"At least he managed to get some sleep," Restil sighed. "I guess we all feel guilty. Hakkon wanted to punch heads. I explained why that would have been a bad idea."

"Hakkon is as transparent as Jon is opaque." Kordas shook his head. "How I managed to end up with three so very different children is a mystery to me."

"It was a collaborative effort," Isla chided. "I was there."

He opened the door to the Council Chamber and waved Isla in first; Restil followed him inside.

As expected, the Lord Martial was already there. What was not expected was that young Hakkon was with him. Kordas raised an eyebrow. "Pinching my second son, my lord?" he asked archly as he and Isla took their chairs.

"Just borrowing him." The Lord Martial cracked what passed for a smile for him; it looked genuine enough. "Thank you for the loan, Majesty. I've actually been in need of an aide-de-camp I know I can trust not to run about spilling secrets. Your son will do perfectly."

Hakkon blushed a little, but looked pleased.

"I am delighted to hear it. And equally delighted that he showed initiative in coming to you and offering." Kordas nodded at his second son. Hakkon blushed even deeper, and straightened up. *Huh. He already looks more grown-up.*

By now the rest of the Councilors were filing in. When they were all in their places, with Hakkon sitting behind the Lord Martial with a bit of plank and some palimpsest to make notes on, the Lord Martial stood up and cleared his throat. "Before we begin, I'd like to introduce you to this young man as my new aide-de-camp. I'm sure all of you know Prince Hakkon, by name if nothing else. If you need me and can't find me, find him. He'll know where I am, if I can be disturbed, and as I am sure you already know, he can be entrusted with secrets."

He sat back down again, as the other Councilors acknowl-edged Hakkon's presence with brief nods. They looked like they approved of the selection, which cheered Restil, since this had been his idea.

"An official reminder, one and all: We will only discuss generalities here. No operational details that would be of use by saboteurs or spies. However good we fancy ourselves, there is always someone out there better. So keep secrets secret. First order of business: at Restil's suggestion, I am moving Herald Menalus to the northern border. As you know, Menalus was a member of the Guard here in the Palace until he was Chosen. He is skilled with several weapons, and is used to leading small groups of inexperienced fighters. And the main point—with him there, thanks to the Mindspeech that all Com-panions share, we will have *instant* reports from the border."

Well, that certainly made everyone sit up and take notice! Restil thought with satisfaction.

"In addition to that, I am informed that he has the Gift of Farsight. So while things are quiet, he's going to take a day or two and scout a bit beyond the border so he is familiar with the territory." Kordas smiled at the Councilors' murmurs and nods. "That should enable him to give us a day or two of warning if a hostile force approaches."

"Doesn't it take time to learn how to use such Gifts?" asked the Seneschal, cautiously.

"It does. But his Companion will be helping him. And we won't be relying on it; as we discussed, there will be other measures in place. Now, I hope that some of you have other measures to suggest to me." Kordas leaned back in his chair and waited for some answers.

"Why don't we also send my cousin Hakkon along with Ivar the explorer, and Sergeant Briada Fairweather and her brothers Bret and Bart Fairweather?" Restil asked. All eyes turned to him, since he very rarely spoke up in the meetings.

"They are all experienced explorers, good mappers, and very stealthy. They can probably get quite near the Adept's city, and will be able to determine the most likely route that any attacking force will take to reach us. That way we'll know where to best concentrate our attention and our defensive measures, and Herald Menalus won't spend time riding up and down the border for—well, who knows how long?"

"Dressed in white on a white horse doesn't seem optimal for sneaking around," Ponu commented, "so having others do the stealth work seems wise."

Heads nodded all around the table; Restil was pleased that they approved of his suggestion.

"Lord Martial?" Kordas asked. "The Fairweathers are under your command."

"Approved," the Lord Martial said. "I assume that you can talk Ivar and Hakkon the Elder into this, Majesty?"

His father laughed, and listened to Ardatha for a moment. "Ivar has been begging me for 'something to do' for some time now. It might take some persuasion for Hakkon to tear himself away from Jonaton, but I think we can manage it."

:Hakkon has been very attentive to Jonaton because of Sydney, but asked Kordas last evening for something that would get him some time away from Jonaton. He loves him, but I understand he can be intense,: Darshay said to Restil. *:Sending a Seneschal to scout danger is normally an indescribably stupid move—and technically, this still is—but it is also emotionally politic. Plus, he is well-skilled for the task.:*

:I see the logic hidden in it. It's clever. Hakkon will get time away, but Jonaton will undoubtedly spy on the group's safety, so we will have warning if something befalls them. And it will refocus Jonaton, which I think will outweigh the risk,: Restil replied.

"Pebble is very near there," said Isla, thoughtfully. "Could he, do you think, be persuaded to do some . . . landscaping?"

"Are you suggesting that Pebble create some of those traps we talked about?" Kordas asked, clearly already liking the idea.

:I like the idea too,: said Darshay. *:Pebble will work without bringing harm to anything. Granted, this deep into summer it is unlikely that there are any animals with young that can't be moved, but if there are, he'll work around them. You humans can't do that very well.:*

:A fact that is sad, but true,: Restil acknowledged. *:We would dig up the land that a burrow or nest was in. Pebble can move it wholesale.:*

"And re-shaping the landscape to suit us," Isla said. "Cover for archers. Even better cover for mages. Perhaps some rock towers with a simple battlement for both to hide behind. Channeling traps; I remember we used them a few times on our journey when hunting game. I'd very much like him to give us every advantage that he can."

"Well, as Pebble has grown up in age and size, he's grown up in understanding. I believe that if someone can explain anything in a way he can understand it, he can and will create it." Kordas pulled on his beard a little. He stopped for a moment, got that increasingly familiar look that meant Ardatha was talking to him, and nodded. "Ardatha agrees. And Celamir can probably explain things very clearly to him. This would be a good time of year to do this kind of thing; he might leave the earth bare where he sculpts it, but with some seeds, cuttings, and mage-work to accelerate the growth, it will look like the ground cover has been growing there for years."

"And with our exploration party figuring out the line of march, we won't chance putting our traps in the wrong place." The Lord Martial rubbed his hands together in great satisfaction.

Kordas looked up and down the table. "Now . . . can anyone think of anything we could do to buy us more time? The longer we have before the Adept moves on us, the more preparations we can get in place."

"Armies need food," said the Exchequer, tentatively. "Is there any way our mages can create a crop failure?"

Both Kordas and Restil shook their heads emphatically. Kordas deferred to Restil, which gave him a little bit of a thrill. "Aside from the ethics of it—it would most harm those who aren't the target—things like that don't stay in one place," he pointed out. "Whether it's insects or a disease, it will spread beyond their food crops and eventually reach ours. While we probably *could* get something like the green beetles or nim-worms to decimate their crops by creating a way to attract them there, that will also feed the pests, which will multiply, and the next place they'll look for food is Valdemar."

Everyone around the table made some sort of unhappy face. Everyone remembered all the pest plagues. No one wanted to repeat them.

His mother blinked, as if something had occurred to her. "Herald Palonia is a weather mage! She could likely engineer a very large thunderstorm with hail. And if she is careful about it, she can keep it raining right on into fall. Not only will that ruin the crops, no one wants to slog through mud with an army, even a small one."

But Kordas shook his head. "We're dealing with an Adept. She can disperse anything Palonia can produce over her own territory. If the Adept is able to tell that *we* sent that bad weather, and she probably can, that might accelerate her plans to attack us. Let's save storms and hail for our defenses. I very much doubt this Adept is going to leave her city. As we all know, mages in general like their creature comforts, and are loath to leave them."

"Hey!" Ponu and Wis objected together. They looked at each other. "Well," Wis admitted. "That's fair. But we're also individuals, and for all we know, she's a bloodthirsty creature who wants to see a slaughter at first hand."

Kordas drummed his fingers on the table. "The problem here is that we know almost nothing about her. The Hawkbrothers undoubtedly know more of her than we do, but they haven't contacted us yet." He pointed at Ponu and Wis. "You mages see what you can learn about her and the army she is creating without her discovering you. I want that lack of discovery to be a higher priority than information gathering; when in doubt, stop watching. Unfortunately all our agents learned was that she's an Adept, she wants Valdemar gone—or perhaps subjugated—and she is building a conventional army. Not much else, although to be fair, they were concentrating their attention on our defectors, not the Adept."

The debate went around and around for some time without anyone coming up with any more solid ideas. They all adjourned for the day, with the Lord Martial and Hakkon going off to find the Fairweathers.

The three royals left together. "Let's check the royal library before we get dinner," Isla suggested. "If Jon is up there, we'll probably have to drag him away."

The room designated as the "royal library" was a pretty massive one, and some people had grumbled about "all that space wasted on books," when they were unhappy about their own Palace quarters. It was a very good thing that those people seemed to have managed to get their own manor houses built relatively quickly, and had moved out, to mutual satisfaction.

Fortunately, although the books were not in any kind of order, they were all on shelves, and no longer in tottering piles on the floor. Jon was indeed in there, and absorbed in doing something at one of the shelves, while referring to freshly written notes. It was a very plain room; the walls were of the creamy "stone" that the Mother created, the floor and ceiling the same. Eventually, Restil knew, there were plans to make floors, walls and ceiling paneled in wood, but for now, it was more than serviceable. No open flames were ever allowed in here, so the place was lit by mage-lights.

Jon looked up when he heard footsteps—they'd have had to sneak not to make any noise, given the stone floors. "Have you made a plan for tackling all of this?" Isla asked.

"I'm organizing each shelf in alphabetical order by title," Jon said. "Then I'll start moving the books in the whole room so that they are in alphabetical order across the room rather than across individual shelves. Should I organize further by category?"

"Maybe, if you keep things to just a few categories. Magic, history, geography, tales, and poetry, perhaps?" Isla suggested. "I don't think we have very much on maths in our personal library . . ." She winked at her husband. "If we did, I am sure I would have noticed Kordas using them to put you lot to sleep while you were younger. Organizing the materials in those few categories would be enough for someone to know exactly what shelves to go to in order to find something. However, right now, you need to find some dinner, and so do we."

Restil could not help but notice that Jon looked considerably better. He thought about asking about Sable and her kittens, but then . . . *let's not remind him of Sydney.*

"Maths aren't boring," Jon replied, and rubbed the back of his neck. "I am awfully hungry. And . . . I think my eyes are tired."

"Then Darshay and Ardatha want you to come out to the field after dinner and see if the Companions can talk to you, *Chronicler* Jon Valdemar," Restil said, putting emphasis on Jon's new appointment.

Jon lit up. It was all he could talk about through dinner; he all but inhaled his food and very nearly ran out the door, dodging around latecomers to the meal. Restil already knew that Darshay and Ardatha would be waiting for him right at the fence—

And that was when he realized that the bond went both

ways. *Good heavens. I'm in her mind as much as she's in mine! This is astonishing!* He knew exactly where she was and what she was doing, and if he just opened his mind a *little* more—

He watched Jon running across the bridge through Darshay's eyes, face shining with amazement. "I can hear you, Ardatha!" he shouted as he ran. "I can *hear* you!"

Restil looked over to his father and mother, and saw that both of them were smiling. "Well," Isla said. "That's certainly sorted. Our son, the first Chronicler of the Heralds."

The little expedition to and past the northern border went out the next day. As the Seneschal, Hakkon already had a deployment plan written up. The band found themselves with aides and runners gathering and packing everything they'd need for a fortnight's foray, polished and weather-protected. The staff utilized a staging room near the stable supplemented by folding tables outside, directed by a quartermaster and clerk. It was distinctly similar to how the hertasi worked, and no wonder. Valdemarans were pretty smart in general, and were wise enough to adopt superior methodology when they could—in fact, they even had shortcut tunnels as part of their newest architecture. This was a rehearsed task for the staff by now, and the rehearsals had become a kind of sport. For the past five years, each biannual drill had featured more difficult, quirky, and puzzling elements than the last. There were even spectators! Most of the senior participants had learned improved methods from the endlessly resourceful lizards, like priority packing, tag-based duty boards, and more in the settling days before the Tayledras and hertasi departed.

Hakkon and Ivar led the band. Herald Menalus went with them as far as the border, with Laramir as their guide. The Fairweathers were serving as guards, although everyone hoped that they wouldn't need to do much other than hunt game for meals. Although these lands had been cleansed by the Hawkbrothers, in no way did that mean they were safe—it only meant the dangers there would not be warped into chaotic monsters. There were still plenty of nasty surprises out there, and a giant boar could do as much damage as an ambush by humans or a mage could. Kordas was more than a bit surprised that they managed to get themselves organized so quickly—

But then again, it's Ivar and Hakkon. They're experienced at this. They both probably keep expedition packs at the ready at all times. As for the Fairweathers, he knew from experience that they were always prepared for almost anything. He found them inspiring in that way; they had a family tradition of raising children in constant lessons, honing skills for resourcefulness, resulting in the most clever family he'd ever met. They taught how to evaluate problems, to solve for the best-informed answers.

The band had left Haven marks before the royal family even made it down to breakfast, and this morning the royal family all went down in a group. Restil came over from the Herald's quarters to join them.

"I don't want to cast a pall on perfectly good food," he said cautiously. "But . . . shouldn't we be doing something more about this Adept and her army than just sending out—"

"We are," Kordas promised him.

Delia tossed a grape at Restil, who caught and ate it. "I leave to catch up with Pebble as soon as breakfast is over. It's a hidden benefit to being a Herald—sleeping in, because Companions are fast enough to make up the difference."

"The Lord Martial is shifting some of the Guard from the south, east and west today, sending Heralds with the orders since they can travel so quickly," Isla told Restil serenely. "And the mages—ah, here's Sai, he can tell you."

Sai sat down without waiting for an invitation and helped himself to bread, cheese, and a handful of fruit. "Jonaton, that clever bastard, has opened the smallest of Portals in the air *above* the Adept's city. Even smaller than the ones he used to use to help himself to other people's belongings. About the size of a quail's egg. He got the location from Laramir's mind. He said that apparently, the Adept hasn't bothered to ever look up past the shields she has on the place. We have a bird's-eye view of the entire city, and we'll see any troop movements. But I have to tell you . . . I don't think those troops are going to be moving any time before late fall." He shook his head. "Their drilling looks . . . well . . . sad. If she *is* dumping military information into their heads, she's not doing a particularly good job of it."

Kordas stopped eating for a moment and stared at him. "Are you sure?" he asked. "But even if she knows nothing about an Imperial-style army, she has Lord—"

And then it hit him, and he had to chuckle. Ardatha picked up what he was thinking, and evidently passed it on to Darshay, Valiance, and Dendalin. There was no mistaking when the Companions passed it in turn to their Chosen, because first Restil, then Isla, then Delia began quietly laughing too.

Sai, Hakkon and Jon stared at them. Sai got a cross look on his face and said, pointedly, "It's not polite to whisper among yourselves. Are you going to share with the class?"

"I'm sorry," Kordas apologized. "Lord Legenfall attended the same military theory classes that I did . . . but thought advanced warcraft classes were a waste of his time. What you've seen makes perfect sense now. He doesn't know one end of a pike from the other. He's never actually *trained* any fighters, or trained as one himself. Unlike me, he never actually watched any of the Imperial units drilling. His idea of a commander is someone who stands in his tent over a sand table and pushes counters around. I will admit that he was quite good at that, but he has no idea how quickly a plan can break down when a real enemy is involved. He won't have an Imperial-sized army, he won't have Imperial resources, and he's never actually faced an insurgency-type battle, even on a sand table. He doesn't actually know the field he'd send troops into—no wonder he hated us so much. Life on the frontier put him amidst conditions people believed he would excel in, based on his bluster."

Hakkon burst into derogatory laughter that had heads turning in their direction. Sai cast his eyes upwards. Jon snickered.

"We can't count on this situation lasting," Sai cautioned them. "But . . . yes. And historically, an Adept is a poor sort of war leader. Their knowledge tends to be very deep, but very narrow. Specialists. They generally leave anything that doesn't have to do with magic to non-mages. They tend to throw damaging spells and unpleasant creatures at their enemies randomly rather than engage in any sort of tactics or strategy. She may not realize what is lacking at first. Eventually she'll probably demand Legenfall's own Lord Martial and use *him* for her information source, but that buys us yet more time. Yet more, if Legenfall doesn't actually have a Lord Martial. Don't worry, we'll keep our little eye in the sky watching. If training suddenly improves, then we'll know."

A troubling thought gnawed at Kordas. *If the Adept doesn't know how to use an army—ignoring supply, camp, recovery, and so forth, thinking numbers are enough—she may very well send the lot of them into a slaughter.*

"Well, if I have anything to say about it, Pebble and I will have quite a bit of work done by then," Delia told them all, getting up from the table. "And the sooner I can get to him, and get him to sculpt some basic defensive positions along the border, the happier I am going to be. That will leave Menalus free to make sure all the settlers thereabouts know where to go and what to do when that army shows up, and organize the general defense in case they don't try to head straight for Haven."

"Good luck, Delia," Kordas told her. "Safe journey."

She sketched a little salute, and headed for the door.

Maybe I should have gone along too. Second thoughts, third thoughts, should have, would have, could have. He never seemed to be able to free himself of them. Even though, in the next instant, he was scolding himself for not trusting the people he had previously determined were the right people to handle a job. *I can't be everywhere. I can't do everything,* he reminded himself. Again. As he always did.

:And so you always will. It is in your nature to analyze everything, and want to be in direct control of it all. But Kordas, when have any of the people you trusted to perform a task ever failed you because of incompetence?: Ardatha asked, as he and Isla got up, followed by Restil, and headed for the Council Chamber for the first meeting of the day.

He mulled that over. *:Not often. Maybe never. When they fail, and it's rare, it's because of something completely unforeseen. And most of the time, they back up and find a new solution.:* Admitting that made him take a deep breath and relax.

The morning Council meeting was often a short one. This morning, all that they needed to handle were the updates. The mages were raising stout supports out of the river—using something akin to what the Mother did, but with magic rather than organically. They had two of a planned total of ten to the point where the tops had just broken the surface of the water. Projections for the midsummer harvests were good, and the protections against pests were holding. The schools across Valdemar had very good attendance; not a hundred percent, but close enough that this generation of Valdemarans high *and* low was going to be literate, which could not have been said of the same people back in the Duchy. The Empire was not fond of literacy, although it was not forbidden. Literate people asked questions, and were inclined to think for themselves, things that the Emperor discouraged.

And in general, if only they had not had that looming

concern about the Adept and her "army"—this would have been shaping up to be a good year.

Ardatha remained mostly silent during the meeting, but Kordas felt him listening and watching with interest. It was anything but an uncomfortable feeling. In fact, it felt rather like having a friend at your back.

"Well," Kordas said, when most of the business had been concluded. "Here is the dangerous question. Should we warn everyone of this impending danger? I think we should. In fact, I think we should make sure every farmstead and population center is armed."

"They already are," the Lord Martial told him, with a wry look. "Mostly bows, arrows, and pikes, but they are. When things stabilized, I made plans for that, made sure there was at least one weapons maker in every population center that was a village or larger, and made sure to keep the prices low with subsidies from my budget. And for the last four years I've made it mandatory that everyone old enough to handle a weapon safely practice together for half a day or so once a sennight. But I agree, we should send out a warning. Nothing that will terrify people, but something they take seriously."

:Send your remaining Heralds,: Ardatha said, speaking up for the first time. *:Confer with the Lord Martial, write up a decree, and send them out. This is one of the things they should be doing from now on.:*

"You and I will confer this afternoon after dinner and write up a decree. I'll send our Heralds out with it," Kordas said smoothly.

He looked around the Council table, saw no dissent, and dismissed the meeting.

The business of running a Kingdom, or a Duchy for that matter, never stopped. Right after the morning Council meeting were Kordas's and Isla's Courts. They each held one; the Seneschal generally decided whose petitions or grievances were best addressed by the King or the Queen. And those

petitions or grievances were not going to vanish just because
there might be an invasion at some point soon. It did irritate him
a little that because of tradition, if common folk had a problem, they had to first address it with their local "authority"—
village headman, local squire, or local lord—and only if they
found no redress, could they first bring it to an official judge
in Haven, and then come to the Palace and place their petition
with the Seneschal. This was a long and complicated process
that the highborn could bypass entirely, so most of what he
and Isla saw were "highborn problems" that could have been
addressed with a mediator or a judge. But tradition was tradition, and even the Empire had followed this one. This morning,
however, he got mostly *genuine* problems that needed sorting
out. Isla tended to handle familial disputes, he tended to handle
monetary disputes, and that was by design. In a familial, emotional dispute, people seemed to take bad news better if Isla
delivered it.

It was a short Court. Two breaches of contract, three inheritance disputes, and a fairly contentious situation with two of
his highborn lords that threatened to break out into a feud if
he didn't settle it decisively. The latter took a lot of negotiation,
and in the end, neither lord was entirely happy, but both had
the impression that the other lord had received the worse end
of the decision.

*The essence of a good negotiation is that both sides agree
to being equally disappointed.*

Again, Ardatha just lingered in his mind, observing, which
seemed to be his habit when Kordas was holding Court.

:*I seem to have some time to spare before dinner*—: he
thought to Ardatha.

He got the sense of a chuckle. :*No you don't. The old Portal
is opening and you are about to have a visitor.*:

:*So! The Tayledras saw our flag! Sooner than I had hoped!*:

It wasn't a good idea for a King to run, but Kordas certainly
set a new record in speed-walking as he hastened down to the

postern-gate that led outside the wall to where the old Portal was.

The Portal was not something *anyone* could use to go wherever they chose, not even a mage, because it had been irrevocably locked to the Portal wherever the new k'Vesla Vale was. Kordas didn't actually know the geographic location, which was exactly how the Hawkbrothers wanted it. Despite that, caution had dictated that when the Mother built the wall complex, the Portal should be outside it. Just in case someone did somehow manage to hijack it. So when the Hawkbrothers came and went—visits that were less and less frequent as time passed—they had to wait patiently outside the wall until someone with authority would let them in.

They didn't seem to mind. Probably because the precautions seemed reasonable to them. Kordas didn't know exactly what protections the Tayledras had on *their* Portal, but he suspected they were formidable to say the least. Something that could stop the Portal from opening—or maybe something that stranded an unwanted or unanticipated passenger in the terrifying "between" until the Tayledras could verify the in-comer as harmless. And leave them there if they weren't.

That . . . would be a horrifying fate. Every time Kordas transited through a Portal, he got the feeling there was something just outside his sensing range that was watching him. Hostile? Neutral? Definitely not inviting. He wasn't eager to find out what it was, either.

"Majesty?" one of the two guards on the Portal said in surprise, as he dropped his dignity and sprinted the rest of the distance from the postern-door to the Portal. And it was only just as he got there that the first physical signs of the Portal opening manifested in the form of a mist that filled the gap between the two curved uprights. :*Ardatha—how did you know the Portal had been activated before there was any sign here?*:

:*We are much more sensitive to the movements of magical energies than humans are,*: Ardatha confirmed, as the

Companion strolled out of the postern-door in a much more leisurely fashion than the King. *:I suspect that will be useful.:*

The mist thickened, then became the rippling, reflective, water-like expanse that signaled someone was about to step through. Kordas waited, a little impatiently, because he had the shrewd notion that the Hawkbrothers had not been unaware of the entrance of the Companions into the world, had waited to confirm that whatever the phenomena was, it wasn't dangerous or hostile, and then had decided that it was a good time to respond to the hawk banner.

But he was exceedingly glad to see Silvermoon k'Vesla step through that watery surface, and not someone else. First, because Silvermoon was a great friend, not only to Kordas personally, but to all of Valdemar. Second, because if Silvermoon had come, the Hawkbrothers had confirmed that there was nothing inimical about the phenomena they'd detected.

And just to verify that assumption, Silvermoon was dressed in his Hawkbrother finery, showing this was a visit in which he anticipated no trouble, with his white goshawk resting on a thick shoulder-strapped gauntlet on his left arm. Today he wore green in all its possible variations, in the form of an intricately pieced long vest, tunic, and wide-legged trousers, his pure white hair long and loose, ornamented with strings of delicate green beads. Even the green leather belt at his waist was tooled and embellished, as were the pouches and his weapon-sheaths. Only his green gauntlet remained plain—as plain as the hertasi would allow, which meant dyed patterns—probably so that the bird didn't get his talons caught. That goshawk was easily twice the size of a "natural" bird, because it was Silvermoon's bondbird. Bondbirds were magically enhanced, and quite intelligent.

But Silvermoon wasn't alone! The shadow of a second person appeared behind the surface of the Portal, and then the second figure stepped through.

It was a young woman, about Restil's age, Kordas judged,

dressed less ostentatiously than Silvermoon in a gray-and-blue tunic and trousers, a wide gray fabric belt around her waist and a narrower gray leather belt slung at her hips, holding several pouches and weapons, and with a bird of her own on her wrist. This one was a sooty buzzard in its normal colors, broad of shoulder and hips, with a naturally white breast. Unlike Silvermoon, the young woman's hair wasn't white, it was a pure, deep sable, and her eyes were so dark a brown that the pupil almost vanished.

Kordas stepped forward as Silvermoon launched his bird into the air. It soared over the wall and presumably found a place to perch to its liking. Kordas had no fear for the chickens and pigeons of the Palace; Tayledras bondbirds were well-mannered, and didn't hunt domestic stock—although the Palace servant in charge of the chickens, pigeons and rabbits had now and again given one of them permission to "dispose of" particularly aggressive roosters that had somehow missed getting turned into a capon.

"Silvermoon!" he exclaimed, holding out both arms, and the two men embraced without delay. "I presume you came here about—" He jerked his head at Ardatha.

"—that wonder," said Silvermoon. "Indeed. So *this* is the form that the favor of the gods took." He released Kordas from the embrace and stood back a little to run his gaze over the Companion. "Greetings, Bright Soul," he said, with a little bow.

:Greetings, Elder of your people,: Ardatha said, apparently able to Mindspeak to Silvermoon, which should not have surprised Kordas in the least. *:And yes, we are the manifestation of the intervention of the gods. I am Ardatha.:*

"So there are more of you?" Silvermoon replied. "Good. This is excellent news. Truly excellent news. Kordas, Ardatha, this is my cousin, Starbird k'Vesla."

The grave-eyed young woman moved her left arm further from her body to accommodate the buzzard, bowed slightly to Kordas, and more deeply to Ardatha, but said nothing.

"So, you put up the banner, with the designation that this was not a request for a social visit, and I am fairly sure you would not have done that merely so that one of us would come to examine your new—" He paused, significantly.

:*Companions. We are calling ourselves Companions.*:

"—Companions," Silvermoon finished smoothly.

"No, but I'd prefer if we continued this discussion in the comfort of the Palace." Kordas did not want to make his guards uncomfortable by coming out and *saying* he wanted to be away from long ears. These men were only human. Part of the guards' daily ration was beer, and people were known to drink a little too deeply and talk a little too much as a result.

Silvermoon addressed the two guards. "Thank you for your vigilance." Taking her cue from that, the young woman clicked to her bird, and the buzzard launched from her gauntlet smoothly when she raised her arm.

"I would be very pleased to see the Palace up close. Let us take ourselves there," Silvermoon agreed. He nodded at his cousin, and all four of them made for the Palace at a more leisurely pace than Kordas had set to get to the Portal. Kordas hadn't missed the implication in Silvermoon's precisely worded comment—"see up close" indicated he knew it from a distance, implying that he surveilled it periodically. It wasn't a detail a listener would understand, as such, but the Hawkbrother preferred to speak subtly. Ardatha trailed behind at a distance that was neither awkwardly far nor uncomfortably close, aware that he had a possibly intrusive "presence." While they walked, Kordas kept up a running dialog about what he had done at what they were now calling the Grove, why he had done it, and an abbreviated version of what had happened there the night the Companions appeared. Silvermoon listened attentively, asked a few questions, and mostly listened. His cousin said nothing, but Kordas sensed that she was concentrating on his every word.

He paused when they were equidistant from the Palace and the pasture. "Do you want to have our conversation inside, or do you want to go examine the place where 'it' all happened?"

"I should like to visit this Grove, if you don't mind," Silvermoon said. "I'd like to see more of these Companions, and to tell the truth, I sense there is something you want to say that is not for every ear. It's easier to see a curious eavesdropper in the open."

:Oh, we wouldn't let anyone get near you,: Ardatha told him.

"I concede that many stones' weight of annoyed divine horses will make an effective barrier against snoops and gossips," Silvermoon laughed. His cousin finally cracked a smile. He whistled sharply and made a circling motion above his head, then pointed at the pasture. Two very large raptors left the roof of the Palace and flew in that direction. "And forgive me for calling you 'horses.' No offense meant."

:None taken. Kordas, Restil wants to know if you will permit him and Darshay to join us.:

"Tell him yes," Kordas replied.

Silvermoon smiled. "Useful," was all he said, but Kordas took his meaning. Having a pocket Mindspeaker with every Herald was, indeed, exceedingly useful. And if that had been all that the Companions could do, it would have been enough. But the fact that they could do *so much more* made them invaluable.

"Very," he said, dryly.

Just as they reached the Grove, Restil trotted up, riding bareback on Darshay. He slid down easily when he was near enough, looking as if he had never bothered with a saddle in his life.

"It's good to see you, Silvermoon," he said, with a little bow and a glance at Starbird.

"It is just as good to see *you,* young friend," the Hawkbrother replied. "This is my cousin, Starbird."

"And this is Darshay," Restil replied, gesturing toward his Companion. He tilted his head to the side. "Cousin-cousin, or cousin by blood? If you don't mind my asking."

Finally Starbird spoke. She had a very nice contralto voice. "Cousin by blood," she told him, and smiled a little. "It must sometimes be confusing when we refer to all elders as aunt and uncle or grandmother and grandfather, and everyone else as cousins. At least, when they aren't a brother or sister, mother or father. Our relationships between cousins are—not as scandalous as you might assume."

Oh, she's testing Restil. As subtle as a slap, but that's the play. Crafty.

"Well, I suppose it does make a Vale feel like an enormous family," Restil replied diplomatically. "I did enjoy that aspect."

And he replies, "I am not new to this."

"And here we are," said Kordas, pausing at the entrance to the Grove. "Shall we?"

He led the way without waiting for them to respond, and as soon as he entered the clearing, he got a surprise. Where grass had been, there was now a square section of pavement with a raised edge around it, in the creamy "stone" he recognized as the work of the Mother.

"It looks as if the Mother approves," Silvermoon observed. "I assume you had a notion of putting a building here?"

"A universal temple was the thought," Kordas replied.

"And it is a good thought. This will make an excellent foundation for such a thing. And that edge will serve very well as a bench for now." Silvermoon passed through the break in the raised edge, where, presumably, a door would be, and sat down. He placed one hand on the stone beside him, and indicated to Starbird that she should come in and take a seat herself.

She sat, and got a thoughtful look. "The Mother is finished here," she observed. "The rest of the building will be up to you. She must have intuited from one of you that you had plans for the sort of building you wanted."

"Very likely," Kordas agreed. "But that's not key right now. I put up the banner because we have a situation a-building. It's not a current threat, but it will become one eventually, and it is quite possible that trouble will rear its head in late fall."

He explained what his spies had learned: that the leader of the city to which his defectors had gone was an Adept, that she was cultivating an Imperial style "army"—although by Imperial standards it was going to be hardly more than a battalion—and what the Valdemarans were doing to counter her.

Silvermoon frowned deeply the moment that Kordas mentioned that their foe was female and an Adept, but he waited until Kordas was finished, and took a deep breath.

"Well," he said, with what sounded like resignation. "So that's what she has been up to."

Kordas stared at him. "You mean—you know about this Adept?"

"Adepts are rare. I find it vanishingly unlikely that k'Vesla would lose one, and that a different one would turn up in the direction we lost her. So. We can assume they are one and the same. Technically, she *is* one of us." Silvermoon paused, and Starbird fidgeted uncomfortably with the edge of her right sleeve. "*Was* one of us. Have you ever known any Adepts?"

"The strongest mage I know of is Jonaton, and he's not an Adept," Kordas admitted. "The history of the Empire says that the first Emperor was an Adept . . ." He bit his lip, as he thought. The trees of the Grove muffled sound to an uncanny degree, and there was nothing in here but the sounds that they themselves were making. The birds had all gone silent, probably because of the presence of the bondbirds. "Succeeding Emperors collected every mage they could get their hands on. Father and Grandfather always suspected that the Emperors killed any Adepts they found, or at least used them in ways in which it was not obvious that they had control over an Adept, which is why they never appear again in Imperial history. I don't even know how a mage becomes an Adept."

"They don't," Silvermoon told him. "In most cases, Adepts are born, not made. They have to *learn* magic wielding, just as every other mage does, but they are born with an incredible capacity to manipulate power from literally any source, including ley-lines that you and I would not dare touch, or we'd be sizzling little bits of charred meat on the ground."

"And you think this one is from k'Vesla?" Kordas ventured.

"Yes. And she disappeared early—*very* early—in her training. She was barely into her teens. We knew that she left the Vale under her own power. . . . We didn't know why, and we tried to track her, but from being a very beginning apprentice, she seemed to have acquired all the skills of a mature, full Adept overnight, and so far as we were concerned, she vanished without a trace." Silvermoon looked more somber than Kordas had ever seen him before. Probably with good cause. Bad enough that there was an Adept with plans of conquest in this area, but that she was a Hawkbrother? It didn't reflect well on k'Vesla, and Silvermoon took these matters personally. "She was—" Silvermoon paused a moment. "—favored by me, and well liked by many."

"That . . . is alarming," Kordas said slowly, the hair on the back of his neck going up.

"That is more than alarming," Silvermoon acknowledged. "We lost track of her completely for years. To be honest, most of us hoped she was dead—that would have been a tragedy, but all too often, death is a mercy. What the Pelagirs can do to someone is unspeakable. If she was alive, why would she have avoided coming back to the Vale unless she was up to things she knew we would not tolerate? And now here she is again. In charge of a city. We knew of temple complexes and keeps, but no cities, north of you. I cannot personally think of any way she could have undergone that drastic a transformation—without us finding trace of it—that is *not* alarming."

Kordas felt cold all over, despite the heat of the sunshine in the sheltering Grove. "Possession?" he ventured. "I mean—I've never actually seen anyone who was possessed. . . . In the Empire, possession is a sort of wonder tale you relate around a winter fire to scare everyone. Though . . . some say that all succeeding Emperors allowed themselves to be possessed by the spirit of the first Emperor when they felt the need. But no one could ever confirm that."

"We simply don't know," Silvermoon admitted. And then he looked at the two Companions.

:That is not knowledge that has been shared with us,: Ardatha admitted. *:I am very much afraid that we don't know everything.:*

"Do you know anything at all about her?" Silvermoon asked boldly.

:No. I wish that we did. But I hope you understand that we have limitations, by design.:

"So we'll muddle through as best we can," Kordas said, raising his chin. "For now . . . let's make a visit to the Old Men. And Jonaton will be very happy to see you again, and meet Starbird. They at least have a view of her city. Maybe your eyes can make out something we haven't."

Silvermoon stood up. "That is as good a plan as any," he replied.

Kordas turned to his son. "Restil, get your mother, and both of you go meet up with the Lord Martial and work on that proclamation the Heralds are going to take out. If he has any questions, ask me through Ardatha."

Restil jumped to his feet. "Yes sir," he replied, and immediately swung up on Darshay when she knelt, and headed for the Palace at a trot.

"Before we panic, let's discover what we can," Silvermoon

cautioned. "It might not be her. She might not be as powerful as we fear; she may not be an Adept at all, she may simply be *claiming* that she is. And—there are two things in our favor."

"She doesn't know about the Companions—" Kordas offered.

Silvermoon nodded. "And she knows very little about you, other than what your defectors have told her. So we have advantages."

"Then we'll have to make our best use of them." He headed for the mages' quarters, which were, of course, in the wall. "And the sooner we start, the better."

Restil had been afraid that the Lord Martial would not accept the substitution of himself and his mother for the King, but he soon discovered that he needn't have worried. Evidently the Lord Martial was perfectly happy with a Queen instead of a King.

Then again . . . he sat in Council, and he had a very good idea of what the Queen could do, and how intelligent she was.

They turned up at his makeshift office, which was in the barracks section of the wall, arriving together. With their Companions, of course, though Darshay and Dendalin remained outside. The Lord Martial—his name was actually Lord Ventis Endimon, but almost no one ever referred to him by anything except his honorific title—was in there, sitting at his desk, with a page accepting papers as he signed them. He had been Kordas's Lord Martial back in the Duchy, having taken over from his own father when Kordas became Duke. He was older than Kordas by about twenty years, and his job was, and always had been, the organization, training, leading, and disposition of whatever quasi-military force the Duchy fielded. Unofficially, of course, because officially all that a Duke of the Empire was allowed was a private force of guards, usually no more than was absolutely necessary to safeguard their property and provide a bit of strong-arm over any recalcitrant highborn under the Duke's authority. And technically, that force should only be under the authority of the Duke himself. But pretty much everyone from the position of Duke and above had had a Lord Martial, and this was one of the very few things that the Empire turned a blind eye to. Mostly because in a pinch, if the Imperial forces ran out of officers, they could commandeer as many Lords Martial as they needed.

Lord Martial Endimon looked every bit the military man, as he should, since he had been trained in the Imperial Military Academy as a youngster. Unlike Lord Legenfall, he *had* weapons training, and *had* done some field commanding with the Imperial Army before being released to return home when his knee blew out during maneuvers in impossible terrain and the Healers could not get to him before there was permanent damage they could do nothing about. He had taken that discharge gratefully, since so far as he was concerned, a blown knee was a small price to pay for going home.

His hair had been cut aggressively short, and what was there was iron-gray and had been for as long as Restil had known him; square-jawed, with penetrating dark eyes, he had not put on a pennyweight of fat since his "retirement." That blown knee was no handicap to him in combat, and he had been invaluable on the trek here, keeping the back half of the convoy of barges in order while Kordas managed the front half. Since the establishment of the "New Valdemar," he had been far more than invaluable. He habitually dressed in brown, as being the color least likely to draw attention and collect dirt; his clothing was usually canvas in summer and leather and wool in winter and identical in cut and style to the Guard uniform.

His office consisted of a single room on the first floor, with nothing in it but the fireplace, a desk, his chair, and two chairs across from the desk. But the walls were papered with maps of the Kingdom, covered with cryptic markings Restil couldn't even pretend to understand, in different colors. Restil didn't think the markings were in ink—maybe artist crayons—and what he assumed were unit markers were wax-backed decals. Easy enough to peel up and move.

The Lord Martial looked up as he signed the last of the papers, and handed a stack to the page. "Ah, Isla and Restil. Come in place of the King, I presume? Good. I'd rather it was you two. Kordas tends to overthink everything." He made a shooing motion at the page. "Off you go, Ternly. Drop those with the Seneschal-in-command. And tell the pages they don't need to quake in their boots because Hakkon put me in charge of them until he comes home. I'm not a bear, I won't eat them."

Ternly, who evidently knew the Lord Martial well enough to know that he was, in fact, surprisingly gentle with the pages, grinned. "Sir, yes sir," the lad said smartly. With a pile of loose papers in his hands, he couldn't salute, but he did click his heels together. "Beggin' your pardon, sir, but it might be a good thing to put old Asterdil in charge of the page's dormitory while Master Hakkon's gone. He's fair, and he gets respect, and with his back actin' up, he ain't good for long Guard shifts."

"Wait—don't go—" The Lord Martial grabbed two pieces of parchment and hastily scribbled down some orders, signing and stamping them. He placed them on the top of the pile. "There, done. One for Asterdil, reassigning him, and one for the sergeant, verifying the order. Good suggestion, lad. Hate to lose you, but when Hakkon gets back, I think it's time you moved up to squire. We'll do that as soon as one of the squires moves up to knight. Which will be soon. The more knights I can field if Legenfall turns up, the better. *He* won't have any . . . or if he does, they'll be on foot. He got *no* chargers, and the horses he has aren't up to a knight's weight."

The boy brightened considerably at the suggestion he

might become a squire. There were not a lot of knights in the Guard at the moment—the Empire didn't approve of a Duke having more than a token number of elite fighters—so this meant that there were not a lot of squires yet, either. This would be a big step upward for the boy.

As Restil had learned as a page in his brief lessons on heraldry and the hierarchy, small "s" squires were assigned to knights, both as helpers and as "apprentices" of a sort. Large "s" squires, like the Young Squire, were something else entirely. Short for "esquire," it was a hereditary title, lower than lord, technically lower than knight, higher than "village headman."

"Knights" were made; the title wasn't hereditary. Most highborn who kept knights "grew" their own, although the Empire had its own college of knights. You took all the younglings in the Court whose parents could spare them and who wanted to train, and made them pages. Let them train part of the day and see who was good at fighting, at least at the youngling level. Elevate them to squire, and pair them with a knight. When they were ready, make them knights. You could have as many knights as you could afford heavy horses. And, of course, Kordas had no shortage of horses.

It was a good place to put highborn youngsters who otherwise didn't have a lot to do. And you very soon sorted out the lazy, those who were unsuited to fighting, and those who refused to be under the authority of anyone else.

There were twenty knights in Kordas's service now, and the shock of twenty heavily armored men and animals against a line of light-armored troops would be more than enough to disrupt and dismay.

When they had first arrived here, Kordas had had only three knights, because any more would have attracted unwanted attention from the Emperor. As soon as the basics had been established and they had a bit of stability, he had started raising more knights up out of the squires, figuring one day he'd need them against a conventional army. Before, a squire was a dead-end sort of position. When you reached adulthood, you just left the squires and did whatever your family deemed appropriate. Now, well, every page had the potential to become a knight if they were worthy.

The page stopped long enough to even up the edges of the stack of papers, tied a bit of string around them to keep them in place, and headed off on his errands.

The Lord Martial gestured at the two spare chairs in his painfully neat office. "So, we need to create a proclamation that will put the folks outside of Haven on the alert and ready for trouble, without scaring them into racing for the city and demanding shelter inside the wall. Have I assessed that right?"

"Perfectly," Isla told him, dropping into the chair farthest from the door, leaving the other for Restil. "Since you've been successful at getting them to practice fighting and shooting, perhaps we should begin with that? Something like . . . 'We have cause to believe that your fighting skills may be put to the test some time within the next six moons'? That will remind them that they are not helpless, and that they can rely on their own walls and skills to hold off enemies until a larger force can come to help."

"Let me tinker with that a bit, Majesty," Lord Endimon said in return, and between the three of them, along with some suggestions passed on by Darshay and Dendalin, they hammered out a document that satisfied all of them in about a mark.

"Good!" the Lord Martial proclaimed. "Kordas would have tried to make an inspirational speech out of this, which is all well and good, but that sort of thing falls flat when someone else is reading it. This is better. Short, informative, to the point. Puts people on alert without making them panic. Leave the inspirational speeches to their local leaders—or the Herald in question, if they feel up to it. Now, does this go out under the royal seal or mine?"

"Both, I think," said Isla, and held out her hand for the original, complete with its scratchings-out and corrections. "I'll take this back to the Palace, get the scribes to make copies, and have the Seneschal-in-command stamp it with both seals. Then I'll pass them out to the Heralds after we assign who will cover what areas." She paused, and looked at both Restil and Endimon. "Should we have Kordas mage-impress the seals?"

Both Restil and the Lord Martial shook their heads. "No need for something like this, Majesty," the older man said. "Especially not something where there is more than one copy being sent out."

"It's too likely that the proclamation will be discarded," Restil added. "Easy to steal that proclamation out of the discarded documents meant to be scraped and re-used. Too easy to 'lift' the seal with a hot knife and apply it to something else." He shrugged. "Best not to put temptation in the way of people who are all too easily tempted."

"Good points," the older man agreed. "All right, I'll leave that in your hands, and start on requisitions and supplies of weapons to go out to those villages. Arrows, mostly," he added. "Good thing we've been stockpiling against this very thing."

"Because *you* insisted on doing so from the moment we got here, sir," Restil pointed out.

"Well, well, that's my job, Prince." The Lord Martial actually cracked a bit of a smile. "I trust you don't need escorts back to the Palace?"

Isla sniffed. "When have I ever needed an escort?"

"Personally, I don't think anyone has been of the opinion that you need one since the day you blasted that wyrsa that came over the wall and landed at your feet, Majesty," Endimon acknowledged. "Opened some eyes that day, you did. And now? You have half a ton of potentially lethal horsemeat on your side. You are more at risk *inside* the Palace than outside."

"One tries," she replied archly, and she and Restil left. "I'll take this to the royal scribes and get the seals attached," she said. "I think that Beltran might be best suited to deciding which of the Heralds should be sent where."

"Beltran *and* me, I think," Restil countered. "Menalus is off and so is Delia; everyone else is back from their last message run. Can the Kingdom stand doing without me for a day or three? Because obviously you and Father can't go out, so that only leaves fourteen of us to make this run, if Beltran goes out, and I think he should."

His mother stopped in the path and pondered that for a moment. "I think we have to. But I want you in the south, not the north."

Restil started to protest, but Darshay had something to say before he could. :*She's right. We don't know anything about this mage; what if she knows what you look like and tries a long-distance attack on you far from the protections of Haven?*:

He sighed, but nodded his agreement. "I'll find Beltran and we'll work out who goes where."

When Isla wanted a thing done, it got done in a hurry. The copies of the proclamation were all written and seals attached by breakfast of the next day, and the Heralds scattered to the four winds to deliver them as soon as they had eaten. Restil was, indeed, sent due south. And for the first time, he discovered just how fast Darshay was, without the distraction of trying to figure out how to save a boatload of children. Very, very fast. It was like riding the wind, and Darshay's pace was so smooth he could have been on a palfrey, at the walk. He made it all the way to the southern border in a third of the time it would have taken if he'd not only ridden a truly fast Valdemar Gold, but had been able to change horses regularly when one tired.

Thanks to Darshay, it didn't take long to get to the southern border towns and villages, read the proclamation, say a few reassuring words, and be off to the next. Restil saw *nobody* who was unimpressed by seeing the Crown Prince and Darshay; the general reaction was one of sacred novelty, like glimpsing a holy artifact passing through on a faith-tour. This was the first time many of the villagers had seen a Herald and Companion, and even if they didn't know what that meant, it was a remarkable sight. People weren't happy to learn that about half of the guards stationed in their villages were being pulled off to go north, but they understood. In fact, more than one mayor or headman said, with resignation, "Well, this is no different than when we had no guards at all. We'll manage."

Not all of them were that sanguine, and some got as combative as they dared to with a representative of the King, but in the end, they understood they had no choice. Restil's retort of "Well, you *could* be in the north," generally quelled the argument. Not once did he mention that he was the Crown Prince, and that was a deliberate choice. Partly it was out of caution—no point in advertising who he was out there. The last thing he needed was to paint a target on his own back. But the biggest reason was that he wanted to establish that the Heralds were, essentially, without rank. That no Herald was more important than any other Herald.

But one excellent thing came out of all of this. Time and time again he was approached by people who wanted to volunteer to help defend Valdemar. After a quick check with the help of Darshay the first time it happened, he was able to tell them that they would be welcome, and the Lord Martial would arrange for their training, and they could start for Haven immediately. Darshay said that what the Lord Martial had in mind was to put them on the walls of Haven, replacing the guards he was sending north. Since virtually everyone Restil's age these days was good with a bow, that seemed very smart to him. The gods knew they had bows and arrows in plenty, thanks to the Dolls virtually robbing the Imperial armory in the days before their escape.

All told, he was about two days on the border, without Darshay showing any signs of tiring. She probably could have kept up a steady gallop (at "fastest Companion" speed!) all night—but he, at least, needed rest. And besides, people got testy if you turned up at midnight and expected everyone to assemble for the reading of a proclamation. So he'd begin at false-dawn, and once it was past early evening, he'd stop at the first place that had an inn or guesthouse to stay in, or even someone willing to give him a place on the hearth to sleep. Inns were few in all of Valdemar, but the fact there were any at all was a testament to how the young country was faring now. Two days was all it took, and he was done by the evening of his third day.

He began his return well before dawn of the fourth day, and thanks to Darshay's incredible speed when she was on a straight run, by afternoon he was within sight of Haven. While they raced home, Darshay kept up a running commentary on who was still out, who was back, and what the reception of the warning had been.

:The folk in the north are frightened, but determined,: Darshay reported. :And the first wagon-loads of arms and weapons have started arriving in the townships nearest Haven. Once the additional guards arrive, perhaps they will be more confident. Menalus is doing a very good job of organizing defenses.:

:Any dissension?: he asked, slowing her to a canter as they approached the outskirts of the city. On this trip he'd been able to get a lot more practice in Mindspeech, and now it felt comfortable.

:Not open. I wonder if the dissenters will just pick up and move back to Haven, or try their chances with the Adept?:

:A few might try, but they'll have to abandon everything they've built, and most people are reluctant to do that,: he pointed out. Then he shook his head. *:That's not something we can do anything about. And if they come, of course we will find them shelter. There are still barges left over. And we can certainly find them jobs. Potentially, if they are proven trustworthy, we could replace all of the guards at the Palace and in Haven with some of them, and send the Palace guards north. Are the mages headed north yet?:*

:A group of six, plus six apprentices. Koto is leading them. Three of them are green mages, so that once Pebble is done reshaping the landscape, they'll make it look as if it is entirely natural. The Lord Martial sculpted the whole thing on a sand table with your father's assistance, and Dendalin sent the plan to Delia via Valiance. Delia and Pebble are already moving along the border right now. I gather from what Valiance says that Pebble could move a great deal faster than he is doing at the moment, but he doesn't want to separate from Delia.:

By this point they were nearly to the wall and the main gate to the Palace. He already knew how many of the Heralds were back; Darshay had been keeping him updated as they returned. Deep inside him was a core of anxiety he was doing his best to keep in check. Packs of monsters, insect plagues, and uncertain crops were one thing, but this was the first time that the new Kingdom had faced anything like a real enemy. The ongoing Imperial wars had been far away—and anyway, he had been too young to really understand any of them at the time. The attack of the Red Forest *would* have been terrifying— if he'd seen any of it. But he and all the other children, and those who were too frightened or utterly inexperienced in combat had all been hiding in the hertasi tunnels while it was going on. The only evidence of a battle had been when the earth trembled, and even then, he'd had no idea what that meant.

But now, for the first time, *he* was going to be in the front lines of a conflict with actual hostile forces. Granted, the "army" could not possibly be "Imperial-size" large; even if every one of the dissenters over the age of twelve or thirteen had been placed under arms, it would be less than a battalion, and even adding conscripts from the Adept's city would scarcely bring it up to full battalion size. But Valdemar didn't have a battalion's-worth of trained troops; there were not enough guards in all of Valdemar to face them one-on-one.

And there was no telling just what other things that army would have with them. Would the Adept defy expectations and come against them herself? Maybe. Would she send magical weapons and monsters? Almost certainly. And his imagination was populated with all of the terrible things he had read about the Imperial mages using. Poomers and Spitters, of course. Catapults that could toss glass vessels full of captured, inextinguishable mage-fire. Potion-mists that infected fighters with intolerable fear. Potion-mists that killed everything they touched. Granted, potion-mists were known for killing both friend and foe, but would the Adept really care? What if she could steer the stuff? The list went on and on.

If he thought about it, he'd be limp with terror, so he tried not to think about it.

:It's all right to be afraid. You would be foolish not to be. I will help you be brave.:

But now that he and Darshay were heading up the twisty road to the Palace, passing through the manors both completed and partially finished, some of those fears receded. Traffic was light, and Darshay could move faster than a trot.

His spirits and heart rose to see the Palace gate, and the guards there. Guards who were still not used to seeing the Companions, so that when he got within hailing distance, they got all starry-eyed to see Darshay present herself.

The guards just waved them through, at the same time that Darshay said, :The King and Queen know you are here, and will welcome you themselves as soon as they are free. I expect that won't be until supper.:

:Well, not to be rude, my love, but I want to be out of this

saddle and onto something flat for a while. Maybe with a hot
bath before I get there. I'll heat the water with magic myself.:
     :Then just stop at your quarters. I'll go straight to the stable
and charm a groom into unsaddling and grooming me.:
     :You are a star.:
     :Yes, I am.:

One hot, soaking bath and a couple of marks flat on his bed
later, and Restil was on his way to the royal suite. Already he
had gotten very used to being away from the family, and he
liked it very much. Beltran and Delia were excellent company,
and they were near Rothas and Lythe, so he could at least
keep an eye on Rothas and make sure that their tentative
friendship didn't fall by the wayside. A lot of his concerns
about the budding Bard had been alleviated, partly because
the mages were all drumming ethics into his skull at every
opportunity, and partly because the Companions all cautiously
approved of him.

In fact, as he headed for the Palace and supper, he encountered Rothas on his way as well. "Back already?" the young
man said, guilelessly. "I thought you'd be gone at least a
sennight!"

"Companions are fast," Restil told him. *"Incredibly* fast.
And Darshay says she's the fastest of the lot."

"Well, while you were gone, I made two more Sydney songs,
and I think I have the song about how the Companions appeared mostly worked out. But I don't want anyone but Lythe
to hear it for now. Not until it's ready." Rothas took a deep
breath. "The Syd songs are one thing. They are supposed to be
funny, not accurate, and not . . . *inspiring.* This has to be
perfect."

Restil nodded with approval. But Rothas was not finished

with him. "Is there really going to be a war?" the Bard asked, hesitantly.

"I wouldn't call it a *war,* exactly," Restil told him—because, after all, this was not exactly a secret. "But it is going to be dangerous, it will definitely be terrible on the border, and if things go wrong, Haven itself might be endangered." Then he gave Rothas the shortest possible explanation.

The Bard frowned. "Fighting is only interesting when it's in the past and didn't happen to anyone you know," he said unhappily. "I didn't like it much when villagers got into fights with each other. I *really* don't like this. What did you do to make this mage so angry with you?"

"Exist, as far as I can tell," the Prince told him. "For some people, that's all that's necessary, I guess. In exact terms, we don't even know if she's hostile, and we don't know for certain that this army she is raising is meant to attack us—but she is dangerous enough just by being an Adept that we'd be naive to assume friendliness."

Rothas continued frowning as they walked toward the Palace. "I have some ideas," he said, just as they got to the door that would lead to the Great Hall where supper was probably being laid out. "I'll let you know if Sai thinks they're any good."

The heady smell of fresh-baked bread wafted out of the windows and the door when they opened it, and the bell in the Palace bell tower rang to announce the first serving. Rothas headed for the hall; Restil headed for the royal suite. The King and Queen usually ate at the second serving; the first was for all the hardworking folk serving in the Palace. Occasionally some highborn snuck in to the first serving—they weren't actually barred from eating then—but mostly they waited for the second serving, which was for the highborn and their personal servants. The reason for this? The highborn and their personal servants were habitual lingerers over their meals.

Most, if not all, of the Palace servants, which included the gardeners, the laundry workers, the stablehands, and the cleaners rose extremely early and were hungrier by the time that supper came, and many wanted to go straight to their beds. Those that did not used the fading daylight after dinner to tend to their own needs, and weren't inclined to waste a moment in gossip or gawking. No one was going to do *their* mending or other domestic chores for *them*. If they were still wakeful and had nothing pressing to do after the second serving was over, they were welcome to enjoy whatever entertainment there might be after supper from the gallery above the Great Hall.

As for the kitchen staff and the servers, they ate first, before the food went out to the Great Hall. That was Isla's doing. It had been the same way at the Ducal manor. She felt that it was unfair for people to be working around food when they, themselves, were hungry.

Since moving in with the Heralds, Restil generally ate at first serving, but Ardatha had passed on that his parents wanted him to eat with them. Since Darshay had kept everyone up to date on exactly where she and Restil were, and how the proclamation was being received at every stop he made, there wasn't anyone he needed to report in to.

Another wonderful thing about Companions. Well, there were just so many wonderful things about Companions that he could be all day listing them. And right now, rather than think about what was looming in front of them, he decided he'd see the family.

That got him as far as the door to the royal suite, where the Guards gave him little deferential nods—the King had scolded them for bowing too much—and one of them opened the door for him. The first person he saw was Jon, sitting in the boat that had been converted into a couch, with three kittens climbing over him.

Jon started to jump to his feet, remembered he had a lap

full of kittens, and put the kittens down on the floor where they toddled over to their mother, falling over their own feet a few times. "You got back *fast*! We weren't expecting you to be back before tomorrow!"

"Darshay is the fastest of the Companions," he said proudly (and maybe a little smugly). "How is the library coming?"

"Things are going faster now that I have each shelf organized in alphabetical order," his brother said, combing his dark, curly hair out of his eyes with his fingers. "I haven't been able to get most of the Heralds' stories yet because you all scattered to the four winds, but I am getting a lot from the Companions that haven't Chosen yet, and from Ardatha." Jon practically glowed with happiness when he said that, which made his brother both pleased and relieved. "I spend most afternoons out there with them. I can't believe they want to talk to me, but they do."

"So now you *have* got your own circle of friends," he replied, clapping Jon on the back. "Instead of people, you have a circle of Companion friends!"

"I . . . guess I have." Jon ducked his head shyly. "They're . . . rather wonderful, aren't they?"

"Yes. Yes, they are."

:*Indeed we are,:* Darshay laughed in his mind. :*But you can go right on reminding people of that.:*

:*Vain horse!:* Restil shot back.

Both the King and the Queen came in at that moment, shortly followed by Hakkon, and there was a bit of babble as they all studiously avoided the subject of the looming conflict in favor of trivialities. But Restil could not avoid noticing that Hakkon was unusually sober behind the banter, and he reckoned that being in on the Lord Martial's preparations had driven home just how serious the situation was, and how little they actually knew. That last would be greatly troubling his lordship, and he would not have hidden that from Hakkon.

So brother Hakkon is starting to understand that not even

Father is in control of everything. The day that Restil had figured that out had been a sobering one for him. And a bit frightening. And that had been the day he became very determined
to do what he could to help, in whatever way he could. It looked
as if the revelation was having the same effect on Hakkon.
*And Jon figured it out before either of us. I think he may be
smarter than both of us combined.*

Restil did a great deal of the talking, with little details
about every hamlet and village he'd passed through. Jon
looked as if he was longing to take notes, but refrained.

:Don't worry, I'll retell it all to him tomorrow,: Darshay
offered.

:You'll remember it all better than I will,: he admitted.

Just before they ran out of things to say, the bell sounded
for second serving, and it was with a great deal of relief on
Restil's part at least that they all went down to eat.

He was more than a bit surprised to see that Silvermoon
and his cousin Starbird were there, and when the places were
sorted out, Restil found himself sitting next to her. He had
expected them to leave shortly after he had—after all, they
hadn't brought anything like belongings with them, except for
the clothing they wore and their birds. Starbird seemed just as
reserved as she had been when the two had first arrived, and
he decided to introduce himself a second time, since it didn't
appear that she was going to make any overtures.

She was not what his mother would have called "conventionally pretty," but since the Queen often used that term as a
pejorative, that wasn't necessarily a bad thing. He liked how
she looked; she had a composed expression that appealed to
him a great deal. Her features were sharply defined, sculp-
tural, which gave her a look not unlike her bondbird, and she
had bound up her long black hair into a knot at the top of her
head, which was skewered in place by a couple of dagger-like
hairpins.

Or for all I know, they are *daggers.*

She wore a similar outfit to the one she had arrived wearing, but in green. Silvermoon was all in grays. So evidently while he'd been gone, they had decided to stay, and gotten changes of clothing. *I wonder how long they're planning to be here.* He hoped it was for at least a sennight more.

"Hello," he said, in his very best Tayledras—because of course he and his brothers had been given the language along with the King and Queen within the first few days of being at what was then k'Vesla Vale. "We met a few days ago, but we weren't properly introduced. I'm Restil, the King's oldest son, and Chosen by Darshay." There wasn't actually a word for "King" in the Hawkbrother language, but there was something that meant "ruler," and he figured that would do.

"I know who you are," she replied. "I remember you riding up on your Companion when we visited the Grove for the first time. And your accent is very good." She smiled slightly. "You just returned from the southern border."

"Yes, I did," he confirmed. "This afternoon. Are you and your cousin going to stay for a while?" He found himself hoping that she would say "yes." She intrigued him no end. Not the least because she was his age—and yet he distinctly recalled that there had not been *any* children of *any* kind at k'Vesla when the Valdemarans had arrived. And he'd *looked* for them as a child, and wondered where all the Hawkbrother children were. There didn't seem to be any—but before he could find out, the Tayledras had removed themselves to the new location of their Vale, and he never got a chance to discover where they were—or if the Hawkbrothers had already moved them to the new location of the Vale before they offered the old location to the Valdemarans. So if she was indeed k'Vesla, and she was almost certainly his age, where had she sprung from?

But it would be very rude to just come out and ask that. The Hawkbrothers were quite secretive—no one in Valdemar even knew where the new location of k'Vesla was—and this was probably one more thing they were very secretive about.

"I'm not sure," she said, looking down at her food. "I—I'm not sure. He hasn't told me."

He decided to be a little bold. "Would you like to stay?" He hoped he didn't sound too pushy. He hoped she didn't take it wrong.

"Actually, yes, I would," she said, finally looking at him. "The Companions fascinate me. The Grove does, too. And I want to learn things from your Healers that my teachers did not know."

"Oh! You're a Healer, then?" He paused. "In the Empire, all Healers wore green, and we more or less kept that, because that makes them easy to identify."

"I'd wondered! That was why I chose this to wear." She smoothed the skirt of her tunic with her free hand. "I didn't know if it was polite to ask."

So . . . she wasn't at k'Vesla when our Healers and theirs were neck deep in exchanges. So where was she?

"My cousin asked me to come, because he wanted me to learn directly from your Healers what they taught the k'Vesla Healers." She smiled a very little. "He says that information obtained secondhand is like wearing secondhand boots. It's never quite right."

"Well, I can do you a favor, then," he said, pleased that he was going to be able to . . . well, maybe not *impress* her, exactly, but certainly please her. "My cousin Delia started a project of copying all the important books we could get together, and I know there must be books by Healers among them. I could take you to the scriptorium and, at the very least, you'll be able to read those books and take notes, even if there isn't a copy to spare. If there is a spare, I am sure they'll let you have it."

"That would be very kind of you!" she exclaimed, as if she was surprised that he had volunteered something of that sort.

"I would be very grateful! I did not know there were extra copies of such texts, and your Healers guard their books like bears guarding a den!"

He smiled back at her. *I think this is going well.*

He glanced up to the head of the table. Silvermoon was deep in what looked like serious conversation with the King and Queen. "Do you remember Lythe Shadowdancer?" he asked her. "She works in the scriptorium at night while she's awake. With a good, bright mage-light you can work as late as you please, but of course, most of the scribes prefer . . ."

"Their evenings to themselves," she said, when he hesitated. "So they can actually have a life outside of books. Yes, I remember Lythe, although I didn't talk with her myself. I sincerely hope that you have managed to at least temper that misery they were both projecting, if not eliminate it." She shook her head in a way that almost made him laugh. It was clear she had no patience at all for what she probably thought was self-indulgent emotional wallowing.

"Well, yes," he replied cheerfully. "In fact, that's one reason why she's in the scriptorium. It's wonderful what having a productive task can do. Honestly, some of her problem was that Rothas did have work when they were with you—he performed, and he composed—but she had nothing at all. To make matters worse, once night falls, people tend to break into small groups to socialize, and she was left out of them."

Starbird nodded. "I expect that was true."

"And once they came here, Rothas had even more to do, learning new instruments, learning exactly how to use his Gifts, and he had a much bigger audience. What could Lythe do?" He shrugged. "I certainly wasn't the one who had the idea—Father did—but the first thing we did was give her a job. Initially, that was helping to patrol the Palace walls at night, because she didn't have any obvious skills."

"She can dance," Starbird said dryly. "That was all we ever discovered."

"Well, as it turns out, Father discovered that she has Animal Mindspeech. And Delia worked out that she enjoys doing detailed work, and tried her on copying books." Starbird seemed interested, so he continued. "So besides working in the scriptorium, which she very much enjoys, she's learning to use *her* Gift and is making a good job of it too. She works with our Master of Hounds to get puppies to understand what is wanted of them much faster, and to discover what exactly is ailing sick or injured dogs. She works with the cats occasionally too, though—" He shrugged.

"I know. Cats." She nodded knowingly.

"And horses. Regular horses, although the Companions talk to her as well. And besides that, we learned that . . . after the initial giddy rush, neither of them was particularly happy about being lifebonded to a complete stranger. Especially not when they only saw each other for a mark or so at sunrise, and another at sunset. The lifebond was dragging them together, but their natural inclination was to resist. So there's that." He waited to see what she would make of that.

"Oh. Dear." She pursed her lips. "I don't think that even occurred to any of us. Very remiss of us. Something we should have picked up on."

"Don't be too upset with yourselves. With all that melancholy oozing out of both of them, it would have been difficult to ferret out the causes." There, that was probably diplomatic enough. "Silvermoon did the right thing by bringing them here. They both got things to do to keep them from dwelling too much on their own unhappiness, and that meant they actually started talking to each other. And we *are* making some headway on breaking those curses, now that we know what happened. The mages tell me it's going to take some very specific timing, but if anyone can disentangle the magic, I think our Old Men can."

"And once they can have normal lives again, it will just be a matter of reconciling themselves to the lifebond," she concluded. "In the meantime, interesting work that you are actually *good* at is a spirit-lifter for most people." She smiled fully, then, and he found himself smiling back.

"Rothas will probably perform after everyone eats," he offered. "He does most nights. He's gotten to be a very fine Bard, in fact! Do you want to stay and listen?"

"I've already heard him, and yes, he's remarkable." He expected her to decline, but instead, she added, "I'd enjoy that very much. And then we can visit the scriptorium, when everyone else is gone and Lythe is awake."

"Perfect," he said, and would have said more, except at that exact moment, Rothas appeared in the doorway of the Great Hall, and anything he might have said was drowned in enthusiastic applause.

16

Jonaton's recitation to the King of what he had been up to regarding his partner was just a little short of smug. A little. Kordas was more amused than anything else. While Jonaton might be more than a little erratic, the one thing Kordas could always count on would be that he was brilliant at coming up with solutions to problems most people didn't even realize were problems.

"I've been working on subtle, self-powered scrying charms off and on, for about a year. Something 'quiet' enough magically to go unnoticed by anyone seeking such things, because they work at low power over only a short distance. But what they show is relayed through a second, larger object nearby, with more power. From that comes the link for the remote scry. Should someone feel like spying on someone else's business, their agent could wear an innocuous mirrored pin or a badge, a quarter mile from the larger item. I made Hakkon wear a mirror-backed badge on his helmet that is linked to a new saddlehorn I gave him. The saddlehorn has an adjustable magelight inside the cap, with a pretty mirrored compass underneath," Jonaton explained to Kordas, as they both gazed into a mirror on the table between them that showed a slowly changing landscape with an occasional glimpse of a Fairweather. "That way there's a chance that someone detecting it will assume the energy signature is just from the magelight, but the item is attached to a saddle, so no one will just pocket it. I didn't tell him what the badge was for, but he probably guessed. He's seen me fiddle with it."

"Does that badge work both ways?" the King asked.

Jonaton sat back in his chair, and sniffed. "What do you think? I'd make something that shows me views of him getting into trouble, but doesn't let me help him?"

"Help get him *out* of trouble, or help get him *into* trouble?" Kordas joked back.

"You know by now, I do as I must," Jonaton chuckled. *Gods and Powers it's good to see him laugh again.* Whatever had broken him out of his grief, whether it be having to keep track of Hakkon, listening to Rothas's songs about Sydney, or—well, it was possible that the black cat that had met Kordas at the door of Jonaton's quarters was there because of Lythe. And if that was the case, he owed the girl another debt. She had *more* than paid off all the effort they were putting in on her behalf.

The mage looked a great deal different than the Jonaton that had arrived here. It had been with great regret that Jonaton had put away all of his elaborate clothing in favor of the plainer stuff they were all wearing. The k'Vesla hertasi had adored him, because he was always wildly enthusiastic about anything they made him—especially outfits with pockets and pouches. But once they, and their superb laundering services, were gone, he had to resign himself to dressing "quietly."

Jonaton loved to collect small things, habitually in fact. If something especially memorable happened, he was certain to filch a stray smoking-pipe, little figurine, spoon, or the like. Jonaton had finally told Kordas why years ago, when his psychometry study bore fruit, because he explained that objects carry impressions enough to seek out specific times. His trinket collecting was a habit he had gotten into in his youth, with predictable reprisals. Learning about psychometry had become an obsession for the boy, especially when his elders fought each other so much. He thought it would let him look back in time and see who was really right or wrong, so he could navigate his youth better. It gave him hope for a future when he finally could be sure of things. Touching and taking things was his way of "sticking a flag" on events, to make them easier to search for later when he'd mastered psychometry. He stole little objects as a way of preserving his memories.

So the more pockets, the better. But alas, none of that Tayledras finery was going to hold up to being laundered with the basic laundry they had now—nor did the laundry workers have the time to devote to cleaning fancy stuffs the way they had back in the Duchy. So now, just like everyone else, Jonaton wore a plain brown linen gown in summer and a wool one with linen underneath in the winter, which he had painstakingly trimmed himself with strips of fancier material, brocaded, beaded, or embroidered, cut from clothing he'd ruined before he realized his favorite outfits weren't going to survive until there were more people and better facilities at the Palace.

The Six Old Men lived in the Palace, but the rest of the mages, Jonaton included, had their own section of the wall. Jonaton had one of those four-room setups for himself and Hakkon, except that they'd taken down the upstairs partition to make one big bedroom. Downstairs was his workroom in the place of a third bedroom, and the partition between it and the kitchen was solid stone with a very stout wooden door, backed with iron plates. That was where he and Kordas were now. It was windowless, and even with the door standing open, Kordas still smelled faint hints of past experiments, a very strange aroma with touches of herbs, bitter, sour, and metal.

Jonaton hadn't outwardly changed much since they first arrived here, other than his clothing, but Kordas knew that under that clothing he was a great deal fitter than he had been. The general lack of servants had meant that they *all* were doing work that would have been "beneath them" in the Empire, and most of that was physical labor. They pumped their own water in the bathing rooms, and heated it themselves if necessary, even if that meant heating it in a wood-fired boiler and painstakingly carrying buckets of hot water across the bathing room and decanting them in the tub. They delivered their clothing themselves to the laundry and picked up clean clothing from the same place. They swept and tidied their own rooms, leaving only heavier cleaning for servants. They laid their own fires in winter (although the servants cleaned out the ashes), and brought their own wood up from a common stack kept at each outside door. When they wanted food outside of mealtimes, they fetched it from the kitchen themselves. Between that, and a great deal more walking than they had done before, every person quartered in the Palace was in better shape, even those who had been in good trim before the journey.

One of the things that the defectors had most objected to was the "servant work." Kordas had to wonder how they were faring now, since a lot of their servants had slipped away and come back to Valdemar to join the Palace staff or set up some enterprise on their own.

Jonaton had never allowed a servant to do anything in his workroom, however, so it looked much the same as his workroom back in the manor. It looked disorganized, but it wasn't. Jonaton could put his hands on anything he wanted or needed without any hesitation. So there must be a system there, though Kordas couldn't see it. The walls were lined with shelves crammed with things Kordas couldn't recognize. There were chests under the shelves. There were books on bookshelves set at angles to the wall. And a table and four chairs dead square in the middle. Kordas could not help but note the scorch marks liberally decorating the tabletop.

"So far, they've been fine. Didn't even need me." Jonaton sounded just a bit . . . put out with that. "But I haven't taken my eyes off them. Sai is watching the Adept's city. Have you had a look at it yet?"

"No, actually," Kordas admitted.

Jonaton frowned. "It doesn't look like it started as a city," Jonaton said, calling up a teaching spell, which drew glowing lines in midair to match what Jonaton had in his memory. "There's some kind of big building in the center that looks more like a temple or a monastery than a manor or a palace. Then everything outside of that is kind of randomly built, haphazard, not laid out the way Haven is. Then there's a wall around the main part of the city, then more structures built outside of the wall. Outside of the wall is where they settled our defectors, and that's where all the training is going on. Such as it is." He shrugged. "I'm leaving that assessment to people who know about training fighters. The weaponsmaster has been in there watching a couple of times, and the Lord Martial. The Adept definitely has something like a Hawk-brother Veil or shield over the whole thing, and I did consider that she might have created some sort of illusion over the top of that, but no. It's just a huge shield that does what the Veil did: keeps the temperature inside it at early summer, and immediately hardens into a very strong defense when attacked." He frowned again. "And that's kind of odd. It's big, it's power-ful, but it's nowhere near as refined as the Hawkbrothers' Veil. It burns a *lot* of energy that it doesn't need to burn. Or maybe I'm just overthinking this. If she *is* an actual Adept, she doesn't need to worry about wasting power, because she can tap into plenty to waste. There's probably a big ley-line running right under that city, so she can just squander power without thinking about it, like a drunkard that just came into a big inheritance."

"Well, that *does* seem to suggest she's a genuine Adept," Kordas replied thoughtfully. "It would match what Silvermoon speculates—that she was merely an apprentice before. That would mean she never learned anything complicated, or how to finesse things. I wonder if everything she does is like that?"

"You mean crude, but powerful?" Jonaton nodded. "I think that might be the case. Of course, it doesn't much matter to the fly if it's smashed by a hammer or a beautifully crafted, jewel-handled swatter. It's still smashed."

"Point taken. But it does suggest gaps in her knowledge we might be able to exploit." He pondered that. "Gaps in knowledge and experience—as I understand it, she would have somehow skipped the journeyman years completely. Something to talk with the Old Farts about, if they haven't—"

"They have," Jonaton laughed. "They're trying to figure out what else she might have done around there so they can examine it. If the Hawkbrothers weren't so damn secretive about their magic—well, we asked Silvermoon to weigh in, and he just made a face and said that he had no idea how she got that kind of knowledge when she was only an apprentice when she left."

Kordas grimaced. "I can't blame him, but it wouldn't hurt him to have a look and say 'Yes, she's doing crude work that has a lot of holes in it that we can exploit' or 'No, it might be crude, but it's solid.'"

"I know, right?" Jonaton dispelled the teaching diagram, although he left the scrying mirror active. "Another thing I'm trying with this scrying method is that the objects are sensitive to whatever the wearer is interested in. So the view follows." Right now, the mirror showed a huge hare, sitting up on its haunches. A moment later it showed the hare toppling over, an arrow through its neck. "Well, there's dinner for them," he remarked, showing that, even as they spoke, he was still keeping an eye on his partner.

Kordas rose. "I'll have a word with Silvermoon," he told the mage. "Maybe I can shake something out of him."

"Good luck to you. He's as slippery as an eel when it comes to magic. Doesn't give anything away, but with you he might barter. I need him to see some simulations I started, too. Sooner is better." Jonaton went back to watching the scrying mirror as Kordas took himself out, stepping around the big black cat aloofly guarding the doorway.

:*Ardatha, do you know where Silvermoon is?*: he asked as he hesitated just outside Jonaton's door.

:*In fact, he and Starbird are here in the pasture. I think you might want to be here too,*: the Companion told him.

Well, *that* wasn't alarming at all! :*What's going on?*: he demanded.

:*We don't know yet,*: came the cautious reply. :*Maybe nothing. It's going to depend on a number of factors. This was not anticipated. We are, as you might say, "making it up as we go along."*:

He groaned silently, and suppressed the urge to run.

But when he arrived at the meadow, he saw Starbird and Silvermoon leaning over the fence, facing a small herd of not less than seven Companions.

They were all as silent as if they were statues, although there was very little doubt that several of them were Mindspeaking. Silvermoon looked over at him and broke off from the group.

"Can you think of any reason why the Companions would be interrogating my cousin?" he demanded—a great deal more brusquely than Kordas was used to, coming from the usually debonair Hawkbrother.

"Well, they can't be asking her about Tayledras magic," Kordas replied, furrowing his brow. "She's a Healer, I'm sure she only knows as much about magic as she needs to live in a Vale—"

"It's not about magic," Silvermoon replied. "They're asking her . . . personal questions. Does she have a mate, for instance. What are her duties in the Vale. Is she *happy* there." He sounded rather agitated. "I don't understand why they are asking her these things."

But Kordas certainly had one idea. . . . It seemed preposterous, but it did match the questions. And it matched the code of ethics the Companions seemed to operate under. "Oh . . ." was all he managed to say.

Then all of the Companions stepped back. Except one. A mare as slim and supple as a dyheli. She stepped forward until she was almost nose to nose with Starbird.

:Are you sure?: he heard in his mind. *:Are you absolutely sure? This cannot be undone except at great cost to both of us.:*

"Yes," Starbird replied aloud. "Yes. Very sure. Please."

The Companion's eyes seemed to glow from within. *:Then I, Radiant, Choose you, Starbird k'Vesla.:*

Starbird pressed her forehead to the Companion's forehead as Silvermoon uttered an audible gasp.

"Well," Kordas said into the silence. "That was unexpected."

Silvermoon wore an expression Kordas had never seen on his face before. He was completely and utterly befuddled. Starbird, of course, was deep into that terrifying, exultant, indescribable communion with Radiant that Kordas knew so well, and he envied her for experiencing it for the very first time for herself. Once Chosen, the communion "settled" into something easy to live with on a day-to-day basis, but that first time . . . definitely the closest thing to a life-altering religious experience *he* had ever had.

Ardatha moved along the fenceline to Silvermoon. *:I cannot say that I am sorry,:* the Companion said so that both of them could hear. *:Because I am not. Starbird knows what this entails, and wants it, but, as you care for her, I understand your* *agitation. Starbird and Radiant are more than compatible, they are perfect for one another. But somehow I feel I must console you, because when we came here, it was with the intention of only Choosing those of Valdemar.:* Ardatha also sounded a bit befuddled. *:There must be a reason for this, but I don't know what it is. You heard us, Silvermoon. We made certain that she had no commitments to k'Vesla that could not be undone, and that she was willing to uproot her life to live it here. We made sure she understood how different Valdemar is from the Vale. She understands. She is sure. You heard her.:*

Silvermoon broke out of his fugue state and rubbed the back of his neck as if it ached. "Well, she is her own person. She is a full adult, and you *did* make sure she knew her own mind . . ." He sighed. "You Companions are the Gift of the Star-Eyed, at least in part. I just do not quite know how to explain this to the Elders of k'Vesla."

:Leave that to your Goddess,: Ardatha told him.

"That's easy for *you* to say," Silvermoon retorted, then flushed with embarrassment, realizing whom, or rather, *what,* he was talking to.

But Ardatha just made a whickering, chuckling sound. *:Why yes. It is.:*

"This isn't going to be a diplomatic incident, is it?" Kordas asked Silvermoon, sounding plaintive and anxious even to his own ears. Starbird, of course, was still deep in communion with Radiant. *I wonder if she's been taken to the Moonpaths,* he thought fleetingly. "She just became Valdemaran right in front of us. Being Chosen makes her a Herald, so she'll be in the service of Valdemar. You must have a hundred questions about loyalty and secrets."

"She's an adult. She's entitled to make her own decisions," Silvermoon repeated, just as Starbird's sooty buzzard soared overhead and spiraled down to the fence, where she landed, then sidled along the fence rail until she could press herself up against Starbird's side. Then she went as still and quiet as the young woman and her Companion.

"Looks as if the bird approves," Kordas offered. "I suppose she could fly on the Moonpaths, too."

Silvermoon pinched the bridge of his nose. "The Moonpaths. Gods and Powers, if I may use a Valdemaran phrase, it feels like every time I come here something unprecedented happens. I . . . I must admit there are more good things about this than bad. In fact . . . there are no bad things. Just . . . it's an inconvenience. Her family will want explanations, but thank the gods, that is *not* something I need to supply. And if the Companions actually *did* make all the drawbacks clear to her—"

:We did,: Ardatha told them both. *:There was a great deal we said to her that was not for any ears but hers. Actually, I would suggest that she and Radiant make a farewell visit to k'Vesla Vale so she can make her own explanations.:*

Silvermoon threw up his hands. "Then it's clearly nothing I have any business poking my fingers into. Starbird will become a Herald, and will join you all here. It's not as if we can't spare a single Healer." He sighed. "I just hope she's happy. Your world is very different from ours."

"Maybe that's part of the attraction," Kordas offered. "Not that I mean anything offensive by that. It actually seems quite equitable to me. Three of *my* people decided to join themselves to Tayledras mates and go with you to k'Vesla, and one of them was one of my mages."

"Truth," Silvermoon admitted. "And you interrogated them quite thoroughly to make sure they knew what they were getting into."

"Just as the Companions did," Kordas pointed out. "Nobody is going into anything blind."

Silvermoon turned his gaze on to his cousin, who was still deep in her communion. "Naive maybe, but not blind. A mage for a Healer," he said, finally. "Seems fair, if we were to look at them by avocation. But—*your* three became Tayledras because of love. I wonder what her reason is."

Mostly, Restil and Rothas chatted outside, which was where they were now—sitting in one of the pea-bowers, enjoying the breeze and occasionally stripping a pod and popping peas into their mouths. Even though when they were in their spellbound slumbers, you couldn't wake Rothas or Lythe if you dumped cold water on them, shook them like rattles, and yelled in their ears, Rothas didn't like talking in their kitchen because—so he said—it might give Lythe disturbing dreams. And since the conversations with Rothas often involved things that were quite personal, Restil didn't care for chatting in his own kitchen, in case Beltran came by looking for something. Or Delia, but right now, Delia was far enough away that wasn't an issue.

Today Rothas was catching the Prince up on the progress with removing the sleeping curses. Granted, Rothas didn't know all that much about magic, but from what he was saying, Sai and Ponu might have hit upon a way to unravel the magic. The problem was, apparently, that since both these curses were—as Sai put it—"hedge magic created by amateurs, powered by ridiculously strong Cataclysm echoes, and complicated by unknown factors"—the unraveling was going to have some very specific and as yet uncalculated requirements that normally would not be necessary.

"They explained it as, and I think they tried hard to explain it so it made sense to someone as uncultured as me, like somebody using whatever was nearby at the moment to make a door, versus a woodworker with specialized tools and experience. They might both fill a doorway, but the first one will have serious drafts," Rothas explained. "Then he said, if they dismantle that door, it could collapse because of its strange properties of mismatched construction. I allowed as how both of us would prefer not to collapse."

Restil rubbed his chin. "That sounds to me like what the Hawkbrothers do in the Pelagirs. Cleansing. They take in chaotic, unpredictable magic and straighten it out so it's predictable," he muttered. "So I guess Sai and the others have to clean up the curse before dismantling it. So it falls apart without taking anyone with it."

"Hey, I could have done without that!" Rothas exclaimed. "This seems a lot riskier than I thought it would be!"

"Sai and Jonaton hardly *ever* explode anybody, you'll be fine," Restil teased. "But—"

Restil stopped in the middle of talking to Rothas and held up his hand to forestall any questions as Darshay informed him what had just happened across the river. His expression must have been one of complete shock, because finally Rothas poked him tentatively in the shoulder and said, "Is it bad? Is it terrible? Is a giant army of soldiers and monsters about to strike us?"

"No, it's nothing like that," Restil managed. "In fact . . . I think it's good. It's just . . ." He shook his head. "Never in a thousand years would I have predicted this."

"What's *this*?" Rothas demanded. "Come on, Prince, you cannot leave a *Bard* hanging, wondering what has happened! We're composed of curiosity!"

"Well, it seems that one of the unpartnered Companions, named Radiant, has Chosen Starbird," he said, the words feeling strange in his mouth.

But Rothas was puzzled. "I don't see the problem," he said, scratching his head. "Why can't a Companion Choose a Hawkbrother?"

Restil ran through a dozen reasons in his head and decided on the simplest. "Because the Companions came for Valdemar, not the Vales. And because Hawkbrothers have their own concerns to deal with that don't involve Valdemar."

"Huh." Rothas tore a pea-pod to shreds and put the mulch at the base of the vine. "So—how does that work out?"

"Evidently . . . she's staying here," Restil told him. "From what Darshay tells me, she got interrogated by several Companions, including Ardatha, and she knows what she's getting into by staying here."

"Well, a Vale is very nice to live in, but I like *here* better, and so does Lythe." Rothas shrugged. "Even if the Palace doesn't have the Veil, or the hot soaking pools. Or hertasi." He made an odd little grimace. "All right, I *do* miss hertasi. I wish you had some."

"You are certainly not the only one. And I miss having the Veil. But the cost of having these things is that you are expected to tame extremely dangerous magic that could probably set you on fire from the inside if you don't do things *exactly* right. And, of course, you have a goddess watching over your shoulder to make sure you are keeping your part of Her bargain." He got up and looked around for Darshay, who appeared, as usual, seemingly out of nowhere. "I should probably go look into this up close."

"I'd go with you, but I don't feel as if this is a story that needs my telling," Rothas replied. "And besides, it's time for another lesson in Barding from the Old Men. Barding? Being a Bard? I suppose it's the same thing."

"Bardicating? Bardonic pursuits? Bardology? You're the one that's supposed to be a master of words!" Restil said, laughing at him.

He grinned. "Then, Barding it is. Well, let me know what happens. I'm still curious, even if I don't think I'll be making a song about it."

Rothas sauntered off in the direction of the Palace. Although he made light of the lessons, Restil knew he was taking them very seriously. Although the Old Men were not by any means masters of Mind-magic, the disciplines they had learned applied to Rothas's Bardic powers. And what they couldn't teach, a couple of the Mindhealers absolutely could. Outwardly, Rothas wasn't much different than the somewhat careless young man who had arrived here. Inwardly, though, Restil was aware he had become a great deal more serious. He understood just how seductive, how insidious, and how dangerous his Bardic Gift could be, and he was determined to do good with it, rather than simply exploit it for his own gain.

Lythe had undergone a similar transformation, though hers was more subtle than his. Instead of waiting to be asked to do something, if she saw a need she could fill, she filled it—just as she had by bringing Sable and her kittens to Jon, and making sure the cat knew all the rules of living in the Palace. From merely tolerating them, Restil had grown to consider both of them his friends.

So as he watched Rothas saunter on his way, he smiled a little. That bit of a swagger didn't fool him at all. Rothas was not nearly as devil-may-care as he looked, and having to learn how to assess and evaluate an audience had carried over into the rest of his life. He also wasn't quite so boneheaded anymore.

:Are you coming, or not?: Darshay asked with mock impatience. *:Not that you're* needed, *but I get the feeling you want to know a lot more than I can tell you about Starbird.:*

He felt himself blushing a little, but suppressed it quickly. "You don't have to come too, you know," he said aloud. "You can just hop the fence back into the meadow and join your friends."

:Oh, but I want to be there.: Darshay didn't say why, but Restil knew. She wanted to see what his reaction would be to whatever Starbird told him. If she told him anything at all. Which, of course, he would also react to.

:All right, I admit it. I like her very much. I'm very happy that she will stay here. It would be . . . .: He groped for words. Because you really could not lie in Mindspeech, and she would know if he wasn't being truthful. *:It would make me extremely*

happy if we were to get closer, and I can't say that about any other lady I've met since I got old enough to be interested in ladies.:

:I'm not enough for you?: Darshay replied in mock outrage. *:I am shocked! Shocked, I tell you!:* Then she got serious. *:Not that I'm looking into the future, because I can't. Not that I'm trying to steer your life, because I won't. And not that I'm privy to what Starbird might be thinking about you, because I'm not. But diplomatically speaking, an attachment to each other would solve a lot of problems that haven't yet arisen. It creates a permanent bond with the Tayledras. You are both Heralds now, and you both are aware of the intricacies of the Herald-Companion bond, and if you are going to have any sort of successful relationship with someone, it has to be someone who completely understands that bond. And, frankly, who understands responsibility. As a bonus, this will completely cut short any Court intrigue over you, because you are the Crown Prince and your highborn—and some commons!—have been vying for you for their daughters. They'll finally leave you alone, if you have an existing attachment.:*

:That last, all by itself, would be a personal gift from the gods.: Of course he was aware of how desirable a marriage to him would be. Of course he had noticed—and politely ignored—all the overtures, subtle and blatant, that were being made to him by single women inside the Court and out of it. And of course he was acutely aware that who he married or even paid attention to had the potential to unlock all sorts of disasters.

But this was the first time an opportunity to avoid *all* of that had presented itself. And it certainly didn't hurt that Starbird was the sort of person he could see spending his life with.

He set off across the garden, trying to control his blushes, and trying also to control his own somewhat tangled emotions. As cold as it might have seemed to put what *might* become a romance into such logical terms, Darshay was right.

And marriages had been arranged on far flimsier grounds than that.

Darshay wisely kept quiet, and just let him mull that over. Which of course only led to internal questions. *What if she isn't interested in me? I mean, it seems like she is, but that could just be me misinterpreting Tayledras customs for something else.*

He put all those thoughts aside as he neared the fence where his father, Silvermoon, and six or seven Companions had surrounded Starbird, her buzzard, and Radiant. From the dazed look on her face, Starbird was just emerging from that magical trance being Chosen put you into.

The other Companions drifted off, leaving only Ardatha and Radiant. The bird unglued herself from Starbird's side, shuffled off a little way, roused all her feathers and then produced a monumental poop. *Slice,* he reminded himself. *It's called a slice, or a mute. Falconers are fussy about that.* Was that the bondbird's commentary on the situation, or did it mean nothing at all?

"That was—intense," Starbird said, finally, looking at Silvermoon. "I am sorry, cousin, but—I want this. I want it *very* much. I like these people, and I want to help them. You cannot imagine how much I envied these Heralds their bonds with their Companions when I learned of them." She shook her head. "And it's everything I had dreamed it was, and more. Besides, I am just one junior Healer among many at k'Vesla. Now I can be *much* more than that."

Restil's pulse quickened a little, because as she said "I like these people, and I want to help them," she cast a look at him that seemed significant.

Silvermoon nodded, as a breeze picked up and stirred his hair. "So I have been informed. Ardatha was *quite* emphatic that the Companions made sure you knew what you were getting yourself into."

"I do," she said firmly. "Though if I had known what this

bond meant to my heart . . . I would have been flinging myself at every unpartnered Companion here and begging them to take me."

"I'd laugh, but I feel the same," said Restil, earning himself another of those sidelong, approving glances.

Silvermoon sighed. "Oh, you Valdemarans. Nothing but trouble." But he said it in a tone that meant he didn't mean any of it.

"So this is not going to be a diplomatic incident?" Kordas said, deadpan.

"No, this is going to be a further cementing of the alliance, of course." Silvermoon snorted, and turned back to Starbird. "But don't come crying to me, cousin, when you miss the Veil's comfort in winter, and you find yourself wading through knee-deep snow just to get your breakfast. And there is *nothing* here like our heated pools! You haven't experienced life without hertasi! You may still come to regret this decision, when you are wearing bland clothing and inspecting your bed for unwelcome visitors before you go to sleep!" Silvermoon looked at Kordas. "Not that I mean anything offensive by that, of course."

Kordas just laughed. "No, you're right, of course. But some things are worth a little suffering for."

"Yes," Starbird said firmly. "They are."

Restil took it upon himself to get Starbird settled in with the Heralds. Of course he had an ulterior motive, as Darshay reminded him, not once, but several times.

:You're not fooling anyone, you know,: she teased. :Probably not even Starbird.:

:And I should take the advice of a creature that has literally never had a body before—just why, now?: he retorted. :I don't *think the best source of advice on the first stages of courtship is someone I had to explain the concept to.:*

Her only response was to laugh at him.

He was not deterred. The first thing he did, while Starbird met with the other Heralds, was to check with the acting Seneschal to find out how many housing units in the wall had been tentatively assigned to Heralds. When it turned out there were completely empty ones, he arranged for her to get one of them all to herself. That seemed the most prudent course of action to him, since she really didn't know any of the others.

When he returned to where she and the other Heralds were slowly getting acquainted, he asked Darshay to ask Radiant if Starbird wanted to share with any of the others that had spare rooms.

:She says, "not really,": Darshay relayed. *:She's used to having her own ekele, and prefers it that way.:*

:Well then, let her know that when she's done here, I'll show her to her new living space,: he replied, feeling smug. *:I'm going to go round up some furniture.:* The spare furnishings, or so the Seneschal had told him, were all being stored in one of those empty spaces. He trotted over there to look through it and see what he could find.

The heaviest pieces were on the bottom floor; he selected one wardrobe, a kitchen cupboard and pantry, a bedstead in pieces with all its pegs in a bag, a couple of chests, and a wool mattress from a tall stack. Tables and chairs were upstairs, as were spare curtains, and with some sweating and swearing, he eventually assembled everything he thought she'd need in the front of the storage unit. At that point, probably prompted by Radiant, Starbird and three of the other Heralds turned up to help him wrestle it all into her new home and set it up. She chose a few more items after the basics were in place. Just as they got most of it in, four servants from the Palace arrived, almost invisible under piles of fabric.

"The Queen sent us with supplies and uniforms," said one, muffled by the featherbed he was carrying.

Sure enough, Isla had found a featherbed and down duvet somewhere, to soften the wool mattress that had come with the bed, and had found Starbird some linens for the bed, towels, and other soft goods, as well as a stack of the uniforms that the Sempsters and Leatherworkers Guilds had made. Another turned up shortly with crockery and pans. He had no idea where these had come from, but Darshay did. *:Palace storage,:* she told him. *:Wood furnishings won't attract rodents, but fabric would invite nesting. And the kitchen stuff is just safer away from where it might get contaminated by mice.:*

"You are *very* well organized!" Starbird said, with gratitude touched with a hint of surprise. "As organized as hertasi, it seems!"

Herald Temon, Chosen by Kiellie, laughed. "Not nearly. This is all due to the generosity of the Haven guilds, after we did that ferry rescue."

Herald Merissa, Chosen by Lengstin, nodded. "They not only rigged all of us out, they came back again with more loads to take care of at least a dozen more new Heralds. Your uniforms probably won't fit all that well."

"I can sew," Starbird laughed. "Not *all* of us depend on hertasi for everything. It will be fine."

"You can thank Restil for getting this all started," Merissa added. "We were just standing about and chatting while he was wrestling furniture down stairs and out of doors. I didn't know that 'furniture moving' was part of the Crown Prince's duties!"

He snorted. "Before I was a Crown Prince, I did whatever Uncle Hakkon or any other adult authority told me to do. And yes, wrestling furniture was part of that."

"Well, Starbird, I don't suppose the hertasi might be willing and generous enough to gift us with some . . . nicer uniforms?

At some point." Temon scuffed his toe in the grass. "If it's not too big a thing to ask? Just so we have something that wouldn't disgrace a fancy event."

"I'll ask," Starbird replied, with a small smile. "But I don't think it's an impossibility. What am I to do for boots?"

"Wear what you have, until the leatherworkers can get your measurements," Restil advised. "There's nothing worse than boots that don't fit."

"Truth!" said Temon.

Starbird had decided that she'd use the downstairs room behind the kitchen as her bedroom. Although it was windowless, like Delia she felt that the extra protection from the winter cold would be worth it. "You know," she said thoughtfully. "What if we put things to sit on upstairs and took down the middle wall? I wouldn't mind hosting gatherings and parties up there. If I got tired of you all, I could just go back downstairs and leave you to enjoy yourselves."

:*Did Radiant advise her to say that?*: Restil asked Darshay.
:*No, that was her idea.*:

"Sometimes Tayledras overbuild their ekeles just so they can do that," she continued. "I think it would be nice for Heralds to have a little social space just for Heralds."

"I vote for that!" Restil enthused, and earned himself a smile.
:*You are shameless.*:
:*I am seizing the moment.*:

Starbird had been at the Palace long enough to know about meals and the like, but when the bedroom and kitchen had been arranged, and they were all discussing just how to set up that "gathering room," the bell rang for dinner, so they all went in with the entire group of Heralds. Restil could have sat at the high table, but he preferred to sit with the Heralds. Starbird got a taste of the camaraderie that had sprung up among them, and he could tell she felt welcome and accepted.

Altogether, though the fare was a lot simpler than anything you'd get in a Vale, Restil thought she enjoyed the meal.

And finally he took her and Radiant to the stables and got Radiant fitted with a good saddle and a hackamore. Darshay ambled along, and he showed her how to put the gear on Radiant.

"And now the question: do you ride at all?" he asked. "I never saw horses when k'Vesla Vale was still here."

"I do, but I rode dyheli. They don't care much for saddles and won't tolerate anything on their heads." She eyed the gear on Radiant. "How do you—"

"Watch," he said, and demonstrated mounting using the saddle. "Go ahead, try."

Before he had finished the sentence, she was in the saddle. "Oh . . . my," she said. "Oh, this is *much* more comfortable than a dyheli."

He chuckled. "I've seen them. You could cut yourself on those backbones. Come on, let's see how you like riding a Companion. I think you'll never want to ride a dyheli again."

He led the way, first to the field, then over the fence and into it, but it was very clear that she was quite comfortable on Radiant's back, comfortable enough that she took a very high jump without so much as a wobble. So he and Darshay increased their pace to a trot. Then a canter. Then a gallop.

And then, because there really wasn't anything better than putting Darshay to her fastest pace, and because she didn't need any urging, Darshay obeyed his impulse and poured on the speed. Starbird was able to keep up for a little, but not for long. He looked back over his shoulder and saw her dropping back, even though Radiant really was doing her best.

:Told you I'm fastest.:

:And I believe you!:

They doubled back to where Starbird and Radiant had slowed and were coming to a stop, completely unable to keep up.

"This is incredible!" she shouted with glee as they neared.

"This is *so* much better, smoother, and faster than any dyheli can manage! Even a King Stag!"

"And they can do this . . . well, I wasn't able to find a moment when Darshay was tired when I went out with that proclamation," he told her, pulling up alongside. "I don't think there is a limit to how long they can gallop. The real limit is how long we can stay awake in the saddle."

"Radiant was doing her best," Starbird replied. "But you two just shot off like an arrow from a bow! And I think you have your Tayledras name now."

"Oh really?" He grinned, feeling absurdly pleased. "Something like 'Recklessidiot'?"

She made a face at him. "No, of course not. Windrider. You are definitely Windrider."

He didn't even try to hide how fantastic that made him feel. "I'll take that," he said. "And I'm honored." He felt warm all over under her approving gaze. "You're probably one of the best riders in the Heralds."

Now she blushed. "I'm glad you think so. And as much as I would like to keep riding, I still need to finish up my quarters. I don't suppose you want to help, after all you did earlier?"

"Of course I do." He could not help grinning now. "Let's get to it!"

:Absolutely shameless.:

In the past near-fortnight, Starbird had fitted herself so well into the Herald corps that she could easily have been among the first Chosen. That, alone, would have been fortune enough, given the strengthening of the alliance between the Tayledras and Valdemar, but Restil had every reason to think that Starbird regarded him as something more than a friend by this point. Or, at least, she regarded him as a best friend. And if only they were not Heralds, he would definitely have pushed those boundaries as far as he dared. Come to think of it, she probably would have pushed first. The Tayledras, in general, weren't shy about showing interest in someone.

But they were Heralds, and he was a Crown Prince with additional duties, and they were both kept busy enough that once she'd settled in, he didn't get to see her nearly as often as he would have liked. At meals, generally, although she often ate dinner with the Healers, who had their own separate building and kitchen. Herald she might be, but she was still pursuing the learning that had brought her here in the first place. She didn't particularly need weapons training, but she did keep up her practices, and those were not at the same time as Restil's. Restil was still sitting in on Council meetings, and now often at Kordas's Court as well. And in accordance with the planned duties for the Herald corps, they both, along with the other Heralds, often got sent off when there was a new law or ruling that affected the entire Kingdom, though other Heralds got the more distant parts and Restil and Starbird were never sent out on journeys that took them more than a couple of marks at their Companions' fastest pace.

Except for the frustration of not being able to spend time in Starbird's company, Restil would have been pretty contented with his lot in life—*but*—

But there was that looming storm on the horizon. The Adept out there was still pursuing the formation of an army of her own, and it was an army that was growing. At this point it was the size of a full genuine Imperial battalion. Where were the additional fighters-in-training coming from? Frustratingly, there was no way of telling. All they could safely do was watch through Jonaton's tiny Portal and worry. The training that they could see showed the soldiers to be, if not *good,* no longer terrible. There was no sign that Lord Legenfall had been replaced by someone more competent, but there was also no sign that he *hadn't.*

Restil knew his father was increasingly worried—well, so was *he.* But there wasn't anything that either of them could do about this situation other than what they were already doing.

The only progress that had been made was that Hakkon, the Fairweathers, and Ivar had returned with the good news that there was only one reasonable line-of-march that an invading force could take to get to the Valdemar border, thanks to terrain that was not particularly hospitable to a force of armed men on foot. Rocky ground, threaded with a lot of small streams, suited mostly to grazing, which was how the few holdings Hakkon and the others had found out there used the land. So they had a good idea of where on the border an army would appear, and where to sculpt their ground, and Pebble was already on the job. So were the green mages, who were following behind Pebble making sure that the alterations to the ground were camouflaged by what would look like the growth of decades.

Herald Menalus was on permanent assignment to make sure that all the Valdemarans up there kept in practice with weapons, and held evacuation drills about once every fortnight. Roughly half the Valdemaran Guard had been sent up there as well—not as a single force, but trickled in by squads and quartered in villages and farms near where Pebble was working, just in case the Adept was doing some long-distance spying of her own. The joint verdict of both the Six Old Men and Silvermoon was that if the Adept observed Pebble working, she really would not recognize what the Elemental was doing. No one out here in the records of the Hawkbrothers had *ever* tried to enslave and exploit an Elemental, even a youngling, so she would assume Pebble was amusing himself.

And the favor of all the gods wouldn't help her if she had a go at Pebble. Pebble's mother would appear, and her wrath would be terrible.

Menalus would be able to spot any invading force when it was at least a day away by virtue of his Farsight, which would be plenty of time to assemble the Guard on ground of Valdemar's choosing.

But anxiety and tension only increased with every day that passed without any idea of what the Adept was going to do. Farmers looked over their shoulders, brought in harvests as early as possible, and made plans to hide their stock, their valuables, and themselves. The citizens of Haven made no long-term plans, and their short-term preparations included securing valuables as best they could and having evacuation bags packed and at the door so they could run for the safety of the Palace if invaders got as far as the capital. And as for the highborn—they relocated themselves from their manors back to their crowded quarters in the Palace, and no one complained about the conditions. In fact, the weapons-practice fields were in use from first light to last, as everyone who *could* use a weapon of any sort made sure their skills were no longer rusty. Court sessions were much, much shorter these days; those with bones to pick with other highborn were concentrating on the young Kingdom's first martial threat, rather than picking fights with each other. Mysterious illnesses, insect plagues, and the troubles of the farmers hadn't made much of an impression on them, but an army on the border? *That,* they could understand. And it didn't hurt that this was something they themselves could combat. This was particularly true among the ones around Restil's age, who were still naive enough to think that they would be the great heroes of any battle they took part in, and in between practices, had a lot to say about "glory" and the amount of it they expected to get for themselves.

If the weaponsmaster had any thoughts on this, he was keeping them to himself. Or at least, he wasn't voicing them where Restil could hear them. Uncle Hakkon, however, had had a few choice words for the King about "expensively dressed arrow magnets."

Rothas was invaluable; his Gifts kept spirits up, and by day he circulated around the city performing anywhere he could, returning only to the Palace in time for the last serving of supper in order to do the same there. And Lythe had recruited a little army of her own in the form of night-birds, who kept a watch to make sure the Adept didn't slip anything into Haven or the Palace under cover of darkness.

So matters stood, as summer became autumn, and nerves, if not yet frayed, were under a great deal of tension.

———————

:Your father particularly wants you at second serving tonight, to eat with the family,: Darshay reported, as she and Restil

made their way back through the purposefully winding streets of Haven to the Palace. Kordas and the Lord Martial had planned from the beginning to make it difficult for an invader to get through the city to the Palace. Invading forces would have to make their way through constant street-fighting with no direct way to get anywhere. Yes, this made it a little inconvenient for people trying to cross from one side of Haven to the other, but there weren't a lot of people actually doing that, and what was inconvenience for a single person would be a nightmare for groups of fighters.

Some bright spark in the mayor's administration of Haven itself had gotten the idea of replacing the guards stationed in the city with a force of their own—the Watch. Right now it was composed primarily of people too old or unfit to serve in the Guard, but who were perfectly willing to patrol their own neighborhoods for whatever problems might arise, from theft to drunken fighting to neighbors clashing. And, of course, to lead the street-fighting in the event an invading force got as far as Haven. Making already known and trusted people into a sort of defensive command would help to keep casualties down, while professional fighters did the grim business of warring. Kordas had encouraged this plan, and Restil had been assigned to make sure that the Watch wasn't composed of bullies looking for a "legitimate" reason to shove people around, but instead were folks with a genuine interest in keeping their neighborhood safe. He'd weeded out a few bad apples, but most of the people who had volunteered had been not just well intentioned, but pretty well suited to the task.

:Did he say why he wants me to eat with the family?: Restil asked, because after a solid day of traipsing around the city, inspecting the little neighborhood groups, he was more tired than he'd been after that run to the southern border. It wasn't just a physical exhaustion—he generally liked people no matter the occasion, but in his rounds there were plenty who were

awed at being within speaking distance of the Crown Prince . . . but not awed enough to keep their opinions to themselves. So speak, they did.

His own side of that was that he'd been trained how to be safe in neighborhoods, and how to interpret particular gestures as incipient assaults—and that training screamed at him all day. And there had been no attacks! But there were endless quick moves and arms swinging about, and the noise of people's excitement got shrill before long.

:Dear heart,: Darshay spoke gently in his mind, :That doesn't make you self-important or arrogant. You have been around well-disciplined people for most of your life. Life isn't like that for regular people. Their lives are more random in nature, and when something novel happens their emotive displays are much more pronounced than you are accustomed to. Your reputation carries weight among the people. They show you approval and respect—but many of the ways they do that are unpleasant to you.:

:It's starting to rub my nerves raw. Probably none of this would bother Hakkon and Jon, but I was just old enough to get all the lessons in danger about being too loose-tongued around strangers who might be Imperial spies. And that made me see risks hidden in the slightest gesture, you know? Sometimes I miss being on the barges, in convoy on the river, feeling sunlight and seeing wonders. New lands, trees, birds, but safe in a cozy cabin or comfortable deck.:

:No clusters of star-struck admirers trying to touch you.:

:That, too.:

:Imagine how I was feeling as an enchanting, gleaming, soft-eyed white horse with amazing proportions. I had so many children around me I was afraid I'd step on one!

:You truly do have the hardest life possible,: Restil jabbed back.

And really, all he wanted was to boil an egg in his room,

toast some bread and cheese at the fire, drink the last of his apple cider before it turned, and go to bed, the desire to see Starbird notwithstanding.

:As to your question, Ardatha didn't say why you are summoned to the family table.:

:So it's probably that Father wants to show the entire royal family acting calm and composed.: He sighed, and resigned himself to putting on an act.

:Very likely. There was a bout of hysterics and catfighting earlier. Nothing that couldn't be smoothed over, but—:

:But highborns will be highborns and convinced that the universe revolves around them, and that they *are in the most danger, and are the likeliest targets.:* That was somewhat unfair . . . but only somewhat. And Restil was not in the mood for tempers or tantrums right now.

:Indeed.: The details of the altercation drifted into his mind from Darshay, probably via Ardatha. All the Companions were very well acquainted with the vagaries of the courtiers by this time, presumably from sharing their Chosens' impressions in context to the other Companions. A few had naively assumed that in the face of threat, *everyone* would be on their best behavior. They quickly learned that people didn't "work that way," and adjusted their own behavior and expectations accordingly. Restil suspected that the unpartnered Companions were serving as a repository of information on every single person, from kitchen boy to the Seneschal, that lived in the Palace, so that the rest didn't *have* to keep track of who was likely to have an outburst at any given time. That kept the Herald-Companion pairs within the Palace walls from being blindsided. Usually those outbursts were limited to semi-hysterical demands for information no one actually had, but sometimes they escalated, and being forewarned kept things from getting out of hand. That catfight, for instance, had been a completely unneeded brawl between two highborn mothers

who were intent on securing the services of the Palace blacksmith on behalf of their offspring, for armor alterations, and both were adamant on "jumping the queue." Selfish? Absolutely. Understandable? Absolutely.

Restil had an odd thought that Darshay picked up on immediately. *:If all Companions are Mindspeakers, and all Companions can share their memories, does that make all of the Companions together into one big mind with everyone's memories?:*

Darshay seemed impressed. *:Aren't you clever. We all have minds of our own, but you are close. And yes, the more Companions there are, the more memories and insights there are to draw upon.:* She added, in a more serious tone, *:We have our vulnerabilities, too. Our state of mind carries over when sharing thoughts, so we take sanity very seriously. Derangement can be—infectious for our kind. That is why Repudiation exists; it is to cut off the Chosen's madness from spreading through us. Just the thought of it is heartbreaking. No one should be pushed away when in so much need. But that is a risk we simply cannot take. It is the conundrum of the swimmer and the drowning man who seizes him and threatens to pull him under.:*

:But just how much madness are you talking about? Some of our best friends are pretty strange.:

:Weirdness is embraced, as are those differences that often put someone at odds with those around them, and so forth, but we are on our guard about self-destruction beyond—how shall I put this—beyond the amount that comes with self-examination. There are specialized Healers of the heart and mind that can pull someone back from doom, but we are not they. We would like to be all things, but we cannot be. We want and need our Chosen to be healthy, in mind, heart, and body, without losing who they are.:

Restil pondered for a few moments. *:There are so many*

things I learned about the Hawkbrothers that would seem mad to a regular Valdemaran, but I feel like they're understandable, just different from our ways. I don't know if I could live as they live, but I am happy for them.:

:I know. And by that, I mean, I know. However aberrant, chaotic, or embarrassing your imagination may get, we understand. A Companion is the best of friends—someone who knows you for exactly who you are, and loves you anyway.:

:Hah! That will take some getting-used-to, but I trust you. I'll still blush sometimes.:

Darshay whickered. *:I know that, too.:*

:All right, let's get you up to the Palace and out of your gear so I can get cleaned up and presentable.: It was even odds whether the stablehands would be around to help, or off practicing their bow and pike skills, so Restil would probably be the one taking care of her. Not that he minded. If anything, he was just a bit resentful that he wasn't going to be able to spend a leisurely mark or two grooming her, as he almost always did when he got the chance. It was soothing for both of them.

By a miracle, there *was* a stablehand available. Her face lit up when she saw Restil approaching, though her eyes were entirely on Darshay, not her rider. In fact, when he dismounted, the Crown Prince was greeted with a dismissive "Don't worry, Herald, I'll take care of everything" and a proprietary hand on Darshay's neck. She didn't even look at him to see which Herald he was.

Restil clamped his jaw tight to keep from laughing out loud and took a moment to compose himself before he could thank her gravely and go on his way.

Darshay, of course, could not help but comment, but at least she waited until Restil was out of earshot. *:You have been snubbed, Prince Restil.:*

:Not exactly. No one pays attention to a mere Prince when there is a Queen in view.:

:Hah! Save that silver tongue for Starbird.:

He trotted to the Palace, grinning. He kept a couple of spare clean uniforms there for moments like this. Heading straight to the royal suite to bathe and change was going to save a lot of time.

Supper was uneventful, though in the end, he was glad that the King had hijacked his plans, because the soup was one of his favorites, a nice squash soup made with herbs, butter and cream, and garnished with bits of bacon. And it was only the royal family and Sai, uncle Hakkon, and Jonaton; Silvermoon had gone back to k'Vesla a fortnight ago—and amusingly enough, the hertasi had taken advantage of the Portal opening to kick a trio of large carts through before it closed. Jelavan hadn't been through the Portal to visit, but Restil had seen that Delia did have packages waiting in the hertasi bundles. The first cart through was heaped with rolls of cloth, baskets with tagged plant clippings and bulbs, sturdy boxes of special crystals and other who-knew-whats for the mages, and a sealed box addressed to Jonaton. The other two carts were laden with a couple of tightly packed bales of handsome new Herald uniforms. Actual bales, about the size of a big wardrobe trunk. When the dense bales had been cut open, they spread out into an area three times the size of the original bale. Now everyone had a "best" set of uniform clothing: white doeskin with a light ramie shirt for summer and a white lambswool shirt for winter. Of course the tunics, trews, shirts, and soft boots were ornamented liberally, with embroidery, fabric manipulation, and tooling, but it was subtle, all white-on-white. Starbird assured them all that the hertasi were aware that the laundry facilities were not up to hertasi standards, and that everything had been "treated" to prevent dirtying and staining. How, Restil was not sure. Magic, perhaps? Or perhaps the hertasi had managed to unravel the secret of the Doll canvas.

Each bale also bore a secured stack of identical, glossy white boxes on top. The boxes sported shiny protected corners, edged with steel rails and handles like miniature luggage, each adorned by painted Valdemar crests. A note from the hertasi inside every one read, "May you live to be a thousand years old." Inside each box was a full "casual" Herald uniform of Doll canvas and white canvas gaiters to go over the more sturdy and practical boots that had not yet been replaced by the leatherworkers, which made Restil giggle. Hertasi, it seemed, didn't understand "formal" or "informal" like Valdemarans; they just understood "more impressive" or "less impressive." Apparently, they understood "uniform" as meaning that every outfit was supposed to match—and so they did, down to the smallclothes with little Valdemar crests embroidered on them. These uniforms had less ornamentation, but that didn't mean no ornamentation.

They made us ornate casual-wear uniforms. That may be the most hertasi *gift ever.*

As he had suspected, this evening's display was to show the courtiers that the royal family was taking the situation seriously, but not panicking about it. But alas, Starbird was not in sight; she must have eaten with the rest of the Heralds at the first serving, or was still with the Healers. But that meant that he was seated at the King's left hand—the right being reserved for the Queen—so they made a nice block of pristine white in the middle of the high table. The only one missing was Delia, who was still up north with Pebble.

When dessert—the usual fruit and cheese—arrived, the King finally turned to him. "What would you say to going up north to get eyes on Pebble's progress?" he asked.

"I'd say I thought you didn't want me anywhere near that border," Restil replied.

"Well, with half the Guard up there, I'm not as concerned as I was. As for borders, what we think of as our border likely isn't what they think of as their border. There's a good bit of distance between the area that city is served by, and us. A wilderness buffer." Then his father paused. "Well, we had better talk to Jonaton after dinner to see what he has to say about the idea."

Restil did not groan, although he was tempted to. He preferred to have a word with Starbird, then go to bed to sleep for a year. But . . . this was not a request. This was a not-at-all-veiled command from the King to his son, and from the King to his Herald. So he nodded, steeled himself for another mark or two of not-sleeping, and waited until the King and Queen rose to leave.

Kordas passed by Jonaton and murmured something too low for Restil to hear. Jonaton nodded, said a word to his tablemates, and got up and followed them.

So much for getting to sleep.

But at least Kordas led them back to the royal suite instead of all the way across the grounds to Jonaton's workroom. "My other sons are certainly going to stay and listen to Rothas and the other entertainers, so we'll have some privacy for a while," Kordas said, as he gestured for all of them to take seats among the couches and chairs near the fireplace. "Jonaton, before I consult you on something else, you told me right after Silvermoon left that you had something to show me. I'm sorry I didn't have time, but why don't you show me now?"

Jonaton's body language expressed relief, though his face displayed displeasure. "I will, though it was hard-won. I wanted to be wrong about it, so I spent myself confirming as best I could. Just before he left, I finally got Silvermoon to myself. I showed him what I had on that anomaly that happened during the coronation, and, you know, just came out and asked him if the Hawkbrothers had anything to do with it." Jonaton made some gestures in the air and brought up a sharp illusory teaching diagram. Fortunately Restil knew how to read it, or he probably would have been sorely confused. "He said no, and gave me some instructions and information that helped me refine the diagram. He showed me how to fan radiance filters across mage-tracery to see them as a solid shape, and how to move other filters over that. It's brilliant. It makes images like in a teaching spell, but from actual readings, not approximations. With that, I was able to walk around the readings' illusion, examining it like a sculpture, and it proved out what I was hesitant to tell you unless I was sure. I didn't have the readings of the Red Thing itself, but I did have detailed readings of its effect on the Tayledras shields. So I reversed the—" He paused. "You stopped listening a while back, didn't you?" His expression was both exasperated and resigned.

"No, no, I follow so far," Kordas nodded, but Restil left his expression a bit on the stupid side. He had a vague idea of what Jonaton was talking about, but combat magic had everything to do with knowing what to do instantly, not faffing about trying to analyze things while you were trying not to be killed.

"All right. Aside from what that will mean to us in the future—since I think this method of visualizing pattern qualities is completely unknown to Imperials, should we need it—I could understand the textures of the magic by experiencing tastes. Seeing a flavor. The different series of spikes, their patterns of force, or the lower undulations and reverberations—I began tasting them."

That sounded familiar. "We've heard you talk about the flavors of magic before," Restil offered.

"I was trying to name something we had no name for yet. It fit, as an explanative term, but this imagery, when I concentrated on the finer patterns, I could actually taste them on my tongue. Like hearing a sound and you can feel a memory associated with it on your skin, only another sense was suited to interpret what was now being said." Jonaton waited for a response.

"That's amazing," Kordas flowed in as if rehearsed. "It's because you're a very remarkable person, Jonaton. No one else would have understood that with all their senses."

"And I'm still not sure I'll tell Silvermoon about the

implications. We can keep at least a few secrets for ourselves, Your Majesty?"

Kordas frowned a moment. "You know how I am about sharing lifesaving knowledge," he said defensively.

"I do! I do know, Kordas, and I love you for it, but while there are forces in this world that can take over people's minds, curse them, and ensnare and inhabit their bodies, I am going to come up with ways to stop everyone I'll ever know. It's merciful, to me. If an ally or courtier suddenly turns on us, it will be handled quickly." Jonaton licked his lips and continued. "Which brings us to why the flavor is important—I can understand what *structural* principles a spell field is built on, and deduce its intent. Maybe unsurprisingly, magic meant to heal is pleasant, and magic made to destroy tastes acrid. The secondary notes in the taste give further detail. So here it is, and believe me, it tastes rancid."

Jonaton showed the Coronation Day protective fields as illuminated yellow, and barely any stray energy flared from it all despite its power. A red circle appeared in the north, above the Palace and in midair. Moments later a representation of what must have been the Red Thing hurtled out of the opened Gate. It appeared to be a ball of woven vines. Jonaton made the representation larger and there were—*people* woven into it.

"Gods and Powers—" Kordas began, and Restil felt suddenly both bolt-awake and queasy.

:Calm, calm, Chosen,: Darshay's Mindvoice implored. :I am sad to say it, but it is what it looks like. Living sacrifice to power spellwork is a foul and cruel enterprise by its nature.:

Jonaton didn't say anything, but reduced the Red Thing to the previous scale and tracked its path from the sky, in a clean arc to the shields over the Palace and city. "The circular shape tells us it was a mid-air Gate. The trajectory tells us the Red Thing was launched with considerable speed. I'd guess it went down a ramp to gain speed, with the Gate entry at the end. This is when it hit," Jonaton said gravely as if he had a bad taste in his mouth. The impact broke the sphere outward into a larger, but still cohesive, ball of energy that rebounded away off of the shields' curves and continued to fall. Jonaton paused the diagram again. "This eruption on impact was cut short. I'd guess it had a failsafe based upon its speed—it was supposed to have hit the ground and detonated, but it hadn't fallen enough yet when the shields slowed it. It wasn't an explosive as most would understand it. It was made to . . ." and he licked his lips again, ". . . *dismantle air*, is the best way to put it. As it spread outward, it would have killed everything breathing in a league's radius in moments. Everything, down to the insects."

Kordas's face went immediately grim, and Restil felt a big, cold ball suddenly form where his stomach was.

"The Palace—" Isla breathed. "And Haven."

"I was waiting for you to have time to look at this before I finished the refinements, so . . . might as well do it now." He frowned at the diagram and made some tweaks and alterations. The diagram shivered, then changed. And Restil made an inarticulate sound of horror as he thought about all those people, innocently watching what they thought were pretty illusions.

The diagram continued to move, showing now what had actually happened. "And this is what happened to it. It stopped expanding in mid-eruption because the casing broke prematurely upon impact with the shields. It rolled off, and we all thought it was a lightshow as part of the festivities." Jonaton manipulated the illusion with his fingertips. "Here, the flavor changes." He tapped at the image. "And here, it is halfway changed and maybe twenty, twenty-five horselengths from the ground. By now it has rolled along the shield dome, across the river, and into the pasture's little forest. When it hits, it isn't the same flavor of magic at all. It has the *absence* of flavor. It's completely purified."

Kordas frowned, and Isla looked puzzled. It was Isla who

spoke. "Wait, you mean in a sense, right? Not literally. All the texts say that 'purified' magic is supposed to be an idea, an impossible goal to strive for. We mortals try to get close on our best days."

"I said what I said," Jonaton replied, apparently miffed that their tiny Kingdom had hosted something so monumental as a true purification without him being any part of it at all.

"The Grove," Kordas said, but it needn't have been spoken. They all knew, which meant the Companions now knew too. "Some Power *purified* what would have killed us all, and used it to transform the thing into the circle where the Companions could enter the world. That must be why the grain was so tight, and vertical—it was in motion when it was used! I should have seen that."

Jonaton looked sympathetic and shrugged. "Took me a while to figure it out, too."

"I can only think of one entity that would do something that—mad," Isla said into the silence.

"The Adept?" Kordas asked tightly.

"Most likely," Jonaton replied.

Kordas turned to face his son. "I've changed my mind. I don't want you going north," he said, his voice a little uneven. "It's too great a risk. I—"

Restil held up his hand. "Are you still going to send another Herald?" he asked. "Or are you going to pull Delia and Pebble back?" Obviously they needed Menalus there—but Menalus was moving around a lot. He was a swiftly, and erratically, moving target, if he was even a target at all.

And Menalus wasn't the Crown Prince.

"I'm leaving Delia and Pebble until their job is done, and yes, I am sending another Herald," the King replied, eying his son speculatively. "Why?"

"Then send me. If you are sending a Herald, send me. We talked about this before, Father. How will people feel about risking *their* sons in danger if you won't send *yours*? And besides," he continued, as his father started to reply, then closed his mouth on what he was going to say, "people will know by this that we Heralds are not just pretty messengers. And people will know you are confident in Valdemar's defenses. This is a crucial point. It's not a *crisis* point, but it's a crucial one. And the answer to it needs to be the right one. I think sending me is that right answer."

He looked at his mother, expecting to see her ready to raise an objection. Her eyes were too bright, but she nodded slightly. "I agree," she said quietly.

Kordas looked at Jonaton. Jonaton shrugged. "I'm not a mind reader, Kordas. I don't know what that Adept is thinking. I don't know what she's planning. All I know is that she hasn't tried anything else and she *seems* to be concentrating on her new army, so maybe she's given up on trying anything magical against us. But I do think Restil is right. You do need to show people that the Heralds are more than messengers, and you need to show them that you won't ask them to make sacrifices that you, yourself, won't make."

The King took in a deep breath and let it out slowly. "All right, then," he replied. "Restil, you'll go, but I want Starbird to go with you. If something does happen, you'll have a Healer right there. She needs more experience with ordinary Valdemarans. And she needs our sort of practical field experience; she knows how the Hawkbrothers do things, and . . . gods only know what that is . . . but she hasn't seen how we operate."

"There is another shading of meaning to all of this," Isla continued. "We know the weapon was transformed. We certainly know why and by whom, even if the gods have been chary about taking credit for this—call it what it is—miracle. But something else occurs to me." She waited to see if Jonaton would interrupt her, but for once, the mage didn't. "It is very difficult for mortal folk to see the future, because the future is always in flux," she continued, sounding like someone who was very sure of her ground. "That is why those who are said to be Gifted with Foresight can see only a limited way into the future, and any attempts to look further are composed of many future paths vying with each other, with little way to tell which is the most likely. But gods are not subject to the limitations of mortals when it comes to knowing what the future most likely holds."

Jonaton was wearing that face that said "Is this going somewhere?" but the Queen pointedly ignored his expression.

"However, as the Companions have told us, the gods are limited in what they can do for us. I am very much inclined to believe that. And creating that doorway through which the Companions came—and giving the Companions a mortal shape and form—would have required a *tremendous* amount of magical energy." She aimed a gimlet eye at Jonaton. "More than 'allowable,' if you will. *But.* Seeing the future, they knew there was going to be a source of magic heading for exactly the right spot. All they had to do was transform it and use it, then wait for Kordas to ask the right question for the right reasons."

Jonaton's mouth gaped a little. "But—but—but—" he stammered. *"The people—"*

Restil completely understood his mingled fascination and horror. Because if his mother was right, the gods had just allowed those people to die terribly so the Companions could enter the world. He went cold all over. If true—

Isla's mouth turned down in a frown. "Those people were already dead," she said.

"You can't know that!"

"Actually . . . I can," she replied, in a tone he had never heard from her before. Absolutely authoritative. Brooking no argument. "Since you already have the information—the 'readings,' as you call them—I can prove it to you with your own diagram if you insist on seeing it."

Jonaton's mouth worked for a moment, but no sound came out. Instead, he finally dropped his eyes, sighed, and murmured, "I'll take your word for it."

"If you ever bothered to *talk* to a priest . . ." she began, then sighed. "Never mind. The *point* is, the Adept was going to murder those people regardless. Since the gods are held to certain constraints, the gods could not intervene to save them. So why not make their sacrifice mean something? Why not use it to improve the world by putting the Companions into it? Turn a weapon of terrible evil into a force for good?"

Jonaton looked as if he had eaten a raw worm. "If only you knew how much I hated what you are saying even while I agree with you."

"It's a decision not unlike some I've had to make," Kordas said softly, his eyes haunted. "I hated what I did, even while I understood it was the only way I could make things better for everyone."

Isla reached out and laid her hand over one of her husband's. He clasped it tightly.

The cold feeling had drained out of Restil in the time it had taken his mother to say all that. By the time the Queen had ended the last sentence, Restil had regained his composure.

"Just as we both hate sending Restil north, even with Starbird, because we are potentially sending our son into great evil. But doing so will make things better for everyone, because the faster people come to trust the Heralds and Companions, the quicker it will be to rally the people at need." The Queen's voice was steady, but Restil knew she felt as much doubt and pain as the King, if not more.

Then her voice lightened. "Besides, I suspect that Starbird has a number of tricks not even an Adept can guess at. One should never anger a Healer. They know how you are put together, and that makes it easy for them to take you apart."

There's the bloodthirsty Mama I know and love so well.

Darshay chuckled in his mind.

So now that his composure was back, he was able to think about other things. Like the fact that he was going to be all alone with Starbird for as long as it took them to reach the border. He tried to remain sober and serious, but inside he was giddy.

So giddy, in fact, that he completely lost track of what Jonaton and his father were saying. All he knew was that when he started paying attention again, Jonaton had dismissed the diagram, and the two were discussing all the things that the hertasi—and probably some of the Tayledras mages—had sent along for him.

"—clever stuff," Jonaton was saying. "I only wish I had time to study the 'toys' more. I've mostly concentrated on things we can use to bolster our defenses or that might be useful in sniffing around that Adept without her detecting anything."

Then he glanced over at Restil. "We're not taking *any* of this lightly, lad. But we're operating with too many unknowns. We don't even know the scope of what we don't know. So realistically, all we can do is wait for her to make a move besides sit in her city and brood. I mean, I guess she's brooding. For all I know she could have decided that we're too much work, and now she is concentrating on another target altogether. That may be why she forced all the defectors into her army—it's a good way of getting rid of people who are probably going to make trouble, without just having a wholesale massacre of them." He frowned again. "She probably used criminals—and for all we know, they were *real* criminals—and dissenters in that spell-ball of hers. And her people would probably be all right with that. But they would probably balk at the wholesale slaughter of allies, even if they are foreigners."

Restil wanted to ask, "Is that even likely?" but he knew better. Jonaton had just said he didn't know, after all. In Restil's experience, Jonaton hated saying he didn't know something more than he hated saying he was wrong.

"This tells us we thought too small," Kordas muttered. "The enemy is now confirmed as an enemy, with lethal intent, but desirous of possessing our city rather than razing it. We know they can craft a major weapon and its launch device, and use a midair Gate to attack from the side. They're cunning enough to not simply drop it on the Palace, assuming we would have especially sensitive Gate detection above our capital. Now we know they have Gate capability, and that skews every defense we've thought of so far. They don't need to march an army or have a supply line when they have Gates, and we don't know where a Gate will open."

"Maybe not now," Jonaton offered.

"I think it makes the construction of defenses to our north a fresh target," Restil ventured. "They may see a force gathered there, but it won't be treated as a threat as long as it's building them fresh infrastructure to seize." He felt a little guilty saying it, because that's what he would do in the enemy's position. "Once the forts or towers are built, bomb them with a Red Thing and they become empty of opposition and ready to move into. Or send in an overwhelming force by Gate to give their troops some field practice for Haven."

Isla darted an appraising look at her son. "Disturbingly reasonable."

Kordas commented, "Parasitic expansion is not unknown in Imperial strategy. Legenfall would no doubt favor it. Knowing his units are limited in experience, he'd want them to train more, rather than use them as a labor force. So, use the enemy to do the work, and eliminate them as an exercise." He made gestures similar to spellcasting, but Restil knew his father well enough to recognize that these were a byproduct of him moving concepts around in his mind. "Truth be told, we don't have any Gate detection running. We should. And we should have a perimeter of Gate disruption if we can manage it, but we'll run out of mages, fast."

"A ring of Gate disruption," Jonaton suggested immediately. "Or rather, a dome with a hollow part in the center, so we can still use Gates stabilized by uprights, and the one to the Hawkbrothers, in that inner dome." He frowned. "We need a way to communicate with the Hawkbrothers, better than flags. Would the Companions have input on that? And we need to know who and what this Adept was before she went missing. Silvermoon did not want to talk about that, but I don't think he was being covert. He may have had a personal connection to her. In fact, now that I think of it, he took care to never use a name for her at all."

"Hawkbrothers are secretive," Restil offered. "Their most common diplomatic answers are, "I'll look into that," "No," and "I won't tell you." Can the student mages be shunted over to enchantment? The Gate ring could be made of enchanted objects, for the sake of efficiency. Maybe it's my own fatigue talking, but every mage will need time to rest. Linked objects could be monitored by fewer mages, and hidden from view."

Jonaton looked proud for a moment. "The students make the teacher validated," he replied. "Good thinking, Restil. We needn't make the objects forever-permanent, either. Let's say, a quick fabrication meant to last five years, with a limited range, enough to overlap each other in case one goes down. How about placed in a rosette, perhaps two hundred junctions or so? Use river silt bound into concrete for an insulating matrix, a steel pole for grounding. No, iron would do, enough to disturb magnetism, but tunable—"

"Well, I'll go get my traveling gear together," Restil said, standing up. Best to leave now while Jonaton had a challenge to solve. He turned to his parents. "I assume I am to wait until you tell Starbird before I talk to her about this?"

Kordas nodded. "That's probably best." And as Restil found himself erupting in an unexpected yawn, added, "You probably shouldn't be doing anything before you get some sleep, anyway. I want you here after breakfast. Ardatha has told Starbird the same. We'll go over what plans we can before the morning Council meeting."

Restil yawned again, and all the energy that Jonaton's revelation had given him drained out of him so suddenly he almost staggered. "Yes, sir," he replied obediently. Then added, "If she's going to have to put her traveling kit together tomorrow, there's no hurry to see to mine, is there?"

"I shouldn't think so," the King said.

"Then if you don't mind . . . I think I'll sleep in my old room."

His father's serious face was almost—*almost*—turned to a smile, as the King nodded his permission. Isla's openly smiled.

Restil staggered off to his room, which looked extra inviting right now—and just about got his uniform off before falling into bed. The last thing he knew was hearing his boots hit the floor as he dropped off to sleep.

It was rather nice to be able to wake up in his old bed, saunter into the bathing room where a boiler of hot water was already waiting, and get a morning bath without having to heat the water himself. A small thing, but pleasant, especially when his muscles ached a little from all that unaccustomed walking. Yes, he did indeed walk a lot, and train, but he'd been walking for many more marks than he was used to down there in Haven, and on hard, paved streets, not turf.

Perhaps because he had gone to bed as soon as he could, and long before his brothers came up from the Great Hall, he was awake even before his parents were. So he had his leisurely bath in peace, and took his time dressing. Jon was up next, flew through his bath and threw on his clothing, and after an interval of crooning over his cats, was ready to dart out the door when Restil intercepted him.

"What's the hurry?" he asked.

"I want to catch Starbird and get her Herald story," Jon explained. "She always eats in the first serving, but since Father wants her to eat with us, I can catch her before she starts, get what I need, and be done before we all need to be at the head table."

That gave Restil pause. Something about this plan bothered him, though he couldn't put his finger on why. So instead, he said, "I'll come with you. Darshay will tell Ardatha and Father will know where we are."

Jon gave him a sly look that said, *You just want more time with Starbird,* and Restil wasn't about to deny that—but he also wasn't going to allow his youngest brother to twig him over it, either. So he raised an eyebrow, which Jon interpreted correctly as *Don't. Just don't.*

Who needs Mindspeech when you have Sibling Speak?

So they clattered their way down the stairs to the Great Hall and intercepted Starbird as she followed the rest of the Heralds into the hall.

She cocked her head at Jon's exuberant greeting, but gave Restil a warm look that gratified him no end before turning her attention back to Jon. "I am happy to see you, Jon, but what is so urgent that you have risen this early just to speak with me?"

"Well, you know the King made me the chronicler of everything to do with the Heralds, right?" Jon said, motioning with his head that they should step aside and not block the door. She followed him a little way down the hall, with Restil following her.

"Of course, we all know that." She gave him a slightly doubtful look.

"I've got everyone's story but yours—" he began—and that was when she raised a hand to stop whatever else he was going to say.

"And you will please leave me and Radiant out of your chronicles," she said, firmly, and steadily.

Jon was clearly taken aback. "But—but—"

"No 'buts.' We must not be in your chronicle. Radiant agrees."

:I do, too.:

"So does Darshay," Restil relayed. "I don't know why, but she does."

"But *why?*" Jon demanded. "What reason could you possibly have? You being Chosen is . . . almost as big and important a thing as the Companions themselves! It means the Hawkbrothers are really our allies—"

"And that is precisely *why* we must not be in your chronicles," Starbird said patiently, brushing a strand of her black hair across her forehead and back into place. "If the Tayledras are known far and wide as allies, we lose much of our effectiveness *as* your allies. Instead of being a factor of uncertainty, we become something your people will think they can depend on. Instead of being something they do not want to cross, we become something taken for granted. Secrecy is part of our armory. We will not give it up under any circumstances." As Jon's face registered his disappointment, she looked as if she was inclined to pat him on the head, but instead, just softened her expression to one of sympathy. "I understand that this is very important to you, but this is not something I am prepared to compromise on."

"But what about—"

"You may make up a new Herald, Chosen by Radiant. You may give her whatever background you wish. You may ascribe what we do to Radiant and her Chosen, the Herald you made up. You just may not make that Herald *me,* or say she is a Hawkbrother." She paused. "And Radiant says that Ardatha says that the King agrees. As your father, he understands your disappointment. But as your King, he orders you to abide by my wishes."

Jon heaved an enormous sigh. "But what about history?"

"What we know as history changes over time, little brother," Restil said with the authority of being the eldest. "It depends on who is telling it, why they are telling it. People will edit out, add, or change a lot of things in twenty years, let alone a hundred. And no one actually *needs* to know that one of the first Heralds was a Tayledras. I mean, in fact, once we are in the uniform, we are all just Heralds and none of us is any more special than any other. That's why we have a uniform." He thought about it a little more. "In fact, the only stories that *need* to be told are those of Heralds who came out of poverty or modest circumstances, because that will mean people will know that this is not confined to the wealthy or highborn. Other than that—it's nice to know, but in twenty, fifty, or a hundred years, it won't matter."

"Especially not if, in twenty or fifty or a hundred years, what my people *want* is to be the frightening, spooky people that no one knows much about, who live in the Pelagirs where no one else will." Starbird gave him an earnest look. "Much of our work revolves around keeping the unwary *out*. Because the Pelagirs are dangerous, even to the wary, much less the unwary. In the future, we will inevitably move apart from you, and perhaps another clan will be nearer than us, a clan that has no interest in you. That is our culture. That is part of our Goddess-appointed task. And in that future, we don't want people reading your chronicles of the first days of the Heralds, then wandering around in those dangerous lands, looking for us. *I* do not want to become an exotic icon—and we don't want romantic young idiots interfering with the job we must do because they're hoping to find someone like me. We want to be the people they are actually afraid of encountering. Do you understand now?"

"I do," Jon sighed. "I don't like it, and it seems wrong to keep such a momentous thing out of the chronicles, but since Father agrees with you . . . I guess I'll just make someone up, like you suggested, if you do something I need to write about."

"Thank you," she said, then added, with mock seriousness, "because I would really hate to have to kill you to prevent you. Your cats would never forgive me."

"The King wants you to have breakfast with us," Restil

said, relieved that what could have been a "situation" had been dealt with so easily. "He has some things he wants to discuss with you."

She looked curious, but didn't ask any questions, merely nodded her assent. The three of them made their way up to the high table just as the rest of the family got there.

There was no talk of the trip at breakfast, which he found odd, but at least the King relayed through their Companions that he wanted them to follow him when they finished. That seemed even odder, and Restil began to worry immediately. And when Kordas took them not to the royal suite, nor to his own privy chamber where he had private conversations, but to the corresponding chamber that the Lord Martial used for the utmost secret talks, Restil's concern shot straight up.

It was not soothed at all when he found that Sai and Jonaton were there, along with the Lord Martial.

It was a very stark little room in the basement floor of the Palace, and windowless; there were silencing spells on all four walls and doubled on the doors and ventilation apertures to prevent any sort of mundane eavesdropping. There were so many anti-scrying measures that to Restil's senses everything seemed a little muffled in here. Even the mage-lights were warded, because scrying via a light was a known thing, although it was not commonly used, and he had only seen it demonstrated once, by Sai.

They sat down around a table with a map of Haven on it.

"I'm calling Delia and Pebble back from the border, and we have changed our minds about sending you and Starbird north," Kordas said as soon as the door was closed, and Sai and Jonaton had laid in still more anti-scrying spells. "Jonaton has discovered some things that have caused us to completely re-assess our defensive plans."

Before Restil could say anything at all, Kordas turned to Starbird. "Starbird, this is a position I hate to put you in, and it is probably going to test your loyalty, but your uncle has been very evasive about this Adept we face, and if you know anything about her, we need you to tell us, regardless of whether or not you've been asked to keep it secret."

She blinked slowly. Clearly this was not anything she had expected. "What do you mean by 'evasive'? I don't actually know what he's told you."

"Next to nothing," the Lord Martial rumbled. "Only that she was a Hawkbrother of k'Vesla, that she 'disappeared,' and that they assumed until now that the wilderness had claimed her life. And despite the fact that he certainly should have more information than that—after all, there cannot be more than a few thousand people in your clan!—he has not been at all forthcoming."

Starbird held up her hand to stop him from saying more. Finally, after a term of silence that seemed to go on forever, she sighed heavily and spoke.

"Radiant says I should tell you everything I know, and Radiant comes from the Star-Eyed Herself. So whatever my uncle thinks, it's obviously my duty to do as you ask." She grimaced, and cast her eyes down. "I'm surprised he didn't tell you . . . and yet I am not surprised. The reason my uncle doesn't want to talk about her is because she was *his* apprentice. He is very ashamed, and considers her defection a moral failure on his part."

The silence that fell after *that* shoe dropped was so profound that Restil found himself feeling as if he needed to break it before he went mad. Fortunately, he didn't have to. Starbird continued.

"As I was told by my parents, everything in Cloudfall's apprenticeship appeared to be normal—though there wasn't a great deal of it. She had only barely come into her powers, though it was clear that she was going to be an Adept. My uncle had just begun to teach her the basics. In fact, just that day he had taught her the spell to create fire, and left her in a safe place to practice it when he knew she could handle it on her own. And that is the last time he saw her. Everyone woke in the middle of the night to shrieks from the bondbirds and fire in the bondbird aviary, where they raise their young. It was a terrible, terrible fire. It nearly spread to the rest of the Vale, and many almost-fledged birds died horribly. Cloudfall's own bondbird was found pegged to the ground with a knife in her heart at the aviary entrance, and Cloudfall herself was gone."

Restil gasped. He knew how close the Hawkbrothers were to their birds; it was a bond not unlike the Herald-Companion bond. For the Hawkbrothers, it would have been as if their own children had been slaughtered.

"Everyone assumed some enemy had somehow penetrated into the Vale, kidnapped Cloudfall, and set the fire to cover their tracks. But immediate spells, including past-scrying, proved that was not true. It was Cloudfall who had done all this, murdering her own bird and setting the fire in such a way that only the adult birds were able to escape. Then she simply vanished. Quite literally. There was no trace of her, not to any sort of magic anyone tried." She licked her lips. "Uncle blamed himself, completely, I am told. He never talked about it. But he looked for her tirelessly for years. A decade at least. And then he gave up."

Kordas blurted, "A decade! How long ago did this happen? He must have been devastated!" He exhaled a tense gust. "I wish . . . we could have helped him somehow."

"It was when you were all still in Old Valdemar. I wasn't even born yet. It was bad on him in every way—he couldn't teach again, his hygiene fell, and Healers came and went from his ekele daily for months. Other mages came to replace them, and it turned out to be wise of them. Adepts' students achieve an intimacy with their teachers that you probably wouldn't understand," Starbird stated bluntly, then she softened the statement. "Different approaches to learning than you may be used to, is what I'm trying to say. Learning the subtleties of high-power spellwork is done by shared senses, and it is—sympathetic. She was someone whose soul he knew a little like Companions know a Herald, which implies of course that she knew him that well too, and had orchestrated an atrocious emotional torment specific to *him* from it."

"I can't imagine how personally he must have taken it all," Restil commented. Starbird met eyes with him for a few seconds longer than she had to.

"It would make lesser souls shatter, but those who loved him stood with his hand in their palms. They did not wish him words from a distance, they sought out what actions would take strain off of him, and championed them like questing heroes. The whole while, understanding his heart was deeply bruised, they took care to not mention Cloudfall in any disparaging way around Silvermoon. Besides, it was still an ongoing mystery—as horrible as it was, we Tayledras deal in facts, and there were too few facts to begin judgment. Like everyone else, Silvermoon surmised that something about tapping into her powers sent her insane—she could have had a stroke, brain-bled, or otherwise damaged her reasoning, and that was why she did—what she did. The whole Vale reeled from it, and I've long thought covering an escape was why she did it. Insane doesn't mean stupid." Starbird frowned at herself for the acidity of her words. "The search for her was thorough, and eventually Silvermoon assumed that she had died somewhere out in the uncleansed lands."

Jonaton's look directly at Kordas was clearly meant to send a pointed message.

Kordas returned Jonaton's look with a subtle double-shake of his head which obviously meant *don't you even start with me.* "Is that—common?" Kordas asked, looking not only at Starbird, but at Sai and Jonaton. "For Adepts to fall prey to madness?"

"It's not unheard of," Sai said carefully. "At least, not in the limited amount of information I've read about them."

Jonaton nodded. "I've heard the same. Why? Maybe when

an Adept comes into their power, instead of having to coax it into being, learning to control just the trickles you first get, then bigger and better sources of energy, it blazes up within you all at once, like fire in oil-soaked wood, and some people can't handle that. Particularly if they are already mentally unstable." He raised his hands and shrugged. "That's just speculation on my part."

Starbird mirrored his shrug. "I don't know either, but it's as good an explanation as any. And if that *is* the case, it might explain why she killed her bondbird and all the young ones. It's one thing to have your bird in your mind when you want to talk to it. It would be quite another to suddenly be privy to its every single thought, and then have all the half-formed thoughts of the fledglings rushing into your head, like being surrounded by shrieking children."

Kordas nodded. "Well, obviously she didn't die. And whether she is mad or not, she's perfectly capable of controlling an entire city. But that is not what concerns me now. Sai, Jonaton—could an Adept *take over* a warded and protected Gate? That sudden fear last night was what woke me, made me wake the Lord Martial, and decide to bring Delia and Pebble back."

Sai and Jonaton looked at each other, and many emotions flitted across their faces. Alarm, speculation, calculation, consternation. "Well," said Sai at last, as Jonaton made a motion with his head suggesting that he deferred to the old man, "yes. An ordinary mage, even one as powerful as Jonaton, no. Or at least, not without alerting every mage in the country that someone was appropriating a Gate. Not even an entire circle of ordinary mages. But an Adept can handle the full power of the largest ley-lines, and with that, she can blast through what she could not ordinarily break. We've permitted ourselves to become complacent about her, and assumed too much."

This time the silence felt stifling. Restil felt as if he was being crushed by a sensation of impending doom.

"We have . . . severely underestimated her," the Lord Martial said, slowly.

"*We* were . . . stupid," Jonaton said bitterly. "We should have thought of that. We just blithely went along thinking that nothing could come through our Gate because we locked it and only we and k'Vesla had the key to it. *It never even occurred to us that she could force it open,* like a thief breaking a lock rather than trying to pick it."

"So," the Lord Martial said, his voice now pitched so low that it sounded like a mastiff growling, "what we have is essentially a wide-open invasion port right outside the walls of the Palace. She doesn't have to march her army across the intervening space and end up on the border. She doesn't even have to make an unanchored Gate on the border and drop them there. She can drop them right at our feet."

Only the King seemed, if not undismayed, *less* dismayed than everyone else. *Then again, he's probably been thinking about all this since he got woken up by his—call it a premonition, I guess.* Knowing his father as well as he did, Restil figured that he had run through every single possibility he could think of, with special attention to worst cases.

"Right." Kordas straightened. "We should assume she's had some way of spying on us—for all we know, she's got an agent inside the Palace walls. So outwardly, except for bringing Delia back, which we would have done about now anyway, nothing changes. She actually doesn't know that we've trapped the northern border—"

He looked inquisitively at Starbird.

"Hawkbrothers do not have *anything* to do with Elementals," she said flatly. "We were rather shocked by all the *vrondi* you had with you! We leave them strictly alone. And as for Pebble and his mother . . . well, to our minds, their intervention was practically as much an act of the gods as the Companions are! So . . ." She blinked several times. "Assume she was watching the Vale. She saw us preparing to hand the territory over to you. She certainly did *see* the attack of the Red Forest and the intervention of Pebble's mother, but . . . her interpretation might not have been the correct one. She might have assumed the only reason Pebble's mother intervened was because Pebble was threatened. Or she might have thought it was a predator-prey situation, that Pebble's mother attacked the forest because it was the sort of prey that she lives on."

"Hope for the best . . . but assume she knows the truth," Kordas corrected. "So . . . what we need to do now is *hide* Pebble when he gets back here."

"You certainly are not going to ask that child to—" Jonaton began indignantly.

"Of course not," Kordas snapped. "I am *not* going to ask Pebble to join our defenses. I just don't want Cloudfall to think that Pebble's mother is going to show up again and in anticipation of that prepare—say—a barrage of what hit us during the coronation. We are unlikely to get divine intervention a second time. We need her to think that we are unprepared for her. We need to somehow hide our preparations for her to take over our Gate. We want her to be as under-prepared as possible."

"And we hope that what she wants out of us is something to conquer and keep, not destroy," the Lord Martial added. "We hope that she has discarded fully lethal options. It is true that the fact she is raising an army suggests that is the case."

"How, if there's an ordinary spy among us?" Restil objected.

"Ah . . . the spy might be ordinary, but the means of communicating with her won't be," Sai said, perking up. "The rest of the Old Men and I can start combing the Palace and Haven looking for a device or traces of magic. Jonaton and all the youngsters can start working on defenses."

"We trickled the guards in . . . we can trickle some of them back out again," the Lord Martial mused. "I'm loath to pull them all back, because she just might just put up her own Gate within an easy march of our border, but we can bring some back—"

:We can help with looking for spies,: said Darshay at last. *:Don't waste the mages' time. There are more of us than there are of them, and all the unpartnered Companions have time to waste. We are very sensitive to the use of magic of any kind. All we need to do is "listen" for magic where no magic should be.:*

Restil was about to relay that, but his father beat him to it.

:No, we are not going to be listening to everyone's thoughts. Not only would that be unethical when there is no cause to suspect an individual, but trying to sift through all the thoughts of everyone in Haven and the Palace would probably drive us mad. You humans have—issues that frustrate us. There is only so much drama we can endure.:

That last had a tinge of humor to it, but given what Darshay had said about madness earlier . . . there just might be a grain of truth in it.

"I just can't believe we were so blind," Jonaton said bitterly. "Or was it stupid?"

"Why not both?" said Sai sarcastically, then altered his tone. "We're in a new place, with new rules and new hazards. We can't anticipate everything. And when the Companions, a literal gift from the gods, arrived, we were blinded by wonder and awe. And maybe a touch of naivete. After all, the gods themselves had just blessed us with these incredible helpers, and I think in the back of *my* mind, at least, was the thought, 'Why would anyone sane want to challenge someone who just got divine intervention to save them?' And, of course, we've been assuming the Adept was sane." He poked a finger toward Jonaton, who replied by sticking his tongue out at his elder. Sai shook his head. "It's very difficult not to make assumptions. We are often forced to do so when there is not enough information." Now he patted Jonaton on the shoulder. "We're fallible, flawed creatures. I didn't think of anything like this either, and I should have. I'm older than you, and I lived in the Empire most of my life. I should have known better."

It was Starbird who interrupted all of this. "I believe that we are all best served by dealing with *now.* We can trade tales of why we are to blame when we have all survived this."

The King and the Lord Martial both nodded. Kordas sighed. "All right. Let's get the people we think we need in here, and start planning."

"We need to talk to Koto and Rothas together," Starbird told Restil when they were finally released so that other people could fit into the room. "Well, Koto first. He is the one doing the research into breaking their curse, yes?"

"He is," Restil confirmed. "And I think we can catch him before he gets hauled into that consultation." He rubbed the back of his head. "Why, though?"

"Because those two deserve to know what is happening, and if it will affect their plan," she replied. "They've earned it at this point. *I* think so, at least."

"Then let's talk to Koto." Almost as one, they both sped up to a trot. "You know what is the most frustrating right now?" he added.

"That we were only consulted because we were immediately affected, and now we've been told to 'run along and don't worry about it'?" She gave him a sideways look, and smiled.

"Well, yes." He sighed. "But our Companions will at least tell us what is going on. So we have that much going for us."

:Why yes, I will. I thought you'd never ask.:

He rolled his eyes, and she caught it. "What?" she asked.

"I have a Companion with a somewhat sarcastic vein."

:It's not a vein. It's an entire mine. Nice of you to notice.:

When they reached Koto's dwelling, however, Rothas was already with him, brow knotted, talking over some tricky business about his Gift. Or at least, that was what Restil assumed he was talking about. Something about "threads," "strands," and "bits."

Koto held up his hand to get Rothas to pause. "Whatever brings you here at this early hour cannot be good," he declared. "Spit it out."

Restil waited until both of them had a chance to establish wards against scrying, then made very short work of describing what the meeting had been about, and Koto nodded all the way through the explanation. Then he sighed. But before he could say anything, Rothas spoke up.

"I guess this means we aren't going to try breaking our curse then, are we?" he said, looking defeated. "We only get one chance after all—"

"Nonsense!" Koto replied. "Why shouldn't we? We still don't know when or even *if* this madwoman is going to attack us! What's changed between now and yesterday? *Nothing.* We just realized that we weren't quite as safe as we thought we were." He snorted, and took the handkerchief he always carried and polished his shiny, bald head. "What does it matter? Better try it! If we wait too long, I might be snake-dog food by the full moon after this one, and then where would you be?"

Rothas blinked at him, bewildered, and obviously unsure what to make of this speech.

"What *are* you talking about?" Starbird asked, looking at Koto askance.

"The magic binding Rothas and Lythe to day and night is . . . well, a tangled mess is the nicest way to say it," Koto replied. "We've been trying to figure a way to untangle it, and there's no way. It's like a hopelessly snarled ball of string. But then, it occurred to me, there's no reason to try to untangle it! It's not as if it was a golden thread we needed to have intact! But there's no brute-forcing it, either. So I created a spell that works like a very patient craftsperson. It makes little snips in the tangle—*snip-snip-snip*—" he said, miming a pair of scissors. "Make enough little snips and bits start to fall off. Not enough damage to make the spell backlash into anyone. Not enough damage to make it unravel catastrophically. Just little bits falling off over the course of three days and three nights. Optimum time to start it is at the start of the three days of the full moon. The only drawback is I'll have to seal them into their living quarters for that time. And if they break the shields and the circle to leave, I'm not sure I'll be able to find another solution, because the research diagram *suggests* that all those bits will gather the energy of the broken circle and shields and create a *new* "curse," just as messy as the last, and probably worse to try and undo."

"So that's what you were talking about when we came up here!" Restil exclaimed.

"It wouldn't be fatal if they broke out, would it?" Starbird asked.

Koto shook his head. "No. Not enough power, for one thing, and for another, I haven't seen a hint of lethality, and believe me, I looked!" He cackled. "Sometimes these wild-magic curses have minds of their own and I didn't want it coming after *me*! No, there's some hard specifications in there—that Rothas is bound to the day and Lythe is bound to the night—so it would be something incorporating that." He shrugged. "Other than that, I can't say. Might bind them more tightly. Might bind them more loosely. Might force them to *do* something during the day or night. All I know for sure is that it would be worse to try to take apart a second time without hurting them. As I said, wild-magic spells like this seem to get minds of their own. It might be angry about being taken to pieces, and make it impossible to pull the thing off them without killing them or driving them mad."

Restil did not want to contemplate what damage a mad Bard could do. Rothas continued to stare at Koto, with an expression that suggested he was sure that Koto was going to decide not to remove the curse after all.

"No! I say we do this!" Koto continued. "I can do all the

energy-hungry work now, and leave it ready to activate at twilight on the first night of the full moon. I'm sure you two can figure out how to cook a few things over your fire by then. You'll have fire if you need it, plenty of water, lots of free time to write more songs and practice." He paused. "You'll have to have Lythe's pets stay outside, though. Can't have them, or anything, crossing the circle. Good thing Lythe has Animal Mindspeech! She can warn everything away except bugs, and we've got a good repellant that we can paint around the doors and windows. Some people would call that 'having a nice rest'!"

Rothas's expression cleared, and he nodded. "As long as you're sure . . ."

"I'm never *sure* of anything! Magic is all about playing the odds and hoping you stay lucky! But I'm determined!" He polished his head again. "You go trot down to the kitchen and have someone teach you how to toast bread and boil an egg or something! I'll get things started, and when I need to, I'll show up at your quarters and start laying in the foundation."

Rothas began babbling thanks, but Koto waved them away. "Just remember, what you heard from Restil is secret! Don't go making a song about it! At least, not until after we're sure we're rid of the problem permanently!"

"And while we are on the subject of songs," Starbird interjected. "No songs about a Hawkbrother Herald. No songs about Hawkbrother allies. In fact, your only songs about Hawkbrothers should make us sound . . ." She hesitated.

"Stern guardians of the forest, unreadable, unpredictable, and a little bit frightening?" Rothas suggested, one eyebrow raised.

"Yes," she replied gratefully. "Your songs are far too memorable, and there are many reasons why *that* is the image we want going into the future."

He nodded, but looked pleased with himself. *Well, he should. There can't be too many musicians who wouldn't be pleased to hear, "Your songs are far too memorable."*

Rothas stood up. "If that's all, I'll go get some cooking lessons. If nothing else, there is always beer, bread, cheese, and vegetables. It will only be for three days, after all!"

He eased past the Heralds and sauntered off, and was soon out of sight. "All right then," Koto said into the silence. "Close the door, and I'll activate the wards on it, the windows, and all the other openings into this place." He made a face. "And on the fire and the mage-lights. And reflective surfaces. What a nuisance! There are far too many things that could be used to scry."

They did as he told them. A couple of mage-lights in glass holders on the wall slowly came to life as the light from the open door got cut off.

When Koto was done, he got a couple of giant cushions from a stack in the corner of the room and threw them at the two of them. *Old habits die hard,* Restil thought, as he and Starbird picked places to sit on the floor and arranged their cushions there. *I wonder why the Old Men are so opposed to actual furniture?*

The cushions Koto threw them were not as fluffy as the one he took for himself, but . . . well, Restil and Starbird were many decades younger, and Koto had next to no padding on his skinny frame.

"So, I've more or less been in charge of helping the Herald-Mages learn how to integrate their powers with those of their Companions," Koto said to both of them. "Restil has been taking lessons from me, but I'm not sure where your powers and Gifts come into defending this Palace, Starbird."

He gave her a quizzical look, and one that invited her to say more.

"I'm not sure either," she confessed. "I'm probably of more use as an archer. I do have some tricks there."

"Well, what about your Companion?" Koto persisted. "Can Radiant join forces with a Herald-Mage's Companion and boost their powers further?"

Her eyes widened, as if she was surprised. "Radiant says that she can," she reported.

Koto looked very pleased with himself for having thought of that. "Well, good! In that case, when it comes to a fight, mount up, find a Herald-Mage, and stick to them! You could just plan on it being Restil! I don't think you'd find him difficult to work with!" His eyes twinkled a little, and Restil felt himself flushing. "And his specialty *is* combat magic, after all!"

"And I have been well trained," Restil replied, happy to steer the subject away from that particular hot chestnut.

Starbird nodded solemnly.

"With extra energy at my disposal, I can certainly keep a shield on two people and their Companions *and* fight," he continued. "It was easy enough to do so on myself and Darshay when Young Squire called us for that monstrous bear two weeks ago." *I wish we'd had that at our disposal long ago. Would have saved me and Father a few bruises and gashes!*

"There, that will leave Starbird free to stick as many arrows into things as she can." Koto nodded wisely. "And of course, her Healing Gift will be mightily useful when the fighting gets hot."

Starbird's lips twitched a little. "It's also true that if an enemy gets close enough, I can do more than just stick arrows in them," she said a bit grimly. "Healers among my people are trained to use their Gift to take people apart as well as put them back together. Not all of them do, because not all of them are comfortable with the idea of dealing harm as well as healing—but I do. Joints," she added thoughtfully, "do not like bending backward. And there are these soft little disks in spines that can cause immense mischief if they rupture."

Koto blinked at her owlishly. "I do believe I like you very much, Starbird!" he declared. "You are sufficiently bloody-minded even for me! It's a good thing I'm not younger! I'd snatch you away from all these young stallions! I was quite the handsome devil at your age, and very much a risk-taker! I would need a Healer of my very own!"

Starbird smiled slightly. "You are quite the handsome devil *now,* Koto," she replied. The old man preened.

"Well, well, I'm far too old for you now, young lady." He sighed dramatically. "A tragedy for both of us!"

Then he sobered. "Well, well. I can tell you what I would like. The thing about Adepts, you see, is that they only think *big,* and often miss small magics and even things non-magicians can do—like you snapping knees, Starbird—in favor of very large magic. Now, while the Companions can certainly boost their Heralds, I'd like all of you to get together as a group and start making strategies based around the small—and *Mind-magic!*—especially boosted Mind-magic. Because that's something she won't be looking for, and won't guard against. Oh! And station one of those unpartnered Companions at the Gate at all times! You've said they're sensitive to magic; they can warn us if the Gate is opening."

:Darshay, will the unpartnered Companions help us in a fight?: he asked, as Koto was finishing that sentence.

:Absolutely. The unpartnered Companions won't be able to boost people as much, but they will make a difference. And, of course, we are prepared to fight. I am reminding Ardatha of this so he tells your father. And we will have unpartnered Companions at the Gate as forward-guards.:

Well, that was good news in a sea of grimness.

The three of them threw many ideas around the room before Koto needed to go make the initial preparations for breaking that curse. Some were good. Some seemed good at first, but there were problems that appeared on closer examination. Like, for instance, seeing if Lythe could summon a few giant boars to the battlefield.

"Imagine what would happen if they slipped her control," Koto said, regretfully. "The best that would happen would be that they would run away. The worst that they would attack *us.*"

And of course there was the unspoken question: what if Koto's curse-breaking didn't work? Lythe would only be useful at night.

Finally Koto called a halt to the discussion. He rose. "Time for these old bones to get to work." He made a sweeping motion with his hand that dismissed the extra protections against scrying that he had put up. Restil and Starbird rose too.

He opened the door with a gesture—because he could, obviously. Restil couldn't help but smile. The Old Men never changed. They did like to remind people of the fact that although they all looked ready to die at any moment, they were almost Adepts themselves.

And Koto proved that he was anything but infirm by quickly outdistancing them as they all left his quarters.

:We've called all our Heralds together for the mass meeting,: Darshay said. :Well, all but the King. But your mother is coming, and she's probably better, since she doesn't get bogged down in trying to blame herself for things. We're all going to meet at that pavement at the Grove where the temple will be. The Queen is arranging for luncheon to be brought.:

:Mother thinks of everything,: he replied gratefully, as his stomach growled.

:What she doesn't think of, Dendalin does.:

Starbird must have been talking to Radiant at the same time, because she turned to smile at him, and despite how grave the situation was, his heart turned over a little.

"Radiant says everyone is heading for the Grove already."

"Well, we'd better—" he began.

:Radiant and I are waiting for you at the door into the garden.:

"—go join our 'transportation,'" he said smoothly.

:Transportation? Is that what we are?: Darshay said in mock indignation.

:Among so many, many other things, yes. You carry me, not the other way around.:

:Hmph. Keep talking like that and I might arrange to swap bodies with you so you can see what it's like!:

He chuckled softly as he pushed open the garden door to see Radiant and Darshay standing in just the right light to make them look fabulous.

:Of course we do.:

He put both hands on Darshay's bare back and powered himself up into place. A glance to his right showed that Starbird had done the same. "Let's go see what mayhem we can plan," he said, feeling a bit more confident than he had before talking to Koto.

"Oh," Starbird said, with a sort of vindictive tone that made him wonder if she was now aching to avenge the wrong done to her uncle by his former apprentice, "I am very much looking forward to this mayhem-planning. Cloudfall has had things all her own way for too long. It is past time that she got used to disappointment."

It was the second night of the full moon. Rothas and Lythe were sealed into their quarters, and had been since twilight last night. They could still come to the door or window and talk, they just couldn't leave, and no one could enter. And the unraveling appeared to be working! Rothas had been able to stay awake for three whole candlemarks after full darkness fell last night, and Lythe had been able to stay awake for five this morning.

As he sought sleep, Kordas tried to concentrate on that, rather than on worrying about the preparations for what now looked like an inevitable clash with an Adept. But he tossed and turned, molded his pillow a dozen times, got too hot, then too cold, and finally Isla sat up in bed and threw the covers off of both of them. "I'm going to the fire and making you a sleeping posset," she said. "And you are going to drink it. No arguments."

"Yes, milady," he said meekly, and got up. That didn't feel like enough, so he added the first thing he could think of.

"Pebble finished what I asked him to do today." It had all been underground work, of course. Tunneling where no one could see him unless they knew to scry underground, which was a difficult proposition to say the least. But now there was an escape tunnel from the hertasi tunnels where the children and other noncombatants would hide, a tunnel that would take them very far from Haven indeed. It stretched a league. Inside, Pebble had somehow made the surface just like the roadways he had been laying down, and created tiny ventilation holes that came up beneath bushes or hedges. *Now we just have to hold off an army until everyone gets a chance to get down in those tunnels.*

He followed Isla into the main room, where she put wine, cream, honey, and herbs into a little long-handled pot and held it over the fire to warm. "Oh, I meant to ask you, did you find out if Pebble is a boy or a girl?" she asked, as if that was the only thing in the world to worry about.

He had to chuckle at that question. "No, but not because I didn't ask. He giggled and said, 'I didn't know I needed to choose! I might do someday, but I haven't decided yet.'"

"Well . . . Elementals are by their nature changeable. Many of them can change shape and size entirely, so I suppose it's not out of the question for them to change their gender." She pulled the pot out of the fire and sniffed it. Satisfied it had warmed as she wished, she carefully poured the contents into a tall copper beaker she had sitting on the hearth and gave it to him. He took it and sipped it appreciatively as she went to the bathing room to wash out the pot.

They talked mostly about Elementals in general and Pebble in particular while he waited for the posset to take effect. She was much more widely read in magic than he was—her father's magical library had been absolutely enormous, and his one regret about the hasty way he had come to get Delia was that he had not also taken the time to loot that library on the grounds that the Emperor had gifted the manor, title, and land to the new owner, not the *contents* of the manor. *I wonder what happened to that library. Stupid prig wasn't a mage, I know that for certain, so it's not as if all those books were any use to him.* The thought of making raids on the old Empire for resources like that raised its head again, and he squashed it quickly. Things would be desperate indeed to even consider trying.

"Sleepy yet?" Isla asked, plucking the now-empty tankard from his hands.

"Somewhat?"

"Then go to sleep. I'll tidy up." She looked as if she might say something more, like *We're doing all we can* or *Worrying won't speed up our preparations,* but she didn't. Instead, she took his hand, pulled him to his feet, and pushed him in the direction of the bed. Whatever had been in that posset was effective. He had trouble keeping his eyes open, and while he didn't fall asleep immediately, at least his mind quieted down and allowed him to get to sleep at all. Of course, Ardatha may have had a part in it too.

He was out of bed and standing in his bare feet on the floor when he recognized what had startled him awake, startled straight out of bed before he even consciously recognized what had awakened him. It had been the sounds of the alarm horns on the Palace wall, and the earth-shattering *boom* as the portcullis gates and iron-banded doors on the wall slammed shut. Trumpets took up the alarm out in Haven and outward.

Isla was standing up next to him, shocked awake the same way he had been. She had a stiletto from *somewhere* in one hand, and a pillow in the other held defensively like a shield.

:Ardatha, tell me.:

:A Gate is delivering monstrosities in measured waves and formations. The Palace appears to be the objective.: Ardatha's

Mindvoice was clipped and to the point. :*The Gate does not touch the ground and is deformed at the edges. It's wide, and wavering; forces that trip on its edges are losing feet. It looks like the Adept's city on the other side, emptying staging grounds to here. Guard is delaying engagement but they're tense. Quarter defense is mustering in Haven, and Palace contingencies are being executed. We're meeting our Heralds at the stable.*:

His armor stood ready on its stand. Isla emptied her hands by dropping the pillow and throwing the stiletto into the floor for easy retrieval. Kordas pulled his boots on while Isla retrieved wrapped bars of Ponu's design from the valet stand—black and lumpy, containing nuts, seeds, and outright candy. These were not everyday fare—they were expressly for events when the mind must be sharp, pain blocked, and metabolism at its best efficiency. She started chewing on one while unwrapping another for Kordas, and fed him pieces between pulling on her own trews and boots. It was best to not think about the flavors.

Kordas exhaled loudly between chewing and quipped, "They were good plans."

Her glance showed that Isla was in a similar mood—concerned, exasperated, and angry, yes, but in a seething, tight-lipped way. "It was a gamble all along. Sounds like someone just flipped the table."

Isla served as his squire before his own valet reached the suite. She had helped him armor up countless times before this, and there was a sort of comfort in feeling her sure hands buckling straps and tying off ties. Within moments, he was geared up and out the door, just as one of Isla's former maids dashed in to help *her* armor up. He already knew that Ardatha was waiting for him; *all* the partnered Companions were lining up at the stable to be saddled, but Ardatha was the King's Companion, and as such, came first in line, followed by Dendalin. And sure enough, Dendalin was standing right beside

Ardatha, looking as tranquil as if everyone was just going to a training exercise.

Now that the worst was on them, he somehow felt very calm. Every thought, reasoned, clear, immediate. He grabbed the pommel and leapt into the saddle as easily as if he was still Restil's age. Ardatha raced to the front gate, which was now barred by an iron portcullis and a massive wooden, iron-bound door at either end of the tunnel. Leaping from Ardatha's back, he raced up the stairs to the top of the wall.

He had no idea what he was about to find, but what was out there was much worse than his worst nightmares.

Beneath him was a sea of monstrous creatures. The wyrsa milled around down there, of course, and there were giant boars and snarling cold-drakes, but there were also things he couldn't even put a name to. The horns were still sounding, and it must have been mere moments since the Companion watching the gate had detected the Gate opening and gave the alarm. :*Ardatha? Is the watch Companion safe?*:

:*She lost a few hairs from her tail, but she made it inside just ahead of the barriers coming down.*: Good. He could let that go. One less thing to worry about.

:*Wait—that isn't* our *Gate, is it?*: The open Gate seemed to be in the wrong place!

:*It's not,*: Ardatha replied. :*She's drawing on the same power source, but it's unanchored and about three lengths to the right.*:

He swore. *I should have sealed and locked the power source.* But if he had, wouldn't she just have done what they'd feared she would, and taken over their Gate by force?

Doesn't matter. Concentrate on what's in front of you.

In the distance, the Gate still spewed enemies, obscured by fog on the far side until they reached Valdemaran ground. Disturbingly long-legged, forest-green relatives of the water spiders they'd disturbed at the Red Forest passage stalked out in triangular formations taking horse-length steps, and they were followed by humans. *Probably smart to put the humans behind the monsters. Keep them focused on the food in front of them—us.*

This was not a war. Wars played out over the course of months, even years. There were not enough combatants here for a war. There weren't even enough to make this a "proper" battle by Imperial standards. It wouldn't even last the morning. By luncheon, this would be over, at least for those inside these walls—one way or another. *This is going to be brutish and short.*

And what they needed to do right now was buy time. Time for all the noncombatants to get down into the tunnels, with whatever they had with them or had packed into the tunnels anticipating this moment. Pets had to be evacuated too; Lythe had spent a full week making sure all the pets in the Palace knew what to do when those horns sounded. His stomach knotted up at the idea that even one child would be weeping because they could not find their beloved pet, but Lythe had assured him that this would not happen. The pets, even the cats, had agreed to stay with their people until everyone was safe underground.

And his heart threatened to break at the idea of his people suffering yet more loss.

He surveyed the "army" below, and even with the addition of the monsters, it was still less than two Imperial battalions in size. *Of course, we don't have monsters—but we do have mages. I don't think the Adept does.*

No, the battle would not last long. If they won, people would be eating luncheon in the Great Hall as usual. If they lost—people had been told to collapse all the hertasi entrances and stay put, unless they heard something digging for them, and wait until dark to trudge to the end of Pebble's tunnel.

And pray that the gods take pity on them.

He didn't need Ardatha's wordless warning to know that Isla had just arrived and was coming up the stairs to stand beside him. This wasn't like the time they had fought the Red Forest, and Isla had commanded those who had evacuated then into the tunnels. Restil was a man grown, and out here, prepared to fight, as well; Hakkon and Jon were going down into the tunnels and old enough to take care of themselves. Isla had made it abundantly clear, with very few words, that this time she was not going to hide in a tunnel and wait.

Just as she slipped her right hand into his left, Ardatha gave them another update. :*The archers are deploying.*:

The sounds of dozens of runners sprinting up the stairs behind him confirmed that, and a moment later, fighters spread out on either side of him. Well . . . young fighters. Some were *very* young, though they had turned back anyone younger than fifteen by calling *vrondi* to help and asking the age of every volunteer when they turned up to join the defenders. These were not recruits; every one of them was a volunteer from villages and towns all over Valdemar. The Lord Martial had concentrated on honing their skill with the one weapon every one of them had and knew very well—the bow. Even the people living in towns supplemented their food supplies by hunting, and came out to defend against wild animals or Change-creatures.

They had faced intense training from morning to night without much of a break, and not one of them had quit. Though young, they were now very skilled indeed, and the only fear he had was that some of them might snap under the pressure of real combat, and run straight into worse danger.

If they run, I hope they find shelter.

Now that the walls were fully staffed, some of the archers converged on the little wooden sheds along the top of the wall, and dropped their sides to reveal all the Poomers left after the Battle of the Red Forest Siege, and all of the ammunition, divided up exactly among the Poomers. A second lot of marksmen clattered up the stairs to intersperse themselves with the archers. These were the people trained in using the Poomers and Spitters—all the ones they had left as well. On their backs were baskets full of ammunition, and each one carried a Spitter. They had been saving the Poomers and Spitters all this time for a great need . . .

Well, this was it.

Morning light shone thinly down over the horde below, and still there seemed to be more people pouring out of the foggy Gate, as clouds began to boil up above them all. Behind him, an incongruous sound—the sounds of dozens of muffled bells. He knew what it was, despite not turning to look. It was all of the rest of the Companions, both with Heralds and without, their bell-like hoofbeats muffled by the turf.

:Apologies—we did not have time to sharpen our hooves,: Ardatha commented. *:Hopefully, hard kicks will serve well enough.:*

The Heralds remained below, on their Companions, massing with the Guard at the main gate. Kordas tightened his grip on Isla's hand; a little too much, it seemed, as he felt her wince, and immediately loosened it. She patted his hand wordlessly, but it didn't help. Cold dread crept over him. It didn't matter now what plans they had made. Now was the time when those plans would be tested based upon the progress that had been made up until this morning, and many of those would fall apart.

The monsters were eerily still, even the wyrsa, who were not doing the dodging and weaving he remembered from their attack on the convoy. There were just thousands of eyes staring up at the defenders on the wall, and . . . fewer than that staring down. Inside he felt as tightly stretched as a harp string. From various parts of the creatures, high keening wails rose and fell in staccato notes—a mocking sound, as if the monsters were laughing at what they faced. Some danced side to side in anticipation. They were waiting on something, but

Kordas felt no doubt that they'd turn lethal in an instant once that something occurred.

I see no siege weapons, no defense wagons, or towers to gain height advantage. Maybe they do have mages. A war mage could circumvent or break defenses as surely as any machine, if they were prepared well. *But there's also no relief— no Healers, nor even water wagons. Gods, they're being kicked out against us with nothing but what they're carrying. They either win, or die here.*

Behind the ranks of the enemy were the manors of his highborn, built, half built, and barely begun. He hoped that everyone had deserted those buildings, because at the moment the only purpose they served was to provide the besiegers with something to burn or use for cover.

As for the rest of Haven—well, everyone knew that the Gate was probably where the enemy would invade, and the Gate was between at least a third of Haven and the Palace. That had shot a hole in the plan to evacuate everyone behind the wall in the event of an invasion. There wouldn't be time. There would *just* be enough warning to get the gates closed and barred.

It had been an uncomfortable proclamation, one in which he had confessed he could not advise anyone what to do. Some had just uprooted themselves and the things they thought they could not live without and moved back onto the Palace grounds, re-occupying the quarters in the wall and even moving into the living chambers off the tunnels. Others had turned their new homes into small fortresses. Still others had packed up and moved to farms and towns in Valdemar where they had relatives. Haven was mostly deserted, according to the few members of the Watch that still remained.

Now, in an Imperial battle, or in a wonder tale, would be the time when the leader of these creatures would step forward and make a speech, calling on the Valdemarans to surrender and giving them terms, while they all stood there on the wall like a lot of clay statues and listened. And it would be his place in turn to utter a defiant reply, while the rest all stood on the wall and listened.

Well . . . we aren't going to do that.

Kordas spoke clearly and quickly to the nearest captain, who repeated the orders to a runner as Kordas turned away. Within two minutes, trumpets sang out a single phrase in unison, an Imperial battle call that no one on the enemy side would recognize, except perhaps the defectors. But they were all bunched in the rear of the sea of apparently impatient monsters.

Isla and Kordas dropped each others' hands, and tapped into one of the ley-lines beneath the Palace. Kordas allowed the line to fill him with power until it felt as if his eyes were going to pop out of his head and his skin was going to split. He tasted blood, and a faint red haze rose between him and the attackers.

On the last note, the massed ranged fighters on the wall attacked.

Kordas winced at the thunder from the Poomers; the Spitters barely made any sound at all in comparison. Arrows didn't exactly "turn the sky black," but they certainly looked and sounded like an enormous cloud of angry insects—not unlike the arrowclicks, in fact. They were just as effective as the arrowclicks, too; shrieks and howls marked where arrows and Spitter bolts found their targets, and the Poomer operators launched their scattershot loads into knots of enemies, guaranteeing at least two or three disabling hits per shot as the bodies of creatures human-sized or smaller went flying.

First blood to us—

The mass of monsters raised their voices—or as near to a voice as they might have had—into a cacophony of concentration-splitting shrieks and ululations before the echoes from the

Poomers had even subsided. Every call had its own rasp and tempo. Even Kordas found himself rethinking trains of thought due to the monsters' interference.

Meanwhile, the ragged-edged Gate rose up from its previous spot near the ground, utterly abandoning those combatants terrified by the initial volley who bolted for the Adept's city. One of the defector soldiers made it halfway through before the Gate lifted up, and only half of the soldier stayed on each side.

And that's why we use uprights, Kordas thought. *The Gate itself is ragged, but—oh! Of course! It's a Gate spell that's meant to attach to a permanent receiver. The rough edge is because it's effectively wandering, but someone is keeping it open anyway. Since it's wandering, it can be moved while still open—but it's still unstable. It'll stay open until it shatters, and I can't tell when, or who it'll take with it. Let's hope it won't be used to scoop up our forces, or just cut them down with its edge.*

Once the Gate settled its climb at half a furlong high, the bird-things they had largely seen at a distance—*maka'ar,* the Hawkbrothers had called them—shot through the Gate in a flock and headed for the wall. The Gate crackled with arcs of lightning around its perimeter, but stayed open. The faint distortion of the air around the maka'ar, and how they pushed clouds of smoke and the frost from the Poomers away, told Kordas they had protective shields on them. And the fact that he *could see them so clearly* told him something else. These creatures were big—big enough they might be able to snatch lighter fighters off the wall. Certainly two together could! And their numbers were, in a word, frightening. None of them seemed like they could hold a straight line, so counting them was almost impossible, but there had to be over a hundred.

"The birds are shielded!" he shouted, his words picked up and relayed in either direction, and echoed a moment later by Ardatha's mental "shout," :*The birds are shielded!*: The dis-

tinctive echo of Ardatha's Mindvoice told him that the Companion had just projected the warning into *everyone's* mind, even those who didn't have Mindspeech.

No point in wasting any conventional weapons on the maka'ar. A Poomer shot could fell one, shields or not, but the chances of hitting were minuscule. For this section of the wall at least, the defense would have to depend on Kordas and Isla.

Isla said, "Dust defense," and Kordas knew just what to do. The King and Queen joined their spellwork as easily as joining hands.

Let's see what we can do about those shields.

This was hardly a conventional spell. In fact, it was the equivalent of a street fighter picking up a handful of dirt and throwing it in his opponent's face. When the mages had been stretching their brains trying to think of smaller magic that the Adept would be unprepared for, this was something Isla had thought of, and it had made Jonaton cackle.

With the first gesture, lids flipped open and a thick, nearly impenetrable cloud of dust rose up from bins spaced around the base of the wall behind them—a fine dust specifically created for fire suppression by Pebble, but this series of spells was a wholly different application indeed. With the second gesture, the dust, churning in the air by a magically induced updraft, got charged. This was a variation on the spell to bring down lightning, and no doubt everyone could feel their hair standing up. Small snapping sounds and curses were heard along the wall as the charge built up. In unison, Kordas and Isla raised palms up as if pushing from the ground within the Palace complex, then tilted their palms toward the flying maka'ar, and a strong, broad gust of wind brought the surface of the monsters' *shields* an opposite charge, which was the other half of the lightning spell. A fourth synchronized gesture, looking like throwing an invisible sack of beans, and the cloud of dust flew to meet the maka'ar.

When dust cloud met maka'ar just before they reached the

wall, well . . . if the situation had not been so deadly, Kordas would have laughed. Where there had been a flock of deadly, airborne creatures headed for their position, there was now a giant cluster of fuzzy-looking beige spheres, and squawks of confusion and rage from inside them.

The maka'ar managed to make it over the wall, intent on swooping back to engage, but when the dust cloud enveloped them, their already-meager cohesion abandoned them. Maka'ar hovered in place, tried to "dive" in every direction but down, and some just turned in drunken-looking circles. Defending the wall, the Poomers *boomed*, and the monsters below the walls howled, shrieked, screamed, screeched, or otherwise registered their objection and pain. Above, the maka'ar were doubtlessly gulping in lung-clogging dust, and they couldn't see to attack, they couldn't see to fly, and they couldn't see to land. The only way to enable *any* of those things was to disperse their shields. Would the Adept do that?

Well, they were on the other side of the wall now, and not Kordas's problem—the maka'ar-problem solvers were arriving just now to handle them. Jonaton and the Old Men arrived on the scene by a single-horse narrow wagon, trailed by a dozen students and porters on foot, laden with satchels, midsized trunks, and sailor bags. Jonaton spotted Kordas and Isla up on the wall, shouldered a second bag, and ran for the stairs to join them on the walkway. Wis and Ponu coordinated the porters, and Sai assembled the apprentice mages—a diverse lot from elder to adolescent, and all awestruck by the battle—into circles of six, each around a hastily planted, saddle-sized, folding copper pyramid capped by a device of glass. The students immediately began casting, resulting in completely straight beams of light lancing out, from the glass to individual balls of dust. The lines moved wherever the dust-bound maka'ar wandered, only gaining in brightness over time.

Targeting assistance, visibly tracking the shields. There's much more to light-spells than just spotlighting performers.

"This was quicker than I'd have liked," Jonaton huffed when he reached the wall's top. He set both of his bags down, then set about unfolding the end of the larger one.

"We didn't expect an attack like *this*. We weren't prepared." Kordas frowned to his longtime friend.

"I'm always prepared," Jonaton said, jamming his arm into the bag and, apparently, unleashing a mage-bolt. He hoisted the opened bag between the wall's crenellations, and shook the bag's contents widely onto the monsters below. Almost immediately, loud cracks and shrieks came from an increasingly disorganized cluster of creatures. Jonaton's reaction was a half-smile and a "Heh."

Isla asked, "What . . . ?"

"Animated ropes, made of flexible explosives. They find something living, wrap around it, and detonate. They prioritize the largest targets. Simple." The number of loud cracking noises and cries increased on the invaders' side of the wall. "Now let's get to work," Jonaton said, slapping his palms together.

Kordas met Jonaton's eyes and was about to say something, but was interrupted.

"I know." Jonaton grinned and opened his next bag. "And more coming, when the porters bring them. Students are setting up other fun things. You'll like this one." The mage pulled out a plate-sized, metal-edged ring, thickly edged and clearly lathe-turned. "Remember our little spy hole over the Adept's city? We didn't know all of this was being set up, due to fog, but it made us suspicious. Must have all been staged under that fog. Clever. This is like that little spy hole, but a lot more local."

Jonaton waved his hands over the disc and its center shimmered and gave way to—grass. "So how's the day been?" Jonaton asked conversationally while he pinched his fingers over the disc and mimed pulling something upward. The view inside the outer ring became the battlefield, with the point of view brought up from "ground level" to "quarter furlong." It was a view of the *actual* battlefield, not a diagram.

Jonaton set a pocket brazier out and ignited it. "Sleep well?" he asked.

"I was awakened too early," Kordas answered. He knew this wily old mage well enough to understand, when he acted like nothing at all was happening, big things were happening. "We could use some breakfast," he continued.

"Oh, me too," Jonaton said, pulling out a paper-wrapped box with a cord sticking out from one corner. He touched the cord to the brazier, and the fuse burned brightly. "I get in the worst moods when I'm hungry." With that, he dropped the box into the ring, and they all saw it dwindle into a dot as—out there—it fell among a cluster of the spiders. In a flash of orange and white, there were no spiders, just a hundred pieces of spiders flung from an explosion, which sounded as loud as a Poomer when they heard its report from outside the wall. Jonaton's forelock was blown away from his face by the explosion's noisy rush of expanding air through his tiny Gate. He looked satisfied with himself as he offered the King and Queen a stack of the boxes from his bag, and then he sat down to "fly" the view from cluster to cluster of hostile creatures, and snickered when Isla gave one of the boxes a try. "Now, with this, you use the usual gestures for teaching spells to move the aperture around, and when you pull like this, you can get an overall view of the entire field of battle. Push down to get closer. And, since it's an open Gate, just drop things through when you feel the need. I thought you might like it."

Kordas also knew when Jonaton was avoiding saying something. "And the dangers, Jonaton?"

"Well, after a half-candlemark, it gets hot enough around the edges to start a fire. If it gets too hot, it'll ignite its own metal, and someone could lose their vision. Or a hand, or pretty much anything nearby. And don't get it near a Gate when it's on. Moon above us, it does not play well with other

Gates at *all*." He guided the view through the circle over a knot of wyrsa and dropped a lighted box, then whistled. A half-dozen wyrsa faces looked up at the whistle from midair to see Jonaton's face, which zoomed up out of sight in the next instant. The box exploded in a fireball on the far side of the battlefield, and then there were fewer wyrsa to worry about. "But up until then? I think it's handy."

The three of them rained their "gift boxes" upon groups of enemies, resting and recharging their own magic, until they ran out of the boxes. They hadn't even come close to running out of enemies, but there was no sign of a coherent formation left out there. If there was an active general coordinating that mob, they weren't showing themselves.

"Oh, I have to try this," Isla said to Jonaton, while nocking an arrow. "Find me a neck."

"My Queen, my love for you has never been stronger," Kordas replied, before hearing status reports from a runner. Isla's efforts with a bow were successful after a few tries, but it was clearly difficult to determine range through the little Gate's "window." Jonaton steered the aperture for Isla's murderous pleasure, then yelped as he blistered his right hand. "Shuttering to cool," he warned, while holding the scorched hand to his chest, and he performed the same gestures as before, in reverse, with his other hand. The view through the circle ceased, and Isla laid her bow aside and held his blistering hand while Jonaton hunted up a water bottle from his satchel. Instead of soothing himself, he poured it onto the Gate-circle, which steamed and hissed in response.

And then Kordas, Jonaton, and Isla had a new challenge to face.

The monsters parted and a turtle formation of humans appeared, carrying not just heavy shields over their heads, but a pole-supported structure with a metal roof. They marched it right up to the gate and butted up against it, as arrows and bolts bounced ineffectively off of the structure's roof. ⁂

moment after that, Kordas heard a peculiarly sharp, very loud *pop*, and ridiculously bright white light, together with showers of sparks, appeared at the outer gate's portcullis.

The distinct scents of burning wood and red-hot iron came up to them.

"What *is* that?" Isla shouted over the din.

He called up mage-sight . . . and got nothing. "I don't know!" he shouted back, "but it's not magic!"

Whatever it was . . . heat blasted up at them from the narrow gap between the roof of the turtle and the wall. The howling and babbling of the creatures didn't let up at all, and he knew that it was having an effect upon the morale of the defenders. If anything, now they sounded *eager.*

"They're burning through the main gate!" Kordas added, his heart plummeting. "They're going to get through!"

:Ardatha says the weather is ours,: Darshay reassured Restil.

:That's a relief. What about Jonaton and the Old Men? What about their students?: he replied to her. Restil and Starbird waited about six cart-lengths from the gate, surrounded by the other Heralds and Companions, inside a ring of riderless Companions. To either side of them were two wings of guards, butted up against the wall, so that nothing was going to be able to evade combat by going around the Companions. Storm clouds boiled up overhead as Darshay kept Restil apprised of how matters stood on the other side of the wall. And it was not good—Valdemar was not losing soldiers yet, but they would, very soon. Versus a host of horrors like that, every single soul that could wield a weapon counted.

No one said anything; they all knew what was going on thanks to their Companions. Restil had already put shields up over himself and Starbird; more shields bubbled around the other Herald-Mages, who in turn extended their shields to as many who were not mages as they could.

Thanks to Darshay, they were ready when the cluster of the dust-covered shields blundered into sight and then stopped, the maka'ar presumably loitering in place, trying to figure out what to do next. Beams of mage-light illuminated each of the maka'ar one by one from over by the Palace entry, and juddered about with every abrupt—possibly panicked—movement inside the opaque dust spheres.

"Wait for it!" he shouted, as the Companions backed up, one hoof at a time, until the ground beneath the dust-bubble cluster was clear of any living being. The clouds overhead went black, and a primal fear went through him—no matter how sophisticated Valdemarans might be, everything alive felt fear of a violent storm. His ears popped, twice. The Heralds didn't need the warning to hold, but the guards did. Arrows and lead shot from slings would just bounce off those shields and come raining back down on *them* if anyone took a shot right now.

:What goes up,: Darshay said, *:will come down.:*

Somewhere deep inside himself, under a thick blanket of enforced calm, he was screaming. It was one thing to face a giant boar, even a dozen of them. It was quite another to face an army of horrors, backed by a powerful Adept with unknown abilities. Thus far, the Valdemaran side was *winning*, and even so, it made his stomach lurch.

Suddenly, lightning began striking outside the wall, and near-deafening thunder accompanied each bolt. The noise was incredible. The deep *booms* of the Poomers, the screaming on the other side of the wall, the shouts of the Lord Martial and the Fairweathers bellowing orders on the battlements to those who did not have the benefit of Companions. The smells, ranging from acrid shocks of smoke to, gods help him, savory cooked flesh. The very occasional Mindvoice that was Ardatha relaying information to those who did not have Companions.

Somehow Ardatha managed to keep *that* to a sort of dull whisper, easily ignored if it was nothing that Heralds needed to know.

The clouds turned black, and roiled like a boiling pot.

He felt the magic building between earth and sky; that was Palonia. But she couldn't do anything about the flyers yet, not unless and until the Adept dropped those shields. But by the same token, the maka'ar were blinded and useless unless she did so. They appeared stalemated.

"Wait for it!" he shouted again, just to make sure everyone heard.

And then, between one moment and the next—the dust bubbles became a cloud that blew away on the wind; the maka'ar appeared, looking down at them, trying to get their bearings and pick out a target—

A dust-static-enhanced lightning bolt shot from ground to the cloud above, branching like a magnificent tree made of white light, and the maka'ar were fated to no longer be in the air.

Palonia gestured, and the clouds answered her, with a fist of roaring tempest-wind and a torrent of water slamming *straight* down onto the dazed maka'ar. It was a stupendous sight, because the water looked so gentle at the edges and caught the light, casting rainbows, but inside, it was raging. It was no longer a collection of raindrops, it was a cohesive, seething wall of water half the size of the Palace and a quarter as thick, coming down fast.

With harsh, strangled cries of alarm barely audible through the roar of falling water, the maka'ar found themselves slammed into the unforgiving earth.

The "splash" from the water and wind slammed into Restil's shields, as the guards on either side of them cowered behind their very physical shields. They'd been warned that Palonia might use this spell, and his shouts of "Wait for it!" plus the state of the clouds had given them plenty of warning to brace against what was coming. Even so, it had more force

than he'd imagined. The ground did more than shake, it
heaved upward in reaction to the hundreds of tons of weight
impacting it. People, statuary, arbors, and sheds not flattened
by the shock wave of that much water's impact were rocked by
the intake of air into the downdraft and back out again.

His senses were assaulted by the blast of air that carried
with it the scents of grass, mud, and a peculiar, vomitous rep-
tilian stench that must be the maka'ar.

Now perhaps only twenty screams arose from the broken
maka'ar thrashing on the sodden ground, some half immersed
in the newly dug pond.

"NOW!" Restil screamed, and Ardatha echoed that command into everyone's mind on this side of the wall. Neither the
guards nor the Heralds hesitated; arrows, bolts and balls of
flame, lead shot, and spears torrented into that pile of floun-
dering wings and legs. Three Heralds atop their Companions
broke to the right of him, and ran down the nearby survivors
stuck to the ground, sending man-high sprays of mud with
every hoofbeat.

And then, the unexpected. As the dying maka'ar screeched
and flailed, the earth boiled up, carrying them with it for a
moment—then they disappeared into a seething mass of dirt
and grass clumps. All of them.

Everyone stopped to stare at the place where the maka'ar
had been.

. . . I guess Pebble isn't a vegetarian . . .

But there was no time for anything but that single thought,
because two figures *not* dressed in white or Guard uniforms
ran headlong around the back of the guards and headed for
the stairs to the top of the wall beside the gate. Restil recognized them only at the last moment, and frantically sought for
his Companion's mind. *:Darshay! That's—:*

*:Lythe and Rothas. I've warned the others so they don't get
shot.:*

All he could do was turn his attention back to the gate—

which was going to be breached at any moment. The iron hinges of the door on this side—easily a handsbreadth thick—glowed a dull red in lines where the hinges had been fastened to the stone. Whatever unholy non-magical *thing* the Adept had cooked up to burn through the metal, it was still working, and it wasn't going to be too long before they faced an onslaught of men and monsters.

He glanced over at Starbird, who was carefully putting the arrow she'd had nocked to her bow back in the quiver at her knee.

"Why—"

:Because they're poisoned, and I don't want to scratch myself or anyone else with it. I carry a seedpod with a wool ball soaked in paralytic, and in case of big trouble, I push it to the bottom of the quiver so arrowpoints soak in it.:

His face must have shown his astonishment at hearing her, but he tried answering her the same way. *:Is that going to hurt Pebble?:*

:It appears to be immune to poison. You would not believe what it can eat.: She gave him a sidelong glance. *:I'm glad you have Mindspeech with people too.:*

:I'm glad it's with you,: Restil blurted.

:The gate is about to break. I suggest you keep your minds on the enemy.: That was Ardatha's Mindvoice, and the dry tone made him blush and turn his attention back where it belonged.

Because Ardatha was right. The gate was about to break. The good news was that the tunnel through the wall's gatehouse was so narrow, only a few monsters would be able to come at them at a time. The bad news was, well, that they were monsters. And that they far outnumbered the Valdemarans. And both sides knew it.

:Lythe and Rothas are on the way.:

Before Kordas could respond to that startling information, the two were already on the wall and fitting themselves in beside him and Isla before a captain could yank them away. Immediately, Kordas extended his shield to cover them. "What are you—"

"We're going to help," Lythe said, in a firm tone that brooked no argument.

"But your curse—"

"We don't care," Rothas interrupted. "Besides, if these things get inside the wall, something would break the boundary on our quarters anyway, so we figured we'd break it ourselves. We're going to help. Or at least Lythe will for as long as she stays awake."

They had to speak between the *booms* of the nearby Poomers, and had to scream to be heard. Kordas wished they had Mindspeech.

Lythe shaded her eyes with her hands as the storm clouds

continued to roil overhead. "Why isn't anyone using lightning to strike those things?" she asked.

"I'm working on that. Give it a while. Palonia is keeping the enemy from taking the storm away from her control," Isla said, her hands sketching diagrams in the air before her. "She can only let one of us have a go at a time. It's about to be—ah!"

Her hands shot up in the air and made a grasping motion, and she brought them down again, hard, as if yanking on a rope, toward the invaders. Kordas had seen this before, so he was braced for it, but Lythe and Rothas both jumped and yelped as lightning bolt after lightning bolt lashed the ground in front of the wall, and arced from figure to figure. Thunder shook the wall under them; Kordas had "tuned" his shield to exclude some of the noise, but a sharp scent stung their noses and made their eyes water, and even muffled by the shield, the thunder was almost enough to deafen. It was difficult to see, too, because of the afterimages of so many lightning strikes combined with the irritation of the smoky air—plus, the ma-ka'ar gambit had left everything with a layer of dust to be kicked up with every breeze and blast wave.

It took only a few moments, but that was enough to turn Isla's hair dark with sweat, and bring more sweat to streak her face. She crossed her hands at the wrist to dismiss her control of the lightning, and sagged a little against Kordas, panting. They all peered over the edge to see what effect it had had.

The ground was littered with monster corpses, but other creatures just hauled them out of the way and moved closer, waiting for the moment when the Palace gate would break and they could pour through. Some of the larger creatures picked up the bodies of smaller ones and wielded them like shields, holding them up to take any incoming arrows or Spitter bolts.

Trouble was, the sounds of Poomers and Spitters were becoming more infrequent as their finite supply of charges ran dry. Kordas patted his pockets and found he had spent his, too.

These invaders have a direction—into the Palace—but they're being wasted. It's as if they were told, "Go there," with no further orders. Aside from the wyrsa, and the humans at the main gate, none of them are coordinating defenses or deployment. They're being—spent.

And it has all our attention.

:Ardatha, send four Heralds on perimeter scouting. Fast pace.:

:Ah, you were thinking "diversion" too?: his Companion replied. *:They're formidable, but they're feeding themselves to us.:*

Kordas paused to sum up his thinking. *:Huge force of enemy arrives, heads for front gate. No skilled deployment, no ranged attacks or softening, aside from war fear. The big spiders could climb the wall, but they aren't. We aren't losing soldiers or civilians. No conditions or envoys, no demands. In short, there's an empty space where the enemy's "results" should be. The monsters aren't here to help us, that's for sure, but there's something we aren't seeing yet.:*

Ardatha took that in, and apparently shared it around with the other Companions before replying, *:Pebble isn't coming aboveground at all, and will alert us to any threat from below. Two of the Old Men are watching our shields and intrusion alarms, two are setting new ones. It's nerve-wracking, especially considering what the Adept theoretically* could *do.:*

:Wait,: Kordas realized. *:There is a strategy to it. I'm not taking arrogance into account. If they were deployed in— gods, any formation at this point—the monsters would overwhelm us, but they're not. To their commanders, they're just monsters, set loose to go monstering. They aren't being deployed as troops. They're a mob.:*

He wrenched his concentration back to the here and now.

"My turn," Lythe said. She closed her eyes.

Isla sat down, still panting. Kordas continued to send levin-bolts down among the monsters below them whenever he got a glimpse of an eye for long enough to make it a target. But the damned things were learning, and didn't give him many opportunities. Creatures continued to rally in the distance and spread themselves out further. Other mages sent down fire-bolts and levin-bolts; not too far away he watched a barrel sail out over the massed creatures and upend, pouring something too thick to be water over them. A moment later, they were on fire. Delia, without a doubt, and one of the mages.

He glanced over at Lythe, and wondered if she had fallen asleep. Then he noticed that the creatures immediately below him were . . . twitching. Startling. And clawing at themselves.

That was when he saw the insect swarms converging on the enemy creatures.

Clouds of gnats, midges, and other tiny insects attacked eyes and mouths, and clogged nostrils. So many ants covered the creatures to their knees that their legs were an entirely different color than the rest of their bodies. Enormous horse-flies clustered on their eyelids, biting. Bees and wasps buzzed around their heads and into their ears. To an extent, the Adept's control of her creatures held—but here and there, the torment became too much, and a few broke away and fled.

"Now let's see what—" Lythe muttered. And suddenly, without warning, one of the tortured creatures turned and attacked the one next to it. Another did the same, and another, and another, until about a third of the monsters were locked in combat with their own kind.

"How long can she keep that up?" Kordas bellowed to Rothas, feeling his hope finally rise.

"Until she falls asleep or this is over," Rothas shouted back. "Whichever comes first."

———

The guardhouse gate fell before the humans who had cut it free, and monsters poured into the grounds of the Palace. They would have hit the front lines of the massed Heralds and Companions, except for all the shields held by the Herald-Mages. The invaders' surge crashed against their shields, starting a life-or-death shoving match. The defenders on the wall couldn't turn their heavy weapons around, because there were still more creatures and humans below them than on Palace grounds, and massing lighter weapons stood a good chance of hitting some of their own with deflected shots, or by sheer accident.

But the twenty knights of Valdemar were heavily armored, and so were their horses. And if they were afraid, they weren't showing it. They made short charges at the packed monsters from the side, using their war lances and their horses' hooves, and they were taking their toll on the enemy. The fact that not a one of them had fled was remarkable, considering the enemy's seemingly endless, sheer-horror cackles, screeches, claws, and teeth—alien to anything they had trained for. Then again, in armor on horseback, a feeling of invincibility could come over anybody.

We're on our own. I can hold shields or attack magically. But a magic attack is what that Adept will be expecting. This whole place is only getting hotter—there's enough magic use here that it sizzles. Best not to add to that.

Delia—Restil was pretty sure it was Delia—solved his dilemma for him. A barrel sailed over the heads of the monsters and upended itself, pouring a liquid about as viscous as hot honey down on the monsters nearest him.

:Yes!: He pulled his shortbow out of the sheath on his saddle, nocked an arrow to it, and set the bodkin-point head on fire. Normally, of course, a metal arrowhead wasn't going to burn, but it would with a touch of mage-fire on it. He aimed and released; the arrow hit the nearest monster just below the ear, and flames spread outward from that point, then spread to the next monster, and the next. And while the monsters flailed and bellowed, the ground beneath them churned and

boiled again, and the lot of them vanished, just as the wounded maka'ar had. The surface sealed up smooth behind them.

Restil spared a thought. *:Thank you, Pebble.:*

But a thought was all he could spare, because there were more behind. The guards were holding their spear line. The knights were eating at the edges. The junior mages were reassembling their pyramids, and the senior mages appeared to be working together on something. And the Heralds? Well, they were about to show what they were *really* good for in a fight.

Even with Ardatha's help, Kordas realized that his own strength was fading. He and Isla leaned against each other, supporting each other, as they and everyone else up on the wall tried to keep each other shielded, and at least thin out what seemed to be a never-ending stream of wyrsa and creatures even stranger before they managed to get to the now-wide-open gate beneath them. He was so exhausted that he could scarcely see, and it was actually several moments before he realized that the sound of fighting in front of him had died down.

He staggered to the parapet and looked over it.

He found himself looking down into a familiar face, only half obscured by a helmet.

Lord Legenfall.

His Lordship stood in front of his battalion of fighters, all of them fresh, unwounded, and ready for anything. Kordas could not read his expression, but he was dreadfully afraid that Legenfall could easily read his. And he knew what was written there. Exhaustion. Grief. The face of a man on the verge of defeat. All Legenfall needed to do was lead his fighters in through that gate, and he'd find people on the other side who were just as exhausted—and outnumbered.

And that was when Rothas jumped up onto the parapet, took a huge lungful of air, and began to sing.

"Tell me, oh brothers, just why you are fighting for some-one who holds you and yours in disdain? Tell me, oh sisters, just what are you doing, to bear all the suffering for none of the gain?"

As Rothas sang, his Gift expanded his words, not only in meaning, but in scope. It felt to Kordas as if Rothas was sing-ing directly to *him*, asking him why he was serving the Adept—someone who was tossing away their lives as mean-ingless, and who certainly would do *nothing* about taking care of the ones they left behind when they died. With every word, every note, Rothas pounded that home: That they were noth-ing but arrow-catchers to the Adept. That she would *never* share Valdemar with them, no matter what she had promised. That they were, in any case, unlikely to survive, because after that fight her monsters were going to be hungry, and would probably need more to feast on than just the bodies of Valdemarans.

Lord Legenfall loaded his crossbow and lifted it to put a shot through Rothas, but halted when he heard the swearing from behind him.

The first fighter that broke and ran was one standing right behind Legenfall. Legenfall turned, to see him bolt—he swore and redirected his crossbow, but it was too late, and the shot went wide.

And that settled it. Seeing *their own leader* firing on one of their own, the troops broke, and fled—not into the Gate, but into the city.

Until, at last, Lord Legenfall was left standing all alone, with nothing around him but a few monsters, still battling each other, caught in Lythe's thrall.

It took a moment for Restil to realize that there were no more enemies in front of him. It took several moments, in fact, and "shivering" his shield to get all of the crap, guts, and blood off it, to see that there were no more enemies on the Palace grounds either. Not even dead ones. Pebble was very efficient at cleanup, it seemed.

There were injured, and many dead, but none of the dead were Heralds. His arms screamed their exhaustion, and he felt hollow and empty inside. Starving without being hungry, which was the sign that his magical reserves were completely depleted. It took magic to use magic, after all, and this was the longest continuous use of combat magic he had ever undertaken in his life. It was *so* much worse than training.

Movement beside him caught his eye, and he looked up; Starbird carefully put the last—absolutely the last—of her arrows back in the saddle quiver, and her shoulders sagged with weariness. She held up her arm, and her bird landed heavily on it. The sooty buzzard's talons dripped with blood, and a vague memory of the buzzard ripping open a monstrous eye just as the monster was about to swat at him swam through his mind. But Starbird looked at him gravely. "Is that it?" she said. "That cannot be all. Surely."

"All for now, it looks like."

Starbird looked around, dismounted, and began salvaging arrows from the bodies nearby—including from the quivers of fallen Valdemarans. Without a word, she passed a double handful up to Restil before gathering her own. "Tell everyone to wash any fluids from the monsters off, as soon as they can. Some of it is toxic," she added, "and don't let it get into any cuts."

:Advice relayed. Portal magic is gathering,: Darshay said to both of them, and she wasn't wrong. Restil sensed great energies moving again outside the wall. With only a few breaths of rest, he sat up straighter in his saddle.

:Form up on me beside the gatehouse, Heralds. We still have work to do.:

Lord Legenfall slowly put his sword on the ground and stood up. He looked Kordas in the eyes and visibly took a deep breath, opening his mouth to speak, no doubt an officious declaration about how he was to be treated as a prisoner.

"Stuff it, you shitbird!" Jonaton screamed at him, and Kordas sensed great energies moving in the direction of the Tayledras Portal. "Get the hell out of the way!"

Startled, Lord Legenfall stumbled to the right and pressed himself against the wall. The Portal enclosure that linked the Hawkbrothers and Valdemar was sturdily built, but only looked like a well-made guard post across from the Palace gatehouse to anyone who didn't know its main purpose. It had no guards on it now, of course, though it did have a coating of monster residues probably best not thought about for long. The static Gate shivered and flared for a moment, signs it was about to open.

At the same time, the fluctuating Gate above them dropped like a stone to ground level. It flared and steadied, showing, for a moment, a distant and unfamiliar fog-wreathed city before the entire magic construct silvered over and rippled, its edges included.

Simultaneously, three shadows appeared in the shimmering surface of the static Gate, and one appeared in the surface of the more turbulent Gate.

How in hell are those things managing to stay stable in such close proximity to each other?

:I . . . don't know,: said Ardatha. *:I think the Adept's Gate is somehow tuned to not interfere with a Tayledras Gate? Maybe?:*

Interesting.

The lone figure was joined by a bulky, inhuman shadow, and together they stepped through from *there* to *here.* Even when on this side of the Gate, the creature was out of focus, as if at a great distance, and its elongated head showed two yellow eyes. Then four, then six. By the time the count was past twenty, the eyes were moving in different directions, slowly, across the impossibly dark, fanged face and down its neck. Two, then four, then six tails swept in a long arc as it positioned itself in a dominating posture. Even its number of limbs seemed to change, sliding up and out of the utter lack of light its body seemed to be made of. Its neck flared outward on each side into a hood of symmetrical green lines and motes of yellow light as it raised its snout to hiss a rasping, fear-inducing, rising cry. Immediately, everyone on the wall reacted as if they had a stabbing headache, Kordas included.

It's as big as a horse. That's the—the biggest wyrsa I've ever—it's immense.

:*It's a mage killer*,: Ardatha warned. :*It could do more than all the monsters we just faced, all on its own. It's deadly, Kordas, don't play any games with that. And—I think it's a pet.*:

The pet's owner shocked Kordas even more when she stepped around the disturbing creature beside her.

She was of moderate height, and appeared to be poured into an armored dress that accentuated her enticingly proportioned body. Both hands were festooned with rings, and her wrists with bracelets and chains, and it seemed every other one of them radiated light. They cast an uncanny illumination onto a face of what might have been an attractive woman once, but her skin was marked wherever it was visible by divots and cuts, as if tangles of wire had been wrapped around and over her body, tightened, and then ignited. And where those deep gouges were, light showed underneath, as if her bones themselves were casting yellow light. She was bald, browless, and carried devices of unknown origin and use, from short daggers and necklaces of teeth, to a staff carried by a strap of human scalps across her shoulder. But it was the last item Kordas saw on her that stopped his breath.

On her head was a crown, bearing the likeness of seven wolves looking outward.

"What the fuck*!"* Jonaton screamed, his hands up in exasperation. "Oh, come *on*!"

Kordas recognized it immediately.

There was no mistaking it. It was the Wolf Crown, the symbol of anxiety and fear for much of his life, right *there*. Its presence sparked off panic among the soldiers. Technically they stayed at their stations, but they backed up as far from the sight of it as possible.

How could this be? The Wolf Crown was in storage in the tunnels.

:But what if whoever took *it there was a spy?:* Ardatha replied, which helped Kordas not the tiniest bit.

The figure, who could only be the Adept, had stepped through the Gate with her focus on the static Gate, but Jonaton's scream of pure outrage attracted her attention.

She might still have ignored him, but she couldn't ignore the lightning bolt he called down on her from the clouds over her head.

It was such a massive bolt that Kordas's eyes were still watering when they cleared enough for him to see the Adept still standing there, untouched, in her shields, which coruscated with a thousand tiny lightning bolts crawling over the surface.

"Iss zat all you can do?" she called mockingly, her voice booming.

That's the Crown, Kordas recognized. He'd used that trick to warn the entire Capital City that Pebble's mother was coming to retrieve and avenge her stolen child.

:Shield!: Kordas "shouted" at Ardatha, and grabbed Isla's hand. Together they threw up a shield that covered both of them, Lythe, Rothas, and Jonaton as she made a rolling gesture with her hands and flung the most powerful levin-bolt he had ever seen at them. It hit with enough force to drive them

all to their knees and leave them breathless. It even chipped the Mother's wall. But they struggled to their feet, and Lythe—well and truly fully awake—was the first to act.

Dagger ants boiled up out of the ground at the Adept's feet, and swarmed up over—and presumably under—her clothing. She made a gurgling sound of mixed pain and rage.

"Oh, didn't shield the ground, too?" Jonaton shouted mockingly. "Amateur!"

It took her a moment to gather her wits and her power and send a surge through herself that killed the ants instantly, and another moment for her to shake a shower of dead insects off herself and out of her clothing. In that moment, Kordas heard hoofbeats behind him, dared a glance, and saw the Six Old Men riding bareback on Companions, converging on the staircase up the inside of the wall.

The static Gate shivered, and three Hawkbrothers stepped through, wary and alert: Silvermoon and two who looked to be Elders. None of them were in casual clothing, nor courtly finery; they were armored, with skullcaps of silver and a staff or climbing hook in each hand. Their birds shot through above their heads and made for the wall.

The Magekiller, as it had been appointed, howled in what could only be called *delight*, and hopped side to side, awaiting command from the Adept.

"Ssilvurrmoon! Reunited at laszt," the Adept crowed, and the joy in her voice might actually have been genuine. "I am sszo exsscited, I have sszo many new gamessz planned for you. Onessz we just didn't get to before." She presented her hands, her rings glowing brighter. Negligently, the Adept flicked a finger at Silvermoon's bondbird, and Kordas shouted in anger and despair—

But the bird was shielded, and the levin-bolt glanced right off. In the next moment, all three birds landed heavily on the stone behind the parapet, protected for now.

The Magekiller was already charging the three Hawkbrothers in a display of unnerving acceleration, throwing a rooster tail of bones, body parts, and muck behind it. The Adept snickered when the effluvia spattered her shields and streaked downward—and they had been her own forces. Silvermoon and the two other Adepts reacted by hardening their shields into ramps to deflect the monster's imminent impact away from them, but that was not to be. The monster hadn't even reached them by half, and their shields visibly shattered.

It—ate the shields. Magekiller, *of course, it's a perfect name. It consumes what mages would use to defend themselves, even the shields of Adepts.*

They couldn't attack the thing magically without making it stronger. They couldn't attack it physically at all, because it was just out of range, and the Adept was shielding it. Kordas wracked his brain for something he could do, Lythe sent swarms of insects it just ignored, and Rothas uttered an inarticulate howl that only made it shake its head with irritation.

The Magekiller leapt the last distance to the trio in two bounds, and simply overran the three Hawkbrothers, not bothering to bite or claw at them. It clearly enjoyed what it was doing. Once the Adepts' shields were consumed, the creature played with them, stepping on the nearest Adept until distinct legbone and knee snaps were audible, then stood on the fallen Adept's legs, batting at the other two. Only one of the swats was meant to actually disable, and when it connected, the Hawkbrother didn't make a sound, and didn't move at all when his body landed. That left Silvermoon alone on his back, shakily and painfully levering himself up. It wasn't just the physical pain—which looked considerable—but simple proximity to the creature cost him his grace and coherence.

"I can feel zat warrm Heartssztone already," the Adept quipped, closing the distance toward the fallen Adepts. She turned to speak to the Valdemarans as she walked. "And you! You walked into sszomebody else'ssz war. You were jusszt the *bait*, you clueleszs yokelssz." She stepped up to Silvermoon. "Thissz isz what I wanted!" she shrieked down at him, before jabbing at him with a barbed ring. "Draw you in, crussh you, and play with you later, after I've usszed your own Portal to get into k'Vesszla, you sszweet-hearted relic. I'll kill thessze sszimpletonssz assz a warning."

"Hell you will, bitch," Jonaton muttered quietly, restarting the Gate-circle now that it was cool enough to handle again. He glanced at Kordas, who understood what the mage intended, and hefted his Spitter. "I can set this up once," Jonaton said directly to Kordas. "Are they here yet?"

Kordas deduced what Jonaton meant. "Moments away. You should hear them soon. The entry tunnel's almost cleared."

"All right. Hold them back until we're done, then I'll toss the ring over the side, toward the Palace. That *thing's* appetite can't be sated yet, I'll bet, so it will pull mage-energy from us through the aperture as soon as we're lined up, but I'm counting on this Gate hole being so minor compared to what else is down there that the Magekiller won't even react," Jonaton instructed. "Don't charge your bolt, sharpen it—and overcharge the Spitter for velocity. It needs to punch as hard as it possibly can, even if it's its last shot ever."

Kordas released the bolt stay and passed the bolt to Isla, who rubbed her fingers and thumb together on its metal tip. A sound much like two fine swords sliding edge to edge came from her handiwork, while Kordas opened the slide breach and drew out his final charge sphere from the piston assembly built into the handle for coup de grâce. He'd used every charge sphere he'd had, like nearly all of the troops had, but his Spitter's custom mercy-killer sported its own charge. He recalled grimly how he'd used it on the previous bearer of that Crown.

Isla handed the gleaming bolt back to Kordas once he'd snapped the weapon's breaches closed, and he fit the bolt into place. He caught her eye, and smiled a little despite the tension of the moment. "If this works, will you marry me?"

She kissed him chastely on the forehead and replied, "Only if you treat me like a Queen."

Jonaton cracked a smile for an instant, then said seriously, "With that *thing* alive, we can't throw any magic at the situation. I got a good look at it, and its mouth is made for ordinary meat eating. It isn't armored like the rest of it, and it doesn't do that creepy oily light thing like its skin does. It's just flesh and teeth. You can do this, Kordas, you're the best marksman I know. I'll get you within a few arm's-lengths of its mouth."

Kordas braced himself with the Spitter resting atop his opposite forearm, and answered, "Ready." Lythe, Rothas, Isla, the attending captain, and a runner looked on hopefully as Jonaton set the metal device on the walkway and dialed its view in. The Magekiller's head came closer in the view from above, and the smells of charred earth and worse came up through the ring's aperture. Fortunately, everyone was holding their breath from sheer tenseness.

Suddenly, Jonaton whistled, and the Magekiller looked straight up, its tongue lolling.

Kordas's Spitter bucked back like a horse kick in Kordas's hand. It would never fire again, but it served to provide the very last thing that the Magekiller would ever feel. Jonaton yanked the aperture back, and through the clearing frost cloud from the shot, they saw the monster stagger—thankfully not onto the incapacitated Hawkbrothers—and spasm violently. It didn't scream or roar—its only sounds were those of a huge, dying beast, its hindbrain shot through and its thrashing body unaware it was dead.

:Restil, we're throwing something down to you. Watch out, it's hot. It needs to be near the Tayledras Portal. It's best if it's

under an arm's-length away,: Restil heard relayed through Darshay. *:It's one of Jonaton's toys.:*

:Right. I'll stay alert for explosions, then.:

Restil unnecessarily gave hand signals for the Heralds and Companions to hold position. Cavalry training was hard to let go of. Darshay carried him over to retrieve the ring, which thunked down into the mud as she arrived.

:If I were a dyheli, I could pick that up for you on one horn,: Darshay commented just before Restil remounted.

:And you could stab the Adept with your face,: Restil replied.

:I'd enjoy that. We should have been dyheli.:

Restil rejoined the Heralds and took the colonel position as charge leader. One of the knights rode up and asked for orders, and Restil gave the command to stay within the walls, patrolling and hunting rogue monsters—two troops, one in middle ground, one close by the Palace, and two knights per hunting team. Now came the decision about the Heralds' deployment.

Darshay relayed his orders to the other Companions in the formation.

:The Magekiller is dead. The Adept is furious about it, which means she won't have a mind for subtlety. Let's use that. Make our entry three wide through the gatehouse, form a crescent six horselengths from the wall, and make our presence known. Soldiers on the wall are spent, so rejuvenate them as part of the show. Then split into two troops; Beltran, you take right, and I'll take left. Sweeping flank, closing to ten horselengths between us and the Adept, with two horselengths between each Companion—you want to be far enough apart that only one can be targeted, but still be perceived by the Adept as a group. We want her attacks to spread the energy and be less of a hit on any one of us. Keep moving. Reverse the flank and close to six horselengths. Use your magework and Gifts. Probe and pick at her. Keep her distracted. Make

her bleed. Flank again to three horselengths, maintaining pressure. Close to engage. Loose Companions, close in a second crescent, and weave to confuse, two horselengths' gap from the Herald wave. Our objectives are to get this item close by the Tayledras Gate, rescue the downed Hawkbrothers, and keep the Adept raging, while appearing as if our goal is to thwart her getting through her own Gate. What we really want is for her to flee through it.:

Every Herald, and every Companion, nodded twice in unison.

The moment was here.

:Match tempo with Darshay,: Restil ordered, and called out loud, "Let's go. For Valdemar!"

Darshay stepped onto the gore-strewn hallway through the gatehouse, and within seconds, the ringing sound of Companions' silver hooves matched hers, step for step, echoing loudly enough that every defender could hear them, even after the previous chaos. Thunder rumbled and boomed as the Heralds and Companions exited the gatehouse, but with them they brought a kind of stillness against the background of the invaders' carnage. On the wall, soldiers hesitantly looked out at them, joined by more as moments passed. In Mindspeech, Restil heard the coordination of the formation; the Companions not only matched each other in position, they were in time, stepping at the same pace as when they'd come through the gatehouse.

The Companions began to glow once their crescent was formed. In a moment they were incandescent, and a wave of renewal and rejuvenation flooded outward from them, enveloping the weary Valdemarans, the fallen Hawkbrothers, and the battlefield—and, conspicuously, *not* the Adept. Celebratory shouts and a few cheers came from somewhere behind and above Restil. All over this part of the wall, the defenders straightened up, fatigue wiped out, depleted magic restored.

The Adept was talking privately to Silvermoon, cradling

his head. Even the gesture of a caress was somehow perverse coming from her, and she didn't look up until the bright white light of the Companions illuminated her mutilated face.

The challenge calls of the entire herd of Companions rang out like trumpets.

"Go kill yourself, *bitch*!" Starbird shouted in fury.

And battle was joined. There was so much going on at once that Restil wasn't certain he wanted to ever recall it all. There were flashes of green, of orange; sparks of purple smashing off of shields, and the sensation of falling. Companions fell, Heralds with them. His fists hurt from holding on so tightly, riding the incredible speed Darshay cut loose with. The sharp sound of hooves ringing from smashing at the Adept's shields, and rain of blood—possibly not illusory—and more blades than he could have kept track of, stabbing, slashing, cutting into him. Bright red on white. Lightning. Lightning *close*. Darshay whinnying in shock, and falling backward with more than a dozen dagger-sized thorns in her belly and rump. Pounding headache threatening to make his skull burst. The disorienting struggle to stand.

Bleeding profusely, smeared with battlefield muck, Restil was only one horselength from the Adept, who was one horselength from the Tayledras Gate.

I can use this, he thought. *:Darshay?:*

:Down here,: came the reply, in a tone that suggested it was an attempt at humor she knew wouldn't be funny. *:Just having little lie-down.:*

:Stay down. I need to finish this.:

Darshay essentially gave a mental sigh of resignation, and it wasn't reassuring to Restil at *all*.

Nor was the appearance of the Adept suddenly in his face. "Sshould have sstayed down, hero," the Adept hissed. She was much, much worse up close. The gouges and lines of her skin were acid burns, splitting and dividing, but also—*added to* in years past with deliberate knife cuts. And at the moment, at least, a palm-sized section of brow had been sheared off by a Herald's sword, and the exposed bone *did* glow on its own.

She looked him up and down while arrows and levin-bolts struck her shields. Her sneer suddenly snapped into a smile. "Prrinssze! Ressztil. Hossztage."

She lunged and grabbed Restil by the collar, and with her other hand reached down and picked up the hot metal ring popping and hissing in the filth. Her flesh steamed and sizzled, but she reacted like it might as well have been a massage. She glanced it over and cackled, seeing herself from above. "A viewport! Nisszce! I could ussze that. And hot enough to cook with." She held its edge to Restil's eyes. He felt its heat radiate strongly enough that he knew he'd be blinded if he played this wrong.

"Please. Please don't kill me. I'm desperate. I don't want to be here! I *need* to get out of here," Restil blubbered, faking his plea—and stressing the concept of leaving.

"Surely you do!" The Adept laughed and dragged him along behind her, directly to the Tayledras Gate. "I'll sszee you later," she sneered at Silvermoon. "I'll play with thissz one a while firsszt. You think up all the clever wayssz you'll defeat me next time, sszweetie. Sszurprissze me."

With that, the Adept turned away and dragged Restil to the Gate, the ring sizzling away in her other hand.

She stepped halfway into the shimmer of the Gate to k'Vesla.

And there she stopped.

And there she stayed, frozen in place, trapped by the interaction of Jonaton's ring and her Gate.

Then the ring flared, and her Gate flared in turn for just a moment.

Restil pulled himself away from her grasp, and in doing so, peeled the Valdemar-side half of the Adept's body away from the serene silver of the oscillating Gate, where it fell wetly to the ground, and half of the Wolf Crown with it.

Somewhere up on the wall, a whoop from Jonaton started the cheering.

A sennight after the Adept's messy death, the city of Haven had repopulated itself, with few unhappy incidents. Some of the monsters attempted to burrow in among the residences, some took advantage of unattended livestock, and more had doubtlessly fled into the countryside. The Guard did a good job clearing the threats out, though there were rumors that the fearsome Hawkbrothers deployed their deadly scouts completely unseen.

The k'Vesla Gate restabilized instantly once the ring device melted itself into slag, and a force of mages, scouts, and hertasi came through to retrieve the downed Adepts. Silvermoon chose to stay in Haven, and would not look at the remains of whom he had known as Cloudfall. Squads of hertasi—sporting blue and white ribbons tied like scarves to distinguish them from monsters—dashed to the Palace and into the tunnels beneath it, and were not seen for two days. Once they surfaced, they took it upon themselves to clean out the extensive debris aboveground. Not a window in the Palace was intact after the punishment of the water hammer, the nearby lightning strikes, the storm draft, and more. The same was true of a third of the structures in Haven.

Monster viscera and corpses were dumped into the rapids, never to be seen again. Pets and livestock remained traumatized by the thunder, screams, and smells, and so did a great many people—the memories would not just disappear.

The dead were being mourned after their ceremonies, and honored, as Starbird put it, for "good deaths." The living were tended to by Healers, but even when magic has stitched muscle and bone together again, pain and bruises remain. Heralds were in uniform but a quarter of their number were on crutches, and every one of them moved gingerly. The downed Companions lay in stalls freshened thrice daily, attended by the unattached Companions and the occasional hertasi visitor. The Old Men were looked after by their students, who in turn were tended to by Palace staff, who in turn were—well, anyone who did not have a family to work their stress through with found one.

Some of the mystery of the Wolf Crown was solved by the hertasi, who sorted out how the crate it was in—and more—had been stolen via their old tunnels. Apparently it had happened more than a year ago, and nobody had any reason to check on it until now. Plenty of valuables were missing, too.

———————

Overall, things were returning to normal in Haven. Normal for Haven, that is.

And now it was back to the business of the Kingdom. There were still decisions to make, things to do, projects to finish.

And winter is coming. I'm very glad the Council Chamber has two fireplaces, Kordas thought. *Windows would be good, too.* His skin felt too tight on his flash-burned face and hands, and he did notice his own lack of eyebrows—somewhat like his son, and a score of others who were in the fight. Even now, he could still see negative images of lightning when he blinked.

"Defectors' families?" Kordas asked briskly. Several of the Council members looked as if they had eaten something sour. Not everyone approved of Kordas's clemency. But he was the King. And they'd put him on that throne. There wasn't much they could do about it.

Restil, who had nominally been in charge of the entire operation of fetching them from the Adept's city, consulted his notes. Wisely, he had delegated the travel-intensive parts to those in better shape than he was physically. He didn't have crutches, but he was certainly firmly belly-bound under his uniform. "The last of the highborn have been settled on the farms you gave them on the southern border. That would be Lord Legenfall's closest adherents, himself, their families, and the few servants that cared to stay with them, or volunteered to teach them how to farm." Restil smiled slightly. "*No one* likes them, so *everyone* is keeping an eye on them. The volunteers are enjoying themselves, I'm told. They are there under the Crown's auspices and very much enjoy being able to give Legenfall and his cronies a regular piece of their minds."

Jonaton coughed. If anyone here looked the worst, it was probably him. Burns, lacerations, gouges, abrasions—he had a plaster for it. Clearly, he'd pushed himself far too hard, and Hakkon, beside him, wasn't letting him dare overexert himself again. "I'm keeping an eye on them too. Would it ease the Council's concerns if I told you that the words 'shit for brains' are used multiple times a day by their teachers?"

That evoked a chuckle among the assembled.

"What's the status of the Wolf Crown?" Lord Marin asked.

"Dead as last year's leaves," Kordas replied with authority. "I've looked it over. The Tayledras and the Old Men looked it over. It's not only magically inert, it's so magically dead that it couldn't even be re-enchanted. Magic just treats it as if it were a—" he shrugged, "—a spent flower? Something you just can't fix. A twisted wheel, maybe. It can't be fixed so that it's useful anymore. All it's fit for at most is to be melted down and reused."

Lord Damberlin cleared his throat. "Might one suggest that it be melted down and never used at all?"

"I thought you didn't have Mindspeech," Kordas told him, which evoked another chuckle. "Silvermoon has our piece of it, and the other half is already at k'Vesla. He says they'll melt it down, grind it to powder, and disperse the powder among all the clans to be disposed of."

Lord Damberlin nodded. "I approve. And what of the newest Heralds?"

Within candlemarks of the Adept's death, Companions had Chosen Lythe and Rothas. Common talk had it that being willing to sacrifice themselves had made them worthy, just as it had broken their curses. Kordas was of two minds about that, but the Companions weren't talking. So they would probably never know the truth.

"Heralds Lythe Shadowdancer and Rothas Sunsinger have integrated well into the Heraldic Circle," Beltran said with authority. "There is no trace of their curses. Well, other than the lifebond, if you consider a lifebond more of a curse than a blessing. On that, I have no opinion." He shrugged. "They're not unhappy, or we'd know about it."

"So one completely unselfish act was the condition that lifted the curses?" Damberlin noted. "Yes, I can certainly see how that would have been difficult to contrive or arrange. If you know that doing something will break a curse, how can doing that thing be completely unselfish?"

"The Old Men, Koto in particular, are a bit annoyed that it wasn't *them* that fixed the problem," Jonaton put in, resting his jaw in a palm. "So don't bring it up to them for at least four or five moons. Although I think they mostly wanted to see what would happen."

"And when can we expect the delegation from our deceased foe's city of Restin?" asked Lady Bastien pointedly. She was in charge of hosting that delegation, so she was getting a little anxious about it.

"Another fortnight. They set off today, but they're traveling by cart and mule." That was Beltran. "Herald Merissa is with them, and yes, they are still just as anxious to swear allegiance to Valdemar as they were when we showed up to bring back our defectors. Everything that was salvageable from the late Cloudfall's hoard of books and artifacts—that *wasn't* confiscated or destroyed by the Tayledras, that is—has been loaded into two of those carts."

"I don't know why we let those Hawkbrothers paw through valuable objects like that and carry off the best stuff," Hakkon grumbled.

"I can tell you all," Kordas offered. "It's because the two Adepts that Silvermoon managed to recruit from k'Treva and k'Lyonisse know better than any of *us*—even Jonaton—what's too dangerous to touch. The Adept doubtless left it all trapped, so we negotiated in detail, balancing our favors with the Tayledras. Technically, it wasn't our territory or theirs when these events unfolded."

"And the locals want absolutely *nothing* to do with the Adept, ever," Jonaton interjected. "They say the Adept put the worst amongst them into power, and then they crippled or killed a tenth of their number to consolidate that power. Then everyone supplied materials and labor for the Adept's interests, willingly or not.

"And I know you wouldn't expect it from me, but there are some sorts of knowledge we *shouldn't* have," Jonaton went on. "Some concepts are . . . *poison* is the only word. Once thought about, they sicken a mage's joys, and undermine mercy, and the wickedness of them is, they're so *easy*. They start out with big payoffs from small evils and ramp up from there. It's a temptation where no thought of it had occurred before, or a shortcut that costs an innocent their peace. Some magic in our world is so malevolent, it *wants* to be known."

Kordas could tell that just describing that was putting Jonaton into a sour mood, so he picked up smoothly from there. "The Tayledras are giving us what they find that's probably useful for us, and recovering what was stolen from them. They are taking their lives in their hands to destroy a frightening amount of dangerous equipment, spell storers, and other objects. If something can't be identified or destroyed, they'll store it in a null state." He shrugged. "Really, the only thing

I'm interested in is the books they determined are safe for us to peruse. Some of them are spell research logs, centuries old, but they look like new."

And I hope we can figure out what all those notations signed "M" are about.

The subject turned to the new ally city, Restin, which according to everything that Delia had discovered, had essentially been an eerily preserved, pre-Cataclysm place that had been avoided until a few brave souls had decided to re-colonize it over the last hundred years or so. It wasn't anything special—it hadn't been built by a Mother, for instance, and there was only a single structure within it that had signs of being mage-built. It was something like a step pyramid, and a chute ending in a jump was found built down one side of it, which the mages surmised was how the Red Things had been propelled into their Gates. That pyramid had been taken over by Cloudfall, naturally—in whatever form or appearance she'd taken. Cloudfall had, in fact, successfully passed herself off as male until just within the last year. There was a great deal of speculation *why* she had taken that route, but the easiest explanation was probably that the persona she built was so unlike a young teenage female Tayledras—being a middle-aged, male "Archmage"—she was confident that the Hawkbrothers would not guess who she was until she chose to reveal herself.

As for her "city," it wasn't one by Imperial standards. It only held about three thousand people.

Huh. "Only." That's bigger than Haven.

Kordas was not particularly happy about annexing them, but it was what they wanted and what his Council wanted, so annex them, they would.

It was a complication he wasn't looking forward to. He would have to appoint a governor. He would have to send someone to be Herald-in-residence. And he didn't really *want* to send one of his precious Heralds there. But there was a lot he had to do as King that he didn't like, so he was putting the best face on things that he could.

The rest of the Council meeting was concerned with the mundane chores of running a "Kingdom," and Kordas was grateful for that. There were a great many loose ends that would have to remain loose for a while, until things settled back down into a routine . . .

:And one of those loose ends is that you are meeting me at the canal that Pebble is digging,: Isla reminded him, with a knowing look. *:Which as we both know is an excuse to get on our Companions and out of the Palace and get some damned fresh air for a change. I don't care if it's cold, we're having a picnic. There was a hard frost last night and the leaves are turning and the last three falls there was a toad-strangling downpour right after they turned and everything was ruined so I want to enjoy this year.:*

He glanced across the table at her, and winked.

:To hear is to obey,: he replied.

She sent an image of herself sticking her tongue out at him.

And his Councilors stared at him for a moment in confusion as he broke into laughter.

"Heralds," sighed the Lord Martial, and no small number of the Council nodded, as if that explained everything.

Come to think of it—it does!

The royal family retired to the King's sitting room, and Companions relayed quiet invitations to a few individuals to join them there. Delia sounded especially happy to, and Silvermoon asked Jonaton to bring the present the Hawkbrothers had sent for him, which he'd yet to open up.

Within the candlemark, Delia burst in with her hertasi friend, Jelavan. It turned out Jelavan had gained rank among the hertasi, who nobody knew even *had* ranks, and had started a family, whose long list of names he cheerily recited. Jelavan said that his people had already measured the broken windows, and would trade with Valdemar for new glass plate.

"And rugs. This whole Palace could use rugs," he added, bobbing his head.

Silvermoon arrived, moving slowly. Magically, he had the equivalent of a pulled back, and as if his physical wounds weren't enough, the ring he'd been jabbed with held some kind of toxin that threatened to put him in a coma. Unseen, though, were the wounds inside his heart and mind. He was assisted in his walking by Herald Starbird at his side, and they took up cushions instead of chairs.

Beltran held the door for Jonaton and Hakkon to join them around a low, leafed table, set with delicacies, sweets, and teas. "The Circle sends their regrets for not attending, because they are 'too damn busy,'" Beltran said warmly. "Rothas and Lythe are otherwise engaged. You will have to make do with us."

King Kordas himself walked the table, well out of any illusion of royal authority by his casual clothing, pouring refreshment for the assemblage. His crown was on the table like any other dinnerware, with Isla's and Restil's stacked atop it. When he'd finally poured a cup for himself, he raised it and proclaimed, "My greatest moments have been through your support. My coldest nights were warmed by your smiles. My highest honor is that you all would find me worthy. You are the finest, dearest friends I could ever hope for."

"We know," Jonaton replied, and there were laughs. Restil cast numerous looks at Starbird.

And I am keeping an eye on you, my son. Now that Starbird has given you one of her bondbird's feathers . . . this is going to be an interesting winter.

They swapped stories, and refilled cups. Kordas showed the remains of his Spitter around, pointing out where it had delaminated from that last shot. Praises went around for the Healing acumen of those who had attended to their many wounds. Hakkon and Jonaton passed around their cat pictures. Hakkon's were hand-drawn and showed a remarkable talent Kordas had not expected. Jonaton's were all images magically captured onto stiff pieces of paper.

Everyone was tactful enough not to make any mention of Cloudfall or the loss of life. Silvermoon was unusually quiet, but who could blame him, after what he'd just been through? Yet he sought the company of these people of Valdemar to feel better.

Finally, Jonaton pulled a small box from one of his many pockets and set it on the table. "Silvermoon, you wanted me to bring this?"

"Yes. Open it up," Silvermoon replied, apparently cheered by its appearance. "Take our gift into your hands, and think of what it represents. Fondly, I suspect."

Without hesitation, Jonaton cracked the box, unfolded it, then unwrapped the flax cloth wrapping a palm-sized object.

It was a sculpture of a particularly infamous black cat, curled up sleeping.

Jonaton choked, and his eyes watered up.

"You were in mourning for the loss of a dear friend," Silvermoon began. "I know that sorrow. It can be brutal to bear— but much, much worse to suppress. We Tayledras, for all that we may be mythologized, *are* human." He paused before continuing. "And we give strength to each other by holding our hands atop each other's. I didn't want you to feel so bad, so we made you this. It is as accurate to Sydney as we could craft. He is a new friend."

Jonaton sniffled, and warmed the sculpture while everyone looked on curiously. A momentary expression of delight showed on his face when it began to move.

When he opened his palms, the cat sculpture uncurled, stood up on Jonaton's hand, and stretched the peculiar one-foreleg-opposite-hindleg stretch that Sydney had done all his life.

Wordlessly, Jonaton set the miniature cat on the table, where he walked around as if he owned the place. He leapt onto Jonaton's spoon, flipping it into the clotted cream—which splattered across several faces and outfits—and ricocheted the cream jar sideways into Jonaton's cup, which dumped into Jonaton's lap.

Silvermoon k'Vesla, Elder Adept of the fabled Hawkbrothers, in the presence of Heralds, at the table of the King, Queen, and Heir of Valdemar, had a quirk of a smile, even though he spoke in all seriousness.

"And he is an *asshole*."